MAXWELL
THE OUTSIDER

Other books by Tom Bower

Blind Eye to Murder
Klaus Barbie, Butcher of Lyons
The Paperclip Conspiracy

MAXWELL
THE OUTSIDER

TOM BOWER

AURUM PRESS

Published by Aurum Press Limited,
33 Museum Street, London WC1A 1LD

ISBN 0 948149 88 4

Typeset in Hong Kong
Printed in Finland

To Veronica

CONTENTS

'He that has much to do will do something wrong, and of that wrong must suffer the consequences; and if it were possible that he should always act rightly, yet when such numbers are to judge of his conduct, the bad will censure and obstruct him by malevolence, and the good sometimes by mistake.'

Samuel Johnson, *Rasselas*

'Whatever his weight in pounds, shillings and ounces,
He always seems bigger because of his bounces.'

A.A. Milne, *The House at Pooh Corner*

PREFACE

He stood calmly at the entrance while the packed room fell silent. Over one hundred people had spotted the man who desires immortality but would compromise with glorification. Tall, bronzed and immaculately dressed (bright blue suit, white shirt and dazzling red bow tie), Robert Maxwell, alias 'the publisher', glanced at his watch to judge whether the precise moment had struck for his next public appearance. Behind him stood four uniformed security guards. Hovering in front was his chief of staff, clasping a portable telephone. The publisher places a premium upon instant communications. Noticeably erect on his left, attempting to peer into the room, were two secretaries. Their employer prides himself on churning out decisions at a faster rate than most can speak and requires their constant attendance to transmit his thoughts instantly. At the rear of the hall waited a photographer. Like recent Presidents of the United States of America, the chairman of the British Printing and Publishing Corporation wants a visual record of history-in-the-making and the photographer is on permanent call to satisfy his single-minded zeal for self-promotion. Eight floors above hums the nucleus of a growing empire. Even higher, on an adjoining building, is a heliport for the publisher's favoured mode of transport to and from the capital. In the garage below is an immaculate Rolls-Royce. The publisher has always displayed a penchant for the biggest and the most expensive cars. Scattered elsewhere are a mansion, apartments, offices, factories, a luxury yacht and twenty thousand employees.

Sixty-four years earlier, the dollar billionaire was born into a community whose poverty and hardship would be unimaginable for those who were now witness to his ease amid wealth and power. Most in the room regard him with puzzled awe because his path to fame and fortune is as spectacular and peculiar as the mystery of his origins. None can understand how a self-educated peasant can become a redoubtable financier, publisher, politician, industrialist and tycoon extraordinary. The enigma of his inexhaustible tenacity, energy and bravado inflates their deepest suspicions. His huge frame, his piercing eyes and his subliminally alert gestures as he glances around the room confirm that he is a hunter and to be feared. For forty-five years the hunter has sought acceptance but remains an outsider. Undeterred, his ambition for the last quarter of his life is to impose himself not only upon Britain but upon the entire world. Time is pressing for this aspiring superstar for he is determined to score a chapter rather than a mere footnote in history.

At six minutes past noon on 17 June 1987, on the first floor of the red-topped Mirror building in Holborn, central London, Robert Maxwell began squeezing behind a row of sober-suited men who nodded their welcome as he took his place in their midst. Quietly, he called to order the twenty-fourth annual general meeting of the British Printing and Publishing Corporation. In his lifetime, Maxwell has chaired hundreds of similar meetings and has followed the routine as prescribed by law. The accounts are 'read' and approved, directors are recommended and re-elected and questions can be asked. On some notable occasions, in the more turbulent episodes of his career, the timetable has been delayed by outbursts of enmity and screams of abuse. But on this occasion, the smooth, genial but slightly impatient chairman has no fear of interruption or of embarrassment. As befits the hailed saviour of Europe's biggest printing company, he exudes the self-confidence of a man convinced that his manifest destiny is to command one of the world's biggest communications corporations.

The highlight on this occasion was Maxwell's announcement that in the course of the previous year the corporation had passed important milestones on its way to becoming 'a global information communications company before the end of the decade, with annual revenues of £3–5 billion and earnings per share to match'. For a company which was bankrupt five years earlier, Maxwell's ambitions are audacious. He is promising nothing less than an eleven- to eighteen-fold rate of expansion in just four years. In the past, he has been officially censured for his reckless optimism but he has never conceded any wrongdoing. On the contrary, he has always pleaded that he has been the victim of wilful misunderstanding and much worse. It is a measure of his defiance that his accusers have never enjoyed long-lasting satisfaction. Nevertheless, on this occasion from the audience one shareholder was sufficiently bold to challenge his latest prophecy. To the laymen, the shareholder's query was technical but the cognoscenti gathered in the room immediately recognised its pertinence. Would Maxwell actually promise, he asked, that the share earnings would increase eleven-fold? Maxwell began to answer when a young lawyer interrupted and there were whispered consultations. Maxwell's eyes were suddenly covered by a sheen: 'I'm afraid that I cannot give any assurances because it would be in breach of the law.' The shareholder was puzzled because he had just read that very assurance on the first page of the corporation's glossy annual report. But he found no sympathy among others in the audience. No one present would dare to challenge the chairman. 'Next business,' smiled Maxwell.

A clutch of directors was re-elected and the meeting was drawing to a close when from the edge of the room a stocky, bespectacled, grey-suited middle-aged man interrupted. It was Henry Poole, an analyst at the broking firm of Alexanders, Laing and Cruickshank who, as an expert on the printing industry and BPCC's broker, had recently written laudatory reports about the publisher's 'sense of vision'. His opening remarks made it clear that the intervention had in fact been carefully planned. 'Mr Maxwell', said Poole, 'had given me some notes of what to say but I threw them away.' Alternating his gaze between his client and their audience, Poole then uttered the most grievous heresy: 'Sixteen years ago the chairman was judged to be a man who was unfit to be the steward of a public company ...' A ripple of embarrassment extended across the room as eyes darted from Poole to Maxwell and back again. Maxwell's eyes were covered again by a sheen as he feared that something untoward was occurring which was beyond his control. But whatever eulogy he had intended could not have surpassed what followed. 'But I say to those who are here today who manage the pension and investment funds that they are unfit to be the managers of those funds if they do not recognise the achievements of Mr Maxwell and invest in this company.' Relief and a weak smile from the publisher. The embarrassment was neatly averted and the tension passed. The homage was over. Fifteen minutes later, at the lunch, Poole would sit on the publisher's right hand as the honoured guest.

This is a story about a man who uses and abuses people, who arouses fervent loyalty, fear and disdain among otherwise rational and strong human beings, and whose reputation has suffered the misfortune of his best attempts to offer his truth. His impatience for reform is matched by his aggressive search for the power to dictate the pace of an erratic agenda for change. Unlike in the United States, the trail in modern Britain from log cabin to mansion is a perilous saga. The Isles' ruling gentry look askance at brazen ambition and uninherited wealth. They loathe immodesty more than dishonesty. The rise and fall and rise of Robert Maxwell is a story about the survival of a man who recently approved the superimposition of a halo highlight upon an old photo-portrait of himself for a magazine. The caption beneath read, 'Multi-faceted talent'. Maxwell courts publicity too eagerly to be of profound interest to independently thinking men. His earnest desire to sit in the eye of the world tickles the media's interest but suggests an empire built upon sand. Even the most robust qualities of the most upright citizen are eventually eroded by vanity. Twice in his career Maxwell's vainglory consigned him to commercial oblivion but the same vanity propelled his recovery. Throughout his life the pattern has remained consistent. His personality and methods have never changed. The portents for his last dash for glory are both favourable and ominous.

CHAPTER 1

Robert Maxwell was born on 10 June 1923 in Slatinske Doly (or Aknazlatina), a small Ruthenian village in the midst of extensive, dark forests wedged between the jagged Carpathian mountains and the River Tisza, which marked the Czech–Romanian border. The region of his birthplace was probably the most primitive and impoverished on the whole European continent. According to legend, the six thousand inhabitants of Slatinske Doly could not even afford a cemetery – either they emigrated or the birds ate their corpses from the gallows. Life for these people resembled that of villagers in western Europe a century before. In 1923, Slatinske Doly was part of the new Czechoslovakian state, but to the Prague government the citizens eking a meagre existence in Carpo-Ruthenia were little better than serfs or vagabonds. Spiritually, however, the region was unique. Since the beginning of the nineteenth century, there had grown up a thriving Jewish community, whose attitudes and instincts were inherited by Maxwell and were to propel him through life.

Most of the two thousand Jews who lived in Slatinske Doly, a quarter of the population, were docile and uncommercial, simple peasants who were castigated by the more entrepreneurial Jews in the neighbouring town of Sziget as *Luftmenschen* – people who live on air. Most of the villagers failed to earn a regular income but somehow found ways to survive. Among the poorest was Maxwell's own father, Mechel Hoch, a tall, hard-working peasant who earned a pittance buying cattle from farmers for resale to local butchers and later selling the hides to leather-workers. When times were hard, he supplemented his income by casual work as a woodcutter or a farm labourer especially at harvest time. Mechel was religious though not ultra-Orthodox; occasionally he taught the Talmud to local children and served as an official in one of the village's wooden synagogues. Maxwell's relationship with his father was not particularly close, partly because Mechel spent much of his time travelling around the countryside looking for cattle deals and partly because he was very attached to his mother and her father.

Mechel's wife Hannah Schlomovitch was the classic Jewish mother, managing and ruling the household. Undaunted by the struggle that was her daily life, she was fiercely ambitious for her two sons and five daughters and was renowned for her enormous curiosity. Her nephew Alex Pearl remembers that 'She picked up every piece of newspaper in the street to discover what was going on. She was always interested in everything.' Her cousin Lazar Schlomovitch, now a professor in Los Angeles, recalls that she was 'an exception in the village because she read books. She was almost an intellectual.' Like all wives in the Orthodox Jewish community, Hannah cooked only kosher food and ensured that her children regularly attended the local religious school and went daily to the synagogue.

The Hochs and their seven children lived in two rooms in a rented house. During the winter their staple diet was potatoes but in summer there were other vegetables from the garden, a monotony that was lightened on Saturdays and religious holidays by meat and occasionally gefillte fish. In summer all the children walked barefoot. In winter, the shoes were normally shared: one child would wear a pair to school in the morning while another wore the same shoes in the afternoon. 'We didn't understand "happiness",' says Pearl, 'except on Saturdays when there was different food on our plates.' Maxwell's childhood was dominated by the poverty and by the ineradicable conditioning of purist Judaism.

The genesis of the family name Hoch is characteristic of the culture which surrounded Maxwell. The leading Jewish families of Slatinske Doly bore classic names like Schlomovitch, Shaiovitch and Kra'ama'are. The poor families, especially the new arrivals, were usually nameless. Before 1914, that defect was remedied at regular intervals by Hungarian officials who visited isolated communities to complete a census. For one whole day, the villagers had to remain inside their houses while officials interviewed each family. Invariably among the arrivals were Jews who bore no family name recognisable to the Hungarians. Accordingly, the officials assigned the family a 'name' prompted by the Jew's trade or by any remarkable peculiarity. According to legend, one census in the region was executed on the eve of Yom Kippur, the holiest of Jewish holidays. That evening in synagogue, the village discovered that those families 'named' at the end of the day were all called Weiss (white): the census officials had noted that those Jews, already dressed for the evening service, were wearing their long, white tullis and named them accordingly. In the case of Maxwell's forefathers, the census officials noticed that the head of the family was tall or (in German) *hoch*.

Carpo-Ruthenia's change of nationality in 1919 from Hungarian to Czech directly affected Maxwell's forename. At birth, his father called him Abraham Lajbi but on registration at the local town hall the Czech government official insisted that the birth certificate record a Czech name. Hence Lajbi became Ludvik and the name 'Jan' was added to establish that the newborn boy was a true Czech citizen.

Although Jan Ludvik Hoch personally lived amid gross material poverty, throughout his short childhood he witnessed his isolated community undergoing the most dramatic changes: the Jews were winning their struggle to survive; the hitherto close-knit Orthodox community was bitterly divided by political and religious disagreements; and some Jews in the locality were enjoying an unexpected windfall from smuggling, which earned the village the title of *klein Amerika*. So Maxwell experienced a century's evolution compressed into half a generation. His attitudes towards people, business, authority and family life were all fashioned by the revolution which was affecting the Jews in that remote strip of Ruthenia.

The first Jewish settlers had arrived in the area in 1526 as refugees from the Turkish invasion of Hungary but the bedrock of the community were those who fled Polish Galicia in 1648 to escape the vicious pogroms provoked by the Chmielnicki revolt. Although Slatinske Doly was a refuge, they were still subject to rigid anti-Jewish laws. Maxwell's family, like most of his neighbours, were Maramaros Jews who, according to an historical survey, are distinguished by their particularly 'conservative, strongly Jewish character, strong physique, and their sane though simple viewpoint, as well as their ability and willingness to work'. Jacob Taba became the first Jew to be registered in the village in 1728 after renting a smallholding from an absent landowner. One hundred years later, the registered Jewish community had grown to forty-three families (218 people), most of whom worked for local farmers and owned privately one cow and one horse. United by their religion and by their common language, Yiddish, they lived apart from the indigenous and equally poverty-stricken Russian Orthodox Ruthenian peasants.

Life began to change during the nineteenth century when the huge saltmines in the neighbouring village were expanded to supply the mineral to most of the Austro-Hungarian empire. Jews were banned by law from working in the mines, but they could service the workers who were pouring into the area. Three well-established families in Slatinske Doly were permitted to open a salt mill, a flour mill and a lumber mill. Selected

Jews were licensed to sell alcohol and meat while others supplemented their income by selling groceries, household goods and clothes. All of them subsisted on bread made of oats and maize, except on the Sabbath when they ate white Halle bread, with meat and gefillte fish on holidays. The peasants' diet hardly changed over two centuries.

Despite its economic deprivations, the region enjoyed a diversity of cultures from the steady flow of transients. Over the centuries, Slovaks, Ukrainians, Germans, Romanians, Gypsies, Hungarians and Jews settled amid the Ruthenians and were ruled in turn by the Russians and the Hungarians. Hence Maxwell was born into a world where languages were not a barrier and living among different nationalities was normal. But his religion was quite special.

Endemic anti-semitism pervaded the whole of central Europe, but the Jews in Slatinske Doly led relatively peaceful lives except when Russian Orthodox priests delivered Easter sermons attacking the murderers of Christ. At the time of Maxwell's birth, most of Slatinske Doly's Jews were devoutly religious Hassidim who had abandoned their peasant clothes for long beards, frock coats and the large, round Shtreimel hat which is edged with pieces of fur. The Hochs were not Hassidic Jews but, like all the boys in the village, Maxwell wore a black skull cap day and night, with long ringlets of hair dangling in front of his ears. Under the disciplined leadership of the rabbis, Maxwell grew up amid the distinctive rituals of an Orthodox sect. With his parents and friends, he spoke Yiddish; at the daily religious classes, he learned Hebrew; and he duly learned a smattering of Hungarian and Ruthenian to converse with the neighbouring goyim and some Czech in his teens.

The village's life had been abruptly changed in 1919, four years before Maxwell's birth, by the Allied leaders at the Versailles peace conference redrawing the map of Europe. Tomas Masaryk, Czechoslovakia's founding father, had arrived in France to negotiate the creation of the new state without contemplating the inclusion of Carpo-Ruthenia because its inhabitants were neither Czechs nor Slovaks. But, to his surprise, lobbyists representing the Carpo-Ruthenians who had recently emigrated to America pressured his delegation to embrace their homeland. Masaryk calculated that there were considerable advantages in pleasing the new Americans and agreed to their demands. Ninety thousand Jews who thought they were to become nationals of the Autonomous Soviet Republic of Pedkarpatska Rus, or Sub-Carpathian Russia, became instead citizens of the federal state of Sub-Carpathian Ruthenia within Czechoslovakia's stable democracy. The effect on

Slatinske Doly's Jews was considerable. Suddenly, they were cut off from their neighbours in Sziget on the other side of the River Tisza and they had to shift their focus from Budapest to Bratislava and Prague. Slovaks and Czechs, eager for business, quickly began to search for opportunities, and the Jews, especially those in Slatinske Doly, soon suffered from the influx of investment.

Overnight, the Jews also experienced a fundamental change in their status. To avoid nationalistic tensions and remove any sense of allegiance towards Hungary, Masaryk's government granted the Jews Czech nationality but also allowed them to register as Jewish nationals. The recognition of Jews as a separate nationality coincided with an outburst of Zionism in eastern Europe by which Slatinske Doly, a transit centre for Ukrainian and Polish refugees en route to Palestine, was particularly affected. The new Zionists, who were often also Communists, clashed passionately with Slatinske Doly's Jews. Maxwell grew up amid this unprecedented upheaval among the faithful.

The education of one's children, regardless of poverty, is an important pillar of Jewish tradition; although Maxwell maintains that he is 'self-educated', he, like all the children of the village, received seven years' schooling albeit of a kind unlike any present-day model. To the irritation of the Jews, the Ruthenian schools in Slatinske Doly emphasised Christianity and the indigenous culture, so, since the village was too small to attract government funds, the Jewish community organised its own education. Accordingly, unlike the Ruthenians, Maxwell was literate by the age of eight, initially in the Hebrew alphabet only. To this day, he finds handwriting difficult and his efforts are practically illegible. Children attended the village school only up to the age of eleven; thereafter most families sent their children to secondary religious schools known as Yeshivos in the larger towns. Mechel Hoch could not afford to send his son to the towns nor was he prepared to accept charity of another Jewish household. Maxwell was sent to an inferior Yeshivo in the village, where he is remembered by his friends as precocious, energetic and intelligent. But during the holidays, because the family was so big, Maxwell was sent to stay with relatives in nearby Kosice who worked in the timber business. Occasionally he remained in Kosice beyond the holidays and attended the local Hebrew school. The pressure for self-improvement, characteristic enough of Jewish families, had become more intense as a result of the village's birth-rate explosion coupled with a lower incidence of infant mortality. For Maxwell, one of seven children, it was obvious that he would need to make his own way since there was no family business. 'We always knew that he would leave and make his fortune somewhere else,' says Pearl. 'He would have probably gone to his uncle in America because we all knew that there was no future in the village.'

Maxwell is nowadays fond of ascribing his socialism to his mother's explanation for their extreme poverty. She blamed his father's 'unemployment', says Maxwell, upon the government in Prague and upon the world's economic system. There was of course no such thing as 'unemployment' in a peasant society. It was just that the gaps between Mechel's cattle deals had become longer, because Slatinske Doly was suffering a double crisis. There was a flood of cheap merchandise from Czechoslovakia which had undercut and bankrupted most of the Jewish artisans, with consequent effects on traders like Mechel; at the same time there was the worldwide economic depression. The people of Carpo-Ruthenia probably suffered more than most Europeans since their historical destitution left them without any resources to draw upon. All families in the village, including the Hochs, could rely upon the plethora of Jewish community charities which collected clothes and food and received a steady trickle of donations from the émigrés in America. But Pearl, and Hannah Hoch's cousin Lazar Schlomovitch, are convinced that Mechel was never destitute, especially after 1937 when Hannah's brother arrived from America and bought the family a three-room house. Moreover, as the village's general plight worsened there was a major source of relief – smuggling.

Although Sziget, the nearest town to Slatinske Doly, had become Romanian, contact with its eight thousand Jews, one-third of the population, had been maintained despite the frontier and the River Tisza. Food and clothing prices, however, were never the same on both sides of the border because the Romanian government imposed different taxes. The tax on the slaughter of animals and on the sale of meat was usually higher in Romania and, as the price of meat rose, the obvious source for cheaper supplies was across the border.

For both the Jews and the Ruthenians in Slatinske Doly smuggling was, according to Rabbi Hugo Gryn who also lived in the area, 'an honoured trade' in which the whole community was involved. The village's butchers and cattle dealers were natural suppliers. Undoubtedly Maxwell, watching how the meat smugglers negotiated with their customers, would have been enormously intrigued.

Beneath a full moon, both horses and cattle were taken on to rafts, their hoofs wrapped in sacks and a bag of oats or other food fastened across their mouths. After the beasts had been landed on the other side, the real business began. Horse dealers, like their successors, car salesmen, are notorious for their promises, their exaggerated sales talk and their haggling. Smugglers negotiating in the moonlight would be engaged in even tougher and more ruthless dealings since their customers were well aware that the Czech Jew had little alternative but to sell his beast. The moonlit river-banks of Carpo-Ruthenia were an extraordinary site for a business school, but it was one location where Maxwell learned the style of business which he has employed ever since.

The second teacher was his grandfather Yaacov Schlomovitch, who in many ways substituted for Mechel as Maxwell's father. Schlomovitch was a dealer, a trader and a middle man. Whenever someone in the region had a need, he would seek to satisfy it by buying and selling the commodity in question, making his profit 'on the turn'. Watching his grandfather ceaselessly looking for business and haggling the two sides at both ends to increase the margin imbued Maxwell with the instinctive sense for dealing which refined businessmen in London and New York have come to loathe and fear.

Even if Adolf Hitler had not become Germany's Chancellor in 1933 and unleashed murderous waves of anti-semitism across the continent, it is likely that Maxwell would have employed those skills. In jest, he has suggested that had the war not erupted he would have remained in the village and have become a rabbi. In fact, as Pearl, his closest friend in 1939, says, 'We all would have left for a better life.' The Holocaust caused unparalleled misery, but for a fortunate few the Jewish nation's terrible fate accelerated their careers.

The apprehension of the Nazi threat among the population in Carpo-Ruthenia was gradual. Slatinske Doly was so remote and the Czech government so uniquely protective that the region became a haven, albeit temporary, for Jewish refugees from Germany. By 1938, the climate had changed noticeably. Hitler was demanding the Sudetenland, the German-speaking part of Czechoslovakia, and the widespread attacks on Jews in Austria and in Germany caused the Czech Jews to realise the consequences if Hitler's demands were met. And met they were, under the Munich agreement that September. The following year the dismemberment of Czechoslovakia was complete. By March 1939, when Hitler drove triumphantly into Prague, only the poorer Jews, especially those in the east, remained behind. Most of the others had fled.

Under an agreement with Hitler, that part of Carpo-Ruthenia which included Slatinske Doly was returned to Hungary, and a company of Hungarian soldiers marched into the village on 17 March. Although the Hungarian government would be generally more tolerant than other Nazi-puppet states, the Jews were nevertheless targeted by new, virulently anti-semitic laws which included immediate conscription into labour battalions for most Jews of military age. The fate of those recruited was easy to imagine and the Hoch family, like many of their neighbours, recognised that there was no future for their sixteen-year-old son in the village. After the Passover holiday in April, Mechel and Hannah agreed that their son should look for work in Budapest. There was no heartbreak about his departure since everyone believed he would return for weekend visits. Both Maxwell and Alex Pearl were given money to buy a train ticket and they arrived in the Hungarian capital after a ten-hour journey. 'We were amazed,' recalls Pearl. 'We had never seen paved roads, street cars, big houses or anything like it. It was terribly exciting.' Maxwell was overwhelmed by the wealth he saw. They looked for a room to rent, then found jobs as delivery boys for shops. Soon they were set on breaking with their past. 'We took off our "cuples" and cut our hair so we didn't look so Jewish,' says Pearl. 'After all, when in Rome . . .' Maxwell had abandoned Orthodoxy and Slatinske Doly for ever and was looking at the prizes which the big city could offer.

Maxwell and Pearl were together almost daily until Maxwell suddenly disappeared. Pearl says that he discovered 'days later' that Maxwell had secretly left the city. In the version which Maxwell told Pearl in 1945, he had met a group of Czech soldiers in Budapest who intended to make their way to France. Maxwell lied that he was nineteen years old and, since he looked that age, they agreed that he might join them, on condition that he did not say farewell to his friends. In absolute secrecy, he travelled by train with the Czechs to Zagreb in Yugoslavia and continued on to Palestine.

In the 1960s, another version was issued in a press release on Maxwell's behalf: 'The 16 year old Hoch/Maxwell joined the Czech army, fought the Germans and the Russians in eastern Europe, made a fighting retreat across Europe to the Black Sea with the Czech forces and back to France via Bulgaria and Greece, in time for another crack at the Germans, was wounded and captured by the Nazis in Orleans and then escaped.'

In 1969, Maxwell told the *Sunday Times* that in December 1939 he had been 'tapped on the shoulder at a street corner' in Budapest after he had helped some Czech refugees who were escaping to Yugoslavia. He suggested that at the time he was part of the resistance and escaped a shooting squad for committing treason only because he was under eighteen.

Many other accounts were issued over the following years, until in July 1987 he was the guest on the BBC radio programme *Desert Island Discs*. He explained, 'I led Czech volunteers out of what was Czechoslovakia across Hungary into Yugoslavia on their way to joining the voluntary Czech army in France.' He said that he was arrested, 'tortured and beaten up and sentenced to death as a spy' but escaped the death penalty thanks to the intervention of the French ambassador and subsequently escaped imprisonment because his guard was handicapped with only one arm. Maxwell then escaped 'into Yugoslavia, then Greece, Bulgaria, Turkey, Syria and Palestine to France and into the Czech army'.

The differing accounts are confusing. First, there was no Czech resistance in 1939 fighting the Germans in Ruthenia or Budapest. In fact, there were no German soldiers at that time stationed in Hungary. Secondly, it is hard to understand why a sixteen-year-old Ruthenian who had never previously travelled through Hungary should have been involved in facilitating escapes since in 1939 many Czechs were paying to leave their homeland and travelled through Hungary. It was a favoured route for many Jews heading for the safety of Palestine. Thirdly, since the train journey south from Budapest was legitimate, it is puzzling that adults should need a sixteen-year-old to 'guide them by train'. Fourthly, by recently adding that he actually arrived in France via Palestine, it suggests that Maxwell followed the well-established route of thousands of Czechs who wanted to join the Czech Legion and eventually sailed for France, under British auspices, as an organised army. Fifthly, his latest version conflicts with the account he gave his best friend Pearl in 1945.

The confusion ends at Agde, west of Marseille. In all the versions, it is clear that he landed or arrived in France in early 1940. He told the *Sunday Times* that it was only then that he formally joined the Second Regiment of the Czech Legion in the name of Ludvik Hoch, but clearly if he sailed from Palestine he was already a member of the Legion. At all events, the Legion fought an undistinguished campaign before evacuating from Sète in May 1940 and sailing to Liverpool on an Egyptian ship, the *Mers el Kebir*.

Jan Horal, a Czech air force pilot, met the young Maxwell soon after his arrival in Britain at the Legion's base outside Dover. Horal was recruiting mechanics and was approached by Maxwell who explained that he was desperate to escape from the dreary camp life. According to Horal, Maxwell had every reason for trying to leave: 'His fellow Czechs were chauvinist and anti-semitic and had instinctively little fondness for an uneducated Ruthenian who looked like a ruffian and spoke a smattering of bad Czech.' Horal, who saw Maxwell in Czech clubs several times subsequently during the war, had no doubt that Maxwell was 'deeply disliked but was also not very likeable'. When he turned down Maxwell's application 'because you know nothing about engines',

Maxwell persisted: 'I can learn very fast.' But Horal was adamant. The youth's chutzpah was disagreeable. It is the first recorded instance of Maxwell's ambition and self-confidence.

Horal's impressions are confirmed by a Legionnaire who told the *Sunday Times* in 1969 that the scarcely literate Maxwell seemed like 'a wild young man from the mountains . . . quite unruly, like a young bull'. Another remembered his astonishing curiosity: 'He used to drive everyone wild, because he would follow you like a dog – trying to do anything one had just done, and to do it slightly better. If you jumped over a ditch, he would do so. He has this talent for taking what someone else has conceived and improving it slightly. It's a basic trait.'

In 1941 Maxwell, realising that his future with the Legion was limited, took the exceptional decision of applying to join the Pioneer Corps, known throughout the military as the 'British army's coolies' because there was nothing lower. It was a gamble because the Corps offered only frustrating chores and no chance of fighting, yet it was Maxwell's only opportunity to escape from prejudice and insularity. Posted to a camp in Sutton Coldfield, Maxwell says that he learned English from a local woman in six weeks. Certainly by the end of two years, he had perfected the British mannerisms which he displays today. Unlike many refugees, he had consciously and completely discarded his background and had become a student of the British way of life. His reward, in October 1943, was a posting to the Sixth Battalion of the North Staffs Regiment which was then based in Cliftonville on the south coast of England.

For a Czech national to be admitted as a private to a British regiment, even in wartime, was exceptional. The Sixth was preparing for the Normandy landings and needed German-speaking officers to translate the enemy's intercepted radio messages. Maxwell had volunteered on the basis of his languages for precisely that duty but he had also, during the previous two years, become a fully trained soldier and, in particular, a marksman. Brigadier Gary Carthew-Yourston, the individualistic commanding officer of the 176th Infantry Brigade, which included the North Staffs, took an instant liking to the reformed ruffian and approved his recruitment to the battalion's Intelligence or 'I' section. Carthew-Yourston's decision opened the way for Maxwell's subsequent career.

Maxwell arrived in Cliftonville as Private Leslie du Maurier, a name he had chosen from the brand of cigarettes, to disguise his true identity from the Germans. His serial number was 13051410. Most of the privates and NCOs in the battalion were potters and miners who lived around Stoke-on-Trent and were types with whom Maxwell could strike friendly rapport since their limited education and narrow horizons mirrored his own. Major Albert Mitchell remembers du Maurier's arrival well: 'He looked dark and slim just like his sons now. He spoke nearly fluent English and was assigned to the sniper section. We watched him very carefully in practice sessions and he showed great initiative, moving with agility.' Recollections of the young du Maurier among the ranks are typified by Walter Smith, a sniper. He remembers Maxwell's interesting lectures about escaping from Europe, his keen interest in football and his regular wrestling bouts: 'He was as strong as an ox.' Maxwell acclimatised quickly and, unlike most of the battalion, used his weekend leave to travel regularly to London, earning himself a reputation, according to Mitchell, as 'a great socialiser'.

By his twenty-first birthday in June 1944, Maxwell had been promoted to corporal with responsibility over seven men in a sniper unit; it was unusual for a Czech to be in command of British soldiers. Smith noticed how he relished the insignia of authority and the dispensation of power: 'Commanding people seemed to come naturally to him.' The battalion was denied the excitement of the D-Day landings that June. Delayed by storms in the Channel, the battalion sailed in two groups on D + 16 from Margate and Tilbury, landing near Arromanches.

RSM Norman Champ travelled with Maxwell via Douvres towards the 59th Division, which was located opposite the German lines north of Caen. For the Staffordshire professional soldier, du Maurier was an 'unusual character', especially because he took 'quite unnecessary risks' as a field intelligence NCO. Champ recalls that most nights Maxwell disappeared across the German lines and reappeared at daybreak, often in a German uniform. 'I told him', says Champ, 'that he'd get himself shot. And then I became suspicious. I went to Colonel McWilkins [the battalion commander] and asked him straight out: "This du Maurier, is he one of them or one of us?"' McWilkins agreed to 'keep an eye on du Maurier' and promoted him shortly afterwards to sergeant.

At 4.20 a.m. on 8 July, the battalion launched its first attack against the German lines at La Bijoud. The fighting against dug-in Tiger tanks and 75mm anti-tank guns was bitter and confused, and it remained intense over the following four weeks. After skirting Caen to the west, the division fought against the German Panzers at Thury-Harcourt before heading south-east towards the Falaise Gap. Throughout the battle, the various reported sightings of Maxwell reveal an impassioned and energetic soldier. Jimmy Warrington spotted him in a dip organising the salvage of a Wehrmacht truck; Walter Smith witnessed his fury when he discovered that a group of captured enemy troops whom he was interrogating were Czechs in German uniform; while RSM Champ saw

Maxwell, occasionally using the name of 'Jones', working directly for the 'I' chief Captain Terry, 'constantly disappearing across the lines'. In the battle for Falaise, the casualties were enormous. 'Apart from facing every known form of German weapon,' says Champ, 'we were also rocketed by our own Thunderbolts, machine-gunned from the air and were unpleasantly close to 500lb bombs dropped on the wrong target.' Champ was soon badly wounded, and both Colonel McWilkins and Terry were killed outright when a lorry filled with mines exploded. Maxwell fortunately survived unscathed and arrived in Paris soon after its liberation in September, renamed by then 'Private Leslie Jones'.

Few Allied soldiers who passed through the French capital en route to the Rhine left the city without lifelong memories of romance and splendour. Unlike London, the city was barely scarred by bombs, and everyone there, both liberators and liberated, was overwhelmed by emotion. For Maxwell, there was a happy reunion. Brigadier Carthew-Yourston, who had been relieved of his command of 176th Brigade, arrived in Paris to take command of British troops in the capital. Maxwell reintroduced himself and once again endeared himself to his mentor, who recommended that the young NCO should seek companionship from a French group called the Welcome Committee for Allied Personnel. Among the French personnel, acting as an interpreter, was Elisabeth (Betty) Meynard, the twenty-three-year-old daughter of a Protestant silk manufacturer from Lyon who during the war had traded in vegetables. Reminiscing about the circumstances of their meeting, Betty described the encounter as 'love at first sight'. During the weeks Maxwell remained in Paris, they made plans for the future. 'When we realised that we were attracted to each other,' recalled Betty, 'one of the first things he ever said to me was that if anything ever happened out of our romance, it would happen in England.' Then aged just twenty-one, Maxwell expounded his ambitions to his future wife. 'The very first thing he told me was that he wanted to work in England, for England.' His strategy was bold: 'I want to make my fortune,' he told Betty, 'and then I want to go into Parliament.' Thirty years later, Mrs Maxwell was still astonished that the impoverished refugee had the determination to conceive and realise those ambitions.

Maxwell's ambition also deeply impressed Major-General L. O. Lyne, of the 59th (Staffordshire) Division, who recommended his promotion to second lieutenant. Simultaneously, Carthew-Yourston suggested that du Maurier and Jones were no longer suitable names. The Brigadier proposed a Scottish one, Robert Maxwell. Jan Hoch was not quite prepared to lose his identity completely and therefore adopted Ian as his first Christian name. Long after the war, Ian Robert Maxwell could not quite decide which Christian name to use.

It was usual for a soldier promoted from the ranks to be transferred to another regiment. Maxwell was posted to the Fifth Battalion of Queen's Royal Regiment (West Surrey) then stationed near Brussels. Carthew-Yourston's letter of introduction to the regiment was flattering: 'This man has a very strong personality. He is well disciplined but will for various reasons give far better results if he has a certain amount of freedom of choice and movement than in a post where he is surrounded by too many rules and restrictions. His sense of duty is outstanding and his desire to kill Huns a driving force. I hope you will enjoy his company. I know that you have acquired a most valuable officer.' While waiting for the next battle, Maxwell regularly travelled, on a captured German motorbike with a sidecar attached, from Belgium down to Paris to court Betty. Their relationship was interrupted in December when the regiment moved up towards Holland. In the midst of bitter, snowy weather he arrived at Vloed and introduced himself to his new commanding officer, Major D.J. Watson of 'A' Company.

Watson remembers Second Lieutenant Maxwell as a 'popular and outstanding officer' who quickly displayed the qualities which Carthew-Yourston described. The Fifth were preparing for a push towards the River Roer on a twelve-mile front, codenamed 'Operation Blackcock', which would be supported by three armoured groups. Conditions were worsening as Maxwell's battalion moved forward at 2 a.m. on 17 January 1945. A thaw had turned the snow into thick mud which, combined with fog and the darkness, frustrated their attempts to move their guns across the dykes. By daylight, the Germans were counter-attacking and in the fierce fighting many British lives were lost. During the day, the British position worsened, their casualties increased and the tanks sank further into the mud. It was twelve days into the attack that Maxwell's moment of destiny occurred. During the night of 29th/30th a large number of German troops crossed the river and successfully attacked a village which was occupied by Maxwell's battalion. It was a critical battle which was closely monitored by the senior staff at Corps headquarters. In fierce fighting, two platoons found themselves under heavy fire and effectively cut off. Maxwell, according to Watson, 'splendidly led' his platoon in a frontal assault against the Germans now esconced in the houses. By all accounts, Maxwell rushed a window under withering fire, and after killing the machine-gunner led a counter-attack, forcing the Germans to retreat with heavy losses. Major Watson was impressed by the 'brisk and spirited action which is not mentioned in any history book' and recommended the young officer for an award. His citation read:

During the attack on Paarlo on 29 January 1945, Lieutenant Maxwell was leading his platoon when a heavy artillery concentration fell on and near the platoon killing and wounding several men. The attack was in danger of losing momentum, but this officer showing powers of leadership of the highest order controlled his men with great skill and kept up the advance. During the night another platoon of this company was counterattacked and partially overrun. An attempt to restore the position with another platoon failed but Lieutenant Maxwell repeatedly asked to be allowed to lead another attempt which request was eventually granted.

This officer then led two of his sections across bullet–swept ground with great dash and determination and succeeded in contacting the platoon who had been holding out in some buildings.

Showing no regard for his own safety he led his sections in the difficult job of clearing the enemy out of the buildings, inflicting many casualties on them, and causing the remainder to withdraw. By his magnificent example and offensive spirit this officer was responsible for the relief of the platoon; and the restoration of the situation.

Maxwell had fought courageously. The critical action had been so particularly closely followed by anxious chiefs at headquarters that they warmly endorsed Watson's recommendation. In March, Maxwell was awarded the Military Cross by Montgomery in person. He then drove to Paris, where on 15 March he married Betty. Carthew-Yourston was among the guests who watched the bride in a traditional white dress and veil, which Maxwell had raced around Paris to procure, pledge her vows.

Two weeks later, Maxwell was again in the midst of battle. His battalion formed part of Montgomery's final thrust across northern Germany towards Hamburg. On 8 April, the battalion began a pincer movement against a company of the SS Training Division. Maxwell's own platoon killed no fewer than fifteen SS soldiers and took fourteen prisoners. After disjointed fighting against lacklustre resistance, the regiment entered Hamburg on 3 May. 'When Hamburg was reached,' records the official history, 'the Battalion was weary, but the casualties had been so few that the fighting strength was hardly affected.' Hostilities officially ceased five days later. For Maxwell, it had been a glorious war.

Because he was wounded soon after 'Blackcock', Watson had not witnessed Maxwell's receipt of the MC but he does remember when they next met, soon after the German surrender. Maxwell was based at

Iserlohn in the Ruhr interrogating prisoners of war. Maxwell's sister Sylvia, who had learned of her brother's whereabouts, arrived at the regiment's temporary headquarters but Maxwell had already moved on to Berlin. Sylvia and her sister Brana had remained hidden in Hungary throughout the war, but the remainder of the Hoch family had perished. The Holocaust had ravaged Slatinske Doly, but only in 1944. For the previous five years, the villagers had suffered increasing hardship. Most males were forced into labour units where many died, some as the victims of sadistic games played by the Hungarian guards, such as hosing water on to the workers in winter and watching their painful, freezing deaths. In the village itself, the women were compelled to watch a succession of executions, including those of some rabbis. Increasingly, they heard accounts from Polish refugees of the production-line killing through the gas chambers, but escape was by then too difficult. The true horror began on 17 April 1944 shortly after Adolf Eichmann's visit to Budapest. A ghetto was built in the centre of the village and five thousand people were crammed inside; fifteen to twenty people were assigned to each room of the small houses. The brutality, sadism and torture which the villagers suffered during the ensuing four weeks was, according to the survivors, worse than anything they endured at Auschwitz extermination camp, to which they were transported on 20 and 23 May. Most of those who tumbled out of the packed cattle trucks and saw the flames spouting from the crematoria's chimneys, were gassed the same day. Among them was Hannah Hoch. Her husband escaped the gas but was shot dead. Maxwell learned of his parents' deaths when he drove to Prague in the summer of 1945 to discover the fate of his family. Strangely, for the next forty years he showed little public interest in the Holocaust, but felt guilt that while he had survived and enjoyed a 'good' war, his family had suffered so catastrophically.

For all refugees, the end of the war produced a mixture of emotions – the joy of victory was tinged by sorrow for those who had been murdered. Until May 1945, there is little doubt that Maxwell, like most front-line soldiers, accepted that he would quite probably die in battle. But having escaped the poverty of Slatinske Doly, the Holocaust and the perils of the battlefield, he sensed that he was thereafter living on borrowed time. All the anguish, the humiliations and the defeats which he would endure during the remainder of his life could always be rationalised by the thought that fate, or in his words 'the Gods', had been particularly kind. It is a sentiment which can only be properly appreciated by those who have shared his experience. Consequently, during those first weeks in Berlin, Maxwell's hitherto exclusive preoccupation with survival was replaced, despite the self-confident image which developed in later years, by a temporary uncertainty about his future. Unlike the majority of his fellow officers, there was no home beckoning to him. As a penniless nobody, he was unsure about his ambitions. Only the army, where his status was established, offered glowing prospects.

After Germany's defeat the victors could enjoy almost unlimited spoils. For a single packet of cigarettes, the officers of the occupying armies could buy an extravagant lifestyle. A simple scrap of paper decorated with a military stamp and signature was sufficient to requisition any house, its entire contents and the Mercedes in the garage. Throughout Germany, the most menial Allied officer lived in a style to which he was unaccustomed. Copious supplies of food, alcohol and entertainment were on tap while the Germans themselves struggled to survive starvation and illness. Understandably, for the Allied soldiers who had survived the war and seen the horrors of the concentration camps, there were few pangs of conscience about the way their enemy was treated. Maxwell had more reason than most to dislike the Germans and to relish the privileges which would disappear like melting butter if he returned to London and demobilisation. If he remained in the army in Berlin, however, there were unrivalled opportunities which an ambitious and talented officer could exploit.

The government of occupied Germany (and, separately, of the city of Berlin) was divided between the four Allies. In its own zone, each Allied army wielded sovereign power, subject only to the Four Power agreement concluded at Potsdam in August 1945. In each of the three western zones, there was a sharp distinction between the regular army of occupation which was responsible for security and combat in any future conflict, and the section of the military which had replaced all the former civilian ministries of the deposed German government. That section was called the military government, known in the British zone as the Control Commission. Politically, the Control Commission was answerable to the Foreign Office in London but it was staffed by military officers, who either were on secondment from the regular army or, as was increasingly the case, were civilians enjoying temporary military rank. By October 1945, there were no less than twenty-four thousand British officers employed by the Control Commission whose responsibilities covered education, health, the judiciary, transportation, denazification and housing. In effect, the military government officers were dictators who wielded enormous power with little occasion to answer for their decisions. In the exercise of this almost unfettered discretion they could either enrich or impoverish a German individual or business.

The quality of those temporary British civil servants was dramatically uneven. Initially, among the higher echelons were talented and impassioned idealists who were dedicated to the rebuilding of a sound democracy. Many were middle-aged men unfit for combat but deemed to possess the special talents needed to govern the defeated enemy. After inadequate briefing during the last months of the war, they arrived in Germany ill prepared for their task, if only because no Allied planner had foreseen the sheer scale of devastation and demoralisation which would be inflicted upon the enemy. But as demobilisation rapidly robbed the Commission of those qualified staff, many of their replacements were less able men attracted by the promise of privilege and high reward which would be barred to them in Britain. Unmotivated by any higher calling, they exploited their power. It was in that atmosphere that Maxwell had to work during the summer of 1945.

Initially, Maxwell had continued with Field Security duties of interrogating Germans but he possessed one talent which enjoyed an important premium in the British occupation army – his fluency in eight languages. Few British officers spoke German and hardly any spoke Czech, Hungarian, Russian, Polish, Ruthenian and Romanian. His languages, war record and self-presentation made him an ideal candidate for the army's information control section, which in the British sector in Berlin was organised by a section of the Control Commission known as the Public Relations and Information Services Control or PRISC, situated in Berlin's Klaus Grothstrasse. PRISC's more important task was acting as a cultural licensing agency. Germans who wanted to show films, stage plays or publish books and newspapers had to obtain permission from PRISC, whose discretion was guided by two objectives: first, the eradication of every vestige of Nazi philosophy from Germany's cultural life, and second, the reintroduction among the Germans of democratic aspirations. To that end, priority was given to the reestablishment of diverse and liberal newspapers edited by German journalists. Maxwell was appointed Berlin's press chief by Colonel 'Red' Edwards, head of PRISC in the city. It represented the end of his association with any British Intelligence activities and his introduction to a profession which would shape the rest of his life.

Among those who applied for a licence to publish a newspaper in the British sector of Berlin was Arno Scholz, then forty-one years old, whose proposed newspaper would be called *Der Telegraf*. Scholz was an independent socialist who until 1933 had written for *Vorwärts*, a left-wing newspaper. Soon after Hitler's election he had been arrested and, although later released, he was forbidden to work throughout most of the war. His application was considered by Nicholas Huijsman, the South African-born PRISC officer who was in charge of the press section for the whole British zone, and then by Edwards. After careful vetting, a licence was issued on 12 March 1946. Maxwell's role in that process is uncertain. In 1969, Maxwell told the *Sunday Times*, 'I had nothing to do with licences. I certainly could do no such thing as help get a licence for *Der Telegraf*. It had a licence already.' The actual dates are at variance with Maxwell's version, and Huijsman says that the recommendation for awarding the licence was forwarded to him by Maxwell. Maxwell's reluctance to take any credit remains puzzling.

To obtain the precious permit, Scholz guaranteed to PRISC that both he and his journalists would submit to total censorship by the Control Commission. It was Scholz's good fortune that the officer appointed to supervise the *Telegraf*'s operations in their ramshackle premises spread over the suburb of Wilmersdorf was Robert Maxwell, recently promoted to captain. In theory Maxwell's job was, in Huijsman's words, 'completely negative'. Each article of the newspaper had to be vetted to exclude any offensive comments about the four Allied powers or the Control Commission. The temptation for any British officer was to control the newspaper's balance very strictly but Huijsman is certain that Maxwell was generously restrained and intervened on only a minimum of occasions. At 3 a.m. the young officer would solemnly 'press the button for democracy' and the printing presses would roll. In retrospect, Maxwell's determinedly laissez-faire attitude contrasts oddly with his later interventionist behaviour, but this liberalism was undoubtedly spawned by his admiration for Scholz, with whom he formed a friendship which was to prove as important as his earlier relationship with Carthew-Yourston.

Maxwell's contemporaries in the Control Commission had by then recognised his intelligence, energy and instinct, but inevitably, because of his apparent fluency and self-confidence, overlooked his emotional need for a mentor and father-figure. Denied a respected male teacher (other than his grandfather) whose example and advice he could depend upon during his childhood, Maxwell was naturally attracted in Berlin to anyone who could compensate for that lack. Although Scholz was not Jewish, he did share a certain common heritage with Maxwell, and by all accounts the Berliner spent many hours talking to the Czech, moulding his political outlook and trying to satisfy his appetite for a vehicle which would provide him with both a fortune and power. Like so many others in Berlin, Scholz was besieged by Maxwell's requests for introductions to important people which he obliged because he liked Maxwell, upon whom he depended daily to further his own ambition to create a successful newspaper.

PRISC's licence permitted Scholz to publish the newspaper but did not guarantee him the means for printing and distribution. In common with all German industry amid the post-war chaos, Scholz faced an hourly struggle. Production was constantly interrupted by breakdowns and by the absence of replacements for broken parts of the printing presses. Paper and ink were severely rationed and there were strict daily limits on the allocation of electricity. Often, even these slender quotas could not be fulfilled. Scholz was entirely dependent upon the British military government in the person of Maxwell, who would have to use his influence and ingenuity to find a solution somewhere in the city's devastation. In Huijsman's view, 'Maxwell was marvellous at it.' In addition, to give 'his' newspaper an advantage, Maxwell acted for the first and only time as a journalist, using his rank (according to Huijsman) to 'worm out' from military government officials good stories which the *Telegraf* could publish.

The results were hugely successful. According to a confidential Control Commission survey, up to 260,000 copies of the eight-page tabloid were sold six days a week, making it the best-selling newspaper in the British sector. Sixty thousand copies were sold daily in the Soviet zone and a reported 300 copies were flown to Moscow. Within two months of its launch, it incorporated its competitor, *Der Berliner*. Scholz, with firm British support, was destined to build a flourishing business, coincidentally inspiring Maxwell's appetite to own a newspaper.

Maxwell in the meantime was laying the foundations for a stable family life. Betty had arrived in Berlin and was living in a requisitioned flat in what was known among the British staff as the 'ghetto' – an area exclusively reserved for Allied officers. Other than work, most of his fellow officers felt there was little more to do than to enjoy the endless succession of parties hosted by the military representatives of one of the four powers and by his fellow British officers. Huijsman remembers seeing Maxwell, 'a very handsome and personally very charming officer', at least twice a week at social and formal gatherings, and the two became quite close. When Maxwell's first child Michael was born, both Scholz and Huijsman became his godfather. At the christening party, Huijsman's subordinate confessed his true ambition: 'He confided to me that he wanted to become a millionaire.' Huijsman was apparently unaware that Maxwell had already made his first steps in that direction.

In July 1946, Maxwell was demobbed from the army, but he had already agreed to continue working for PRISC in Berlin as a Control

Commission officer wearing a military uniform and retaining the rank of captain. While in Britain during the summer, completing his formal demobilisation, Maxwell consummated an arrangement he had made months earlier. On 18 September 1945, a small, £100 company had been incorporated in London. It was called Low-Bell Limited, and its founding director was a Czech refugee called Arnos Lobl. The history of Low-Bell is puzzling but it is fitting that the very first company of which Maxwell became a director should be shrouded in a mystery which would be consistently reproduced on so many occasions during his commercial career.

Although Low-Bell was a trading company, during its first year Lobl did not carry out any business. On 22 August 1946, the directors of Low-Bell, notably Arnos Lobl, held an extraordinary meeting and passed two resolutions: first, to double the number of shares issued by the company to two hundred, and then to grant the power to increase the number of shares to a total of 10,000. The following month, on 12 September, Maxwell was formally recorded as owning ninety shares in Low-Bell, while Lobl personally retained a majority of 110 shares. Although Maxwell was still at the time employed by the Control Commission in Berlin and was not living in London, he described himself on the formal document as a merchant who was resident at 21 Stanley Gardens, London W11. The mystery deepened in December when three additional shareholders appeared; again this is consistent with the procedure in Maxwell's later business career, with people casually entering and exiting as directors and employees of his companies. On this first occasion, they were a retired bank manager called John Stratton-Ferrier, Paul Raque from Paris and Ladislau Skaloud, described as a merchant who lived in Prague. Their object was to start trading between Britain and Europe.

Lobl, like many Jewish refugees in Britain, lacked any professional qualifications, but appreciated the enormous opportunities for earning a living in straightforward business deals. Like continental Europe, Britain was suffering acute shortages and there was a demand for anything which was manufactured, imported or grown. Even a modest entrepreneur could earn a decent income simply by knowing where and how to buy. Selling was never a problem.

Maxwell returned to Germany and Lobl rented tiny premises in Grand Buildings, Trafalgar Square. Low-Bell's office was crowded even with only two people inside. There was no daylight because the window was covered by an advertising hoarding for cinema films. When Low-Bell occupied the office the ad was for Ivor Novello's musical *Perchance to Dream* – a fitting motto for the shareholder resident in Berlin.

Whether Maxwell, on his return to Germany, immediately started dealing on Low-Bell's behalf is unknown, but two months later he became the company's majority shareholder, owning three hundred shares over Lobl's two hundred. While Scholz built up his newspaper, Maxwell constantly hunted for opportunities, travelling frequently into the Soviet zone, on one occasion visiting the relaunched Leipzig book fair which in the pre-Hitler period had had the same status as the present annual Frankfurt fair. The trip awakened his interest in the business of books, but when he formally resigned from the Commission on 15 March 1947, he was still unsure how he was to make his fortune.

Maxwell explained his resignation to the *Sunday Times* in 1969 as having been caused by a clash with his superiors. He claimed that he was opposed to the Soviet dismantling of German industry and consequently allowed the *Telegraf* to publish anti-Soviet stories which in the period before the Cold War was against Allied laws. His decision, he said, provoked a row with his superiors but Huijsman recalls a friendly parting of the ways occasioned by Maxwell's desire to construct his peacetime career. In any event, Maxwell packed for his return to England armed with his army gratuity and an idea. On the eve of his departure, he telephoned John Kisch, another Czech working for PRISC as the press chief in Düsseldorf. Although the two had never met, they had occasionally spoken on the telephone and Kisch knew Maxwell's reputation as a man with the ability to 'fix the impossible'. Maxwell suggested to his fellow Czech that they might join forces in a business venture when Kisch returned to London. Kisch agreed.

Kisch arrived at Low-Bell's offices in Trafalgar Square in the summer of 1947 to discover that Maxwell had established a new company, the European Periodicals, Publicity and Advertising Corporation. EPPAC's initial business was to import German newspapers to Britain for sale to German prisoners of war anxious for information about their homeland. Maxwell had seen the value of the idea at the beginning of the year when George Houghton, a senior officer in Berlin, had asked him to negotiate the sale of the *Telegraf* with another London company. But Huijsman had agreed, just before Maxwell left Berlin, that he would be granted the concession, and EPPAC was registered with the military government as an official distributor. Maxwell was in business. Recognising that his future would never be in editing or writing for a newspaper, he had started as a trader.

Using a huge, grey Dodge still bearing its Berlin military registration plates, Maxwell or Kisch regularly collected the newspapers from Victoria railway station and wearily toured around Britain's POW camps, driving as far as Bridgend in South Wales, where the top Nazi generals were incarcerated. Although sales were healthy, both realised that their business suffered the fatal flaw of a diminishing clientele. Maxwell nevertheless applied on EPPAC's behalf to join the Publishers Association, the elite club of British book publishers. His request was promptly rejected.

Kisch noticed that Maxwell regarded the newspaper distribution as just one of several ventures. Every month, as the director of Low-Bell, Maxwell obtained one ton of caustic soda from ICI for £47. Like every commodity, caustic soda was in short supply and Maxwell found no difficulty in reselling his precious allocation in the Far East for £98. That was a monthly income nowadays worth £1,000, ample for a comfortable living.

Maxwell evidently thrived on those first business ventures, applying – it seemed to some eyewitnesses – the same reckless bravery to his pursuit of fortune as had earned him such commendation in wartime. He displayed a natural talent for trading and a bull-like determination to overcome the confusing multitude of banking and Customs controls which dominated international trade in the post-war era. Yet those who knew him in 1947 are convinced that he was, despite his deals, living way beyond his means. They did not know that his uncle was sending regular payments from America. Nevertheless, Maxwell left Kisch and others in cold fear. Only those who understood that his primitive background excluded any sense of embarrassment or fear of poverty could understand the style. But even they found the pace he set daunting.

In autumn 1947, Maxwell travelled to Berlin. He returned with a new venture which was his key to becoming a millionaire. The business needed new premises and he moved out of Grand Buildings and into 3/4 Studio Place, off Kinnerton Street in Knightsbridge. The annual rent at £350 was more than either Maxwell or his partner had ever possessed. Kisch, his nerves outstripped, bid fond farewell and headed for Fleet Street. Maxwell was unmoved. He had new partners in mind for his fortune-making venture.

On 16 October 1947 Maxwell arrived at the delapidated headquarters of the world's largest scientific publishers Ferdinand Springer in West Berlin's Jebenstrasse. At that moment, Ferdinand Springer's business was in ruins, both literally and metaphorically. According to Vernon Baxter, who worked for Maxwell in the early post-war years, it was Arno Scholz who had explained to his protégé the value of German scientific book exports. 'Scholz told him,' recalls Baxter, 'if you help re-establish the trade, the trade will kiss your feet.' What followed would change Maxwell's life forever.

The origins of the Springer publishing house, which has no connection with the Axel Springer newspaper group, were laid in May 1842 when Julius Springer opened a bookshop in Berlin. By 1907, when Julius' grandson Ferdinand inherited the small family business, the revolution in science and engineering was gathering momentum throughout the world. Perceiving that German scientists lacked a specialist publisher, Ferdinand personally introduced himself to selected leading experts and offered his services. Within twenty years, because of Germany's position as a pathfinder in science, industry and engineering, Springer swiftly developed a very lucrative world market for his books. Among his stars, including several Nobel prize winners, were the first works written by Paul Ehrlich, Karl von Frisch, Max Born, Max Planck and Albert Einstein. But his fortune was earned not only in single volumes, but in publishing whole series of books edited by eminent panels of German experts. Springer's Beilstein series on chemistry, medicine, psychology, mathematics, engineering and physics was purchased by every reputable library throughout the world. For practitioners, Springer's publications on the natural sciences were standard textbooks, and after each regular revision the demand for the books was renewed.

Simultaneously, Springer began publishing a wide range of learned journals containing short articles by doctors, scientists and researchers which described their most recent work and their discoveries. Springer found that the same libraries which subscribed to the books were eager customers for his journals. The economics were also extremely attractive: unlike most business payments, subscriptions to journals were paid in advance of delivery, which guaranteed a healthy and positive cash flow.

As the world's interest in science expanded and the demand for Springer's books and journals grew, the publisher realised another bonus. New libraries and universities opening around the world not only started buying Springer's current books and journals, but also wanted to stock their shelves with their past publications. Known as 'back issues', the older journals were by definition rarer than the current issues and consequently more valuable. The earnings on trading single, rare issues or buying incomplete sets at reduced rates and adding the missing journals for resale as a prestigious investment were high. To capitalise on growing demand, Springer printed more journals than he could immediately sell as a calculated speculation that the surplus stock would be sold in the future at considerable profit. In 1932, the last year of free trade, Springer's sales were bigger than the combined total of the remaining world's scientific publishers.

Hitler's accession to power in January 1933 changed Springer's business overnight. An immediate ban was imposed on sharing Germany's scientific secrets with the rest of the world. Although articles describing experiments and theories would still be written, their circulation would be strictly limited. But Ferdinand and his cousin Julius, who was a partner in the business, had a more pressing problem. Both were part-Jewish. By applying the detailed criteria established by the Nazis to determine a German's racial origins, Ferdinand was deemed a half-Jew and Julius three-quarters. For completely assimilated and loyal Germans like the Springers, the shock of being branded an enemy by one's own countrymen was considerable. Like so many German Jews, Ferdinand immediately sought allies among his Aryan friends to protect himself and his business from the law. Initially, because of his worldwide reputation as a prestige exporter, Ferdinand's efforts were successful and the Nazis granted a special permit for him to continue as before. But in 1935, following the enactment of the Nuremberg Laws which explicitly discriminated against Jews, Julius was forced to sell his shares in his company.

The purchaser was Tönjes Lange, a senior manager in the company who had been exclusively concerned with managing the business while the Springers had maintained direct contacts with their authors.

Lange, as Maxwell would discover in 1947, was an exceptionally sensitive and generous person. His arrangement with Julius was that, should they both survive the Nazi era, Julius could repurchase his interest in the company. Soon after, Julius was arrested and sent to Oranienburg concentration camp from which he would later be released. In the meantime, Ferdinand and Lange managed the business. In November 1942, Ferdinand too was finally forced to sell his own shares. He made the same unofficial agreements with Lange as Julius had concluded. At this juncture, Springer's Vienna branch was officially sold to Tönjes's brother Otto Lange for 600,000 marks. Only a fraction of the amount was paid and Otto solemnly promised to return the business to Ferdinand after the war. For a time, while Springer was managed by the two Lange brothers, Ferdinand stayed in Berlin, but in 1944 he fled to a remote farm in Pomerania until he was arrested by the advancing Red Army.

By then Lange, with Ferdinand's agreement, had organised the physical survival of Springer's business. As the Allied bombing of the capital intensified, sixty-three thousand books, the tens of thousands of handbooks and invaluable antiquarian series and journals, together worth in pre-war prices £6 million, had been transported out of the city for safe-keeping. Some went by road to a huge warehouse one hundred kilometres south of Berlin in Lausitz and, to spread the risk, the remaining stock was sent to several other sites, especially to Vienna, where under Otto's supervision the 'iron reserves' were safely hidden in Starein for the remainder of the war.

By the end of the war, Lange's efforts had proved invaluable. Not only had Springer's warehouses in Berlin suffered like most of the city from bombs, fire and flooding, but the publishing headquarters in the Linkstrasse, which had, although damaged, miraculously survived, was sited precisely on the border between the Soviet and British sectors. The building was located in Soviet territory while the front door opened on to the pavement in the British sector. Diplomatic niceties were irrelevant during the first weeks of peace when the Red Army exclusively occupied Berlin, and Lange watched helplessly as a specialist Soviet plunder squad arrived to load £1 million worth of books on to a convoy of trucks for shipment to Moscow. By the time the western Allies arrived, little of Springer's stock in Berlin remained to be looted.

The Allies' interest in Springer's books was not surprising. At the beginning of the war, both British and American soldiers, sailors and airmen had suffered serious disadvantages because the military chiefs' chauvinism had falsely convinced them of the superiority of their own weapons. Yet with the possible exception of radar, German scientists and engineers had outclassed their Allied competitors in the design of military hardware from airframes, jets and tanks to submarines, guns and rockets. German superiority was reflected not only in the new weapons thrown against the Allies, but also in the revolutionary new chemicals, metals, fuels and gases which German industry had invented. In the period between Montgomery's victory at Alamein and the invasion of France, an Anglo-American plan was conceived to plunder German science and industry. Hence, following close behind the waves of Allied soldiers who landed on the Normandy beaches were the first of thousands of specialists whose principal task over the next three years was to investigate the wealth of Germany's scientific secrets. Naturally, Springer's old customers also wanted to know what progress German experts in their particular areas had covered during the twelve years of the Third Reich and Springer was understandably keen to satisfy their demands.

Ferdinand returned to Berlin as a Russian prisoner in April 1945 but he was released one month later. Reunited with Lange, he agreed that they should divide the ownership of the business. Both quickly realised the gigantic hurdles they faced to restart their business. The chaos and devastation in Berlin were overwhelming and everything was tightly controlled by the occupying armies. The Allies, as General Eisenhower proclaimed, were conquerors. They felt little compassion for the Germans and officially none whatsoever for those who had prospered under the Nazis. Nevertheless, Allied policy was to encourage the reopening of non-military industries to prevent Germany becoming a heavy financial burden on the Allies themselves. Springer's new headquarters, in the Reichpietschufer, were located in the British sector, but their initial application for a licence to PRISC in summer 1945 was unsuccessful. Some Springer executives believed that the British were suspicious that Ferdinand, despite his Jewish background, must have collaborated at a high level with the Nazis to survive in Berlin until 1944. There were even suggestions that Lange had made a serious attempt to obtain a testimonial from a Vatican bishop that Springer was not a Nazi sympathiser. But in this case, since it was British policy to encourage scientific publishing, for both Britain's and Germany's benefit, PRISC was ordered to ignore the past and Springer was awarded a licence on 24 October 1945. In practice the licence meant very little. Without telephones, petrol, paper or access to printing presses, Springer's business remained paralysed. Yet orders were beginning to arrive from all over the world for Springer's back issues and new journals. In November 1946, when Maxwell was still an officer in Berlin, the Control Office in London had telexed that there was 'concern about the lack of scientific learned journals coming from Germany to UK. We consider that this should be pressed forward vigorously.' However hard Maxwell attempted to implement that directive, he failed because the resources were unavailable. But he had registered the implications of the urgent messages.

In 1946, Tönjes Lange believed that Springer's best hopes for recovery lay in the Russian zone. In the pre-Cold War period, travel between the zones was relatively easy and Lange's assistant Paul Hövel began negotiating with the Soviet authorities to start printing a series of journals and books which had been planned during the last year of the war. Simultaneously, Lange personally began discussions with the Soviets for releasing Springer's stocks in Lausitz, which was in the Russian zone. But Ferdinand decided that Berlin's isolation hampered his relations with his authors and he moved near to the home of Karl Jaspers in Heidelberg in the American zone to establish a new editorial headquarters.

It is not quite clear exactly when Maxwell met Lange and Springer for the first time but Hövel remembers that during 1946 Maxwell was often approached by Ferdinand or Lange at PRISC for help in obtaining allocations, especially paper. Maxwell's duties would have been to judge the assistance Springer should receive and the company's success in securing its share of the rations depended upon the personal relationship developed with Captain Maxwell. Ferdinand and Tönjes Lange, who were both by nature traditional and conservative, were hugely impressed by the handsome, self-confident, German-speaking British captain. By all accounts, by the time Maxwell formally resigned from the Control Commission, his relationship with the two men was quite close, especially that with Tönjes Lange, whom Maxwell would later come to regard as a father-figure and address with fondness as 'Onkel'.

By October 1947, when Maxwell returned to Berlin, Lange had become desperate. The war had ended more than two years before but his business suffered an insurmountable obstacle. A few new journals were being printed in the Soviet zone and the demand for back issues and antiquarian books was overwhelming not only from libraries but also from astute investors as a hedge against the worthless German currency. Yet he was unable to send the journals and books out of Germany to his customers. An attempt in July to dispatch some parcels had been frustrated by the Allied insistence that all exports had to be in bulk rather than sent as single items. Springer needed someone outside Germany who could distribute the journals to its customers in over twenty countries. On 16 October 1947, with Maxwell's arrival, Springer Verlag was blessed with a golden opportunity denied to its competitors. Maxwell proposed that he should act as their representative abroad. 'Maxwell's arrival and offer', recalled Paul Hövel, 'was at a most opportune moment.' According to Lange, Maxwell's offer was 'the only hope for rebuilding our company'. Others believe that a tentative agreement had already been concluded between Maxwell and Lange in spring 1947 and that this was the cause of his resignation from PRISC to establish the export network. Maxwell's own account is that the initial offer was made by Lange and that his interest in scientific publishing was purely scientific, sparked by the atomic explosion at Hiroshima. Since Hövel's version was recorded shortly after the event, it is likely to be the most reliable.

Despite all the tension and conflict which would follow, Springer was forever grateful to Maxwell: over the following nine years their joint business was worth DM 20 million. 'Never will the Springer Publishing House', recorded an internal memorandum written in July 1959,

forget the help which Captain Maxwell gave us. . . . Throughout that time, Captain Maxwell always had good advice, solved the most difficult problems and was the person who was primarily responsible between 1947 and 1949 for re-establishing us as publishers. . . . In those terribly difficult times after Maxwell made his first offer, the drastic and successful methods invented by the British Captain (with an MC) produced unimaginably successful solutions to overcome those conditions so we could start exporting again.

Springer faced three fundamental problems: first, to produce new journals; secondly, to regain control over its huge stocks which had survived the war; and thirdly, to obtain permission to trade outside Germany. On the first problem, as we have seen, Maxwell as a PRISC officer gave Springer help in the course of his duties. It was Maxwell's successful efforts to solve the second and third problems which became controversial.

The reason why Hövel described Maxwell's arrival as 'opportune' was that Lange had just negotiated with the Russians the release of the valuable stock in Lausitz. Hövel is unclear about the details of transporting the books and journals by truck to West Berlin but it is certain that during the October visit Maxwell and Lange agreed that EPPAC should own the exclusive worldwide distribution rights of Springer's journals and books. Ferdinand, who was always wary of Maxwell, hesitated before endorsing the agreement because he feared Maxwell's total inexperience. The young ex-officer, Ferdinand felt, lacked the staff to wrap and address the packets and lacked the refinement to develop the personal contacts with Springer's traditional and valuable customers. Before signing, he insisted that Lange should try to organise another mass mailing operation of a few copies of its new journals to its most important pre-war customers. With Maxwell's help, a special dispensation was secured to dispatch 369 separate packets from Germany to EPPAC in London for onward shipment. The results, both sides agreed, proved that it was not a realistic, long-term solution. Therefore with Ferdinand's wholehearted support, Lange formally registered the publisher's agreement with Maxwell on 18 November 1947. It fell to Maxwell to secure the crucial export permits and arrange the transport for the contents of the Lausitz warehouse. He launched himself like a whirlwind, desperately keen for his new venture to succeed. 'Undoubtedly,' recalled Hövel, 'it would not have been possible to start exporting on that scale without the influence which Captain Maxwell could exert over key officials.'

Under the Allied laws of the occupation, all Germany's trade was controlled by the Anglo-American Joint Export – Import Agency (JEIA), based in Frankfurt. As part of the Allies' rigorous control of the German economy, everything which was bought and sold abroad had to be filtered through British and American officials at JEIA. The agency regularly published details of Germany's import needs and awaited tenders for their supply from Allied industrialists and businessmen. Similarly, nothing could be exported without JEIA's permission and at an agreed price. Since the only credible currency in Germany was cigarettes or chocolate, JEIA had to ensure that German industry obtained a fair price for its exports and, similarly, that its Allied competitors were not undercut. Consequently the true price depended upon the exchange rate between the discredited Reichsmark and the pound or dollar. The rates in 1947 were not officially fixed, but JEIA's normal rate was thirteen marks to one pound. Although the details of Maxwell's negotiations are no longer available, it is indisputable that Maxwell, after obtaining JEIA permission to export Springer's journals, obtained in early December 1947 the exchange rate of twenty-one marks for each pound, a 60 per cent advantage which would substantially increase Maxwell's profits. As later episodes demonstrate, Maxwell probably used the contacts which he had forged as a Control Commission officer to obtain the satisfactory terms. He most likely convinced officials that since it was Allied policy rapidly to disseminate German scientific knowledge, the journals' prices should be kept quite low. On the export licence itself, an official noted that the special rate was agreed 'after discussion'. But Springer would not get any of the benefits of that exchange rate. Nor their customers. 'Captain Maxwell', commented an astounded Hövel, 'obtained an extraordinarily favourable exchange rate.'

Within days of Maxwell's coup, a formal protest about Springer's contract was sent from a Dutch publisher to PRISC's director Kenneth Kirkness at his headquarters in Berlin. Frans von Eugen, the owner of *Excerpta Medica* of Amsterdam, had been granted by UNESCO the rights to publish medical abstracts for specialists and among them were Ferdinand's new journals officially published in Heidelberg, in the American zone. Maxwell's exclusive deal destroyed the Dutch hopes for a monopoly. 'I sincerely hope', von Eugen wrote to Kirkness, 'that you will use all your influence to frustrate this agreement and any such agreements which would be made in the future as they are ill suited for turning the intercourse between nations in the right channels.' Following his letter, von Eugen arrived in Berlin armed with the claim that even the American authorities condemned both the agreement and the exchange rate. Kirkness evidently was unimpressed since less than one month later Maxwell and the Germans formalised and registered their new deal. By January 1948, it would be worth £2,387. By the end of the year, EPPAC had purchased books and journals valued at over one million marks which, converted at the special rate, equalled £47,750. Converted at present-day values, Maxwell had secured a contract worth over half a million pounds.

By early 1948, Springer's journals and books were arriving in London, transported, according to Hövel and Henrik Salle, another veteran Springer employee, by train from Berlin to Bielefeld and from there by truck. To ensure the transport of 150 tons of journals and 150 tons of books, and to provide for future production, Maxwell had negotiated with the British authorities that Springer should be allocated 200 kilowatt hours of electricity, 20,000 kilos of coal for heating, 150,000 sheets of paper, 500 wooden crates and 50 kilos of nails. Springer was back in business and fast moving ahead of its competitors.

Distribution in London was the responsibility of Vernon Baxter, a German refugee whose original name was Blumenfeld and whom Maxwell had recruited on his return from Berlin in October 1947. When Baxter reported for work on his first day Maxwell had forgotten why he had been hired. 'Maxwell asked me whether I could set up a book department,' says Baxter. 'With great cheek I said that I could, but I had no idea.' Maintaining an accurate mailing list and sending accounts punctually required considerable organisation, and more staff were hired. Most of the employees were Jewish refugees from central Europe, some of them successful professionals before the war and thus over-qualified, but nevertheless grateful for employment despite the low rates of pay and the spartan conditions. Maxwell felt comfortable surrounded by people who shared a similar background and it was important to have German-speakers to handle German publications. 'We were bursting at the seams,' recalls Baxter, 'and then a new recruit arrived. He or she was expected to find a plank of wood and a chair and begin to work.' Over the babble of German, Polish and Yiddish, the young Maxwell ruled serenely, nonchalantly ignoring the blatant improvisation. Sooner rather than later, all his employees recognised that Maxwell would brook no challenge. 'He was the sun,' commented an early transgressor, 'and we were either planets or had to leave.' The only exception was his partner, Peter Orton.

In contrast with Maxwell's extravagant character, Orton was a quiet-spoken intellectual who in Berlin before the war had been a member of the Communist Party. Peter Oppenheim, as he was then called, had gained comical notoriety as the cadre who had successfully robbed a cake shop to fill the party funds only to be arrested on a tip-off from the taxi driver who had driven him to the shop. He had met Maxwell in the Queen's Regiment, where Orton had been the sergeant to Second Lieutenant Maxwell. Their relationship would never change. 'Orton hero-worshipped Maxwell,' recalls another Berliner who worked in the office. 'For Orton, as for everyone else, Maxwell was a born leader.' But behind Maxwell's back, Orton often voiced dislike and criticism of his senior partner's brash gambles. Long before his first major crisis, Orton compared Maxwell to Eva Kreuger, the Swedish match king whose empire had collapsed amid bloodshed. Orton would die in a car crash before he saw his prophecy come true. Yet together they made a good team. 'The difference between the two', recalls Baxter, 'was that Maxwell recognised the advantage of holding someone's coat.' While Maxwell addressed himself to the strategic decisions, alternately blustering or charming officials while wheeler-dealing, Orton tried to fashion the sales organisation which Springer needed.

Ferdinand was at first delighted by Maxwell's efficient transport of the stock to Britain but soon felt that his original misgivings were justified. Whereas the Springers had, over a century, meticulously cultivated a venerable style befitting the publishers of the famous and had constructed a fastidious distribution system, EPPAC's staff and its management, complained Ferdinand, were 'amateur' and their inexperience was provoking Springer's old customers to complain that deliveries were too slow. Maxwell, Ferdinand complained to Lange, did not love books and authors like a traditional publisher but was a trader: he happened to be dealing in books but it might as well have been cattle. Maxwell's system for their distribution was 'inadequate', he told Lange. 'He seems to believe that forwarding a bundle of journals is nothing more than acting as a postman.' Lange did not share his partner's anger.

In summer 1948, when Maxwell arrived again in Berlin, his blooming exuberance and self-importance reinforced Tönjes Lange's favourable impression. His young benefactor reported that he had secured orders from the British government and British universities to buy German scientific journals from EPPAC and had also arranged that Lord Pakenham, the Foreign Office minister responsible for Germany, would open an exhibition of German books in London which Maxwell had organised. Lange, who knew the details of Maxwell's impoverished youth, could not fail to be overwhelmed. In the midst of the Soviet blockade of Berlin which cut the city's road and rail connections to the West, and the Cold War, he was sure that Springer's future depended upon the Englishman. Uncertainty prevailed and he could not possibly have envisaged the prosperity which would explode in the new Federal Republic just one year later. Consequently, during that visit, Lange offered Maxwell another huge slice of Springer's assets. He explained that his brother Otto Lange had successfully recovered control over Springer stock stored in Austria, which could be exploited to expand the publisher's exports. But there was a problem. When the books had arrived in 1944 from Berlin, Austria had been part of the German Reich. At the end of the war, Allied laws banned commercial contacts between Austria and Germany as a criminal offence. Legally, Springer was denied control over what they had called their 'iron reserves'. Lange believed that Maxwell was a possible saviour. If the Austrian company would sell the books to Maxwell in pounds sterling, Springer in Germany could eventually recoup its money. Understandably, Maxwell readily agreed to Lange's plan that the Austrian stock be officially sold to EPPAC, transported to London and resold on Springer's behalf to the rest of the world.

In September 1948, the arrangement was formalised when Ferdinand and the two Langes came to London to sign the agreement with EPPAC. On the same day, EPPAC moved again to larger premises – above a rat-infested banana warehouse in Neal Street, Covent Garden. Within two years Neal Street was to be a mini-empire of fifty employees, and still growing.

Both Otto and Ferdinand were soon unhappy about the proposed deal. Otto feared that he might lose the financial benefits of his legal ownership and be tarnished as a criminal while Ferdinand had become still more upset about EPPAC's incompetence. Throughout the year, as world trading gradually normalised, inquiries and subscriptions had increased, but simultaneously, according to a Springer executive, 'The difficulties and the continuous stream of complaints about EPPAC's methods did not stop.' EPPAC was certainly not the sole cause of all the problems. Both the Bank of England and British Customs succeeded in injecting obstructions at every level; in any case, some foreign customers were jealous that an upstart like Maxwell had secured a valuable monopoly. But, in Ferdinand's view, Maxwell was much to blame. Instead of remaining in London to smooth out any problems, he had dashed around Europe opening subsidiary offices in Paris, Brussels and Basle, so compounding the difficulties. In addition, he had approached Springer's competitors and offered similar deals to distribute their journals and books. His restless ambitions irritated Ferdinand all the more because Maxwell had inherited Springer's invaluable mailing list, which had been carefully compiled in the course of one century and had targeted sixty thousand individuals in universities, institutes and industry. Overnight, Maxwell could use it for the benefit of Springer's competitors. Yet, despite his reservations, Ferdinand acknowledged that he had no option but to signal his agreement if the stocks in Vienna were to be sold.

The 'iron reserves' in Vienna were worth in 1945 prices about £100,000. Springer knew that if the true value were disclosed to the authorities, their export would be banned. At the meeting in London, the three Germans told Maxwell they had decided to undervalue the stock. Springer's contract with EPPAC dated 16 September shows an invoiced price as £4,000 which was later increased to £12,000.

Two weeks later, Maxwell reported that he had removed every bureaucratic obstacle between Vienna, Berlin, Frankfurt and London and was waiting for the first shipment. On 7 October about seventy boxes of books and journals were loaded into a railway wagon destined for London. Among the titles were books on atomic physics, pharmacology, jet engines and medical specialities. But even before the wagon crossed the Channel, the harmony between the three German confederates fell apart. Otto Lange bitterly protested that Ferdinand had broken his wartime promise and had deprived him of reward for all his work and risks. He threatened to renege on the whole deal and blamed his brother in Berlin for allowing Maxwell to benefit handsomely from the favourable exchange rate. Finally, he accused Maxwell of not paying the amount which had been orally agreed in London. Irritated, Maxwell flew to Vienna, accused Otto of breaking his wartime 'gentleman's agreement and his word of honour' to Ferdinand and then flew to Frankfurt. With the three

Germans warring among themselves, Maxwell's own position had immeasurably strengthened.

While in Frankfurt, Maxwell negotiated with JEIA a new, special dispensation for Springer to dispatch books without the time-consuming need for Customs' clearance for each consignment; he then flew on to Berlin to negotiate an improved discount on the purchase price for EPPAC – 50 per cent on books and 40 per cent on journals. With his special exchange rate, Tönjes Lange calculated, Maxwell had by then effectively obtained an unusually high 70 per cent discount. As his success and wealth soared, Maxwell's horizons broadened. During his visit to Berlin in October 1948, he told Lange that he was planning a sales trip to Tokyo to exploit Springer's contacts with Japan's leading book-dealers, Maruzen and Nankodo. For a recently impoverished refugee aged just twenty-five even to contemplate a flight to the Far East just three years after the end of the war staggered the Germans. But by 15 February 1949, when Wagon No. 455 596, the seventh and last of the consignment, left Vienna, Maxwell already had under his control a reservoir of books and journals which would attract the attention of the whole world of learning.

Yet ostensibly Springer received no gratitude from London. Instead, Maxwell forcefully complained that Otto had broken his agreement, which gave EPPAC the sole distribution rights, in 'a most unethical manner'; apparently Otto had supplied other British dealers. Maxwell sent Otto a menacing letter: after accusing Otto of breach of the agreement and denying that he owed any more money, Maxwell suggested that since he had sold a mere £150 worth of books so far, he might ship all seven wagon-loads back to Vienna and in future place his orders like other booksellers. Otto did not reply.

For those who knew Maxwell in London, the smooth self-confidence which supported that threat was characteristic of the image that the handsome businessman presented. Despite the stringent post-war austerity under which the majority of Britons suffered, Maxwell never seemed to be affected by the Labour government's rationing of everything from bread and eggs to petrol and clothes. As he dashed around London, dressed in well-tailored suits, he seemed to have settled upon a lifestyle which few could afford. In 1949, he possessed a petrol-guzzling red Chrysler which he had brought back from Prague, and he would soon exchange that status symbol for a Cadillac which, because such cars were still banned for British subjects, was acquired on temporary import licence and owned by a foreign friend. Maxwell himself rarely drove his cars, but was chauffeured by an enigmatic and swarthy cockney, Bob Oglanby, whose antecedents were, to Maxwell's staff, mysterious. His insatiable appetite for luxury cars reflected his noticeable desire to impress everyone.

If Maxwell's poor childhood had instilled in him an appreciation of money and taught him the simple delight of grinding down his business partner by exhausting negotiations, it remained true that, in post-war Britain, wealth did not enhance one's social status. Maxwell's only social attributes in 1945 were the MC and his wartime rank. Although by custom only professional officers retain their rank in civilian life, Maxwell clung to his and to those bare letters as if his very survival were dependent upon them. Rigidly, Maxwell insisted on being addressed as 'Captain' for nearly two decades after the war. Even in 1969, Springer executives still addressed him in the fashion which, twenty-five years earlier, he had judged would earn some social status among Britain's uniquely class-prejudiced society. In 1949, Maxwell had not finally settled upon his identity. The confusion is evident on his various business notepapers. The heading of EPPAC notepaper showed Capt. R. Maxwell MC, on Springer's letterhead he was R.I. Maxwell MC, yet his private notepaper was headed Capt. I.R. Maxwell MC. To complete the confusion, even when the letterhead stated R.I. Maxwell, he signed the letter I.R. Maxwell.

On one matter, however, there was no confusion. Maxwell was devoted to his family. By 1949, a second child, Anne, had been born. Like the remainder of his nine children, Anne was born outside Paris, France, delivered by Betty's sister, a gynaecologist. All the Maxwell children are French citizens by birth, and have remained so. After Anne's birth, the family had moved into a larger flat in Kensington. The amount of time he spent with his family was limited by his work, but never, by all accounts, by play. His only recreations were the cinema and, on Saturday afternoons, watching Arsenal football club play at Highbury. 'I would love to own a football club,' he told a friend at that time. But in work, despite enormous energy and dedication, the results were still confused. Yaacov Schlomovitch had taught his grandson the talent of negotiating, to buy and sell, but not how to organise an office and staff. Haggling in the fields around Ruthenia did not require chains of management command of the type which Ferdinand Springer required.

In the summer of 1949, Ferdinand's dissatisfaction revived. It had taken one year to unpack, store and catalogue the Vienna stock, and EPPAC's inexperienced staff were still failing to keep proper records, to dispatch orders rapidly and, understandably for the inexperienced refugees, to grasp the importance of advertising. In Germany, Springer's staff, who reverently described Ferdinand as *Der Kaiser*, jealously watched Maxwell's windfall and his encroachment upon their work. Some harboured fears that he might ultimately inherit the whole business. To alleviate their complaints, Lange had decided to send his best dealers to help the London operation. At Springer's expense, Maxwell was learning the business, and he now conceived a scheme which would endow him with increased respectability.

On 14 July 1949 Maxwell suggested to Springer that EPPAC was 'not really suitable for the distribution of your world renowned publications' and proposed to create a new company which would be called Lange, Maxwell & Springer in which the Germans were offered 49 per cent of the shares for £10,000. Tönjes Lange would be the unpaid chairman, Maxwell the managing director and Orton the secretary. The Springer directors were interested in the idea. Although the Berlin blockade had been lifted and Konrad Adenauer would soon be appointed Chancellor, they were still unsure about their prospects and felt that they might gain more direct control over their business. One week later, Lange agreed and effusively thanked Maxwell for the 'honour' of becoming the chairman. Jubilant, Maxwell sent to Lange, whom he now called Charlie, the proposed articles of association with the quip: 'If you are clever enough to understand what they mean, then I lift my hat to you. I think the lawyer's language used in these things is appalling. However no doubt you will send me a complete translation in Chinese, in which case I shall, of course, understand it.'

Maxwell's conception of LMS was a quintessential example of his business acumen. Under his proposed scheme, Maxwell was the manager of two companies which, while theoretically they would work together, could place him in an embarrassing conflict of interest. Under the agreement, EPPAC contracted with Springer that their joint company, LMS, would distribute all Springer books outside Germany. But EPPAC would not cease to trade since it was EPPAC which was officially importing Springer's books from Germany. So EPPAC would sell its stock to LMS but would continue to trade under Maxwell's management while promising not to compete with LMS for the next ten years. It was a simple arrangement which revealed the essence of Maxwell's future operations: namely, compartmentalisation. 'Everyone works in blinkers except Maxwell,' said one of his trusted advisers twenty years later. 'Only he knows the master plan and that keeps changing.' Securing Springer's agreement to that duopoly was a masterstroke which launched Maxwell closer towards the millionaire status which he craved.

To establish LMS on a sound footing needed finance. Whereas nowadays almost anyone may approach a bank for a loan, in 1949 it was the privilege of the rich and the respected. Since status was a commodity which Maxwell did not naturally command, it was a major coup when he obtained an interview with the merchant banker, Sir Charles Hambro, to discuss a loan. Although there are suggestions that Hambro, who was attached during the war to Special Operations Executive, the British sabotage organisation, had met Maxwell in an Intelligence role (since Maxwell would occasionally hint at his connections with British Intelligence), Maxwell says that the meeting was in fact arranged through Major John Whitlock, a former SOE officer and executive of the publisher Butterworths who enjoyed a reputation as a freemason and 'likeable rogue'. Hambro was interested in both science and publishing, so Maxwell, who eloquently portrayed LMS's glowing future, was not disappointed. Hambro agreed to a loan of £25,000, the present-day equivalent of a quarter of a million pounds. Maxwell left the Bishopsgate building ecstatic, and cabled Lange the good news that their new company was firmly operational. He had found a new godfather. 'It was Charles Hambro', Maxwell told Gunther Heyden, an employee in later years, 'who taught me the importance of having a chauffeur. You must think about the business, not about getting to the meeting.'

Yet within days of the new company's incorporation in October, there was a crisis. Writing from Berlin, Tönjes complained to Maxwell that he felt isolated, uncomfortable and helpless and feared that Maxwell was more than ever exploiting Springer's reputation and keeping his German partners in the dark. Maxwell, wrote Tönjes, seemed to ignore advice and was even signing letters as 'chairman'. Worst of all, Tönjes had confided to Orton that he could not always trust what Maxwell said.

Maxwell felt genuinely hurt by the reprimand. 'I value your personal friendship and esteem more than anything else in the world,' he replied to Tönjes, whom he felt had not understood the enormous obstacles he had faced in establishing the business. Even if London was not as physically destroyed as Berlin, there were myriad problems, which Maxwell listed: inexperienced staff, tax disputes, overcoming the legacy of wartime and socialist regulations. 'It doesn't feel good', Maxwell scribbled at the end of his five-page explanation, 'to receive such scoldings from one's "father" and teacher.' Tönjes's distrust irked: 'Should you ever in any way or manner whatsoever feel or say that you cannot trust my statements, then immediately from that minute I would wish to resign from that association.' The crisis was, for the time being, resolved and, as Lange would often repeat, 'Maxwell gave us enormous and valuable help over those years.'

But Ferdinand and Tönjes were convinced that some of Maxwell's more far-reaching ambitions should be curbed. Maxwell had proposed that LMS should also become a publisher. The idea was flatly·rejected. Instead, Springer opted for an invitation from Butterworths, one of Britain's most venerable publishers, founded in 1818, to form a joint company. Ferdinand's motives were simple. Maxwell had proved to be a trader not a publisher, so he would be confined in the new joint venture to simple distribution.

The link between Springer and Butterworths was Dr Paul Rosbaud, a 53-year-old Austrian metallurgist who was the pre-war advisor of Springer's major journal *Naturwissenschaft*. To this day, Rosbaud's wartime career remains a mystery. Although he was credited with aiding the destruction of Nazi Germany's heavy-water programme, some suspect that he was also the source in 1939 of the famour 'Oslo' report which provided British Intelligence with a detailed insight into un-imagined inventions which German scientists had placed at the disposal of the German military. Because the report was so authoritative and suggested German developments which far surpassed British achieve-ments, it was disbelieved, but in the course of the war it proved to be totally accurate. Its authorship has never been officially revealed. Nevertheless, Rosbaud clearly enjoyed good connections with senior British personalities because on 25 November 1946 he was present at a meeting in the Cabinet Office in Great George Street under the chairmanship of Sir John Anderson, an under-secretary.

The government, having belatedly recognised the importance of science, hoped to encourage the development of journals similar to Springer's and wished Butterworths to be the publisher. Most of those gathered at the November meeting were senior representatives of the British scientific establishment and members of the new Scientific Advisory Board. Others present were the merchant banker Sir Charles Hambro, Hugh Quennell, the mercurial representative of Butterworths who, as a Control Commission officer, had met Maxwell in Germany, and Count Vanden Heuvel, alias 'Fanny the Fixer', a wartime Intelligence officer and diplomat and then a colourful businessman whose meagre knowledge of science nevertheless elevated him to the status of expert compared to that possessed by the other laymen present. The result was the foundation of Butterworth Scientific Publications. But the company failed to flourish and so, in 1949, after Ferdinand had rejected Maxwell's suggestion, a joint company was created called Butterworth-Springer. Rosbaud was appointed the editor of the scientific journals and it was agreed that they would be distributed by LMS.

After just two years, Maxwell was the managing director of an important book distributor which was recognised by the City, the publishing world and the government. But it was not enough. Fifteen years earlier, Maxwell had observed that his grandfather Yaacov Schlomovitch never confined himself to a single deal. Unlike his father Mechel who just dealt in cattle, Yaacov always managed a collection of parallel but unconnected deals. He was constantly juggling, keeping as many deals going simultaneously as he could. Instinctively, Maxwell searched for the same.

Tönjes was possibly the first to recognise Maxwell's inheritance of that talent. In later years, he recalled eating in a Berlin restaurant in 1950 with Maxwell when he noticed his associate listening to the conversation in a foreign language at the neighbouring table. Afterwards Maxwell explained that the Hungarians were discussing a barter deal and if he acted quickly he might profit from the information. Tönjes was bewildered but admiring. He had not realised that Springer's worldwide manager was also a player in the barter trade – a testament to Maxwell's natural compartmentalisation.

Barter is the oldest form of trade, used before coinage was invented. For poorer countries, who after 1945 either had no hard currencies or faced politically motivated trade embargoes, bartering their own produce was the only means of obtaining important foreign goods. In its essence, barter is a simple bilateral exchange, but by the early 1950s Maxwell would become involved in hugely complicated, multilateral deals which would embrace several countries and many different commodities – pork bellies were exchanged for wood which was bartered for silk which might be exchanged for a metal. Success in those barter deals required all the skills and guile of a businessman, and more. So much depended on racing to close the circle before any of the interdependent deals collapsed. Like a juggler, the dealer's success was to keep a huge number of balls in the air which required exceptional mental agility. Throughout his career, his adversaries and friends alike have commented upon Maxwell's phenomenal capacity to retain and instantly recall information. Combined with his charm, fluent sales talk and tireless determination, this facility made him exceptionally skilful in constructing the circle for a barter deal. Lange and Springer were eyewitnesses to one refined brand of Maxwell's style, but Gunther Heyden saw another.

In 1948, Gunther Heyden was just twenty years old. Born in Cologne, he had spent the war in hiding in Germany after his Jewish mother had committed suicide. After the war, he found menial jobs with both the American and British armies until he was employed by PRISC in Berlin to supervise the licensing of cultural activities. Over the following two years, he 'quite often' saw Maxwell in Berlin, occasionally dressed in uniform even after he had officially resigned. 'Maxwell dropped into the Commission's press club, discussing business with contacts,' Heyden remembers. 'He was always in and out doing deals.' The deals had no connection with books or scientific publishing but were, on behalf of Low-Bell, for unaesthetic commodities such as brushes and cotton waste. No deal was better remembered than Maxwell's coup to sell paint to German railways.

The German requirement for paint was, as usual, formally issued by JEIA in Frankfurt. At the former headquarters of IG Farben, the German chemical conglomerate, Maxwell was a familiar figure, especially to Paul Lassen, a British officer attached to JEIA who was responsible for vetting contracts in the food and agriculture section. Lassen's office was situated on the so-called 'Polish corridor' where everyone who wanted a slice of the lucrative business congregated. Lassen candidly admits that the potential for anybody to benefit by corruption was enormous: 'I vetted every contract and could have made a fortune.' Lassen's friend, Bill Hickey, who was responsible for the paint contract, was visited by Maxwell and Louis Berger, the paint manufacturer. Twenty years ago, Berger told the *Sunday Times* how impressed he had been by Maxwell's dynamic organisation, by his ability to obtain visas and transport and by his winning $40 in a poker game with American soldiers to pay for their expenses in Frankfurt. Most of all, Berger was thrilled that Maxwell obtained the enormous $1 million contract for the paint. While Lassen believes that Berger never delivered and was never paid, Heyden says that Maxwell delivered not only the paint but also the brushes. The two JEIA officials impressed Maxwell and when their contracts ended in 1950 both were employed by him to implement his more intricate deals.

By then, Heyden, hired by Orton, had arrived from Berlin. On his first day at Neal Street on 2 January 1950, he received a familiar welcome: 'They'd forgotten what they wanted me for.' The confusion was symptomatic but transitory. Maxwell's businesses were booming and Heyden was detailed to supervise LMS's publicity, its mailing list and the printing of ten thousand copies of LMS's first catalogue, which featured 1,000 books and 1,200 different journals. His lack of any experience was overlooked.

On that same day, the new company LMS began formal trading. Besides the five-year agreement which gave LMS exclusive rights to the worldwide sales of Springer's books and journals, Maxwell also enjoyed very favourable terms for the return of all unsold books; most import- antly, Maxwell's own company, EPPAC, could sell its stock of Springer rare books and old journals to the new company on advantageous terms.

The first LMS board meeting, which was held in January and which the Germans attended, was a notable occasion. Maxwell was representing the competing interests of EPPAC and LMS. It was a pattern of inter-company trading which would be repeated many times over the following years. At that moment, any reluctance the Germans might have felt was dissipated: they were grateful for Maxwell's services, they believed that the inter-company sales would be simple transactions, and they knew that moving the stock back to Germany was fraught with difficulties, not the least of them legal.

Springer, however, was disquieted. The previous year, Maxwell had signed exclusive distribution agreements with his competitors Urban & Schwarzenberg, Ernst & Sohn, Verlag Chemie, Thieme and an East German publisher, Akademie-Verlag. JEIA had agreed that the same hugely advantageous exchange rates could be applied to the new contracts. Ferdinand complained to Lange that he, Springer, was bearing the cost and 'taking a great risk' to promote his competitors: 'For Maxwell, it was the means to build for himself a huge business in London and he achieved that in an astonishingly short period.' Springer was worried that it had placed so much of its future in Maxwell's hands. Yet at its early regular monthly board meetings, Maxwell successfully charmed the very precise Germans with evidence of his success, produced by the 'great intensity' of work by his staff of sixty-five. Everything, he claimed, was rapidly becoming more efficient and rationalised, and the empire was expanding. A new ten-thousand-name mailing list had been compiled, a system of Adrema name plates had been completed to speed the dispatch of circulars, and a new warehouse had been rented in the Elephant and Castle district of London. The Germans thought the innovations were 'exceptionally good' but their demeanour changed when the very reason for their special relationship with Maxwell suddenly disappeared.

In early 1950, the new government of the Federal Republic of Germany announced that the Allies' vast network of regulations and controls would rapidly vanish and direct exports would be allowed. Anxious to earn dollars, the Bonn government urged companies like Springer to dismantle their artificial arrangements.

Both Ferdinand and Lange realised that, despite the irksome duplication, Springer's prestige and sales had become too enmeshed with the London operation to be abruptly terminated. Moreover, the Maxwell connection placed them at an enormous advantage over their competitors since Germans were still unable to travel to most countries. Through Maxwell, they could still contact their old customers. At that moment, he was on their behalf energetically travelling around the world, opening new offices and selling Springer's books and journals in Japan, Italy, Spain and Austria. The commercial advantages still outweighed any irritations.

In the cause of Springer, legend relates, Maxwell became the British airline BOAC's first passenger to clock up one million miles. His frequent dashes to Northolt aerodrome were accompanied by pleas from his devoted secretary Anne Dove to 'hold the plane for Captain Maxwell' while Oglanby raced along the Great West Road. If the loyalty of most of Maxwell's staff was won by a mixture of love and fear, Anne Dove was the exception. 'A superior lady, out of the top drawer, with excellent breeding,' is the general recollection of the Jewish refugees who observed their boss's alter ego. 'Dove was more than a secretary to Maxwell,' recalls Heyden, 'she was the most powerful influence on him.' Dove, all the refugees suspected, was the source of Maxwell's phenomenal success in British society. Others were convinced that no one could have influenced Maxwell's performance.

Besides his wife, Maxwell has relied upon two women in his life. Both were secretaries. Anne Dove was the first. During the war, she had worked as a secretary for SOE, first in Baker Street, then in Cairo and later in Italy. Since that organisation appealed to an extraordinary mixture of entrepreneurs, individualists and above all ambitious members of the Establishment who would play important roles in post-war Britain, she had collected during that decade a notable list of contacts ranging across the worlds of finance, politics and culture. In 1950, she returned to Britain and saw an advertisement in the *Daily Telegraph* for a secretary. She applied and after waiting for two hours outside the director's office was on the verge of leaving when she was ushered inside. On one wall of the huge book-lined, mahogany-coloured office, she remembers, there was a 'huge map of the world with all the capitals pinpointed by red lights. Behind a huge desk which didn't seem large enough for him, I saw a big man with jet black hair and large greenish eyes. But what I noticed most was the very warm and beautifully timbred voice.' During the interview, Dove recalls how Maxwell turned the map lights on and 'Whenever I would say, "Have you got an office here or there?" pointing to the various capitals, he would immediately say, "Of course." Some of the offices had not even been thought of yet, but Maxwell went on the maxim that nothing was impossible.' Dove took the job because she was attracted to the idea of constant travel to all the 'offices' and the thought of an endless supply of bananas, her favourite fruit, from the warehouse downstairs. Her boss, she realised, was a man for whom 'there was never enough time to achieve all the things he wished for. His own life was planned in his mind several jumps ahead – ambition being the driving force – and as each ambition was achieved then the next plan was already being formulated.' Dove was quite prepared to place her impressive list of contacts at her boss's disposal. Among them was Charles Hambro, whom she knew from her service in SOE. 'Charles told me that he was pleased that I was with Maxwell looking after things,' she recalls, 'and Maxwell minded very much what Charles thought of him.'

All those meeting Maxwell in 1950 were left breathless by what Dove describes as his 'tremendous life-force'. The size of his desk, they quipped, matched his ambitions. Visitors discovered that their attempts at conversation were constantly frustrated by their host picking up one of his four telephones and ordering calls to China, America or Russia and then switching from one language to another without a blink. Some staff insist that at least two of the telephones were not even connected but were important props for his role as the international tycoon. 'Every time I walked in,' remembers one frequent and sceptical visitor, 'he was shouting down the phone to New York and one minute later picked up another phone and was screaming at Moscow.' According to Heyden, 'You could hear Maxwell's voice booming down the length of Neal Street as he alternately harangued or charmed somebody into a profitable deal.'

His staff were not so much sceptical as suspended between amusement and fright. Maxwell's senses of humour, fun and generosity were engaging qualities. At Christmas he paid for many staff to return to their families in Germany. But the moods easily changed. His appearance in the general office was usually accompanied by the question: 'And what are you doing?' If inadequately answered, there was another dismissal. Those who attempted to temper his approach met with no success. One senior executive who told Maxwell that his staff were quivering on their seats with insecurity was cut off in mid-sentence with a deep growl: 'Rubbish, while they work for me they have complete security.' 'But look at this list of all those who you've fired!' countered the bold employee. 'They're ex-employees and ex-employees have no security,' was the crushing reply.

Springer employees were less intimidated by the extravagant style. After a period of relative calm, they were once again sending their complaints to London, especially about the failure to send money which was owed. By November 1950 the outstanding bills amounted to £115,000 (£27,585 in October alone) and the debt was growing. Although Maxwell was not solely to blame – customers were invariably reluctant to pay their accounts, and compliance with the Bank of England's rigid currency controls presented endless difficulties – Springer's suspicious staff constantly scrutinised every detail of London's operations.

Triumphantly, in November they found some evidence to justify their unease. By chance, Springer staff had seen a document, inadvertently sent from London to Berlin, which showed that Maxwell's distribution deals with their competitors Ernst & Sohn and Urban & Schwarzenberg were signed, not as they believed with LMS, but with Maxwell's own company, EPPAC. Both Lange and Ferdinand were shocked since in their view this was a clear contravention of their agreement with Maxwell which forbade EPPAC to compete with LMS for ten years. They were due to travel to London in mid-November and a showdown seemed inevitable. To avert the crisis, at twelve noon on 1 November Maxwell went to Bishopsgate and successfully obtained a further £25,000 loan from Sir Charles Hambro. But it was not enough to prevent the Germans demanding concessions.

At a meeting on 14 November, Maxwell agreed that Springer could begin exporting books directly from Germany and that he would repay DM 1.1 million in five monthly instalments. The following afternoon, Lange, Ferdinand and Maxwell went to Hambros to confirm the recapitalisation of their company. It was a useful opportunity for Maxwell to demonstrate the support he enjoyed in the City. Relations improved and Maxwell once again addressed a letter to Tönjes as 'My dear Onkel'. Springer, he knew, still depended upon him.

One problem in early 1951 which needed his help was to find a route out of their original agreement. The demand for Springer's books was growing but the supply was hindered by an unpleasant truth that their exports were based on a fundamental deception. Springer had never disclosed to German Customs the true value of the books and journals in the boxes: the value of their exports which were declared on the ECDs (Exchange Control Documents) did not match the true value. Whereas the current certificate was worth DM 30,000, the shipments awaiting dispatch were worth DM 600,000. Lange and Hövel confided to Maxwell that their deception was in danger of exposure.

At first it was argued that the Customs officers would never check the real value of the books, but he was persuaded to the contrary. Then both sides formulated a ruse which they believed to be legal. One hundred boxes awaiting shipment in Berlin and Würzburg would be repacked, relabelled and sold in three parts: Springer would sell to LMS and EPPAC, while Lange & Springer (a separate German company) would sell to LMS. It was the provision of that kind of help which earned Maxwell their gratitude. But the respite was again short-lived

On 28 November 1950, Maxwell arrived in Berlin reporting that business was booming. He disclosed that he had secured a massive £150,000 order for books from Guozi Shudian, the Communist Chinese book-dealer, and that he had been paid in advance. Ferdinand was less pleased. He claimed that Maxwell had overcharged Springer's old customer and warned that the Chinese would eventually discover the truth. Six weeks later, the crisis deepened. In quick succession, LMS's Paris office went bankrupt, the victim of French tariffs and of the state of the economy; the LMS operation in Basle also collapsed because the Swiss insisted on buying direct from Berlin and adamantly refused to place their orders in London; and Maxwell's much vaunted deal with Sansoni of Florence, which featured as a considerable profit in that year's accounts, was proving to be disastrous. Shipping books from Germany to Italy via London was costly, and Springer was faced with Sansoni's complaint that excessive stock had been delivered which he insisted Springer should repurchase. For the conservative Springer team, each case was a major crisis. Together, they seemed to presage the *Götterdämmerung*.

Ferdinand, galled that he should have surrendered so much control over his company's reputation and future, reflected his staff's irritation about the London operation. In early 1951, he sent Maxwell a long reprimand criticising his failure to appreciate the invaluable mailing list. But more revealing were the guidelines which Springer listed as important for a publisher's behaviour: adhere to the prices quoted in the catalogues; do not quote a rare-book price for standard books; and treat a customer in such a way that he will return for a further sale. The more memorable cautionary rules have in retrospect a piquancy. A publisher, Maxwell was told, should not promise more than he can fulfil; it is more important to serve a customer than exploit him; one shouldn't buy more than one can pay for; and one shouldn't offer more than one can deliver. 'You are making the mistake that you are expecting good results based on faulty methods,' concluded Ferdinand. Their personal relationship, he said, was terminated.

The first consequence of the break was a letter from Springer's accountants to Maxwell disclosing that they wanted to scrutinise LMS's accounts. The initial summary sent from London for the year 1949/50 showed a loss of £225. In June 1951 R.A. Meilicke, Springer's lawyer, and Fritz Fuhrmann, an accountant, arrived in London to check the books, especially the sales of EPPAC's stock to LMS. There were good grounds for their suspicions. Maxwell's own accountants had also discovered irregularities.

Over the past year, Frank Beckwith, a qualified chartered secretary and LMS's accounts manager, had been grappling with dozens of untidy files containing invoices and receipts, in an effort to end the chaotic system he had inherited on his recruitment. Reconciling the inter-company trading between EPPAC, LMS and Low-Bell was complicated by the never-ending flow of foreign currencies in and out of their bank accounts and through smaller companies privately owned by Maxwell. Together with Tom Clark, an accountant who would stay with Maxwell for over twenty-five years, Beckwith discovered that their predecessor had been obtaining Maxwell's signature for cheques against false invoices which were in fact payments to himself. Defrauding Maxwell, the two new accountants decided, had not been difficult. 'Maxwell's style of business', recalls Beckwith, 'was like a golfer who liked to hit the big drive down the green but was uninterested in the small strokes at the end.' Others suspected that Maxwell had not shown sufficient care to prevent the chaos developing. Among those was Ferdinand Springer.

Fuhrmann's first impression on landing at Northolt aerodrome was favourable. Oglanby graciously chauffeured the German in the Cadillac to the Shaftesbury Hotel. Compared to Berlin, London was a sanctuary with plenty of food and not totally devastated by bombing. Fuhrmann's attitude changed a few hours later when he heard from Meilicke that LMS's accountants, Moodie & Epstein, had reported that LMS's accumulated losses were £22,618, considerably worse than expected. Fuhrmann suspected the accountants of 'manipulation'.

Fuhrmann met Maxwell at 2 p.m. the following day when Maxwell explained that the proper accounts were not yet ready. Instead of staying in London, Maxwell suggested that the German should fly immediately to Basle. Fuhrmann refused and prepared his own assessment which confirmed that, although the official accounts would show a £22,000 loss, the real loss was only £4,486. The accounts were nevertheless unsatisfactory and the two Germans secretly appointed a solicitor, considered initiating a private investigation, and finally returned home dissatisfied.

The relationship between Maxwell and Ferdinand now exploded. In May 1951, Butterworths decided that their joint venture with Springer was grossly unprofitable although Rosbaud had established three highly respected journals – *Spectrochimica Acta*, *Journal of Atmospheric and Terrestrial Physics* and *Geochimica et Cosmochimica Acta* – and published two standard textbooks. Maxwell bought their shares but it is not clear how much he paid nor whether Springer knew in advance that he had bought the interest. However, on 10 October 1951 he wrote to Springer requesting £7,500 for the Butterworth-Springer shares he had just bought. Ferdinand's reply was stinging and shows that he felt misled. Maxwell's proposals, he wrote, were an 'embarrassing shock' because they broke all the previous agreements. It was 'disreputable for a gentleman and businessman to make those type of demands which were contrary to his previous promises'. Future relations, he wrote, 'were very doubtful', and he ended, 'I deeply regret having to write this letter.' Within an hour of its receipt, Maxwell telephoned Springer in Heidelberg but the secretary was under orders not to transfer any calls: 'Dr Springer doesn't want to speak to you, Captain Maxwell,' she told the evidently hurt caller from London.

Maxwell now says that he paid £13,000 for all the shares. In February 1969, at a graduate seminar on business studies held at the London School of Economics, he said that he paid 'a relatively small sum of money'. Pertinently, the self-made millionaire also outlined to the students how he raised the money to buy Rosbaud's infant publishing house in 1951: 'As I had no other capital other than my gratuity [i.e. on demobilisation from the army in 1947], the capital was provided from three sources. First a loan from Hambros Bank; secondly, a contribution by some of my relatives and friends in America; thirdly, a contract with Her Majesty's Stationery Office to supply them with out-of-print wartime German scientific material for which they paid in advance.'

Rosbaud and his three staff joined Maxwell in Neal Street without celebration. They were given a small office and were instantly forgotten. The only formality was to produce a name for the new company. Orton toyed at first with Athena Press after the goddess of wisdom, but discovered that the name was already registered. He then suggested Pergamon, the Greek town in Asia Minor where stood the Altar of Pergamon, dedicated to Athena. Maxwell summarily approved the suggestion and soon after received from Heinz Götz, a friend, a reproduction of the Pergamon coin found at Herakleia which shows the head of Athena. He gave it to Rosbaud, commenting that it could be the company's symbol. That settled, Pergamon barely featured in Maxwell's thoughts for the next four years. He had embarked on an adventurous scheme which would win him the fame which he desired.

CHAPTER 3

The members of the Garrick Club in London are predominantly men of letters – actors, writers and publishers – and lawyers. It was the natural rendezvous in early 1951 for Arthur Coleridge, the great-grandson of England's Lord Chief Justice and a relative of the nineteenth-century poet, to meet an acquaintance for an early-evening drink. Coleridge, who during the war had worked in the Cabinet Office, was the managing director of an ailing book-wholesaler called Simpkin Marshall which was owned by Pitmans, then one of Britain's major publishers. His host at the Garrick was Count Vanden Heuvel, Charles Hambro's business scout, whose elegant, foreign appearance impressed Coleridge as it did everyone else. Heuvel had suggested that he might have a buyer for Simpkins called Robert Maxwell.

Simpkin Marshall was a unique British institution, acting as the wholesale intermediary between publishers and the retail bookshops. The book trade was, then as now, fragmented, and the cost of ordering and distributing single copies of books to every shop in the country was high. Simpkin Marshall, like their only competitor W.H. Smith, offered bookshops a central warehouse from which to obtain books from every publisher. In the trade it was known as the 'single copy wholesale'. Simpkins' pride was that it stocked nearly every book in print and many books which had been long forgotten, and that any telephone order could be delivered by the following day. Since the bookshop paid the same price buying from Simpkins as it paid buying direct from the publisher, Simpkins earned its profits by obtaining the books from the publisher at a lower price than the shop. With an annual turnover of over £1 million, Simpkins' profits before the war were quite acceptable. That state of affairs came to an abrupt end on 29 December 1940, during one of the worst nights of the Blitz, when Simpkins' warehouse in the City of London was hit and four million books were destroyed. Demoralised, Simpkins' owners decided voluntarily to liquidate their business.

A group of leading publishers were anxious to maintain the institution. They bought Simpkins' goodwill and urged the publisher James Pitman to lease part of a new warehouse which he had built out of speculative philanthropy in Neasden, north London, called the Book Centre. Initially, the publishers and Pitman hoped that the new venture could be run as a co-operative for the book trade but they found little support. Most publishers, before the war, had become unhappy with the narrower profit margin received on the sales which went through Simpkins rather than direct from their own warehouses.

Nevertheless, Pitman, committed to the notion of a central warehouse, tried to rebuild the business at his own risk. A new, more centrally located warehouse was rented in 1944 at Rossmore Court in Marylebone and stocks were gradually rebuilt. Yet by 1947 the new company's modest annual profits had turned to huge losses and the prospects were grim. The warehouse was too small, too much of its stock was printed on poor-quality wartime paper, and its labour costs were rocketing. Moreover, in the new era, the civilised cohesion which had cemented the industry for generations was disintegrating. While the book trade unanimously and piously paid tribute to the importance of Simpkin Marshall, individually most publishers in the face of growing competition took a selfish view of their interests. Increasingly they were unwilling to give Simpkins special discounts and preferred to deliver direct to shops. Even those who sat on Simpkins' board were undermining the business by squeezing its profit margins. By 1951, when Simpkins' debts to Pitmans amounted to more than £250,000, James decided to dispose of the institution. It fell to Coleridge to make the first contact with a prospective purchaser, Maxwell.

Since the Garrick was not appropriate for a business meeting, Coleridge and Heuvel took a taxi to the Savoy Hotel and met Maxwell in the bar. Coleridge, the only Englishman of the three, was immediately impressed. Maxwell, wearing fine-cut tweed, looked and sounded the proverbial English gentleman. The dark, handsome young man with clipped moustache and huge bushy eyebrows gave out a hypnotic quality which 'magnetised' Coleridge. Even compared to Heuvel, dressed in a Savile Row suit, Maxwell shone. The only flaw which Coleridge noticed on that first day was a slight imperfection in the Captain's English: he used plural nouns when singular were required.

Heuvel had judged Maxwell's interest in Simpkins perfectly. Several Jewish refugees had recently established themselves in London as successful publishers because they had spotted the deficiences of the crusty, arch-conservative scions of the British trade. For Maxwell, Simpkin Marshall was a typical example of a good idea which, because of bad management, had turned sour. He recognised that whatever notable qualities the British possessed, they were not blessed with an aggressive sense of business and viewed money-making with distaste. For the refugee, the British disdain for ruthless negotiations and trading reflected an ineptitude which he could exploit. Buoyed with immeasurable self-confidence, he was certain that his energy and talent could revive any bankrupt businesses. In Simpkins' case, he needed only to persuade the publishers not to be shortsighted: after all, German publishers had long supported a central warehouse for book distribution. As he explained to Coleridge in the Savoy bar, he hoped to create the same institution in Britain. His only question to Coleridge was: would he help? Coleridge agreed and without any further questions Maxwell began negotiating the purchase of the bankrupt company from Pitmans. It was a decision which would never cease to haunt him.

One indicator seemed to be favourable. Over the previous financial year Pitman had turned a £23,000 loss into a £17,000 profit. On balance, the deal which was struck seemed advantageous to Maxwell – although, according to one accountant's investigation four years later, Simpkins had actually lost £34,261 that year.

Maxwell paid Pitmans £160,000 for the total ownership of Simpkins, whose assets Pitmans had valued at £250,000. But Maxwell was required to pay only £50,000 (part of which he borrowed from Hambros Bank) immediately. The remaining £110,000 was due in instalments over the following nine years. Significantly, the whole £160,000 was immediately entered in Simpkins' accounts as a debt owed by the company to Maxwell although he had paid only £50,000. Until its eventual collapse, Simpkins' accounts would always show a debt owing to its managing director. That accounting procedure was commented upon adversely a few years later. Pitmans was also owed about £108,000 by Simpkins; this debt was dealt with by Pitmans agreeing to write off £35,637 of its losses completely and account for the remaining £72,590 of the money by using the services of the Book Centre in Neasden. In theory, Maxwell had negotiated a bargain which, if properly managed, would secure for him respectability and a voice among the power-brokers.

Soon after the transfer was finalised, Maxwell issued his very first press statement to the trade magazine, the *Bookseller*. Like thousands of other statements over the next decades, his first was characterised by its optimism, ambition and promises: 'I am determined that this will prove to be a long and successful chapter, founded on an even greater improvement in services to both booksellers and publishers.... Nothing will be spared to promote the completeness and efficiency of this service in every way.' After explaining how Simpkins would be expanded, especially by export sales, Maxwell pledged 'all my energies' to develop goodwill. Two weeks later his confidence was rewarded by the trade. Under the headline 'Man of the Hour', the *Bookseller* sought to dispel the fears of those who were evidently 'a trifle startled' about 'the burning question in the book trade just now: Who is Robert Maxwell?'

The magazine's answer to its own question was glowing. After mentioning Maxwell's courageous war record, it described how 'he was asked by a number of prominent German publishers to help them restart their exports' and how the business had expanded ever since although 'there was nothing to prevent them, had they so wished, from thanking Maxwell for his services and then politely bidding him good-day. The fact that no German publisher has chosen to exert this independence is itself eloquent testimony to the efficiency of Lange, Maxwell and Springer as a selling agency.' Trusted by the Germans, Maxwell was also said to be dynamic, having travelled 800,000 miles since 1947 to speak to his customers in any of his nine languages. All that and more, said the *Bookseller*, would be placed at Simpkins' disposal; 'in particular the remarkable publicity machine which he has built up at Lange, Maxwell and Springer, and which regularly and continuously feeds up-to-the-minute information to the 480,000 people in all parts of the world who have reported their specialised book requirements to L.M. & S., will be placed fully at Simpkins' service.' Maxwell now had to match his promises with performance.

Maxwell's first weeks at Rossmore Court are remembered by Coleridge and others as enjoyable. For those accustomed to the pace of traditional managers, Maxwell's dynamism and especially his speed of calculation – 'always on the back of an envelope' – was inspiring. After two weeks he announced a survival plan which involved selling all of Simpkins' stock, negotiating bigger discounts and persuading publishers to deposit books at Simpkins on sale or return. Everything depended upon overcoming the publishers' prejudice and shortsightedness.

Coleridge was appointed as Maxwell's 'ambassador' to arrange the blitz of introductions. The clubbable heir of a judge and the ambitious offspring of a peasant attended many meetings but won few converts. 'They were a severe, tight community who lived in the Garrick,' recalls Coleridge, 'and couldn't stand the sight of an upstart, especially someone who was so brash.' Nevertheless, Simpkins' turnover did begin to increase and that year's profits headed towards £50,000, but Maxwell was impatient. At the beginning of 1952, he decided that the cause of Simpkins' shortcomings was the division of the warehouses between

Rossmore Court, which was too small, and Neasden, which was badly located. His recipe was to bring all his businesses, including LMS, under one roof by procuring bigger and more impressive premises.

The site chosen as the headquarters of the whole Maxwell empire was a former bottling plant, abandoned by the brewers Fullers, situated on the Marylebone Road in central London which was later rebuilt as the headquarters of Woolworths. Maxwell overlooked its obvious deficiencies – it was old, was built of wood, had few telephones and as a former bottling plant was totally unsuited for a book warehouse which needed vast shelving. He also ignored Simpkins' insolvency. He was impressed by its major advantage which was that it was very big and matched his ambitions. Soon after the purchase, he renamed the warehouse 'Maxwell House', brushing aside those who tried to dissuade him because of the comical comparisons with the brand of instant coffee. But he was unable to ignore the loud demands by the local authorities who threatened to close the site immediately as a fire hazard. He had bought the lease without estimating the price of the necessary extensive rebuilding, which he would later claim had cost £63,000 although Orton confided to Tönjes Lange that the real cost was £140,000.

Those who moved the tens of thousands of books into Maxwell House in summer 1952 have one predominant recollection: 'Maxwell was always shouting, "I want it done yesterday."' Impatiently he strode through the new warehouse tipping up boxes of carefully packed books, cursing about the loss of a day's business. The newly appointed manager of the warehouse, who is today still fond of his former boss, was amazed: 'His personality was like a sledgehammer. He could not adjust it to match his partners.' Within days, Simpkin Marshall was back in business with a lot of goodwill from the staff. 'He represented Simpkins' only hope for salvation,' recalls another manager, who initially wished him well.

Maxwell House was a pot-pourri of nationalities. On the first three floors were four hundred partially unionised Simpkin Marshall employees who worked amid stacking shelves which were strung between old bottling machines. Above them were the staff and stock of LMS. Most of those storemen were former Czech and Polish soldiers who regularly fought among themselves but were convinced that their boss had arrived in Britain with 'pips in his pocket'. On the top floor, across gangplanks laid over the open roofs, was an office set aside for Rosbaud and Pergamon, while over another roof was an office housing Lassen and Hickey, who were deeply immersed in barter deals. Maxwell House would have been better named 'Maxwell's Bazaar': under one roof, deals were being struck in German scientific journals, Argentinian pork bellies and practically every book currently published in Britain. Gunther Heyden, working for LMS, can remember 'a mad combination of refugees speaking Yiddish, cockneys and English aristocrats from Oxbridge. A lot of suspicion between everyone. There were cliques and factions and everyone was convinced that Anne Dove was keeping them out.' Heyden's awareness is substantiated by the confessions of Simpkins' sales manager, who worked on the next floor down and deliberately behaved 'more British than the British' to avoid any taint of the 'Mitteleuropa above us'. Maxwell, of course, was oblivious to any tensions or to the notion that Maxwell House was a high-risk social experiment. Bringing all his businesses under one roof made, he believed, good commercial sense. The rambling building might create confusion but that was ideal for maintaining rigid compartmentalisation and protecting his secrecy. 'He would never want his right hand to know what his left hand was doing,' says Anne Dove. 'Sometimes I'm not quite sure that he knew himself. But it was part of his success which was built by making all his instincts work for him.' Ensconced in a huge office, Maxwell presented himself to the outside world as a tycoon – late-night dinners were often delivered from the Savoy – and ordered Coleridge to relaunch Simpkins with a lavish party.

Throughout his life in Britain, Maxwell has been fond of hosting big receptions. Gauging their success is not easy or even fair because so much depends upon the attitude of those invited. As unashamed snobs, some of those who arrived at Maxwell's parties in the early 1950s might have been reluctant to make a pretence of enjoyment, but even fewer attempted the civil gesture when they were invited to the launch of Simpkins which was 'the biggest party the book trade had probably ever seen'. A huge marquee was erected inside the warehouse and, though the atmosphere was stuffy, there was ample to eat and drink. Suddenly a booming voice was heard from hitherto undetected tannoys introducing 'the managing director of Simpkin Marshall, Captain Ian Robert Maxwell MC', and Maxwell began to address his guests from another room. At great length, in a deep cavernous voice, he extolled the virtues of using Simpkins' services. He wanted publishers to change the basis of their relationship with Simpkins and urged them to deposit their books on sale or return. At the end, most of his audience were fidgeting in the foetid atmosphere and beginning to conclude that their prejudice was justified. 'The general attitude was, "We don't have to trust this man, so why should we?"' recalls one publisher. Maxwell returned to the marquee, ebullient and convinced that his guests had been impressed. 'It did him more harm than good' was the reaction of one staid guest. But John Brown, one of the younger publishers who would later become Publisher of Oxford University Press, was enthusiastic: 'I was making my way as well and I admired his courage for taking on the impossible.'

Maxwell won some successes but the turnover of books was stubbornly stuck. Simpkins' recovery was slower than he had anticipated while his labour costs were mounting. The bloated workforce with its rigid twice-daily tea break and regular strikes was, he decided, an easy target for savings.

For someone of Maxwell's background, the British unions' inflexible habits and the absence of a recognisable work ethic was, to say the least, frustrating. Simpkins' four hundred employees had little sympathy for the financial plight of their employer and reacted accordingly when Maxwell informed their shop steward that he wanted, immediately, 150 redundancies. The shop steward, Bill Pescott, summoned his local SOGAT official, Bill Keyes, then a young trade unionist, whose career over the following thirty years would be peppered by bitter and emotional fights against Maxwell's bulldog resolve.

Unlike most other union leaders whom Maxwell would physically confront in his career, Keyes has something more in common with him than just a stubborn ambition to succeed. Both are tall, forceful men who possess an ability to control their naturally volatile tempers to suit the occasion. Both enjoy their battles and detest contemplating defeat. Like all whose public image is aggressive and uncompromising, both believe themselves to be at heart soft, emotional and caring. As a left-wing trade unionist, Keyes has spent a lifetime fighting on his members' behalf the inaptly named press barons of Fleet Street. Fortunately for Keyes, over most of that era the battle was tilted in his favour because the barons routinely succumbed to union demands. By deploying ruthlessness, brinkmanship and a saving dose of reality, Keyes succeeded in frustrating most of the management's attempts to demolish the print workers' restrictive practices. Accordingly, when Keyes was telephoned late one Friday night in 1952 and told that a certain Robert Maxwell, the new managing director of Simpkin Marshall, not only was threatening 150 dismissals but had selected for redundancy exclusively trade union members, Keyes warmed to the prospect of teaching the newcomer the facts of life. What followed was the curtain raiser to a long and respectful relationship; Maxwell himself once said, 'Look, we both come from the same sort of background' – to which the unionist replied, 'Yes, but I haven't forgotten mine.'

Keyes arrived in Marylebone Road at 8.30 on a Saturday morning. At first Maxwell refused to see him, but he relented soon after. 'He was arrogant when I walked into his office,' recalls Keyes, 'and he just told me that he wasn't going to be told what he could do.' Keyes's response to such a taunt was to threaten a total shutdown. Maxwell's counter-response, which Keyes would hear repeated over the years, was categoric: 'I haven't got any time. I've got to catch a plane to Russia.' Keyes was equally dogmatic: 'Go to Russia, but you won't have a business when you come back.'

Like high-stakes poker, successful negotiations about money among tycoons or with union leaders depend upon many ingredients, but ultimately the outcome is decided by whose nerve cracks first. On this occasion, seeking to impress a left-wing union official by referring to a visit to Moscow positively rebounded. Keyes coolly waited while Maxwell fretted about missing his plane and then conceded the union's demands. 'It was my first fight and first victory against Maxwell,' recalls Keyes.

Keyes's victory contributed to Simpkins' immediate financial plight. The huge rebuilding costs had wiped out the previous year's £50,000 profit and left the company with a massive £98,000 loss. But that year's accounts would also reveal an unexpected item. Maxwell had repaid the £110,000 which he personally owed to Pitmans although under the original agreement it was to have been repaid by instalments over nine years. The reasons for the accelerated repayment will be explained later, but the methods Maxwell used would become controversial.

According to the accounts, it was Simpkins and not Maxwell who repaid Maxwell's personal debt. Because repayment was accelerated, Pitmans agreed to accept £98,000 instead of £110,000. The accounting methods used were ingenious but totally legal. With the help of Hambros, special preference shares had been issued to increase Simpkins' capital, but the cash which Maxwell had invested by purchasing the shares was immediately repaid to him by the company. The result of the money chase was that Simpkins paid Maxwell's debts to Pitmans and left Maxwell in complete control of the company, though he had paid no more than the initial £50,000. The extra money had come from Simpkins' own cash flow.

Maxwell had demonstrated his mastery of accountancy, a character-istic which recurs throughout his life. Accountancy, it must be em-phasised, is not a science but an art, and the classification of any money is, within certain limits, quite legitimately subject to considerable personal discretion by the accountants. The immediate result of Maxwell's exercise of his discretion was that Simpkins' reserves were £45,000 poorer in actual cash than they had been at the beginning of the year. Since the company was still hovering on the verge of insolvency, it was a bold decision to take.

There was no secret why Maxwell was in such haste to repay the debt. In his bid to build an empire, he wanted a base in America where there was undoubtedly a huge market for British books and for Springer's journals. In 1952, he wanted to buy the British Book Center in New York, which was for sale. Pitmans, who had a power of veto over any investment while Maxwell still owed money, could see no commercial sense in the venture. So Maxwell paid off the debt and was free to bid for the Book Center.

Pitmans' disapproval appeared to be well founded because the American company was bankrupt. The Book Center had been founded at the end of the war by B.T. Batsford, a British publisher, with the support of other companies, and ambitiously housed in a five-storey office block on the relatively fashionable East 55th Street. After three years the founders' hopes began to fade and Batsfords sold part of its controlling interest to a Conservative Member of Parliament, Captain Peter Baker MC, a well-known socialite who, everyone agreed, had fought 'a wonderful war'. After demobilisation, Baker had embarked on a mercurial career of establishing a publishing company, investing in a film studio and winning a seat in Parliament. Maxwell was very attracted to Baker, including his political views. For at the turn of the decade Maxwell, who had never lost sight of his ambition to become a Member of Parliament, was in contact with several Tory politicians. Possibly Maxwell saw in Baker an entrée into politics, but his friend's dazzling success was very brief.

In early 1952, Baker was drinking heavily and suffering financial problems. Maxwell lent him £13,500. Just months later, in May, Maxwell agreed to cancel the debt in return for Baker's 1,215 shares in the Book Center, which gave Maxwell a major interest. There still remained a $78,000 (£27,857) debt which the Center owed Batsfords. Maxwell's negotiations produced an apparently good deal. For £7,000 and a further £3,606 he obtained Batsfords' 334 shares and complete control. Although the shares were bought by Maxwell personally, a cheque for £9,666 was paid by Simpkins and charged to the debt owed to Maxwell. It was totally legal because, according to the accounts, Simpkins was still in debt to Maxwell, but the sagacity of that transaction would soon be queried by independent accountants. However, in mid-1952 it seemed to outsiders that Maxwell's success was impressive.

Within one year of the meeting at the Savoy, Maxwell was operating from a major property in central London, and controlled Simpkin

Marshall, LMS and the Book Center. He seemed set to become a major international book-distributor, with a lifestyle to match. He had moved from suburban Chiswick to Claygate, a substantial detached residence in Esher which housed his family (now expanded to four children with the birth of girl twins). His business interests were accompanied by intense socialising. Through Anne Dove he was introduced to a succession of luminaries including two Labour politicians who also seemed set on stardom. The first was Francis Noel-Baker, son of the Labour veteran, and the second was Hugh Gaitskell, the Labour Party leader. Many of Maxwell's former employees remember the stir that Gaitskell's arrival at Maxwell House caused, but none remember it better than Bill Keyes who watched it from outside. Keyes was on picket duty in one of the regular strikes for a wage increase. As Gaitskell approached the entrance, Keyes asked him to respect their picket. 'He just ignored us,' says Keyes.

Coleridge understood why Maxwell was currying friendship with politicians. During one conversation Maxwell confided that his ambition was now to become Prime Minister of Britain. His self-confidence was shared by Betty. 'My husband', she told Coleridge, 'can do anything,' and that included governing the country. Endearingly, Maxwell did not believe that his birthplace and religion were obstacles. Few of those around him, however, especially his fellow refugees, could see any suggestion that Maxwell embraced any particular political philosophy: he seemed to be motivated largely by the desire to increase his wealth. But others like Anne Dove believed that Maxwell wanted power, particularly political power.

Anne Dove understood his ambitions better than anyone and often held parties for him to meet the influential people whom she knew. Admiringly, she watched her boss in action: 'He always made a point of learning something from everybody. It was his instinct.' He always made a beeline for those who were important and, with the skill of a seasoned actor, played a matching role: 'He had respect for power, which was a natural outcome of his character.' He was also, she recognised, abrasive in handling people. Dove pointedly states, 'I often made him undo unfair things like dismissals. It was his best quality. He always knew when he was wrong and quite humble.' But in the euphoria of his success, no one else noticed that characteristic or the appearance of the first cracks in his ambitions. The initial cause emanated from Heidelberg.

Tönjes Lange's first reaction to Maxwell's purchase of Simpkin Marshall had been cautiously optimistic. Although the take-over was effected without his knowledge and was contrary to their agreement about his exclusive employment for LMS, the publicity Maxwell had attracted in London convinced both Lange and even Ferdinand that they were associated with someone who was rising very fast in British society. In particular, they were impressed by the *Bookseller*'s prediction that LMS would become part of Simpkin Marshall and '480,000 clients all over the world will be served specialist books and up-to-the-minute information'. Despite the fear that LMS's fortunes night suffer because Maxwell's efforts would be diverted to his new interests, both believed that there might be advantages in the massive amount of new capital which Maxwell would presumably have at his disposal. Consequently, throughout 1952, they tried to help and advise Maxwell in the organisation of his new business, although to their disappointment he ignored their suggestions. His very ambition, they felt, was a major cause of the friction.

In May 1952, Maxwell opened a LMS office in New York at the Book Center's premises despite Ferdinand's and Tönjes Lange's objections. His motives were to challenge Springer's two American competitors, Walter Johnson and Stechert. To staff the new office, Maxwell hired Albert Daub, a German refugee who was Stechert's sales director. Explaining his tactics to Lange, Maxwell declared his assumption that with Daub he would inherit most of Stechert's customers. He was quickly disillusioned. His prey had no influence with the customers and his former employers were delighted to be rid of him. Another attempt by Maxwell to hire expertise also misfired but in a different way. Charles Hutt was recruited from Butterworths and brought enormous expertise. But months later, he was lured away by Johnson with all his inside knowledge.

These miscalculations were exposed towards the end of 1952 just when Springer's staff were searching through the London files for other reasons to reopen their bid to recover control of Springer's exports. Among their discoveries was the payment of £10,000 for a series of lacklustre 'Book of the Month'–type promotion campaigns which had little connection with scientific books; moreover, sales of Springer's new publications were static, and Shudian of China, Springer's old customer, was refusing to place any new orders because half of his order made eighteen months previously had not been delivered. The case they made against the London connection seemed convincing.

Maxwell ignored Springer's complaints. He was preoccupied by the uncertain finances of Simpkin Marshall, as those in his office recall: 'He was forever on the phone to Sir Charles Hambro.' The banker had loaned Simpkins £74,000 and was still personally well disposed towards Maxwell. But his fellow directors had become uneasy about the bank's link and wanted to end the commitment. At first Hambro resisted and negotiated to secure the loans against Simpkins' assets. But even that was insufficient for Hambro's colleagues and in early 1953 Maxwell was asked to find a new source of finance. Some years earlier he had borrowed money from an Armenian carpet dealer called Nassim Sakuto, whom he had met in Berlin. Sakuto claimed to have sold carpets to Goering and was trying to reclaim his property. It was an unlikely story but he was prepared to lend Maxwell money in return for a share of future profits. On Orton's advice the relationship was terminated and Maxwell now needed an alternative source of money. He turned to Kurt Wallersteiner, a German refugee, with whom he was closely involved in barter deals.

Wallersteiner was a talented organic chemist and chartered chemical engineer who had developed a series of international trading companies, most notably the Watford Chemical Company and the Anglo-Continental Exchange. They met at a lunch at the Athenaeum Club in spring 1952 hosted by Major John Whitlock, the clubbable Butterworths executive with an interest in science.

The two refugees immediately achieved a close rapport, especially since Maxwell still retained an interest in barter. Wallersteiner at the time was supplying pharmaceuticals and chemicals to East Germany, which, like all Communist countries, had little convertible currency and paid instead with East German products. Wallersteiner was attracted to the precarious trade by the big profits earned by deals with the Communist countries at the height of the Cold War. But the perpetual juggling act required skill, and Wallersteiner would occasionally come unstuck, as when he was stranded with one and a half million babies' feeding bottles in a Hamburg warehouse. When the two men met, Maxwell also had a pressing problem. He needed to liquidate the barter 'payments' made by the Chinese and Yugoslavs for the supply of Springer journals, although he seemed better able than Wallersteiner to terminate the juggling act profitably.

Throughout the post-embryo period of building his book-marketing interests, Maxwell had nurtured Low-Bell's business. The era of extreme shortages still prevailed and fortunes could be earned by skilfully negotiating through the tangle of government controls to supply a much needed commodity. Soon after they met, Maxwell offered Wallersteiner the services of his own team, Bill Hickey and Paul Lassen. Lassen, the junior of the duo, recalls that while 'Waller would set the deals up, Maxy would have to rescue him from the mess.' In recognition of his services, Lassen's wages would sometimes be paid by the Watford Chemical Co.

The deals invariably involved a triangle formed by west Europe, China and East Germany. Occasionally, everything went through smoothly, one such transaction being the supply of indigo-blue dye to China via East Germany. Other deals were initiated through LMS's supply of British and American books and journals, which would be part of a normal barter deal. But Lassen remembers a series of transactions which ended in desperate phone calls, frantic flights across Europe, threats to extract money which was owed and endless negotiations to sell a bewildering and occasionally exotic array of foods, chemicals and hardware which were located in Customs' warehouses at ports around the world. Lassen particularly remembers shipments from China of silk, egg-yolk spray and tea. It was a characteristic of the period that obtaining import permits was a precious skill which in the barter trade became invaluable when Maxwell or Wallersteiner wanted to close the circle and collect the money. Lassen was often the fireman who rushed off to 'liquidate' the deal. Successfully he negotiated for the silk, worth more than £1 million, to be sold to Debenhams, and for the egg yolk to be bought by cake manufacturers in the Midlands; while the tea, which had been obtained in exchange for cement, was, he proudly recalls, liquidated within three days: 'I knew nothing about tea but I found a broker in London who put his nose into the sample and said it was excellent. I flew to Rotterdam and air-freighted the cargo to Britain within three days. Maxy was very pleased and gave me a one hundred pound bonus.'

Lassen unsuccessfully fought shy of Wallersteiner's more dubious deals, especially the purchase of the antibiotic streptomycin in America, which were done without Maxwell's knowledge. Washington has always been sensitive about its trade with the Communist bloc and its prejudices were never more intense than at the height of the Korean War. For the sly entrepreneur who managed to break the American trade embargo and supply the Communists' urgent needs, the profits were commensurate with the risk. In 1952, Wallersteiner had bought streptomycin in America, which had been shipped to Holland. Surreptitiously, the boxes were relabelled and, with false shipping documents, forwarded to China. In return more silk arrived in Europe. Lassen collected the payment in East Berlin from 'Diamond Jim' in bundles of dollar notes. According to Lassen, who was 'unhappy' about crossing into the east, 'Waller was caught on that deal and someone in Europe was imprisoned.'

No deal however reached the bizarre proportions of Wallersteiner's shipment of chemicals to East Germany bartered for an assortment of china, glass and textiles which were shipped to Argentina. The Argentinians in turn shipped two thousand tons of pork bellies to Britain but to Wallersteiner's horror the British Ministry of Food condemned the meat as sub-standard. With his costs mounting daily, Wallersteiner searched for a solution. Part of the shipment was sent to Holland for canning while the remainder was sold to Austria under the guise of a bilateral barter deal between two nations. Anne Dove stayed with Maxwell at the Hotel Sacher in Vienna for that complicated transaction. 'It was absolutely hilarious,' she recalls, 'like a music-hall comedy where strange men were constantly coming in and out and hiding behind doors and curtains while Maxwell and Wallersteiner argued about the deal.' It was one of the rare occasions when Dove realised that Maxwell's right hand did not know what his left hand was doing. 'The meat was so old', says Dove, 'that I warned Wallersteiner that he would poison a whole nation but everyone just thought it was a hoot.' Among the strange cast helping Maxwell and Wallersteiner to conclude the deal was Sir George Franckenstein, GCVO, an Austrian-born nobleman, diplomat and financier who was naturalised as a British citizen in 1938 and received a knighthood in the same year. Franckenstein had fallen on hard times but still had enough connections in his homeland to convince Austrian officials that they should accept that Wallersteiner was the representative of the fictitious state of the Oceania Republic and agree to exchange the pork for prefabricated houses. It fell to Hickey and Lassen to find customers for the houses.

In typical Maxwell style, the new project was attacked with gusto. Since the lack of housing in the post-war period was an emotive political issue, Maxwell had high hopes of profits. A prototype, installed with electricity and plumbing, was erected in High Wycombe and government officials were invited for inspection tours. Nobody responded. Four months later, Maxwell's team finally secured an interview at the Ministry where, according to Lassen, 'We were treated like children.' Rejected by the government and also by the building societies, their efforts were deployed to selling the houses to Canada, America and Cyprus.

Meanwhile, the pork, after canning in Holland, was sold to East Germany in return for some thousands of tons of cement. After the British government refused to grant an import licence, the cement was sold to Canada for the foundations of the wooden houses. The chain seemed finally complete, but en route to Canada one Liberty ship sprang a leak that set the cement rock hard. On that transaction there were no profits for either Low-Bell or the Watford Chemical Company.

To the staff in the Marylebone Road, the antics of Hickey and Lassen were barely comprehensible, and, in the compartmentalised world which Maxwell created, that was the intention. Heyden remembers only the 'shadowy' Wallersteiner, who was forever coming in and out, while others jibed about the 'mysterious foreigner'. For those engrossed in rescuing

Simpkin Marshall, the managing director's endless meetings with the ubiquitous Wallersteiner were frustrating. Some surmised that Maxwell was 'keeping his cards close to his chest' because he was reluctant, as an aspiring socialite and book magnate, to be seen in the grubby and unaesthetic world of pork and chemicals. In line with compartmentalisation, Simpkins' accountants did not prepare Low-Bell accounts. 'Barter was not the image he wanted to cultivate,' recalls one of his financial staff.

There were, however, pressing reasons for Maxwell's relationship with Wallersteiner. With Simpkins losing money, Wallersteiner's business was an enticing prospect for easily earned income. One year after their first meeting, on 3 July 1953, Maxwell was formally appointed 'confidential manager' of Wallersteiner's companies and was to be paid 20 per cent of their net profits. In 1969 Maxwell explained his motives: 'I would be able to control him and prevent him from doing any unsavoury business in Iron Curtain countries.' He added that this would add to his own profit and be to the benefit of the national economy. Within five weeks, on 14 August, Maxwell had persuaded Wallersteiner to take over Hambros' secured charge which by then had mounted to £320,000. Wallersteiner paid by way of a debenture which was not redeemable until 1958. Since Wallersteiner had already lent Simpkins £50,000, his commitment to Simpkins' success was greater than Maxwell's own. According to Wallersteiner, they celebrated their partnership by dining together at Les Ambassadeurs in Mayfair.

The following month, on 28 September, Maxwell asked Wallersteiner for more money. Wallersteiner claims that Maxwell assured him that Simpkins was thriving, and on that basis he lent a further £100,000, although Maxwell, by a special share issue, still retained control over the company. But Simpkins' costs continued to mount. A successful strike had led to increased wages while the volume of Simpkins' trade had barely increased. Yet there were limited successes. Two weeks after Wallersteiner's third loan, Maxwell persuaded thirty-five publishers to deliver their books on sale or return. Although he had achieved a singularly important breakthrough, 'The trade was simply suspicious,' says one of Simpkins' executives, 'and they had some grounds.'

In the summer of 1953, Coleridge suddenly resigned, so sparking a crisis of confidence. In the trade, the gossip was that the company was virtually insolvent. Publishers personally demanded that their accounts be settled. The behaviour of Otto Kyllmann of Constable was typical: he arrived at Maxwell House, told the taxi to wait, and burst into Maxwell's office, refusing to leave until he had received a cheque. There were also rumours that books which had been bought for export at a 50 per cent discount and ostensibly shipped to the Book Center in New York had been sold in Britain where the publisher's discount would have been 33 per cent. The fiddle, if it existed, was deemed to be the brainchild of a Simpkins employee who had joined the company before the war, and Maxwell would never have known what the trade long suspected. Although Simpkins had little prospect of recovering from bankruptcy, some observers claim that Maxwell was 'deeply worried', while others assert that there was no visible sign of concern. Simpkins' impending collapse might have been less alarming if his relationship with Springer, which supplied the bulk of Maxwell House's income, had not again been endangered.

Earlier in the year, Lange had summoned Maxwell to Berlin for a weekend discussion, in particular about the delay in payments. Maxwell, it was felt, was spending too much of his time on Simpkins' business at the expense of LMS'. Lange had heard privately from Orton that while Simpkins' costs had increased by 300 per cent, its turnover was up by only 180 per cent. But Maxwell arrived, employed his customary mixture of persuasive charm and salesmanship and departed after convincing his 'uncle' that the suspicions were unfounded because 'sales and profits had increased during the previous year by 24 per cent'.

But by September the reservoir of goodwill had practically disappeared. Orton told Hövel that the local authority in London was once again threatening to order the closure of Maxwell House on the grounds that it was a fire hazard. Maxwell's only hope of reprieve, said Orton, was to use his influence at the Ministry of Labour. Hövel was particularly struck by Coleridge's resignation and by Maxwell's refusal to 'properly exploit' the Germans' advice. 'We regretfully came to the conclusion', says Hövel, 'that too many sales were being lost by poor advertising. It was not completely Maxwell's fault that we felt that it was time for a friendly divorce.'

The formal letter, couched in mournful terms, was sent in November. The official reason cited for the break was the new German exchange regulations which required payment in dollars for exports to America. Tönjes noted with regret that they rarely saw or even heard from Maxwell anymore. Ferdinand, however, was delighted by the break. In a letter to his nephew Bernhard, who was attempting to establish a Springer publishing house in New York, Ferdinand warned against any relationship with Maxwell and Bernhard accepted the advice: 'Maxwell has proved to be a difficult person to do business with.' Maxwell had proposed to Bernhard that he invest in the new company, but Bernhard's rejection was emphatic: 'We don't want him as a person who wields any influence here.'

Legally, Maxwell could have forestalled the break for one year but since he had bought Simpkins without Springer's approval he was on weak ground. That weekend Maxwell and Lange agreed to an amicable, partial separation under which Maxwell relinquished his exclusive selling rights throughout the world but was allowed to represent LMS in some areas. The new arrangement would amply suit his latest ambition: to tap the vast reservoir of scientific journals published in the Communist bloc countries which had never been read in the west.

The first public hint of the strategy which would earn its architect his first million pounds was a small article in *Der Telegraf*, Maxwell's old newspaper, on 19 January 1954. After long negotiations, the Soviet government had agreed to consider Maxwell's proposals to translate and print Russian scientific papers in the west. Since there were no direct flights, the easiest route was via East Berlin. Maxwell arrived at Tempelhof airport in West Berlin, where he gave an interview to the newspaper. He described himself as the publisher and director of the 'world's biggest bookseller, Simpkin Marshall', as the director of a 'London merchant bank' which hoped to conclude some barter deals with the Russians (presumably Wallersteiner's Anglo-Continental Exchange) and as the first publisher from the free world to negotiate for the sale of scientific books with the Soviets.

Anne Dove walked alongside Maxwell in the middle of the night across the snow-covered Kurfürstendamm, watched by armed Russian soldiers, into the Soviet zone. By arrangement a taxi was waiting to take them to the airport. These were pioneering forays behind the Iron Curtain but Maxwell was by then a seasoned traveller. Maxwell and Dove stayed in Moscow for two weeks. The Russians constantly refused to answer Maxwell's questions and to give a date for the next round of negotiations. Between the meetings, Maxwell was confined to the hotel with a minder with whom he played chess. During the negotiations themselves, Maxwell and Dove were plied with vodka. But Maxwell, according to Dove, was always well prepared. 'He ate loads of yogurt to line his stomach. I ate caviar. He knew all the tricks.' At the end, Maxwell could wait no longer and returned to England without a firm contract. 'As we crossed the Channel he breathed a sigh of relief and said how pleased he was to be home. Being British meant more to him than anything else. "I feel safe," he would say to me.'

The contrast between his patriotism and the long trips to the Iron

Curtain countries did not pass unnoticed by the British security services. Soon after their return, Anne Dove received a private call from a source she well recognised. She was invited to come for a 'discreet chat with an anonymous man in an unnumbered room in the War Office'. The purpose was explicit. 'They wanted me to vouch for his loyalty. Of course they trusted my judgement.' It was not the last occasion that Maxwell's good business contacts with the Communist bloc were suspected as a cover for sinister activities, especially after Mezhdunarodnaya Kniga, the Soviet publishing house, granted him an exclusive contract for the western world.

In Neal Street Maxwell was triumphant and began circulating the enormous new offering to potential customers using the LMS subscribers' list. 'As a result of Captain Maxwell's visit to Moscow last January,' it read, 'a wide range of Soviet scientific books is now available.' The letter was written on LMS paper and among the first recipients of his advertisement in June was Ferdinand Springer, who claimed that he knew nothing about the deal. It was another crucial moment in Springer's relationship with Maxwell since they were on the verge of signing a new agreement.

Tönjes Lange had felt considerable doubts about any new arrangement because Maxwell had proved uncontrollable and had avoided summoning a board meeting for the past two years. Nevertheless sentiment and Maxwell's irrepressible charm had always swayed his doubts and he had agreed that Maxwell could retain some exclusive world selling rights. The new advertisement arrived as the lawyers were clarifying some final details. Ferdinand was apoplectic. 'We demand', he wrote to Maxwell, 'an immediate and complete break between us and LMS.' Condemning the 'serious breach of trust', Springer wrote that he regretted taking the final step but blamed Maxwell's 'misuse of our loyalty'.

Maxwell personally negotiated the break on 2 July 1954 in Heidelberg, under which he agreed to dissolve LMS and operate under the name I.R. Maxwell & Co. Ltd. Springer gave Maxwell exclusive rights until 1959 in the British Empire, France, China and Indonesia at the same discounts. Maxwell, seemingly unconcerned, asked only that the break be kept a strict secret and flew directly to New York. On his return he wrote to 'My dear Onkel Lange' and promised 'a smooth handover' at the beginning of 1955.

The divorce was not smooth. Within four weeks Maxwell was protesting that Springer had broken the agreement. Lange counter-charged that Maxwell was guilty of the same; in particular that Maxwell, instead of ensuring the swift disappearance of the name Lange, Maxwell

& Springer had actually printed his new notepaper with the subtitle 'Formerly Lange, Maxwell & Springer Ltd', a clear breach of his promise not to use the name in the future. Over the following months, Springer would repeatedly complain that Maxwell's staff were trying to hang on to old contracts or offer cut-rate terms in territories where they no longer enjoyed exclusivity. But by then Maxwell was fighting for his reputation in London.

The discord with Springer coincided with Simpkins' unstoppable slide into insolvency. In the book trade, the easiest method of directly influencing the apparent financial state of a company was through the accountant's valuation of the stock. Tom Clark, Simpkins' accountant, tried within the law to paint the best picture of the company's financial state, but his view proved to be too optimistic because one year later the stock which he had valued at £180,000 was written off as worthless. Clearly, the accountants were fighting a losing battle. Only Maxwell's determination delayed the inevitable. On 3 May 1954, he turned again to Wallersteiner for help. In a late-night meeting in Marylebone, according to Wallersteiner, Maxwell presented a predated contract which extended his own control of the German's companies in exchange for more shares in Simpkins and a right to 20 per cent of Simpkins' profits. Wallersteiner claims that he signed the following day. The background to what seems like inexplicable generosity or folly appears in Wallersteiner's own explanation to the *Sunday Times* in 1969. The businessman claimed that he feared retribution from western governments and Intelligence agencies for his barter deals with the Communist bloc and that Maxwell had promised him protection. His account must be read with caution because he has subsequently been convicted and imprisoned for several frauds. For his part, Maxwell claimed that Wallersteiner's 'investment' was actually his own money earned by the Watford Co. from the barter deals.

Whatever the truth, soon after signing, the partners had a bitter argument which ended with Wallersteiner, whose total investment in Simpkins was by that time £470,000, threatening to call a creditors' meeting. This was clearly a tense moment for Maxwell because it could have provoked Simpkins' immediate closure. In a pattern which would be repeated on many occasions over the coming years, Maxwell called Isidore Kerman, his solicitor. That night, Maxwell swore a twelve-page affidavit. It was unequivocal: 'Based upon their present trading position, their goodwill and their prospects ... [Simpkin Marshall] are not only capable of carrying on their present business, but can look forward to considerable improvement and increase of their trade.' Then Maxwell swore that Simpkins, 'apart from their considerable fixed assets, have an excess of current assets over current liabilities of approximately £450,000'. The following morning Kerman obtained a High Court injunction which forbade Wallersteiner to endanger Simpkins' survival by alleging that the company was bankrupt. Here was an astonishing state of affairs. Subsequently Maxwell has always correctly asserted that Simpkins was insolvent throughout his ownership, yet his sworn statement suggested the contrary.

In an uneasy truce over the following days, a new agreement was fashioned which froze their respective claims. Maxwell had an effective call on all Watford's profits and Wallersteiner would have to wait four years for repayment of the loans. But Maxwell did agree to accept Brigadier Alfred Critchley as Simpkins' chairman. Wallersteiner had met Critchley, a Canadian soldier and the first chairman of BOAC, through Count Vanden Heuvel and hoped to use his Establishment contacts for future barter deals in North America.

Critchley immediately hired the prestigious accountancy firm Peat, Marwick, Mitchell to investigate Simpkins' plight. Simultaneously, Maxwell hired a smaller firm of accountants, Chalmers Wade, who had direct experience of the publishing trade, 'to investigate [Simpkins'] trading arrangements' but not the company's finances. Chalmers' recommendations were identical to Maxwell's own survival plan, which he had presented to London's publishers four years earlier. But the report did contain one observation of future relevance. A sale of books from Simpkins to another company owned by Maxwell had been entered in the accounts as worth £105,000. But investigation revealed that the Maxwell company had the right to return the books, which somewhat coloured the accuracy of the entry as an irrevocable 'sale'. Fifteen years later, the same queries about accountancy practices would be raised during the investigation of Pergamon's affairs.

A third investigation was undertaken by Wallersteiner's own accountants. Like Peat, Marwick, they would eventually declare the company insolvent but they also reported an unforeseen discovery. Simpkins' biggest single debt, no less than £111,335 (it would subsequently increase to £117,000), was owed by Maxwell's own company, the Book Center in New York.

Peat's report also revealed similar inter-company transactions. In the previous year, Simpkins, despite its parlous state, had lent £211,599 to other companies which were controlled by Maxwell himself and had charged no interest. The money, commented Peat, Marwick, was not a normal trading loan, but amounted to 'financial assistance'. They also reported that Maxwell's affidavit describing Simpkins' surplus as

£450,000 was erroneous. He had ignored Simpkins' debts of £524,813 which, after various computations, left an actual deficit, in their opinion, of £12,173 in net tangible assets. Although every assessment depended on an individual accountant's interpretation, the sharp contradiction between Peat, Marwick's report and Maxwell's unequivocally optimistic version was seized upon by London's publishers.

Before the report was finalised, events moved swiftly. In November, Maxwell admitted that Simpkins was insolvent and appealed to the Publishers Association for support by adopting Chalmers' recommendations. His argument, as explained in two articles for *Time and Tide*, seem thirty-five years later reasonable and sane. 'British publishers', he wrote, 'are now issuing a record number of more than 24,000 books each year. This is larger even than the United States with three times our population. Yet here in Britain publishing is still largely regarded as an occupation for gentlemen. In the United States it is a very big business run on hard economic commercial lines. Why are British publishers so reluctant at facing the facts?'

The facts were, wrote Maxwell, that the publishing industry needed to 'modernise itself and take seriously the promise of giving a better service to authors and the book-buying public ... otherwise the United Kingdom publishers will lose a great deal of their traditional export markets.' In June 1954 there was to be a World Book Fair in Earls Court, but Britain's leading publishers, including Macmillan and Heinemann, were refusing to exhibit, which reflected their old-fashioned, undynamic attitude towards exporting. 'Many British publishers are now congratulating themselves that the American attempt to take over the British publishing houses has been repulsed. But they are wrong in adopting this self-congratulatory attitude. The truth is the American publishers have now decided that there is hardly anything here worth buying.' His ardour for reform was unlikely to endear itself to the Association, whose xenophobia would bar all refugee publishers from a seat on their council for some years. In January, the Association rejected the survival plan. The writing was on the wall, but Maxwell was well prepared. Frank Beckwith was sent to New York to arrange that the assets of Book Center and LMS were legally separated from Simpkins. The earlier appointment of Maxwell's sister Brana Natkin, who was an American citizen, as a Book Center director would effectively prevent the British receiver from gaining access to the company's records. In London, a new office and headquarters for Maxwell's other businesses had already been purchased in Fitzroy Square. The news on 14 April that a petition for the winding up of Simpkins had been presented to the High Court triggered his evacuation plan.

During the night, Beckwith and Clark, helped by Maxwell, loaded LMS's filing cabinets in Maxwell's Humber, shuttling to and from Fitzroy Square. Simultaneously, Lassen moved Low-Bell's files to the new headquarters. Gunther Heyden remembers the 'frantic activity to disentangle the companies and get our assets out of Simpkin Marshall's premises before it collapsed'. During the controlled panic, a fire broke out in the basement, but it was quickly extinguished. The following day, the receiver arrived and Heyden and others would spend hours arguing that furniture and stock did not belong to Simpkins. In the confusion, it was not easy for the receiver to disprove the counter-claims of LMS, EPPAC, Robert Maxwell and Co., Pergamon, International Encyclopaedias, Low-Bell and a host of smaller trading companies all registered at the same address. Even the accountants had not always been certain which of the companies was responsible for which payment.

For Maxwell, based the following day in Fitzroy Square, it was practically business as usual. Once again ensconced in a huge room with a large oil portrait of an English gentleman behind him ('That's my august uncle, Moshe Schlemiel,' he would joke), he seemed to those around him supremely confident. While Lassen fixed the central heating, Heyden was still selling Springer's stock, and in a small office Paul Rosbaud was unobtrusively planning Pergamon's new journals. There seemed sufficient opportunities for the future – despite the excitement, Maxwell had even squeezed in a trip to China. Probably only Anne Dove appreciated Maxwell's real concerns. Resting in the Himalayas on account of a 'blood disorder', she received an endless stream of letters and telegrams from Maxwell about his plight. 'He was really quite worried,' she says. But to others it seemed that Maxwell was unconcerned when the time came for Simpkins to be accorded a proper funeral at a formal meeting of creditors for the bankrupt company.

On 15 June, nearly two hundred publishers, their representatives and lawyers crowded into Winchester House, Old Broad Street to hear the official receiver's report. Every account agrees that there was considerable antagonism towards Maxwell, who was sitting on the platform next to the receiver. 'He was very shocked by the atmosphere,' recalls his former sales manager. 'It was a bruising experience for him,' says another, who vividly recalls how the atmosphere soured and Maxwell's demeanour changed as he was confronted publicly with the consequences of his business management.

To protect themselves from the possibility of Simpkins' bankruptcy, the majority of publishers had agreed to give Simpkins their books on sale and return in the belief that they remained the owners until the books were sold. Maxwell, they felt, had personally assured them that they were safe. But according to the legal advice obtained by the receiver, the stock was in fact owned by Simpkins. The publishers, accordingly, had lost their money. Simpkins owed £656,388 and had just £70,000 in assets to repay its creditors. The receiver announced that he had found one puzzling debt owed to Simpkins, namely £113,000 from the Book Center in New York which he believed was one cause of Simpkins' collapse. 'Captain Maxwell', the receiver told his restless audience, 'has informed the official receiver that the debt is not recoverable beyond about £10,000.... As Captain Maxwell was aware of the financial difficulties of both the British Book Center Inc. and Simpkins when Simpkins was supplying the books and the debt was mounting, [that deal would] require close investigation.' The only reassurance for the creditors was that Maxwell had assured the receiver that he was trying to sell the Book Center and intended to hand over the proceeds rather than cover his own losses. 'It appears doubtful', said the receiver, 'whether the company was at any time solvent. The directors concerned were at fault in acquiring the Marylebone premises and financing British Book Center Inc. at a time when the company was insolvent without making satisfactory arrangements for the introduction of sufficient further capital.' Maxwell was criticised for not having 'considered and decided upon liquidation at a much earlier date'.

Bill Keyes remembers Harold Macmillan, whose family firm was one of Simpkins' creditors, leaving Winchester House outraged. 'We have lost a fortune,' confided the future Prime Minister, 'but my lawyers say we'll never get our money back.' Macmillan never forgot or forgave the circumstances of Simpkins' collapse. Nor did several members of the future Labour government. But Maxwell quickly recovered his composure. In a statement which would add notoriety to the existing dislike, he told the editor of the *Bookseller*, 'I've come down flat on my arse, but I'm going up again and this time I'm staying up.' The Bouncing Czech was born and many British publishers were reluctant to deal with him again.

To this day Maxwell feels that the enormous antagonism which the collapse provoked was unfair. 'I took over an insolvent company,' he told the author in 1973, 'and I did the best possible.' He was, he felt, a misunderstood but well-intentioned reformer. But Frank Beckwith, who was Simpkins' company secretary, noticed a fatal flaw soon after the original purchase: 'Selling books is based on counting halfpennies and Maxwell's style was not suited to that sort of care about precise costs.' In the publishers' view, Maxwell's great sin was his cavalier interpretation of the director's role in a company. 'His problem', says one of his executives, 'was that he couldn't distinguish between his interests and the interests of others. He saw himself as autonomous and not as a trustee of shareholders' interests.' The fate of the Book Center is proof of that view. Eventually the receiver would be paid £14,829 by William Curtis, Maxwell's former manager at the Book Center, as settlement of the £113,000 debt, but the New York building itself remained the hub of Maxwell's future and fast-expanding American operations.

CHAPTER 4

Until the collapse of Simpkin Marshall, Maxwell had shown barely any interest in Pergamon, an aloofness which was welcomed by Paul Rosbaud and his twenty-two-year-old assistant Maria Sachs. Rosbaud and Maxwell had nothing in common other than being refugees involved in scientific publishing. But even in that slender mutuality lay fierce differences. Rosbaud was a cultured, Austrian atomic scientist who, according to Sachs, was 'contemptuous of Maxwell whom he saw as an uneducated Hungarian', and their approaches to scientific publishing were sharply contrasting. While Rosbaud considered himself a true publisher who, in the old tradition, identified with the experiences of 'my authors', Maxwell's reading, Rosbaud alleged, was exclusively confined to books of accounts. 'Rosbaud believed in science,' says Sachs, 'while Maxwell believed in money.'

Rosbaud had therefore been dejected when Butterworth-Springer had agreed in 1951 to Maxwell's purchase of their shares, but since his own efforts to buy the company had failed, he reluctantly accepted his fate. Ferdinand Springer had urged Rosbaud to leave Pergamon, but both were persuaded by Maxwell not to upset the arrangement to save Pergamon from collapse. On Ferdinand's insistence, Maxwell agreed to give Rosbaud a 20 per cent stake in Pergamon, but that does not seem to have been effected on account of Rosbaud's refusal. After the take-over, Rosbaud's fears dwindled. He had been given a small office in Studio Place, which he occupied with Maria Sachs and Eric Buckley, his production manager. Buckley thought Maxwell was an ideal employer. They had met a few years earlier when Maxwell had offered Butterworths the services of his book-binding subsidiary, Maxsons, and ever since they had shared a common interest in improving the technology of printing and had discussed plans for expansion. Even for Sachs, who was deeply devoted to Rosbaud, Maxwell was 'generous, good-natured, with a

Balkan sense of humour'. Caught in the middle, she realised that the relationship between the two men was 'doomed from the outset'. But, until they moved into Marylebone Road, the three employees saw little of Maxwell and rather more of the actress Hermione Gingold standing on the doorstep of her nearby house in a dressing-gown.

Rosbaud's asset was his reputation among those scientists who had fled Nazi Germany. He found no difficulty in attracting Otto Frisch, Laurence Wager and L.H. Ahrens (who were unknown to Ferdinand Springer) to his new publishing house in London. Simultaneously, he pinpointed the British scientists whose work was still relatively unpublicised and offered the formula which Springer had perfected. Among the early recruits were Sir Edward Appleton, Sir Harold Thompson, Rodney Hill, Peter Danckwerts and Kenneth Denbigh, who all envied the proliferation of scientific journals in Germany and were irritated by the monopoly of American scientists in English-speaking publications. They resented, as did many of the younger American academics, the exclusion of their work by the editors of the established journals who, they believed, did not understand their discoveries and were prejudiced against newcomers. The reaction of Denbigh, a pioneer in chemical engineering at Cambridge University, to Rosbaud was typical: 'He offered us something quite special.' He was impressed during Rosbaud's visit to his laboratories by the Austrian's grasp of the theoretical and experimental advances which the British scientists had accomplished. Rosbaud proposed, according to Denbigh, 'a journal which emphasised European achievements. He was the driving force to launch the *Journal of Chemical Engineering Science* and it has remained one of the most successful journals in the field.' Payment, of course, was never an issue. 'There was deep loyalty towards Rosbaud,' recalls Maria Sachs, 'but his commercial sense was zero.'

Throughout their stay in Marylebone Road, that weakness remained unimportant. During brief and irregular meetings, Maxwell cast a quick eye over Pergamon's uncomplicated balance sheet and, according to Sachs, showed 'no interest in the journals' content but only in the financial principles of scientific publishing'. Pergamon was just profitable but remained a very small publisher. During those three years, only two other journals were added to Pergamon's list: the *Journal of Nuclear Physics* and the *Journal of Mechanics and Physics of Solids*, and fourteen books. Like Denbigh, all the editors were personally attracted by Rosbaud and had no contact with Maxwell.

After Simpkins' crash, Maxwell's attitude towards his fledgling company changed. Pergamon enjoyed a good but limited reputation, earning profits of £5,000 a year, which he decided to expand in direct competition to Springer. Sachs recalls that when Maxwell's serious interest in the business started, 'he was surprised by our success, especially because we were selling book rights to big publishers like McGraw-Hill in New York'. She remembers the McGraw-Hill deal in particular because Maxwell insisted on renegotiating the terms. Rosbaud argued that Maxwell's increased demands would destroy his relationships but, according to Sachs, 'Maxwell couldn't leave it alone and in the end McGraw pulled out.'

Maxwell had long realised that it did not require scientific talent to establish a new journal. With a modicum of research, a heavy measure of flattery and plenty of organisational skill, anyone of acumen could identify a field of science which was enjoying particular attention but was not yet served by an established journal. It was then a matter of locating a collection of scientists whose work was the most respected and invite them to form an editorial board whose task would be to commission, select and edit papers for publication in their own journal. This was self-motivated, vanity publishing which depended upon Maxwell's talents to sell. With access to LMS's huge mailing list, the availability of Pergamon's new journals was widely advertised and, although each journal's sales in the early 1950s did not exceed more than a few hundred, the sales figures were less crucial since subscriptions were paid in advance. Financial management could be carefully controlled and there were the back issues as an investment for the future. The formula was well established when Rosbaud first tasted Maxwell's ambitions just a few weeks after the move to Fitzroy Square. A large villa, Maxwell announced, had been rented on Pergamon's behalf in Geneva.

What ensued was the first Geneva conference on the peaceful use of atomic energy organised by the United Nations in 1955. Rosbaud's natural interest in the subject dictated that he should attend. In the wake of Hiroshima, the launching of the world's first nuclear submarine and the earliest construction programmes of atomic power stations for domestic electricity, the conference was a natural magnet for every atomic scientist in the world, if only to meet the American pioneers from Oak Ridge and Los Alamos. It was also a magnet for every other scientific publisher who, like Pergamon, hoped to capitalise on the sudden declassification of America's atomic secrets and commission books for a fast-growing market. To Rosbaud's irritation, Maxwell, whose knowledge of atomic science was limited to recognising the mushroom cloud of an explosion, also wanted to attend, not to listen to speeches but to test the commercial opportunities.

Among the scientists invited to the conference was John Dunworth, the head of the reactor department at Britain's atomic research centre at

Harwell who had been recruited by Rosbaud to be the editor-in-chief of Pergamon's *Journal of Nuclear Energy*. Shortly before leaving for Geneva, Maxwell and Dunworth met to agree on special arrangements for the conference. In Dunworth's name, Maxwell would stage a series of receptions in his rented villa to which every scientist attending the conference would be invited. Dunworth understood the purpose. Maxwell, he says, was 'an enormously engaging companion who was determined to make a lot of money'. At the parties, Maxwell systematically engaged each guest in conversation to establish a relationship and discover the potential for new publications. Geneva, in Dunworth's opinion, 'opened Maxwell's eyes very quickly to the commercial opportunities of scientific journals'. Buckley also could only look on in awe as Maxwell, having absorbed the jargon, held seemingly high-powered conversations with the fathers of atomic science. Maria Sachs watched Maxwell's technique: 'He was smart because he always knew what to offer to buy the person – fame or money.' Rosbaud, however, was inconsolably piqued, infuriated that a businessman should speak as an equal to a scientist and full of scorn for the 'so-called polyglot' who 'spoke a lot of languages, all equally badly'. If Maxwell was even aware of Rosbaud's mood, he brushed it aside because he was too preoccupied in scooping the commercial benefits for himself.

In the normal course of events, the United Nations, as the conference organisers, would eventually publish all of the 1,100 papers prepared for the occasion in bound volumes – 'undigested and unedited'. Maxwell perceived that here was a natural and unexploited extension to the journal business. Pergamon would publish and sell the most important papers in 'critically revised' volumes under the general title 'Progress in Nuclear Energy'. Purposefully, he approached the most eminent of the scientists and invited them to create six editorial boards which would select and supervise the publication of those series. By the end of the conference, he had recruited the cream of American, British and French nuclear scientists. Among the editors of the series entitled the 'Economics of Nuclear Power' was Maxwell himself. He returned from Geneva euphoric, determined that the Pergamon series should appear before the official volumes. 'We worked fast and furious,' recalls Buckley, 'and came out long ahead.' Pergamon was dramatically transformed. 'Overnight we were involved in huge production schedules,' says Buckley. Maxwell also appreciated the lucrative possibilities of taking two bites of the cherry. While the Geneva conference was published under one title, the same papers but 'revised to include later developments' were also sold in another series entitled 'Physics and Mathematics'.

By the end of 1955, in one year under Maxwell's direction, Pergamon was no longer a small publisher. Its output had grown to fifty journals and eighteen books. The production planned for the following year was nearly double. By the end of 1957, Pergamon was publishing over one hundred journals and books. Among its prestigious contributors whose past papers were collected and presented as Pergamon publications were the physicists Max Born and Niels Bohr. The range of topics was also impressive: electrolytic and chemical polishing of metals; the Aurorae and the Airglow; atmospheric pollution; irradiation colours and luminescence; psychosomatic research; neurochemistry and the chemistry of solids. In addition, Maxwell began to take over the business management of established but unexploited specialist journals from learned societies, such as the *British Abstracts of Medical Sciences*, and placed the Pergamon imprint on their cover. It was the prelude to a life of constantly flying around the world to scientific conferences on every conceivable subject to repeat his success at Geneva. Destinations from Stockholm to Santiago, Moscow to Montreal and Peking to Paris were regular stops in his itinerary to offer Pergamon's services to scientific conferences as the official publisher of their papers and proceedings and to present to the scientists the opportunity to create editorial boards to establish new journals. Gunther Heyden recalls his 'total exhaustion. We travelled non-stop and at night, because he didn't need any sleep, he would either talk or play practical jokes to prevent me sleeping. He just drove himself and all of us on and on and, if someone was no longer wanted, he would be fired.'

Relentlessly, universities throughout the world were being offered an increasing range of journals which, because of the prestige of the editorial boards, their librarians were initially eager to buy. Selling depended upon image and Maxwell was a master of presentation. Pergamon was presented as an international company with offices at the British Book Center in New York, in Los Angeles and in Paris. The foreword to Pergamon's catalogue was a three-page description of the history of Pergamon's birthplace in ancient Greece culled from *Encyclopaedia Britannica*. There was even a motto. Amid great laughter, Maxwell directed Heyden to find the Latin for 'We shall find a way or we shall make one'. *Invenimus viam aut faciemus* was thereafter printed on Pergamon's catalogues. Once the initial subscription target had been met and the money taken, there was always the opportunity at the end of the year to fill out the last issue with a collection of papers from an obscure conference or from another Pergamon journal and keep the choicest papers for the new year and another subscription. Rosbaud's intimate business was transformed beyond recognition. In 1958, utterly isolated from the business itself, he left, full of resentment that he was not due a penny.

By then, Maxwell had also capitalised upon his close personal relationship with the President of the Soviet Academy of Sciences. No other western publisher had invested the time and energy in repeated journeys to Moscow to cultivate the Russians. In the midst of the Cold War, few would have dared and the remainder would have seen little purpose. Maxwell, who grew up physically closer to the Soviet Union than most publishers in the west, was pragmatic and understanding about the Communist system. He understood the Russian way of life and could speak the language both literally and metaphorically. Under his agreement with Mezhdunarodnaya Kniga (the Soviet publishing organisation), Pergamon enjoyed the exclusive rights to a wide range of journals which had not hitherto been seen in the west. After translation in Fitzroy Square by 'two Poles and two Cossacks', they were sold in a variety of packages, but demand remained limited until the unexpected launch of the Sputnik in 1957. Overnight, western scientists, prompted by worried politicians, sought every source of information about Soviet science and it was Pergamon which owned the monopoly. As interest increased and Pergamon's profits multiplied, Maxwell restlessly travelled through eastern Europe, particularly Poland, Hungary and East Germany, obtaining similar concessions for their scientific journals and winning their goodwill by placing orders to print Pergamon publications because they were cheaper than British tenders. By 1962, Maxwell's declared annual profit from his trade with Russia amounted to £50,000 and was increasing. With the assistance of the publishers of the Great Soviet Encyclopaedia, he had obtained the rights to edit and publish *Information USSR* which was automatically purchased by most libraries throughout the west. Proudly, he announced that he was the only British publisher to have a stand at the British trade fair in Moscow and claimed to have personally persuaded Khrushchev to soften the strict Soviet attitudes towards western copyrights, although nothing in fact transpired. Maxwell's relationship with the Communists blossomed. He would become a uniquely trusted westerner who was received in the Kremlin by successive Soviet leaders and would publish their autobiographies in translated versions throughout the west. Each volume in the autobiography series was accompanied by an interview with Maxwell, although the questions were often nearly the same length as the answers. But, curiously, many of those Soviet-bloc journals were offered for sale not directly by Pergamon, but through the Pergamon Institute in New York which was described as a 'Non-profit-making foundation under the Presidency of Sir Robert Robinson OM FRS'. In Britain, however, there was barely any suggestion that Pergamon was not enjoying the profits of its monopoly.

Despite the illusion that Pergamon was totally based in London, America was in fact the financial centre of its operations. In about 1951, Maxwell had established a family trust in Liechtenstein which in turn owned a series of private companies in New York. There were significant tax and legal advantages in dividing the business between London, New York and Liechtenstein and the structure satisfied Maxwell's most fundamental principle of compartmentalisation, whereby employees knew only about their own function and Maxwell alone personally understood the overall operation. The most important private company trading on his behalf in New York was Pergamon Press Inc. (PPI), which was founded in 1952. PPI was based at the British Book Center in East 55th Street under Detlev Raymond, a German whom Orton and Maxwell had recruited in Berlin. In parallel with Pergamon in Britain, Raymond, helped by Maria Sachs, established contacts with American scientists, fostered relationships to create new American editorial boards and bought established journals such as *Akta Metallurgica* which enjoyed large circulations.

During his frequent flights to America, he was often accompanied by his secretary, Anne Dove. Unlike Britain, America could not offer Maxwell the commercial and political opportunities he sought because there were thousands of similar hustling entrepreneurs in this nation of immigrants. Dove could see the true Maxwell at the centre of his family and she was surprised. During their first years travelling together, Dove had often asked her employer whether he was Jewish. 'He never gave a direct answer,' says Dove. 'He would jokingly reply, "Can a Jew read the Sunday lesson?" referring to his attendance at the local church in Esher.' But in New York, Dove met his family and notably his cousin, Irving Schlomovitch, who worked for Maxwell. 'One Friday, Irving said to me that Maxwell was going to celebrate Shabbat with him and I said, "But is Mr Maxwell Jewish?" I got an odd stare.' Understandably, Maxwell had decided that unlike in New York, in Britain there was no premium on being Jewish.

America was also a country where the respected British publisher could still trade without fear of embarrassment. Anne Dove was equipped with a facsimile set of the stamp collection of King George V, bound in sheepskin, and she criss-crossed America to sell the collection to American philatelists. 'It was a great success,' she recalls, 'especially in Dallas where Maxwell had notified the British consul to arrange a conference. Hundreds turned up.'

In the smaller, more compact quarters of Fitzroy Square, it was much easier for the staff to observe how Maxwell operated. The hall outside his office was usually filled with people waiting for a long-delayed appointment and often anxious to attract Maxwell into a prospective deal. Those who managed to get inside met a man whose self-confidence had never been greater. He exuded a mixture of generosity and affection for those whom he saw as both talented and loyal, and utter contempt for those who were deemed dispensable. Often the talented and loyal were the same individuals who were deemed to be dispensable. Few observed Maxwell closer than Gunther Heyden, who besides selling Springer's stock was also on a commission to sell *Encyclopaedia Britannica* on behalf of Maxwell's company, International Encyclopaedias Ltd, which owned the agency for sales in Belgium, France, Germany and South Africa. Heyden was challenged by Maxwell to sell one thousand sets with the promise of a £1,000 bonus. 'Maxwell believed that in business you can't be democratic. He would want to see how far he could push people and then they would be dismissed. When the person was on the floor, he would start weeping.'

Like all of Maxwell's employees, Heyden could not fathom the complexity of his employer's emotions, and he gained no further insight when Maxwell was taken critically ill to University College Hospital. Maxwell was suffering from suspected cancer of the lung and was awaiting an operation for the removal of a lobe. He had been warned that he might not recover from the surgery. Among his visitors was Anne Dove, who found Maxwell in his room interviewing a Christian Science leader, 'trying to find an acceptable truth about life'. The visitor was one in a succession of Jewish, Catholic and Church of England ministers who failed to provide an acceptable answer to his question. After his recovery, the fact that he might have died had not apparently changed his attitudes towards mortals or eternity.

His life remained a series of hectic travel schedules and new ventures. In 1952, he had established Harmony Films, whose directors included the producer Paul Czinner, his wife the actress Elizabeth Bergner and the impoverished Sir George Franckenstein. In 1954, Czinner directed the filming of Mozart's *Don Giovanni* from the live performance at the Salzburg Festival and used the same techniques three years later for the visit of the Bolshoi ballet to London. Maxwell arranged with Buckingham Palace that the première should be a Royal Gala Charity performance to which the Duchess of Kent was invited. It was a glittering occasion, which he barely had time to enjoy before flying to China on business.

The Palace was not the only casualty of Maxwell's unremitting pace, and the consequences were costly. On 15 December 1958, Tönjes Lange wrote that Springer wanted to terminate all its connections with Maxwell.

After explaining that Springer would always be 'grateful' for his help in the post-war period, Lange explained that too many customers were 'dissatisfied' with the service from London to continue any further relationship. The verdict was a body-blow and Maxwell's reaction reflected his confusion.

His first reply on 2 January was a straightforward acknowledgement that while he was 'naturally sad and disappointed' there would be 'a great many points to settle' which he hoped would be done in a 'friendly, efficient and fair way'. The following day, however, he sent another letter which was markedly different. 'Your letter', he wrote, 'caused me a great deal of anguish and surprise. Anguish because it means official notice to sever our special relations which have existed over a decade and which have been so dear to my heart. Everything I know, everything that I have built up, everything that I have learned and acquired spring in one way or another from the joint fountain of Dr Ferdinand Springer and yourself and the splendid House of Springer Verlag.' The letter continued with the statement that he would be returning to Springer 'in accordance with our distribution agreement' books worth DM 300,000 and journals worth DM 200,000. Maxwell asked, 'Do you propose to raise any difficulty about their return and credit?'

Lange certainly did raise difficulties. The correspondence, which lasted one year, was inaugurated in twelve detailed pages in which Lange denied that their latest agreement signed on 13 November 1956 supported Maxwell's claim to the money or his proposed return of the old journals. Lange realised that Maxwell was irritated about losing Springer's lucrative trade especially since his warehouse was still full of old, unsaleable stock. But Lange took particular exception to Maxwell's reference to their 'strictly confidential' post-war agreements which was code that Springer's false Customs declarations after 1950 had weakened their ability to make demands. It could have been the beginning of an ugly divorce except that Maxwell was emotionally attached to Lange and did not want a break with his surrogate father. 'Please, my dear uncle Lange,' he wrote on 23 December 1959, 'let's agree to break the Gordian knot in the new year in a friendly and generous fashion.' They compromised, but barely met again before Lange's death in 1960. It was the end of an era but it caused only a slight hiccup in Pergamon's profits.

By 1959, Pergamon's two hundred employees had already outgrown numbers 4 and 5 Fitzroy Square and, following the expiry of the lease of the warehouse in Elephant and Castle, Maxwell decided to move to Oxford for both cheaper accommodation and prestige. In May he rented Headington Hill Hall, on the outskirts of the old town, for £2,000 a year.

The mansion, which was formerly the home of Lady Ottoline Morrell, would also serve as the Maxwell family home. The previous tenants, the Red Cross, had built four single-storey office buildings in the grounds and they were ideal for Pergamon's staff. The move was completed during 1960 but Fitzroy Square was kept to house I.R. Maxwell & Co. who were described as 'international university and industrial booksellers'. The compartmentalisation between the two businesses, selling and publishing, was physically complete.

Oxford was an ideal location to launch Pergamon's expansion in the 1960s, the decade of a boom in education. With the prospect of the Robbins report and the consequent building of a range of new universities, there were endless opportunities for huge profits to supply new schools and universities. In anticipation, Pergamon embarked on new ventures such as a one-thousand-volume library of original works on science, technology and engineering which was sold in paperback supported by a prestigious team of editorial advisers, principally Sir Robert Robinson, Sir John Cockcroft and Sir Edward Appleton. Called 'The Commonwealth and International Library of Science, Technology, Engineering and Literature', it aimed to provide books for African and Asian students in competition with Communist-supplied books which Maxwell believed to be politically slanted. 'I want to help the man in the factory,' he explained, 'who is anxious to educate himself.' Executives at the competing Oxford University Press were surprised by Maxwell's promotion since their own one-thousand-volume 'Commonwealth Library' had been offering similar courses for many years. On that occasion, executives decided to take no action, but in 1962 they did issue an injunction to prevent the sale of another Maxwell publication, *Pergamon's Oxford Dictionary*, which they complained had plagiarised their own standard work. Maxwell quickly retreated but inside the publishing world, where memories of the Simpkins crash were still fresh, the latest juggle added to a new wave of criticisms against a man widely viewed as an arriviste.

The major complaint concerned Pergamon's pricing and publication policy. Editorials published in the *Lancet*, the medical journal, in *Nature* and in the *Archives of Internal Medicine* complained that Pergamon's monopoly and its high prices, which were often three times greater than those of other publishers, were draining libraries of scarce funds. Philip Wade, in a letter to the *Lancet*, complained that as a librarian he was paying for Pergamon journals three or four times as much as individuals were being charged. Wade further complained that, having paid an inflated subscription for the journal *Biochemical Pharmacology*, he expected to receive as promised an abstract of the proceedings of an international conference in Stockholm because Pergamon was publishing all the papers in a nine-volume set to which he had also subscribed. Instead, he found that the journal was filled out with the papers of the conference and, more irritatingly, a brand new journal to which the library had also subscribed, the *International Journal of Neopharmacology*, contained in its first issue exactly the same papers. 'I may stupidly have missed some warning of that [first] duplication,' wrote Wade, 'but I see little justification for a new journal if its first issue must be padded with papers from a congress held eighteen months before a journal began. . . . It is wrong that libraries should be so burdened; and they should be spared buying the same material twice over.' Maxwell replied that instructions had been issued to prevent duplication in the future.

Some authors were also complaining of minimal fees, and, in an unusual and prominent announcement in the *Author* magazine, readers were warned about signing contracts with Pergamon. 'The printed form of contract', the announcement in the Spring 1963 issue stated, 'was in many . . . respects unsatisfactory. . . . The advantages to such an author, from the point of view of academic prestige, of having a published book to his credit may well tempt him to sign a contract which he will subsequently regret. Authors who have been offered contracts by this firm are strongly advised to consult the Society before committing themselves.'

Maxwell rebutted those criticisms from an industry which he condemned as ultra-conservative, uninnovative and self-destructive as 'sour grapes'. Both the professional institutes and traditional publishers had failed science and scientists, he said, and they were jealous about his personal and professional success. 'I don't make a penny from any of the journals,' he told the *Sunday Times*, and when asked why he did it for nothing, he replied, 'I do it because it ought to be done.' Indeed, many of his authors felt genuinely grateful for his generous support. Among them was Sir Harold 'Tommy' Thompson, an eminent and highly decorated professor of organic chemistry and late Master of St John's College, Oxford. Thompson appreciated Maxwell's style since he also had wide-ranging interests, including the editorship of Pergamon's most prestigious journal, *Spectrochimica Acta*. Thompson was also a keen footballer and a chairman of the Football Association. During their many hours together, Thompson introduced Maxwell to the politics of the British sport and so stimulated his later interest.

By the early 1960s, Maxwell felt that he could afford to ignore critics. He was a millionaire with a Rolls-Royce and a mansion. His family life was much closer than in the previous decade when Betty had relied upon nannies and a train of other employees to look after the home and all of her children. There would have been perfect contentment had Michael, his eldest son, not been critically injured in a motor accident in 1961. He would be kept alive on a support system in Oxford until 1968. A daughter had died of leukaemia in infancy. Seven children survived. He introduced into his home life the same mercurial discipline he imposed upon his employees. It was a homespun philosophy called 'The three Cs – consideration, concentration and conciseness'. Maxwell expected his children's behaviour to be in stark contrast to his own. Showing politeness, speaking in respectful tones and diligently obeying rules were precisely what Maxwell senior had steadfastly and proudly rejected. Yet he expected those qualities from both employees and his family. Betty Maxwell has described those years of running a home with seven children as 'always running behind [him] trying to catch up'. Psychologists describe that peculiar condition of demanding from others the opposite of your own character as 'projected identification'. Maxwell, one can assume, unconsciously dislikes some aspects of his personality and reacts violently if he perceives it in others. In his children, he wanted to forestall the development of his own characteristics. Since by all accounts his children are in some respects the antithesis of their father, he was clearly successful. But he strove towards realising his ambitions, carried forward by the sheer individualism which he could not tolerate among others. His next goal was to fulfil the ambition he had confided to Betty in 1944 – to become a politician.

CHAPTER 5

Anne Dove has no doubts why Maxwell became a Member of Parliament for the Labour Party: 'The Tories wouldn't have had him.' Although there is no evidence that he applied to join the Conservative Party, it would have seemed the natural citadel to match his lifestyle and business activities. Under Harold Macmillan, the nation was riding the crest of a boom which had enjoyed the innovation of jet airliners, LP records, transistors, sleek cars and the first computers. Maxwell was as enraptured by that era's affluence which was associated with the Conservatives as he was irritated by Labour's agonised doctrinal disputes about nationalisation and defence, its cloth-cap image and its Little Englander prejudice against business. Some interpreted his friendship with Peter Baker as a prelude to applying to Central Office to become a Conservative candidate. If he had been so minded, there would have been one insuperable obstacle: Harold Macmillan. The Prime Minister had vowed never to forgive or forget Maxwell's stewardship of Simpkin Marshall. If he was to become a politician, there was therefore no alternative but to join the Opposition.

Maxwell's first approach to the Labour Party was in late spring 1959 when the newspapers had begun to speculate that a general election would be held in the autumn. He applied to the local party in Esher which, because of the overwhelming Conservative majority in the constituency, was a relatively moribund association. Paul Vanson, the nominated Labour candidate, remembers the 'big impression' Maxwell created when he first arrived because 'he was interested in being active'. The party's finances were precarious and Maxwell offered to organise a fund-raising dance. 'It lifted our eyes,' recalls Vanson, 'because we weren't used to it.' Vanson 'thinks' that he can recall enrolling Maxwell as a party member.

Cyril Smith, the local party's chairman, relates a very different account of Maxwell's first appearance at the Esher party: 'The rumbustious Ian

Maxwell got up to make a point at a pre-election debate in the King George's Hall and just didn't stop speaking, which made me intensely annoyed.' Smith does not believe that Maxwell became a member of the Esher party. Certainly, Maxwell has never produced his Esher membership card.

In summer 1959, Maxwell was therefore possibly not a member. It was at this time that an employee, Sheila Stratford-Lawrence, confided to him that she was pregnant and, although unmarried, intended to have the child. The father was an American who had been temporarily employed by Pergamon and was returning home. She further told Maxwell that her decision to become a single parent would prevent her remaining as the prospective Labour candidate for Aylesbury and she was resigning her candidature.

Maxwell immediately offered Stratford-Lawrence a deal. He promised to persuade the recently divorced American to marry her if she, in return, proposed to the Aylesbury selection committee that Maxwell should be considered as her replacement. Stratford-Lawrence agreed. But, although both fulfilled their side of the bargain, Aylesbury's General Management Committee did not put Maxwell on the short-list. According to Albert Birch and Freda Roberts, both members, the committee had already made alternative arrangements. But Maxwell clearly made a good impression because an Aylesbury official suggested that he might try for the seat in the neighbouring constituency of North Buckinghamshire where the Labour candidate, Dr Gordon Evans, had just resigned after a serious road accident.

North Buckinghamshire, which was a mixture of 'hunting, shooting and fishing' villages, plus the towns of Bletchley and Wolverton, was an attractive proposition. The sitting Tory member had won in 1955 by only 1,140 votes, making it one of the country's most marginal seats. With the election announcement imminent, there was already a rush of applicants for the nomination although the national polls pointed to the Tories as favourites to win. First reports in Buckinghamshire's local papers spoke of a short-list of fifteen, but only five, including Maxwell, were finally interviewed when the party executive met on Saturday 22 August 1959. Four were local men who represented the constituency's two major industries, farming and the railways; among them was the party's vice-president, who could boast a long record of service in the constituency. In every sense, Maxwell was the outsider.

In the week before the selection, Maxwell gave local newspapers the material for a short biographical profile. As has been the case throughout his life, the variations in his own biographical accounts say much about

Maxwell's perception of himself – he regularly introduces new interpretations of identical events.

In the summer of 1959, Maxwell described himself as a publisher, speaking nine languages, who employed five hundred people and produced 250 books and 50 journals a year. There was mention of the Pergamon Institute, which disseminated 'research carried out in Russia and other people's democratic republics' and a statement that he had produced a film of the Bolshoi ballet. The full account of his war record was: 'got into the army when he was 16, was wounded in the battle of France in 1940, escaped from a POW camp, was commissioned in the field for bravery during the Normandy invasion and awarded the MC in 1945. He was later with the Foreign Office in West Berlin and helped launch three socialist democrat newspapers [sic].' To the uninformed, it would seem that Maxwell had fought throughout the war in the British army.

Persuading the committee was not an easy task for Maxwell. Candidates normally must show long membership and a laudable record of working for the party. He could show neither. According to the local newspaper, he told the committee that the Esher Labour Party was dormant but he had become a member 'twelve months' earlier. In 1973 he said that he joined 'some time after the war. I don't have any specific time or date.' He also agreed that it 'may well be true' that he joined 'only a few weeks before nomination'. Since he was not officially registered at Esher or at Aylesbury, and certainly did not apply for membership just before the selection meeting, it is probable that Maxwell was not even a member when he faced the committee. He did assure its members, however, that he had been 'an active supporter of the party since 1945' and a Fabian since 1956.

The opposition against him was vocal. Some were frankly unsympathetic to a foreign-born millionaire as a Labour Member, while others clearly favoured one of the local candidates. The day before the selection, the sitting Tory MP Sir Frank Markham advised the Labour committee to choose a local man because 'This constituency has never yet been won in any contested election other than by a North Bucks man.' Most of the committee probably agreed with him. But after the five candidates had made their speeches and had been questioned, the stalwarts were deeply divided. Maxwell had, according to Bryan Barnard, the constituency's agent, 'outshone them all by his delivery, the content of the speech and the way he dealt with questions'. Frank Atter, a fitter from Wolverton, a member of the committee and later a bitter opponent, remembers that Maxwell spoke 'very well'. After a marathon eleven hours and three ballots the committee announced that 'Captain Ian Robert Maxwell MC' was their choice.

Hours later Maxwell made a rousing speech, commenting on the 'magnificent turnout of delegates' and defiantly declaring war against his opponent: 'From here on Sir Frank can expect unrelentless [*sic*] trouble and fight. He had better get up early in the morning if he wants to hold on to his seat. Due to Gordon Evans's dreadful accident, he [Sir Frank] has been feeling pretty sure he will walk away once again by fooling the people as he usually does at election time by talking our kind of philosophy and selling the socialist line to the people. But let us not forget that he was a turncoat.' The meaning of the last comment was unclear. After predicting a 'four to six thousand majority' at the election, he promised to 'hold on to the seat for an eternity'. At a press conference on the same day, he handed out a release in which his background was described as a man 'of farm labouring stock [who], with only his army gratuity behind him, started a scientific publishing business'. His brief membership of the party was not mentioned and, when asked about the recent purchase of Headington Hall, he replied that they were 'business premises and I shall not live there'.

The controversy about Maxwell's nomination broke nationally within hours of its announcement. The *Daily Telegraph* reported a NEC meeting at Transport House where Dan McGarvey, a trade union leader, and Tom Agar, a Co-Op representative, allegedly moved motions to oppose Maxwell's candidature because it broke the rule that candidates needed two years' membership of the party to qualify for nomination. James Callaghan was also reported to be critical that Maxwell had not served 'an apprenticeship the hard way', but the party leader Hugh Gaitskell marshalled the majority to approve Maxwell's candidature. Since James Callaghan cannot recollect the meeting and since the others mentioned are dead, it is impossible to confirm the report's accuracy. But, inevitably, the Conservative newspapers saw political capital in the new candidate's background – he was foreign, rich and lived in a mansion in Oxford.

The second source of discord was more wounding. His biographical sketches had not mentioned his birthplace and the local newspapers carried articles suggesting that his foreign background had been concealed even from the selection committee. Atter believes that Maxwell's Czech birth was not known at the meeting but is equally certain that it would have made no difference. Barnard believes that the committee knew. Maxwell admitted to the local newspaper that he had not mentioned his past publicly because 'I have come to look on Britain as my country and did not think it worth mentioning,' and he insisted that the selection committee possessed 'all my antecedents'. The local paper was properly sympathetic to the omission, quoting a supporter: 'Captain Maxwell is no more a foreigner than Prince Philip. Like him he was born abroad, came here as a boy, fought for this country and has been working for its interests ever since.'

At his adoption meeting in Wilton Hall, three hundred Labour supporters stood and applauded their candidate. Gordon Evans, despite his injuries, spoke for Maxwell in a tape-recording and praised the party for choosing a candidate 'from another small country' who had risked his life for Britain. Maxwell responded with a grand gesture, the 'Buckingham Plan for Nuclear Disarmament', which proposed that the nuclear powers should place their weapons 'in trust for the United Nations' and that they should pledge themselves not to test or use their bombs and ultimately to hand them over to the UN. Copies of his anti-unilateralist plan, he told his new supporters, had already been sent to President Eisenhower, Nikita Khrushchev and Hugh Gaitskell. North Bucks had not previously been a launching pad for the world stage but its new Labour candidate was ambitious. The following day, the election was called for 8 October.

Barnard describes the party's organisation as 'poor'. The constituency covered a large area containing the two towns, Bletchley and Wolverton, and dozens of villages. Over the previous years, canvassing of the electorate to discover Labour supporters had been patchy and the organisation of the party in the villages was practically non-existent. For a marginal, where every vote counted, it was a serious handicap. But Maxwell was undaunted and set off in military style, driving a Humber Super Snipe, with his headquarters, a caravan, trailing behind. At night, a tent could be attached to provide sleeping accommodation. His campaign would not suffer from a lack of energy or determination, but any aspirations to lofty ideals were dashed within the first twenty-four hours. Maxwell's ambitious peace initiative was buried and forgotten beneath an onslaught against his personal credibility. He became the victim of unadulterated racial prejudice.

The first intimation of trouble was the news that Tom Mitchinson, the vice-president of the local Labour Party who had been rejected as the candidate, had signed the nomination papers of the Conservative MP, Frank Markham. Mitchinson claimed that Maxwell had definitely not told the selection committee that he was born in Czechoslovakia and that he, Mitchinson, was therefore 'dissatisfied' with the procedures. The Tories naturally jumped for joy over the defection and began openly to solicit support for their candidate on the basis that he was 'English through and through'.

By the second day, Mitchinson's desertion sparked a wider whispering campaign which questioned Maxwell's business reputation and the collapse of Simpkin Marshall, and even raised doubts whether he had really won the MC. By the third day, a printed list of questions had been compiled by Markham's team which Tory supporters were urged to put to Maxwell at his meetings. All were personally damaging – about his experiences in the Czech army, his name when he won the MC, about Simpkins, and why he employed non-union labour at Pergamon. Wounded, Maxwell protested that he was the helpless 'victim of a smear campaign', but clearly his original autobiographical account had contributed to the suspicion.

His quickly prepared rebuttal fuelled the controversy. The Military Cross, he explained, was awarded when serving in the '7th Armoured Division (the Desert Rats)'; he obtained a letter from James Pitman declaring that there was 'no blemish attached to Captain Maxwell's career in the matter of his scientific book career', which was not relevant to the collapse of Simpkins; and he said that Pergamon's staff were 'all encouraged to join their trade unions', which the Tories disputed. The election campaign degenerated into what was politely described as a 'fierce' fight and by locals as a brawl, since Maxwell took his defence into his enemies' camp by personally attending Markham's meetings to hurl questions at his detractor. Their battle formally ended at the count in Buckingham's council chamber, the day after the election, amid 'unprecedented . . . noise and din'.

Since Harold Macmillan's Conservative government was returned to office with an increased majority, Maxwell had no chance of winning his own election. Sir Frank Markham was re-elected with a slightly increased majority of 1,746 votes, although proportionately the vote for both Markham and Maxwell fell. But Maxwell could console himself with the knowledge that while nationally the swing to the Tories was just over 1 per cent, in North Bucks it was less at 0.6 per cent – which was a positive reflection of the campaign he had fought. At the end of the count, Maxwell was undaunted, but he was still bitter and refused to shake the victor's hand. To loud cheers and even louder boos he tried to make the traditional thanks but his voice was drowned when he claimed that victory would have belonged to him 'had the Tories fought cleanly'. When the uproar finally subsided, Maxwell shouted, 'Long live socialism and victory!', and after revealing that he had served writs alleging defamation on three Conservatives attending the count, he went to a meeting of rail-workers where he pledged himself to 'stick with you'.

Like all defeated candidates, Maxwell suffered an anticlimax after the defeat but it was brief. Barnard recalls that 'Elisabeth was particularly hurt but the bitterness had made him more determined than ever.' The prospect of waiting four years for another election was not a depressing one since, unlike most aspiring candidates, he had not had to suffer the tedious process of establishing his credentials with successive constituency associations and with the party leaders. He had started at the top and needed only to fertilise his new roots in Bucks and at Transport House.

By the turn of the year he had found a small house in the constituency and with Barnard's guidance began attending the necessary functions to court his supporters and to prove that he would be a worthy candidate at the next election. Simultaneously, he and Barnard organised an elaborate canvass of every voter; it would take four years to complete but could be guaranteed to pay rich dividends. Under Maxwell, the constituency would be managed like all his other businesses.

At the national level, Maxwell was already known and admired. Merlyn Rees, subsequently to become Home Secretary, who had just been defeated for the third time and despaired of ever entering the Commons, recalls asking a senior party official in 1959 whether he knew of any suitable work for a failed candidate. 'I was told that a brilliant chap, very similar to Stafford Cripps, had recently come into the party and taken it by storm. He planned an encyclopaedia on social sciences which seemed ideal for me.' Rees took the job after an interview with Maxwell and anticipated moving his family to Oxford. After the first day, he telephoned his wife and ordered, 'Halt. This isn't going to work.' Rees felt unable to work for someone with 'so many balls in the air who played God on five telephones'.

Richard Marsh, who would also become a Cabinet minister, recalls first meeting Maxwell after the election defeat at the party conference in Brighton. 'I couldn't forget the first meeting. Outside was his red Rolls-Royce with personalised number plates which were my initials and he kept asking me, "How did you become a Labour candidate?" as if it was like a business transaction. It seemed to me very strange because he had no history in the party.' As the two became better acquainted Marsh concluded that 'they didn't come any tougher but he had limitless charm when necessary and he needed it because in the Labour Party there was a predisposition against wealth'.

There was also a strong hint of the messianic in Maxwell's first major appearance at a Labour Party rally in Vauxhall Gardens in 1962. Hugh Gaitskell was addressing the Festival of Labour when an aide whispered that 'Captain Robert Maxwell MC is arriving to deliver a message from the electors of North Bucks.' The leader nodded and then heard that the messenger was arriving by helicopter. 'He was', said another future minister who witnessed the arrival, 'like a Harrier jet: all power down to get upward thrust.'

But Tam Dalyell, like other young Labour politicians, 'liked him from the word go for his boundless energy' after they first met at the party conference in 1963. Maxwell had by then established his credentials as a specialist in science, an area which Harold Wilson, who had become the party leader after Gaitskell's sudden death, intended to emphasise in Labour's next election manifesto. With Dalyell, Maxwell was co-opted on to Labour's science committee, which was chaired by Richard Crossman, the brilliant and unpredictable academic who instinctively admired mavericks. For Crossman, 'any man of foreign birth who had fathered nine children and who was decorated in the field must be exceptional.' The senior politician was impressed by Maxwell's 'tremendous organising capacity.... An explosive, enormously dynamic man'. Maxwell and Dalyell met regularly as they toured the country attending conferences arranged by Dalyell at which Crossman could meet scientists and university teachers. But Crossman, whom Maxwell occasionally described as his mentor, never thought of his protégé as a socialist or even as a natural politician. 'You've got to understand the Labour Party, Bob, if you want to succeed inside it,' said Crossman in 1963, but he felt that his advice had fallen on deaf ears.

The proof of that obtuseness was a speech Maxwell delivered in 1967 to a party conference about Labour's education policy, during which he attempted to justify sending two of his children to public schools. 'I only send those who are in need of going there' because of inadequate family circumstances or low aptitude. His views would be greeted with incredulity and catcalls by Labour party stalwarts who realised that he failed to understand the intellectual philosophy which required the complete comprehensivisation of British education. From the outset, his insensitivity plagued his relationship with the majority of the party. Even those, like Crossman, who might otherwise have been sympathetic admirers came away confounded by the sophistry. He was a millionaire who drove a Rolls-Royce and had moved into a lavish home having spent £350,000 on building works. Visitors to the aspiring socialist politician were met by peacocks strutting across the lawn and booming tannoys, summoning employees to the phone or to urgent meetings. Yet he apparently championed the cause of the underdogs against financiers like himself. Regularly, he attacked the Conservative government's proposals to remove Resale Price Maintenance which, he claimed, would cause the 'murder' of small traders. On one occasion he began his speech by disclosing that, only hours earlier, 'I cancelled my flight to Miami to be with you tonight.' His audience, a group of poor farm workers, were told, 'I know what it is like to go hungry because for over twenty years my father was on the dole.' Some in the party were enthralled by the singular power of an individual who could crush any expression of doubts about the contradictions. Others accepted that, while he was not an ideological socialist, these were the sentiments of a radical pledged to reform who was against inherited privilege and wanted the poor to have a fair chance.

To soften the edges and modify the image, in 1963 he presented his business activities more as philanthropic dedications. He offered to subsidise *Isis*, the Oxford University newspaper (of which his son Philip became an editor), to fund a scholarship at Balliol College and to establish a chain of bookshops on university campuses to be launched with the rousing flourish 'Books must replace bombs'. Yet all his bookshops eventually failed, the *Isis* subsidy was withdrawn, but four of his children did graduate from Balliol – 'The same as Asquith,' he would boast. Altogether, his multifarious activities created confusion about what he represented. But in 1964 his self-confidence knew no limits.

In July, Ansbachers, the merchant bank, floated Pergamon as a public company. Twenty years' work was capitalised by selling 1.1 million shares to the public for $3.5 million. Maxwell and his family trusts retained 2.9 million shares. The sale showed that Maxwell's stake in Pergamon was worth roughly £10 million. His other interests in America can be valued at several more millions but their true worth was hidden in the secrecy of Liechtenstein trusts.

With that money secured, Maxwell began looking for new business opportunities. His motives, he explained, were his altruism and his ambition for influence. In 1964, the *Daily Herald*, a staunchly pro-Labour Party newspaper, was suffering huge losses. Fifty-one per cent of its shares were owned by the International Publishing Corporation (IPC) and the remainder by the TUC. IPC's chairman Cecil King had announced that its shares were for sale since the company wanted to launch a new paper, the *Sun*. When no buyers appeared, King delivered an ultimatum that the newspaper would be handed to the TUC for nothing. The Labour movement, who deemed it vital that the party should enjoy the unequivocal support of at least one Fleet Street newspaper, was shocked. The problem was how to save the *Herald*. Maxwell produced a survival plan.

His proposal, which stood out as a sensible balance between capitalist reality and socialist principles, was his first attempt to break the costly stranglehold of the print unions over Fleet Street. He suggested that a new print plant should be established with a government subsidy in an area of high unemployment. During the day, when the presses were not printing the *Herald*, they would be used for general contracts, especially a slice of the £11 million which was spent annually by the trade unions. If his plan were accepted, he predicted, the TUC would earn £750,000 profits annually. Since the trade union movement had never managed to engage itself in business ventures, it was convenient to ignore his plan.

It was a passing rebuff in what was certain to be a momentous election year and an era of political and social upheaval exemplified in the Orpington by-election and Beatlemania. The Conservative government in autumn 1964 seemed worn out by office and shattered by a series of embarrassing scandals which had culminated in the resignations of John Profumo and Harold Macmillan. The new Prime Minister, Sir Alec Douglas-Home, who seemed as relevant to the Swinging Sixties as a penny-farthing bicycle, stubbornly refused to call an election. The Old World seemed to be dying while Wilson promised a Kennedyesque vision of technological revolution which he had called 'the conscious, planned, purposive use of scientific progress'. Maxwell felt that he epitomised that brave new world and his conviction was reinforced when George Brown, the deputy leader of the Labour Party, visited his constituency. Party members were assured by Brown that Maxwell 'was bound to play a very major role indeed in a new Labour government' because he 'represented very much the kind of new look which we think has to be brought into the country'. Maxwell had every reason to believe that Brown spoke for the party leader and that his talents would soon be used for the nation's benefit. He felt, in Christopher Booker's phrase, that he would be part of 'the dream after the storm'.

When the election was finally announced, Maxwell was automatically nominated as the candidate. Over the previous five years, he had earned an impressive reputation in the constituency for his hard work, while nationally it was recognised that he had revamped Labour's National Fund Raising Organisation at Transport House to improve the party's finances. Even Tom Mitchinson was quoted as saying that he would vote Labour because Maxwell had proved himself worthwhile. The local association's coffers were full thanks to Barnard's regular lotteries, and the agent could report a record 90 per cent canvass of voters. In the biographical-profile material provided for the local papers Maxwell described his birthplace as Slovakia, mentioned that he had travelled two million miles to win export orders and to attend scientific meetings and listed his presidency of the National Labour Party working committee to improve productivity as evidence of his contribution to the party's manifesto.

At his adoption meeting on 25 September 1964, he made a long, rousing speech promising that the campaign would be fought on issues which he spelled out in the most patriotic terms. 'I cannot believe that the British people have become so content with their betting shops and bingo clubs that they are prepared to watch our once great nation slip into third-rate obscurity.' He appealed for the expansion of business and the 'zest for a fight' in a mixture of images evoking the buccaneer and Churchill: 'We were only recently the richest nation on the globe. During the last twenty years we have shrunk back in terms of world-power to our condition before Trafalgar and Waterloo, a small country with a smallish population among greater and more powerful nations. Now we are back with Drake and Nelson, with Cromwell, Marlborough and Wellington, living hard and dangerously and surviving as a nation only if, like them, we are tougher, more austere, better at our jobs than our competitors.' Maxwell believed that a Labour government would radically galvanise Britain's lethargic industrial performance.

Politically, he could not quite subscribe to every aspect of Labour's policy. There would be no 'foolish renationalisation', he promised, beyond steel, and he expressly excluded British Road Services from state ownership. 'We will not interfere with the right and liberty of the individual who can do a job that is vital to the community.' His promise that grammar schools would not be abolished similarly reflected Maxwell's own views rather than the party's. Yet on defence he was leftish: 'We are prepared to give up the pretence of an independent nuclear deterrent which is neither independent and doesn't deter.' Finally, he expressed the hope that personalities and smears would not feature because the 'constituency had a basinful of that type of campaign in the last election'. He beamed as his supporters stood and cheered, certain that the next of his ambitions would be realised within three weeks.

The major local issue was the survival of the Wolverton railway workshops which under the Beeching reorganisation plan to reduce the rail network's losses was threatened with closure. 'Now,' he bitterly complained, 'our prized workshops are going to Steptoe's Knacker's Yard for pennies.' Yet one of those benefiting was Maxwell himself, who had negotiated to buy a part of the very same Wolverton workshops.

His acquisition had only been discovered in September. A local newspaper confronted Maxwell and obtained an admission and a promise. Robert Maxwell and Co., he conceded, had bought workshops and land from British Rail with an option to buy more. He refused to confirm that the price was £360,000 but pledged that the buildings would be used to provide '1,200 jobs in twelve to eighteen months', mostly for engineering workers living in Wolverton, although 'the nature of the product is for the moment confidential'. It was the type of 'regeneration' which Labour was promising, but it looked surprisingly similar to a plan which he had announced six months earlier for a printing plant for 1,200 employees in Dundee which was not yet realised.

For sheer energy alone, Maxwell deserved to win the election. His daily whistle-stop dash around the villages of Buckinghamshire in a red Land Rover, and occasionally in a helicopter, delivering impromptu speeches, generated unprecedented enthusiasm. His organisation and self-presentation as plain 'Bob' (the 'Captain' had been dropped), demoralised his new Conservative opponent, Elaine Kellet. Even when his birthplace became an issue with the jibe 'You're not going to vote for a bloody foreigner, are you?' Maxwell had his rebuttal ready: 'I am as British as His Royal Highness Prince Philip and so far as I know the Queen seems to be very happy with his services and so is the country.' The cheers continued until long after the result was declared.

Despite the microphones, the returning officer's voice could barely be heard above the roar when the crowd realised that Maxwell was elected. His majority of 1,481 was a resounding victory, a 6 per cent swing, much higher than the national average to Labour and the first time that Labour had held the seat since 1951. The headlines in the local newspaper spelled out his great success. Under the headline, 'Party Workers' Tumultuous Welcome for Mr Maxwell', the report described 'scenes of great enthusiasm' as, engulfed by his supporters, he and Betty marched through the centre of Buckingham to the party headquarters. There he told the cheering crowd, 'Harold Wilson has watched the result with great care and it will be a great relief to him that Labour has kept its promise and won the seat.' The Labour government had won by the slender majority of four seats and one of those vital seats was his own. Robert Maxwell had little doubt, as he spoke, that the nation's collective attention was fixed upon him and was concluding that, as destiny had ordained, he was indeed the man of the hour. If he looked, according to the local newspaper editor, surprisingly calm, it was, he later admitted, because he felt 'humble, grateful and very tired'. To reaffirm that he would not forget why he was elected, he promised that he would fight to keep a local station open and that a maternity hospital would be built at Bletchley before the end of the following year.

The new MP arrived at Westminster on the first day of the New Parliament, determined to make his contribution to save the nation from bankruptcy. His relationship with the new Prime Minister encouraged his confident belief that he would be offered an appointment. Wilson had been 'stunned by Maxwell's formidable achievement of winning Buckingham'. But Maxwell mistook Wilson's respect for colourful, self-made risk-takers as indicating that he was being considered for ministerial office. He could not see that his pushy and flamboyant personality offended Wilson's natural bureaucratic caution, nor did he take into account the fact that among his fellow politicians were many Labour Members who had worked over the previous twenty years for the opportunity of office. Among them was Crossman. Only days after the election, Crossman had taken his friend aside at a bar in New College, Oxford and told him, on the basis of his knowledge of Wilson, 'You have no chance whatsoever of a job in this government.' Crossman explained that both as a newcomer and 'with your past and your temperament, you'll have to be satisfied with the backbenches'. According to Crossman, Maxwell was 'very, very crestfallen' but he was 'grateful' for the honesty. So Crossman gave his friend one short piece of advice: 'Look, Bob, whatever you do, when you get in there, lie low for six months.'

The first day of the new Parliament was a historic moment. Amid pomp and ceremony, the Queen, as was customary, declared that a new Parliament was in session and read the new government's legislative programme from the throne in the House of Lords. After she left, MPs filed back from the Lords into their own chamber. After thirteen years of Conservative rule, the House of Commons was filled with tense and excited politicians. Former Conservative ministers, suddenly shorn of the power and prestige of ministerial office, sat grimly in their new positions on the Opposition benches. Across the floor sat the nation's new masters, brimming with anticipation of exercising power. After a few courtesies, at precisely two minutes past five on that very first day of the new Parliament, Robert Maxwell stood up to make his maiden speech, the first maiden speech of all the new entrants and the first backbencher's speech of the new Parliament. The whole ministerial bench writhed in outrage. Sitting on the front bench, next to the new Prime Minister, Richard Crossman felt positively embarrassed: 'It was absolutely disastrous. There he was trying to bash his way to fame in the first twenty-four hours.' Wilson's fury was worsened by the smiles of Rab Butler and Alec Douglas-Home. Throughout the Labour benches there was dismay at Maxwell's impetuousness. After a full twenty minutes he resumed his seat. Harold Thompson quipped to Dalyell that night, 'Let's just be thankful that Bob waited until the Queen sat down.'

Maxwell's solecism was not just that it was an inopportune moment for a maiden speech but that it had lasted three times too long. He boasted openly of having 'got in first' and was oblivious to the notion that he had 'left a bad taste in everyone's mouth'. It would take Maxwell many years before he recognised his folly and admitted, 'I thought I was the cleverest thing on two legs there.'

In content, Maxwell's speech was sound. After appealing on behalf of his constituency for improved civic amenities, help for the railway workshops, improved conditions in the brickworks (which were 'shocking') and a plea to keep a local railway line open, he introduced himself as the nation's foremost scientific publisher and launched into a critique of the failure of applying science in Britain. His financial success, he believed, gave him a special status among politicians to pontificate about the nation's salvation. British industry, he complained, was failing to apply the 'results of research faster' and the country's future productivity and profitability depended upon improvements. Attitudes had to be changed, he said, and wasteful government research contracts for defence and civil industry needed to be terminated. Concorde, especially, he insisted, should be cancelled because there was no 'real social or economic demand'. Having made the point, he then continued in the same vein despite the growing restlessness of those around him. The relief when he sat down was temporary. Over the next few days, he repeatedly stood up, interrupted speeches and shouted jibes to score political points until the Conservative Member Edward Du Cann castigated him bluntly: 'I have never heard anybody make so many speeches as he has in the last two days.' According to Crossman, 'I don't suppose there's anybody who is less aware of the impression he's created when he tries to create a good impression and it's no good trying to warn him. He wanted to shine.'

Disraeli also made an appalling debut in the Commons, but the similarity between the two men goes no further. Parliament is a reservoir and generator of every human imperfection, especially jealous rivalries exaggerated by the importance which its Members attribute to themselves. The businessman in Parliament is never a happy animal, especially a maverick who is accustomed to respect from his employees and shareholders. For a boardroom dictator willingly to accept the lowly status of a junior politician requires substantial self-awareness, and the humility which Maxwell described when he won the seat had already disappeared. The new Member was impatient to change the world and even more impatient with Parliament's time-wasting traditions. There was a conviction which ran through all his speeches that, if only one hundred other Maxwells could be marshalled, the nation would be saved. He exuded an ambition for power but no one was certain how he would use it. Some even wondered whether Maxwell knew himself.

Soon after his victory, Harold Wilson told the nation that it faced a grave economic crisis. His drastic cure included import surcharges, a range of new taxes and heavy borrowing from the International Monetary Fund. The remedy provoked hectic speculation against sterling, a crisis which preoccupied Parliament and the media. During those tense weeks, Maxwell was bursting to speak – and he succeeded, but his reward was the evaporation of his ministerial dreams.

First, he suggested that Labour MPs should contribute 10 per cent of their salaries to Transport House, an idea which was not welcomed by the non-millionaires in the party's ranks. Then he loudly accused the previous Tory administration of 'cooking the books' on the use of an obscure technical term that described an army unit. He was accurate but it was an irrelevance. Then he complained that printing of the Commons voting lists which were provided 24 hours after the vote was too slow. Again he was right but his manner grated. Finally, he attacked Parliament's traditions and his own ministers for conspiring with the Opposition to approve the annual cost of Britain's embassies without a debate. The vote to approve the costs was to have been a formality to clear the way for a major parliamentary debate, but Maxwell protested amid shouts and insults, mainly from Labour Members, 'I did not realise, until I came into the House, how much of a rubber-stamping organisation the House of Commons had become.' He continued to speak for nineteen minutes while the crammed and agitated front benches waited to start the debate.

During his many forays abroad, he complained, he had been irritated by the condescending and dismissive attitudes of the public-school and Oxbridge types who then dominated the Foreign Office. Britain's diplomats were not helping to promote exports at a time when exports were falling 'alarmingly'. For them, trade was grubby, and Maxwell, like so many businessmen, was given short shrift in those citadels of class prejudice. 'What worries me considerably', shouted Maxwell above a rising clamour of complaints and abuse, 'is the extraordinary complacency and smugness.' Unfortunately for the messenger, the same blindness afflicted his audience who in unison shouted 'Nonsense' when he claimed that Britain was finding it harder to export its manufactures and the Foreign Office's attitude was destructive. When he finally sat down he was praised by the Tories and derided from the Labour benches.

Maxwell was unaware that the Tory support arose out of glee over the government's embarrassment.

The price he paid was severe. 'Crossbencher' in the *Sunday Express* dubbed him 'the biggest gasbag in the Commons.... This handsome, debonair 41-year-old made the first maiden speech of the new Parliament, and he has scarcely sat down since.' Crossbencher advised the newcomer 'with a touch of old-world courtesy' to 'Belt up'. In the Commons, he was snubbed and mocked by his colleagues. 'I am ambitious to get things done,' he said, but few were listening.

At the end of his first year, he presented his local party with an annual report of his activities. He had spent 3,260 hours working on constituency business, including 1,580 inside Westminster. There had been 92 contributions or interventions in debates and 65 questions; he had written 215 letters to ministers and had led 20 deputations to ministries; he had written 4,000 letters on behalf of constituents and met 780 constituents on personal matters; he had attended 115 public meetings, made 6,000 telephone calls and travelled 15,000 miles. Few politicians would expect to be judged on statistics but the daily reports of the Commons proceedings in Hansard reveal his unconventional approach. Regularly he walked into the chamber, bowed to the Speaker, strode to his bench and either shouted a remark or rose to speak without knowing what had just been said. Repeatedly, he was rebuked: 'If the honourable Gentleman had listened to the debate' or 'That is a point which is not in dispute' or 'The hon. Gentleman cannot walk into the Chamber at about a quarter to nine and expect to be allowed to interrupt. He is always doing it; I have watched him frequently.'

This was the period when Maxwell won his reputation with the wider public by actively seeking media coverage. At the Commons bar, drinks were always on Maxwell. If his guest asked for a single, a double was ordered. Desmond Wilcox, then the executive editor of BBC television's *Man Alive* programme, recalls that 'Maxwell would always, at that time, make himself readily available for a TV appearance.' He wanted recognition for himself and his theme which was that Britain's businessmen should follow his own example and export more, curb their accumulation of capital and increase their investments. As will be seen later, throughout his parliamentary career, he vigorously expanded his own business interests. The media publicity was not confined to his political pronouncements but was mixed with his commercial coups, negotiated either from Fitzroy Square or from his office in Parliament.

No business opportunity was ever missed, including those offered in his constituency. At the beginning of 1966, after buying a large factory at

Fenny Stratford and the site of Bletchley Printers, he bought a 50,000-square-foot building at Olney with surrounding land. It was sited adjacent to the Wolverton railway workshops, where his promise to create 1,200 jobs was still unfulfilled. His plans were frustrated, he explained, because he could not obtain road access to the site. This latest acquisition was completed just after he spoke in a Commons debate where he had praised the proposed Land Commission. 'For too long we have seen marketeers and land speculators holding the community to ransom,' he said. That speech echoed a previous attack during a constituency meeting in April 1964 against 'land speculators [who] have already cashed in on a gigantic scale'.

Land was an issue which found Maxwell confused. Since the early 1960s Whitehall had mooted a new town for North Bucks which would be built on 27,000 acres of agricultural land and be called Milton Keynes. Initially Maxwell opposed the compulsory purchase of the land, the denial of compensation to tenant farmers and indeed the whole scheme, arguing that the expansion of existing towns would be preferable. But at the beginning of 1966 he changed his views and clashed in particular with the railway workers in Wolverton. 'He told them frankly that they were old-fashioned and uninspired,' recalls Barnard, his agent, 'and began telling them how they should run their local council to take advantage of the new town. They didn't like his interference very much.' It was a slight hiccup which was temporarily forgotten in the excitement of a new general election.

Harold Wilson prided himself on his sense of timing and the announcement of the election in March 1966 coincided perfectly with graphic newspaper accounts of disarray in the Conservative ranks. Few departing Members of Parliament doubted that a Labour government would be returned with a working majority and that a ministerial reshuffle would follow. Maxwell left Westminster hoping that Wilson, having paid off his political debts, would finally recognise his talents and invite him to assist in the rescue of the economy. On the eve of his own departure, Maxwell re-entered the chamber of the Commons and waited until just before the last formalities were completed to jump up and say farewell. Two days later he proudly told his local newspaper that the chance of speaking the first and last words of a Parliament 'must be millions to one'.

The confident Labour candidate fought the election with a new agent, Jim Lyons, since Barnard was himself standing as a candidate. Lyons inherited a highly tuned election machine and was presented with the campaign slogan, 'Let Harold and Bob finish the job'. Maxwell rushed around the constituency, extolling his record and his achievements, which included raising the money for a hospital and keeping a local railway line open. He was rewarded with an increased majority of 2,254 which, as Lyons said, was due to 'an outstanding Member of Parliament, the enthusiasm of our members and their will to win'.

For Maxwell, the victory was a personal triumph but his return to Westminster was an anticlimax. He was not invited to join the government and it seemed unlikely that he would be given the opportunity in the lifetime of that Parliament. 'You're neither a trade unionist nor an intellectual socialist,' Crossman told Maxwell. 'So Harold won't have you.' Tam Dalyell, reflecting a common view, says that 'The problem was what job Harold could have given him. It would have to be important and that was too difficult.' According to Merlyn Rees, 'He had been too rude to people but one had to feel sorry for him.' Maxwell accepted that he would remain a backbencher for the next five years and launched himself in every direction. 'He was like the charge of the heavy cavalry,' says one of his party colleagues. 'He whooshed past with enormous speed and strength but one had absolutely no idea where he was going.' Restless and ambitious he seized every opportunity regardless of the effect on his credibility.

In 1966, the publishers Calder and Boyars were prosecuted for publishing Hubert Selby's *Last Exit to Brooklyn* on the grounds that its description of a homosexual affair was obscene. Bernard Levin described it as 'a dreadful, savage and shockingly moralistic book about a corner of New York where, to quote the British publishers, "nothing matters except the precarious dollar and the pleasure of inflicting violence on someone weaker than oneself."' Most of London's legal and cultural elite opposed the prosecution and hoped that it would meet the same fate as the case against D.H. Lawrence's *Lady Chatterley's Lover* in 1960. Their overwhelming opposition made the prosecution's task of finding expert witnesses who could evaluate the book's literary merit particularly difficult and it was therefore relieved when Maxwell was prepared to testify in what everyone accepted was a watershed case. Described as a publisher, politician and family man, Maxwell appeared at Marlborough Street Magistrates' Court and condemned the book as 'brutal and filthy' and added that he was 'horrified to be a member of the same association' as the publishers, who 'disseminate this muck for profit'.

Maxwell's appearance as an expert on literature was puzzling. He had never previously shown an interest in novels and it was reliably rumoured that some of his shelves in Headington contained purely decorative book facias. Maxwell's condemnation of profits was also peculiar since he boasted about the pursuit of money, and his own bookshops had been selling the very book whose ban he demanded. The prosecution was successful but the conviction was later overturned on appeal. Maxwell's reward was to attract the added dislike of publishers who had not experienced the Simpkins crash. Two years later he admitted to the *Daily Express*, 'I'm probably the most unpopular publisher among publishers. But I pay no attention to these matters. It's largely sour grapes. Remember, publishing is a trade for gentlemen. It's supposed to take three generations and 150 years to succeed.' The same article quoted an 'acquaintance' about Maxwell: 'He's really incredibly complicated – megalomaniac, naive and sensitive at the same time. On the whole I admire him. He's nearly all hot air.' Fifteen years later Maxwell made a bid to buy *Mayfair*, the sex magazine. 'With consistency a great soul has simply nothing to do,' said Ralph Emerson, but Maxwell's inconsistency was driven by self-promotion, to cement his self-esteem.

Like so many entrepreneurs, Maxwell had watched in frustration as Britain's industrial performance slid uncontrollably, and he blamed both the managers and the unions. Before the election of 1964, Wilson had often spoken about the need for technology and dynamism but the promised revolution had still not materialised. 'If only the nation would follow my example,' Maxwell was often heard to say, 'so many problems would be cured.' All that talent was at the nation's disposal but was rejected by the Labour Party, which was still steeped in the emotion, mythology and philosophy of state control. Maxwell was not in tune with much of the party. In particular, he could not understand the Labour stalwarts from the north who had graduated from the coal villages or the industrial slums. Their single-minded sentiment and political credo, which was ingrained with the bitterness of their local communities' fight against a pernicious class system, was alien to him. His own worldwide travel had exposed him to industrial and technical revolutions which were unknown to most workers from Bradford and Birmingham, but to his irritation they relished their ignorance and spurned his experience. They regarded Maxwell as an arrogant millionaire; after all, when charged with dangerous driving for shaving while driving at 90 m.p.h. in his Rolls-Royce, he failed four times to appear in court to answer the charge. The dialogue never began. 'His success and wealth annoyed people,' recalls Richard Marsh, who had been appointed Minister for Power and who would invite Maxwell to ministerial parties.

Marsh regularly hosted receptions for foreign delegations at Lancaster House and because budgets for interpreters were limited was grateful if Maxwell agreed to attend. On one occasion, as Maxwell strolled from one group to another changing languages to crack jokes, he arrived in front of

Marsh and Sir Robert Marshall, who was then the Deputy Permanent Secretary at the Ministry.

'I hear that you speak German,' began Maxwell.

'Yes,' replied Marshall.

'Any other languages?'

'French.'

'It is extraordinary', replied Maxwell, 'how you educated people can only speak two foreign languages. I speak eleven.'

Forlornly, Maxwell waited for an appointment, although his politics seemed too varied for him to be identified with a group within the party who needed to be rewarded. For example, at the ceremony in 1966 to receive on Pergamon's behalf the Queen's Award to Industry, he told his audience that the pound would never be devalued because it would cause a 1929-type 'calamity'. When the pound was devalued one year later, he hailed it as 'the greatest opportunity for British exporters'. In autumn 1966, he urged import quotas and a freeze on wages but when the government imposed draconian tax increases to rescue the free-falling economy, he lectured Wilson from the backbenches on his own survival plan which contradicted those policies. The government, he said, needed to produce a plan to increase productivity, to scrap its prices and incomes policy and to join the Common Market. Nothing he said had much effect, not even a sane 117-page report which recommended that the state should use its discretion in procurement to improve industry's efficiency, remove restrictive practices, encourage productivity agreements, retrain labour and boost exports. Crossman sympathised with his predicament and produced what he genuinely hoped would be a helpful solution. He asked Maxwell to become the chairman of the House of Commons Catering Committee.

In 1966, the annual deficit of the Commons' kitchen had soared from £10,000 to £33,000, creating a combined overdraft of £53,000. The Catering Committee blamed the losses on paying too much for food, on the abundance of waste, and on a complete lack of control over the movement of food and money through the kitchens. In summary, there was gross inefficiency and wholesale theft. Chairing the Commons Catering Committee was not a prestigious task and, as Marsh reflects, 'No one was queuing for the job and I was surprised when Bob took it.'

Maxwell's solution was radical. He negotiated a grant from the Treasury, fired a large number of the staff, reduced the quality of the meals and, at the price of eternal opprobrium, sold the entire cellar of vintage wines. At the end of the financial year, he claimed that his entrepreneurial skills had turned the huge deficit into profit.

His success, instead of enhancing his reputation, aroused the very antagonism he might have hoped to assuage. Question-time in the Commons was peppered with exchanges which were cannon-fodder to both wags and journalists anxious to poke fun at the millionaire socialist. He was asked about the substitution of powdered milk for fresh milk, the introduction of processed chips instead of fresh potatoes and the total weight of sausages consumed during one year (6,800 lb). Regularly, MPs used the occasion to deliver embarrassing blows by asking why *oeuf en gêlée* was no longer on the menu or why the tea room no longer served 'decent plain biscuits, only nasty cheap sugary ones'. It was demeaning, and although he claimed that the £33,000 loss had been reversed to an annual £20,000 profit, the MPs who remained on the committee would claim that his achievement owed much to accounting. If the Treasury grant and exceptional items were deducted, the annual losses had actually increased from £33,000 in 1968 to £57,000 in 1969. Crossman was nevertheless very pleased with Maxwell's performance.

Maxwell retired from the committee after one year, a year which coincided with the post-devaluation crisis, a wave of strikes, Cabinet splits and by-election defeats at home and the bitter wars in Vietnam and Nigeria. It was the nadir of the Labour government and, according to Cecil King, Maxwell was among those who wanted to be counted among the dissidents. 'Maxwell', he wrote in his diary, 'has been pestering Hugh Cudlipp [the editor of the *Daily Mirror*] with phone calls and letters. He really will have to be given the brush-off.' In public, Maxwell spoke about 'leading the nation away from the British sickness' but he lacked any following. So when Wilson appealed for the 'Dunkirk spirit' as the cornerstone in the fight for Britain's economic survival, Maxwell, driven by instinct and patriotism, was among the first to rally to the slogan. 'Once their energy and talent is liberated [*sic*],' said Maxwell about the British workers, 'nothing will stop this country regaining its place in the world.' His sentiment was genuine. It was only a short step from there to his association with a new campaign which won him national recognition.

On New Year's Day 1968, five typists at a heating factory in Surbiton, Surrey pledged themselves to work an extra half-hour every day for no pay as a real contribution to rectifying the country's perilous economy. On 3 January, *The Times* carried a full-page advertisement from an advertising agency thanking the girls for the idea of an 'I'm Backing Britain' campaign. For a nation shivering in anticipation of economic decline, the typists' gesture was seized upon by the newspapers as a 'sunrise' issue for their readers. Editors and journalists were delighted to have a new and positive story in contrast to the daily diet of economic gloom. But eight days after the campaign had started, Maxwell decided that it was in danger of faltering because there was nothing new to report and because its new government-appointed sponsors, the Industrial Society, had adopted a moderate and unflamboyant style. Maxwell stepped in with a competing campaign and later told the Society's director, 'The trouble with you is you're all trying to be virgins – whiter than white. I've succeeded in raping you all along.' He would also tell the journalist Nicholas Tomalin that he had thought of the idea at the same time as the Surbiton girls: 'That's the thing about me. I'm quick off the mark.'

In the House of Commons, Maxwell launched the 'Think British – Buy British' campaign. The launch guaranteed him appearances on that night's television and brought an invitation to meet David Frost, who was then basking in glory as the nation's pre-eminent satirist. Accompanied by a few trade unionists and employers, Maxwell breakfasted two days later with Frost and was invited with his supporters to present their views to the nation that weekend. Over the next few days the publicity was terrific and the names he collected seemed to covet public association with the campaign. Among them were the businessmen Joe Hyman, Sir Max Aitken, Sir Billy Butlin, Bernard Delfont, Lord Thomson and Arnold Weinstock, and the trade unionist Frank Cousins, an admirer of Maxwell's, who withstood the complaints of others in the Labour movement that it was a 'pure gimmick'. That Saturday night, Maxwell earnestly explained to the nation that everyone should 'think before buying. Buy the home product or service first whenever you can even if it means buying less for a time.' Minutes after he finished, his associate Joe Hyman, the chairman of the textile manufacturer Viyella, exploded that he could not approve of anything 'so stupid which would provoke a trade war'. Maxwell was undaunted by the evident split. 'I move fast,' he told Tomalin. 'It is both efficient and politic. When there's an object in my way I smash it down, or race around it. And I move so fast that when people put bombs on my road I'm a hundred yards before they explode [sic].'

Maxwell now wanted to amalgamate with the Industrial Society, but the latter refused since he seemed to want to entrust them with the work while he took the credit. So Maxwell, with the help of an advertising agency, launched his own campaign with a poster headed 'Sell British – Help Britain – Help Yourself'. Using the names of his famous supporters, the newspaper advertisements listed '100 uncranky ways you can help Britain'. It included the suggestion that children should not drink their free school milk. When it appeared on 7 February, the campaign fell apart. None of the famous had been consulted by Maxwell and they had not given their approval. Weinstock called the advertisement 'incredibly silly' and Delfont said, 'I'm amazed. It shows what happens when you let people run amok.' Delfont wanted his name taken off: 'It's a pity such a good idea has started off so badly.' Overnight, Maxwell became a target for ridicule, especially when he justified printing Pergamon's books and journals in eastern Europe because 'it's cheaper'. He did not understand his inconsistency but blamed 'Britain's "professional knockers" who just turned their attention from Britain and directed it against me'. When he wrapped up the campaign in March he sat alone, but he claimed nonetheless that the response had been 'phenomenal'. The campaign had amounted to a recorded telephone message urging support for Britain; the collection of signatures for a petition; the establishment of community baby-sitting groups; and the creation of a 'clearing house' for complaints about shoddy British products and services. 'Much has been achieved,' said Maxwell. 'It needed just one more heave' – but unfortunately he would not be able to take the campaign through to its completion because of pressure of other work.

The campaign's only discernible achievement was to turn Maxwell, courtesy of television, into a nationally recognised personality. Since there is little Fleet Street enjoys more than a Labour politician who can be lampooned, a bevy of defamatory tales began circulating. His stock fell. When a newspaper reported that amid the strikes and chaos the socialist supporter of the 'I'm Backing Britain' campaign had, despite all the government's currency controls, spent a holiday on the luxury yacht *Shemara*, owned by Sir Bernard Docker, his stock sank still further: one week's charter cost more than the average Briton's annual wage.

So, by the time Maxwell returned from his luxury cruise, his political career had passed its peak. Yet sadly it was the moment when he finally held the attention of all politicians in the Commons chamber. On 26 August, in a specially recalled session, members discussed the Soviet invasion of Czechoslovakia. The 'rape of Czechoslovakia' was one of those benchmark events by which history is recounted. The world was shocked. Over the previous four years, the sight of Maxwell rising to speak in the intimate atmosphere had increasingly provoked sniggers and sighs, but on this day everyone was quiet. 'As is well known,' he began, 'I was born in Czechoslovakia.... I remember well the betrayal that I, though very young, and the whole nation of Czechoslovakia felt at being let down by Great Britain and France at Munich....' To rapt attention, he outlined his escape and his decision to come to Britain, because 'when the chips were down, Britain was willing to stand against Hitler alone'.

His advice was measured and moderate, and surprised the Tories. The government should take no reprisals which would disturb detente but should leave it to individuals to cancel their contacts with the Soviets to show their disapproval. It was a speech which moved the House.

By 1968, Maxwell had certainly made an indelible mark in the Commons, but not in quite the way he had intended. His weaknesses and strengths were tellingly revealed in a sympathetic profile written by David Wood, the respected political editor of *The Times*, which perfectly encompassed the vices and virtues of the man. Wood had been invited to meet Maxwell and his family at the mansion in Oxford and was impressed by the strong bonds which united the large clan. Surrounded by affection and respect, Wood had difficulty in equating the brave refugee with the much maligned public persona.

During the course of their interview, Wood asked Maxwell about his early years and faithfully reported the anomalous answer: 'His own account of his christening as Ian Robert Maxwell is typical of the man. At the end of the war the army wanted to send him to Berlin on a mission and the officer who briefed him said that he had better find a respectable name to go with. Maxwell had no suggestions to offer. "Then you'll be a Scotsman with my family name," said the officer.' This was an example of Maxwell's romanticising which Wood recorded faithfully. Maxwell's secondment to the Control Commission was not 'a mission' but a regular transfer; in any case, when he received his MC in January 1944 he was already called Maxwell. Exaggeration is one of Maxwell's vices and Wood identified the others which had by then sabotaged his political ambitions.

Robert Maxwell swept into the House . . . and gave every impression to the old hands that he was mounting a takeover bid for the place, lock, stock and barrel. He was loud and thrusting and probably no M.P. came new to Westminster was so little overawed by the surroundings. So far as there was a takeover bid intended Mr Maxwell has failed. In the House he is still regarded as a maverick, a millionaire of unusual antecedents who obviously knows how to be a business tycoon but who will never understand the art of winning men.

Probably Maxwell did not, even in private, acknowledge the accuracy of Wood's summary, but in the midst of his next commercial sortie he effectively admitted its implications. While his bid for power in Parliament was failing, he was simultaneously undertaking a substantial expansion of his business empire. In October 1968, he thought that he had finally secured a power-base in Fleet Street. He announced a bid for the

News of the World and told inquirers that, if he was successful, he would resign his parliamentary seat. 'The first we knew about that', said Frank Atter, the party official in Buckinghamshire, 'was when we read it in the papers.' Maxwell the aspiring tycoon, rather than Maxwell the politician, dominates the remainder of this story.

CHAPTER 6

There was never any secret why Maxwell wanted to own a newspaper. The barons of Fleet Street were automatically granted influence and prestige, and Maxwell's bids for the left-wing *Daily Herald* and four years later for the right-wing *News of the World* indicated a consistency not of principle but of ambition. His disappointment at not winning office, contrasted with his enormous and accumulating wealth, laid the ground for a condition which the American politician Adlai Stevenson had aptly described five years earlier: 'Power corrupts, but the lack of power corrupts absolutely.'

In 1968, Pergamon was booming. Trading profits had risen from £145,000 in 1962 to £1.3 million in 1966, and in 1967 they increased again by 35 per cent. Pergamon's assets had, in four years, tripled in value to £6.9 million and the price of its shares had doubled over two years. Regardless of the setbacks in Parliament, Maxwell appreciated that his new wealth unveiled golden horizons.

The company's phenomenal expansion had not been effected without some difficulties. A five-year agreement with the Macmillan Company of New York for the exclusive distribution of Pergamon books had been terminated in August 1964 amid acrimony, two years before its expiry. Macmillan had bought £3.7 million worth of Pergamon books (which added enormously to Pergamon's profits) but had sold only 57 per cent of the stock. Macmillan claimed that 'the quality and saleability of the books which we were expected to buy fell below our expectations' and blamed Pergamon for selling its own translated versions of books earlier than previously agreed. Maxwell was naturally disappointed because Pergamon's success depended upon exports (40 per cent of its sales were in America) and blamed Macmillan's sales force.

Maxwell's privately owned American company, Maxwell Scientific International Inc. (MSI Inc.), bought the outstanding stock of books from Macmillan for £1.6 million so that Pergamon suffered no losses. When Maxwell was questioned in January 1966 about this apparent setback by Oliver Marriott of the *Sunday Times* he dismissed any suggestion that Pergamon's sales might suffer and boasted about the 'quite abnormal profitability of Pergamon' which had been 130 per cent and 116 per cent pre-tax on the net capital employed over the previous two years. 'These are the sort of returns', wrote Marriott, 'which all industrialists dream about.' Despite Maxwell's assurances, Marriott queried whether Pergamon could continue to perform so brilliantly.

Ebullient as ever, Maxwell dismissed the cautionary note and waved aside any doubts. He was set on a buying spree to build an empire, and to raise the money to finance his expansion 1.1 million Pergamon shares which were owned by his family trusts had been sold on the stock market after the flotation at a much higher price than that at which they had been issued, although some were immediately repurchased by nominee companies to ensure that Maxwell and his family retained absolute control of the company. His targets for purchasing were companies with printing and educational interests. The first was a venture into a field where he had absolutely no experience whatsoever.

On 1 December 1965, Maxwell paid £1 million in cash for the subscription-books division of George Newnes, which published two well-known encyclopaedias, Chambers and Pictorial Knowledge. Encyclopaedias, as a by-product of the expanding educational revolution, were in vogue in the 1960s, especially among the aspiring working and lower-middle classes, who had been convinced that knowledge was the key to improving their children's prospects. Chambers encyclopaedias were well written, but the technique of marketing the fifteen volumes had aroused widespread controversy.

Since the traditional method of selling through shops was unsuitable, encyclopaedia publishers had recruited freelance salesmen who, provided with lists of potential customers (usually parents of young children), arrived unannounced on the doorstep of the unsuspecting client. Doggedly and emotively, the salesmen sought to cross the threshold as the first step to persuade the client to sign a contract whose huge expense was partially concealed because the monthly repayments over three years promoted the illusion that the total investment was substantially less. Since the salesmen were paid purely on commission – no sale, no pay – the pressure exerted on the potential customer was sufficiently strong to provoke demands that Parliament should enact legislation to protect the weak and the gullible. By the time that Robert Maxwell, then a Labour Member of Parliament, made his first investment in the business, encyclopaedia salesmen enjoyed dubious reputations. Cecil King, IPC's chairman, who had sold Newnes to Maxwell, said subsequently that he did not think that selling encyclopaedias could be profitable unless methods were used which were not 'ethical'. Maxwell had a different view, although his own advisers cautioned him against the purchase on commercial grounds.

Chalmers Impey, who were Pergamon's auditors, had advised that the business contained a 'higher speculative element' than Pergamon's traditional interests and pointed out that Newnes's profits over the past five years had substantially declined and it was making a loss. Their opposition was supported by Ansbachers, Pergamon's merchant bankers. Maxwell ignored them both because he believed it would be a very profitable venture.

When Maxwell bought Newnes, the fourth edition of Chambers had already been printed but it took a further twelve months before sufficient volumes had been bound for Maxwell's newly recruited team to begin a concerted sales drive. Newnes's direct competitor was the New Caxton encyclopaedia, a twenty-volume work owned by Caxton Holdings who, under the management of Hedley Le Bas, had pioneered the foot-in-the-door selling technique which had earned the business such a notorious reputation. To maximise their profits, Caxton also sold the same encyclopaedia in parts to the British Printing Corporation (BPC), who marketed their version under the title Purnells New English encyclopaedia. Consequently, in 1966 Maxwell was in competition with both Caxton and BPC in completely alien territory. He had never handled a similar product and he had never been involved in direct selling.

Whatever criticism might be voiced about Maxwell's commercial behaviour, it is indisputable that he never hesitates to mount a challenge in the market. More than most businessmen, he instinctively seeks to defeat his competitors. Chambers was such a venture. Maxwell felt that he had 'bought a bargain' and was optimistic that he could transform Chambers' recent losses into profits. 'The encyclopaedia business', he later explained, 'was 97 per cent in U.S. hands. British encyclopaedias were just as good but weren't being properly sold.' Accordingly, Maxwell reported in a circular to shareholders that his huge investment would show a 'satisfactory return' and set out to fulfil his promise by increasing his share of sales throughout the world, naturally at Caxton's expense.

On 8 January 1967, in an atmosphere of intentional melodrama, Maxwell called a press conference to announce that he was about to set off on a 50,000-mile world tour to promote the sales of the new edition of Chambers. After stating that he had already sold 3,500 sets in Britain, he explained that exports were his dream. 'There is a tremendous thirst for knowledge all over the world,' he told the assembled journalists, 'and we have the right people and product to cash in.' In every respect, it was a highly unusual event. First, most businessmen would never speak publicly before embarking on a speculative tour but would wait for the results. Secondly, it would be unusual even for a Conservative MP to summon the press to promote his business interests but it was rare for a socialist to do so. Yet Maxwell was abundantly confident of proving to Britain how he could win exports. It never occurred to him that what generated interest was the incongruity of a socialist peddling a disparaged product.

The first stop on the world tour was India, where he was greeted by Jawaharlal Nehru, the Prime Minister, an honour which set the pattern for the whole tour. In each country which he was to visit – Thailand, Japan, Hong Kong, Indonesia, Malaysia, Australia, New Zealand, Mexico, the USA and Canada – he had arranged to meet either the Prime Minister or the President, who would be given, in the presence of a photographer, a specially bound set of the encyclopaedias. In each of those countries he had also arranged to meet leading book-dealers to conclude sales contracts and had set up an unlimited number of 'media opportunities' for interviews.

As he toured the world, Maxwell reported back daily to his headquarters in England a succession of record sales. Philip Harris, the vice-chairman of Buckingham Press, the Pergamon subsidiary which had bought Newnes, followed his success with amazement. Without consulting Maxwell, he took the initiative and began to plan a new print of the encyclopaedias, reasoning that even the available stocks of 13,000 sets were grossly insufficient to satisfy the huge upsurge of demand which the tour was generating.

For Philip Okill, who was travelling with Maxwell, a different picture was emerging. Okill had just been promoted to head Newnes's international sales force when Pergamon had bought the company. Okill had taken a different route around the world from Maxwell's, but they had arranged that they would meet in predetermined capitals to compare results.

As a quiet-spoken, slightly built, methodical man who enjoys stroking cats, Okill would be the first to admit that he had little in common with his new employer. The first six months of operating under Pergamon had passed uneventfully, but the changes which Maxwell introduced immediately afterwards were, Okill believed, drastic and dangerous: 'I was expected to jump or dance when the maestro called the tunes, the maestro of course being Mr Maxwell. And Mr Maxwell's ideas of running a subscription-book division were quite different from anything I had experienced in twenty-odd years.'

Okill was a cautious salesman with limited horizons. When Maxwell told him that his objective was to make Buckingham Press 'the largest bookselling operators in the world' he was startled because he believed that his employer did not understand how to manage the operation: 'He seemed to be fired with ambition but he had no experience.' Okill's fears were confirmed during the tour. His task was to follow Maxwell and to complete the legal formalities for the sales which Maxwell had won. Yet in Calcutta where Maxwell had claimed sales of five hundred sets, Okill heard from a Mr Pripittia: 'No, we haven't placed an order. Mr Maxwell offered us some sets of Chambers encyclopaedia and told us we didn't have to worry about paying for them. That could be dealt with at a later date.' Okill left without an order and discovered that India would never place an order because the encyclopaedia's map showed the disputed territory of Kashmir as belonging to Pakistan.

Maxwell returned to Britain on 23 February, before Okill. Promptly, he called another press conference at the Dorchester Hotel to announce the sale of seven thousand sets of Chambers worth £1 million. It was, he told the summoned journalists, a momentous achievement which was 'a lesson for the rest of the British business community'. His 5 per cent target, he declared, was 'easily achievable'. The headlines were fulsome and amusingly included his own quip that Maxwell, 'when broken down into Chinese, means Mr Ma, a man of great thoughts'. Another of his philosophical comments, that he had realised the secret of the Japanese economic miracle when he had seen a newspaper delivery boy running, rebounded upon him. Cynical wags wondered whether the wretched fellow had not simply got out of bed late. But gratifyingly to Maxwell, the numerous newspaper accounts contained the impressive statistics he had compiled: 'In seven weeks I travelled 70,000 miles, I visited 11 countries, 22 cities, held some 400 meetings and was interviewed on radio, television and by newspapers about 140 times. I obtained £1 million worth of orders for British books with some £3 million worth to follow and on my return received a telegram of congratulations from the President of the Board of Trade.'

He then went back to his office and summoned Harris, who expected some praise for his percipient planning for a reprint. The contrary, according to Harris, occurred. He was told by Maxwell to cancel all plans because his claim of seven thousand sales was just for publicity. Okill was stunned when Harris relayed the news. Soon after, he was sitting with

Maxwell in Fitzroy Square when Maxwell said, 'Okill, you don't seem to like me, you don't seem to trust me. Why don't you?' Okill replied, 'Because, Mr Maxwell, you're the sincerest liar I've ever met.' According to Okill, Maxwell laughed, 'because, I genuinely think, he took that as one of the nicest compliments I could have paid him'. Okill claims that the world tour resulted in no sales other than to a Pergamon subsidiary in New York. Maxwell denies the allegation and insists that, with the exception of the Calcutta order, the sales which he announced were all genuine and were delivered. Okill's version was later supported by the government's investigation into Pergamon's affairs.

Maxwell was unconcerned by their disagreements since he was impatient to increase sales of Chambers and challenge his competitor, Caxton. Over previous years, Caxton had successfully established a strong sales team and was earning enticingly high profits in South Africa which contributed a quarter of the company's total income. Maxwell immediately began to search for ways to capture that money for himself. What followed was certainly controversial but definitely not illegal. On 13 November 1966, Maxwell recruited L. C. Schilling, who for the previous six years had been Caxton's secretary, to be the credit controller of Buckingham Press. Events then moved very swiftly. Just before Maxwell had left for his world tour, the head of Caxton's South African sales team had flown to London and had likewise agreed to work for Maxwell. Two months later, in February 1967, days after Maxwell returned to London, Maxwell sent Philip Harris to South Africa to recruit a new sales team. Harris returned to Britain forty-eight hours later, having accomplished his mission. The major casualty of Harris's spectacular success was Caxton, whose complete sales team had deserted their old employer. Harris was quite candid about the instructions Maxwell had given him on the eve of his departure. He was to 'knock off the Caxton sales force'. But Harris went even further and also alleged that Maxwell's true ulterior motive was to 'bankrupt Caxton so that he would buy it cheaply'. Maxwell strongly denies that claim.

By the time Harris came to make his allegations in 1970, he had become a disenchanted critic of Maxwell, but there is no doubt that Caxton was terminally crippled by the collapse of its sales in South Africa. The following month, in March, Maxwell made his first approach to Caxton's chairman, Hedley Le Bas, with an offer to buy his family's business. Not surprisingly, Le Bas was furious to find himself so quickly outclassed by his new competitor, and sought help from his partners, the British Print Corporation (BPC).

BPC was Caxton's natural saviour for three reasons: Caxton's encyclopaedia was printed by Hazell, Watson and Viney, a BPC subsidiary; BPC sold part-issues of Caxton encyclopaedias; and Caxton owed BPC a substantial sum of money. Yet at that precise moment, BPC, which would feature so massively throughout Maxwell's career, was jolting through a major management crisis.

BPC's turmoil had started the previous year. The company was an unhappy marriage created in 1964 of two printing conglomerates, Purnell & Sons and Hazell Sun. Just months after Purnell's chairman Wilfred Harvey, a swashbuckling individualist, had become chairman of the new company, he was overthrown in a public and very bloody board-room coup after the discovery that he had illegally profited from earlier mergers and that he had arranged to pay himself the astronomical salary of £270,000 per year plus £600,000 in commissions. In 1966 BPC's management were still reeling, and they left Le Bas in no doubt that they could not offer him any help.

Consequently, in April 1967, Le Bas began negotiating with Maxwell. On 3 May 1967, Bruce Ormrod, the joint managing director of Henry Ansbacher, announced that Maxwell had bought Caxton Holdings for £1.1 million. In a jubilant public statement, Maxwell estimated that there was a £200 million world market for encyclopaedias of which he aimed to capture 5 per cent. Considering the enormous sales he claimed to have won during his recent world tour, his optimistic prediction was accepted as forecast.

Eight days after the merger announcement, Maxwell formally approached Sir Charles Hardie, the chairman of BPC, and Victor Bishop, the managing director, and suggested that BPC should join forces with the new Pergamon/Caxton company to sell encyclopaedias together. The negotiations and the agreement which followed were crucial to the dramatic and very public collapse of Pergamon's own merger with the American company Leasco two years later.

BPC was keen to stay in the encyclopaedia business since the company printed both the Chambers and Caxton encyclopaedias, and Maxwell succeeded in persuading the BPC directors to unite and fight. On 17 August 1967, they signed a memorandum of intent which anticipated that the two companies would merge their interests into a new company called International Learning Systems Corporation Limited, a very grand name for an encyclopaedia-selling operation. Their agreement contained one very important proviso: Pergamon guaranteed BPC that the new company's combined pre-tax profits would not be less than £500,000. Maxwell agreed that if the profits fell below that amount at the end of the first year, Pergamon would make up the shortfall in cash. Similarly, BPC guaranteed that the profits of its subsidiary Purnell until 30 June 1968 would be at least £98,000. The board of management reflected the merger. Hedley Le Bas was appointed ILSC's managing director, Maxwell was to be the chairman and chief executive and three BPC men were also appointed to the new board – Michael Pickard and Victor Bishop, who were both deputy chairmen of BPC, and Ralph Pollock, who was a BPC director.

From the outset, ILSC inherited from its three procreators the major problem which was endemic to the encyclopaedia business: the head office was always uncertain whether the sales reported by its freelance teams were accurate and whether the customers would honour their contracts and make regular monthly payments. To compound the uncertainty of the new company's financial position, the salesmen were paid their full commission promptly on receipt by ILSC of the signed contract and they bore no responsibility if their quickly forgotten clients defaulted in their monthly payments. Since some salesmen earned as much as 40 per cent commission on a contract which would be paid over three years, ILSC's potential bad debts were ominously large. Okill claims that at Newnes the cancellation rate was on average 9 per cent, yet at Caxton under Le Bas it amounted to 40 per cent. The marriage of the two companies was beset from the outset by a clash of personalities and practices.

ILSC's board met for the first time on 19 September 1967. Le Bas gave an assurance that on balance the new company's forecast profits would be 'very nearly met'. Even on the basis of the information then available, Le Bas's assertion was inaccurate because the ILSC's accounts and book-keeping were in a 'deplorable state', their overseas branches having failed to keep proper records. Maxwell endorsed those accounts, although it was only one year later that he was officially informed by ILSC's auditors about the true state of affairs. But by then he had publicly exploited Le Bas's assurances of ILSC's future profitability.

During the summer of 1967, Maxwell was planning his next acquisition. With Pergamon earning huge profits from its scientific journals and assured a big dividend if the forecast profits of ILSC materialised, Maxwell could afford to finance his next bid by offering Pergamon shares instead of cash. It was a much cheaper way to fund takeovers but depended upon the price of Pergamon shares remaining at their high level, which in turn was determined by Pergamon's high profits.

On 11 October 1967, Pergamon announced a bid for Butterworths, the venerable publishers with whom Springer had twenty years earlier unsuccessfully attempted to begin a joint venture. Since that failure, Butterworths had steadily expanded its own prestigious scientific, medical and legal publications, but its profits had, on its own admission, increased only 'marginally'. Over the previous five years under a new chairman, Richard Millett, diverse attempts had been made to restructure and galvanise the old-fashioned publisher, but with only limited success. Millett was particularly anxious to avoid the clutches of unwelcome American predators able to recognise the real value of Butterworths' assets. To protect the company, Millett repeatedly but unsuccessfully sought possible mergers with other British publishers until on 10 October 1967 a letter was delivered by hand from Bruce Ormrod of Ansbachers announcing Maxwell's bid. Ormrod's letter did not come as a complete surprise. Commercially, the merger had positive merits since Pergamon's and Butterworths' publishing activities had much in common, and over the previous three years Maxwell had made repeated gestures towards Millett, suggesting friendly negotiations.

Millett was appalled. He harboured a deep suspicion of Maxwell which was on the verge of obsessional and stemmed from the days of Simpkin Marshall. After reading Ansbachers' letter, he spontaneously wrote to Maxwell telling him, according to Butterworths' official history, 'to get lost'. To *The Times* Millett said, 'I would want to know a lot more about Pergamon before any merger and would be very reluctant to accept Pergamon paper under any circumstances.' For the first time in Maxwell's career, a takeover battle became ferociously personal. Millett hired private detectives to scour the world for any details about Pergamon's activities, which Maxwell answered by a High Court writ. But within one month it was all over. Millett had also launched a frantic and wide-flung search for an alternative bidder and Cecil King offered substantially more for Butterworths than Maxwell, who reluctantly conceded defeat. Ormrod recalls that Maxwell accepted he had been beaten by a bigger fish but felt that at bottom it had been determined by prejudice: 'He couldn't sit at the top table, as Macmillan would say.' Maxwell had suffered a loss of face which would soon have been forgotten if the offer document issued by Pergamon for Butterworths had not contained statements about ILSC's finances which later proved to be seriously inaccurate.

The problem of consolidating ILSC into a coherent company was a difficult one. Unifying the production and printing of three organisations made commercial sense but arranging the financial operation required time and skilled management. At the outset, none of ILSC's directors knew much about the financial health of their company. Four weeks after Maxwell had made the bid for Butterworths, Cooper Brothers, the management consultancy firm, wrote personally to Maxwell pointing out the absence of reliable information about ILSC's finances. Both John Pickard and Victor Bishop, BPC's deputy chairmen who were ILSC directors, later admitted that the information they received about ILSC's finances, especially its bad debts, was until spring 1969 both 'irregular and insufficient'. Yet the formal offer presented by Ansbachers on Maxwell's behalf for the Butterworths bid contained a very reassuring statement about ILSC's finances. After explaining Pergamon's guarantee that ILSC's combined pre-tax profits for the first year would be 'at least £500,000', the offer document stated that the target would be met: 'The Board of ILS has informed Pergamon that sales and profits for the first three months of operations are running at the level forecast when the arrangements were negotiated.' This statement was crucial to fixing an estimate of Pergamon's profits and therefore to establishing the value of the shares it offered in exchange for Butterworths.

Bruce Ormrod, the Ansbachers banker handling the bid, admits that he never saw the relevant letter from the ILSC board to Pergamon containing that important assurance. 'I was entirely at fault in not getting that as a copy for my own records,' he later admitted. In the rush to make the bid, Ormrod said, he had relied entirely on Maxwell's promise that the letter did exist: 'I was informed by Maxwell that he had obtained it.' The BPC directors later claimed that they had not signed such a letter nor had they ever seen or approved the assurance which Maxwell gave Ormrod. In contradiction, Maxwell insisted that all three BPC directors had visited him at Fitzroy Square and had approved the whole document including the forecast about the profits. Whatever the truth, the profits forecast was wrong. It was a reflection of the style of operations at ILSC.

In December 1967, in response to Cooper Brothers' warning to Maxwell that ILSC's accounting system was unsatisfactory, Harold Moppel was appointed the company's financial director. On arrival, Moppel received optimistic assurances from both Maxwell and Le Bas that ILSC was 'running at enormous profits' because of the high sales. Moppel however judged that ILSC was in a state of chaos and that in reality no one knew what profits would be earned. 'No accounts had been produced of any nature,' he said three years later.

During 1968, as Moppel and another accountant, George Hazard, grappled to organise the accounts, both became disenchanted with Maxwell's style and especially with his interference in their work. As in the affairs of Pergamon, Maxwell was reluctant to allow his employees to dictate to him how the financial position of a company which he owned should be presented.

At that time, no accountant was more aware of Maxwell's interest in his professional decisions than Peter Bennett, Pergamon's financial director. On 2 September 1966, Bennett wrote to Maxwell two memoranda about the purchase of Newnes. Although the binding of the Chambers encyclopaedias was still not completed and few sets had been sold, Bennett reported in the first memorandum that the 'net profits' amounted to £105,000 and in the second that they would reach £222,000. How Bennett arrived at those unrealistic figures is subject to dispute, although their effect on the overall image of Pergamon's profits was extremely favourable. When asked about the second memorandum in 1970, Maxwell recalled that he had 'honestly believed' that the profits were 'properly made' and emphasised that 'Mr Bennett took the initiative in these matters' supported by Chalmers Impey, Pergamon's auditors. Bennett admitted that his views were 'an error of judgement on my part', but he added, 'my recollection is that these views were heavily influenced by Mr Maxwell'. Maxwell also believed, according to Bennett, that the £1 million he had paid for Chambers was £200,000 less than it was truly worth. He wanted that money reflected in the accounts. Bennett claims that he 'thumped the table and said: "Tell me where the £200,000 profit is."'

It also fell to Bennett to prepare Pergamon's annual report for 1968. This stated that both Pergamon and BPC had been paid two dividends by ILSC. In December 1967, each had been paid £112,000 and in June 1968 each was to receive £187,000. Although both parent companies immediately returned the dividends to ILSC in the form of loans, the payments as presented in official reports effectively concealed the chaos at ILSC. Moppel and the accounts department did not know whether ILSC was even earning any profits on which to pay a dividend; although by April 1968 they realised that whatever the profits these were considerably lower than officially anticipated.

By mid-1968, Maxwell suspected that ILSC was in serious difficulties and that the bad reputation earned by the encyclopaedia salesmen was reflecting upon him. In one attempt to stem the criticism, Maxwell appeared on BBC Television's *Braden's Week*, but when surprised by the concrete examples of abuse, agreed to investigate the complaints. Maxwell blamed in particular Le Bas and his Australian manager, Rod Jenman. In Australia, it was said, the list of new customers could be read off the tombstones in the Sydney cemeteries. The situation, recalled Maxwell, 'was absolutely disastrous' and in the summer of 1968 he fired both men and three other senior officials for alleged incompetence (although the report of the Department of Trade and Industry inquiry would state that Maxwell's allegations were erroneous). Maxwell took over ILSC's daily management, which – combined with his many other interests – placed a hugh burden upon him but did not stop his repeated public recommendations about how Britain's sluggish economy could be improved nor his boasts about his own qualifications for the task.

One example that year followed the collapse of Craven Insurance, a company which sold motor-car policies. A winding-up petition was presented in the High Court by the Board of Trade but to the government's embarrassment Maxwell counter-petitioned the Court and insisted that the company was in fact solvent. Amid great publicity, he pledged that he would save the insurance policies of 65,000 motorists and promised to inject £200,000 into the company; he would also become the chairman. Few outsiders could understand the motives of a scientific publisher and encyclopaedia salesman who was also a Labour politician, a public figure at the forefront of the 'I'm Backing Britain' campaign, becoming involved in motor insurance. Two months later, Maxwell admitted that Craven was indeed bankrupt and blamed his original intervention on 'grossly misleading facts'. Having lost all his money, he admitted to being 'very angry and very upset for myself, my associates, the policy-holders and the staff. This is certainly my worst disaster ever.' Board of Trade officials were not amused.

When Maxwell presented himself on 7 June to the Pergamon shareholders for their annual general meeting, his 'worst disaster' was already forgotten. The company's profits, said the chairman, were 'a new record', having increased by 33 per cent after tax during that year. Twenty-one new journals had been published and Pergamon's book list contained six thousand titles, a figure which would increase by six hundred over the following twelve months.

In the company report, Maxwell stated that ILSC 'is already making a contribution to the profits of your Company'. The source of those profits, reported Maxwell, was the outright sale of 15,000 sets of Chambers encyclopaedias in one year and the anticipated sale of another 15,000 sets in the following year: 'This rate of annual sale is approximately 400% higher than that achieved by the previous proprietors.' The £100,000 paid as a dividend by ILSC and immediately returned was counted as a profit.

Maxwell also sent shareholders a separate circular which asserted that 'The Board of ILSC has informed Pergamon that sales and profits . . . are running at the level forecast. . . .' Since the ILSC board had not given Pergamon that information and since there was, at the time, only a vague notion about ILSC's actual profits, Maxwell was characteristically optimistic. But his assurance had been supported in writing by his financial director, Harold Moppel, who, like the chairman, believed that the recent devaluation of the pound would produce an enormous windfall. The price of Pergamon shares increased accordingly, encouraging the strategy of paying for any acquisitions by offering valuable Pergamon shares. His next major opportunity presented itself in the summer of 1968.

Jacob Rothschild, then a partner of the merchant bank N. M. Rothschild, was seeking a purchaser for 25 per cent of the shares of the mass-circulation Sunday newspaper, the *News of the World*. Maxwell, who as we have seen had already made an attempt to take over the *Daily Herald*, did not conceal his enthusiasm when he telephoned the banker. Tantalisingly, it was an opportunity to launch a take-over bid which, if successful, would transform him in one swoop into a press baron with six million readers. The doors to the Establishment's citadel would open in a manner that mere membership of the House of Commons could never achieve.

Rothschild was acting for Professor Derek Jackson, an eccentric cousin of the incumbent chairman of the *News of the World*, fifty-six-year-old Sir William Carr. Jackson, who was enjoying his sixth marriage, divided his time between France and Switzerland and had little affection for the Carr family. Initially, he had offered the shares to his cousin but Carr's price of 28s which Hambros the merchant bankers described as generous was, he felt, derisory and he was not averse to the idea that the family should therefore be discomfited by a take-over bid. Maxwell's agreement to pay 37s 6d for each share (they were trading at 29s 3d on the Stock Exchange) was welcomed as providing a good profit – and an ideal weapon in the family feud.

Sir William's family had edited the paper since 1891 and controlled 27 per cent of the shares. The remaining 48 per cent were mostly owned by twenty-eight individuals. The City institutions owned a negligible interest. Considering the dismal financial performance of the company under Carr's management during the previous years, Maxwell was confident of persuading an extra 26 per cent of the shareholders to sell to him at the higher price. With his new merchant bank adviser, Robert Clark of Hill Samuel, Maxwell calculated an offer which crucially depended upon the new peaked price of Pergamon shares, since the bid would be based on a swap of Pergamon shares for *News of the World* shares with a cash alternative.

By 1968, Carr had been chairman of the group for sixteen years, using the public company to provide the luxuries to which he had become accustomed. His opulent lifestyle, his personal golf courses and his horse-racing were all paid out of the company's meagre profits. The *News of the*

World, under his dictatorial control, had continued to publish a consistent cocktail of rape, marital infidelity and saucy scandal but its circulation had fallen during his tenure by two million copies a week. Similarly, the group's other interests such as Eric Bemrose, a Liverpool subsidiary equipped with the latest gravure machinery for colour printing, and thirty local newspapers had also suffered from his persistent neglect. Carr was unperturbed by his declining fortunes, if only because he was invariably drunk by half-past ten every morning, a habit which had earned him the popular alias 'Pissing Billy'.

On the morning of 16 October, Robert Clark arrived at the offices of Hambros, who were the advisers to the Carr family, and purposefully slapped an envelope down on Harry Sporborg's desk. The Hambros director found inside Maxwell's offer of 37s 6d for each share, a £26 million bid. 'It came as a total surprise,' recalls an eyewitness. When the news reached Carr, in bed at the time stricken with influenza, he requested that a particularly stiff drink be served immediately and rapidly became unavailable for any discussions throughout the remainder of that day. On the Stock Exchange, the excitement of the unexpected bid pushed the price of *News of the World* shares immediately up from 29s 3d to a dizzy 40s 3d with expectations that the rise would continue. Few insiders had believed that the Labour MP could mount such an expensive bid.

While they gathered their thoughts, the Carr family issued a terse announcement that shareholders should do nothing until the board had properly considered the offer with Hambros. For his part, Maxwell told the press that he was confident of success because he believed that some members of the Carr family would desert to his camp; and, to the great surprise of his constituency, he announced that because of the extra commitments he would not seek to be renominated for the next general election. Informally he told newsmen that his aim was to be the 'Arnold Weinstock of the printing and publishing world – a tough business man who can squeeze more profits out of assets than anyone else'. The public comparison did not endear him to the cool, analytical industrialist but it was an adroit one for that 'modernising' era. His real motives were easy to guess: having failed that year to buy Butterworths and having been personally denied the opportunity to purchase a stake in BPC by Max Rayne, this was just his latest attempt to build an empire. But the publisher who had within recent memory supported the prosecution of the publishers of *Last Exit to Brooklyn* announced that he would not interfere with the paper's salacious editorial policy.

Nothing Maxwell promised could ever placate Sir William Carr and his long-serving editor, Stafford Somerfield. While Harry Sporborg began to consider the formal defence against the bid, the chairman and the editor published their own considered reply four days after Maxwell's bid was announced. That Sunday, millions read Somerfield's emotional and xenophobic riposte on the *News of the World*'s front page. Headed 'We are having a little local difficulty', Somerfield's piece continued, 'Why do I think it would not be a good thing for Mr Maxwell, formerly Jan Ludwig [*sic*] Hoch to gain control of this newspaper which, I know, has your respect, loyalty and affection – a newspaper which I know is as British as roast beef and Yorkshire pudding?' Somerfield answered his own question by describing the paper's editorial policy, maintained by just six editors since 1891, as independent but right-wing. Unlike the Carr family, he wrote, Maxwell had no newspaper experience and was a socialist. There was, Somerfield claimed, no chance that Maxwell's promise of impartiality could be maintained. 'I believe that Mr Maxwell is interested in power and money. There is nothing wrong with that, but it is not everything.' But the possibility of socialist interference was nothing compared to the peril of a foreigner taking control: 'This is a British paper, run by British people. Let's keep it that way.'

By any standards, Carr had gone beyond the pale. Even his supporters were shocked by his uninhibited display of anti-semitism, especially against a man who had fought so bravely for Britain and was a Member of Parliament. Unfortunately for Maxwell, the tone set by the newspaper reflected the defensive tactics which were to be adopted by Carr's professional advisers in the City.

By 1968, Maxwell was by no means a stranger in the Square Mile, but this was the first time he had played in the First Division. It was ironic that opposing him was Hambros, the merchant bank which had financed his breakthrough twenty years earlier. But as Sporborg himself had taken the initiative in persuading Charles Hambro to break with Maxwell, any lingering sentiment between the two sides had disappeared by the end of the first day. 'It was', admits one of the bankers advising Carr, 'a thoroughly dirty battle where everyone played as hard as they could.' As far as Maxwell was concerned, however, the players on the other side did not stick to the rules and the City Establishment tilted firmly in Carr's favour.

In the 1960s the City's reputation still basked under the reassuring slogan 'My word is my bond'. Although its inhabitants' nepotistic hegemony was already under strain, most of those employed in banking and broking were still self-styled patrician gentlemen whose families had known each other for generations. Insider dealing and tax-evasion schemes flourished behind the comforting myth that the City's self-policing mechanisms were preventing any dubious profiteering.

At the time Maxwell made his bid, the City had experienced two years of unprecedented mergers and take-overs. No less than 70 per cent of Britain's hundred biggest companies had been involved in bids concerning nearly one-quarter of all British firms. British financial and commercial experts, as in other western capitals, were gripped by the fashionable nostrum that only giants, especially the newly termed multinational corporations, could hope to survive the coming technological revolution. The merger-mania had transformed the normally sober clientele of the Pall Mall clubs into replicas of the gun-slingers in a Wild West saloon. In their desperate urge to win individual take-over battles, prominent companies, having placed their bid at one price, were rigging the share market, crucially changing the nature of their businesses in the midst of a bid, and giving favoured treatment to the more important shareholders, so destroying the cardinal rule that after a bid is launched all shareholders must be treated honestly and equally. By the end of 1967, any pretence of self-policing had been destroyed as evidence of deception by industrialists and their advisers provoked howls of outrage, yet never any suggestion of punishment.

To avoid government intervention, the Bank of England finally commissioned four experts to recommend a new code of practice which would guarantee fair play. Among those four draftsmen was Robert Clark, one of Maxwell's advisers in the *News of the World* bid. In March 1968, a new code was introduced, with a supervisory panel under the chairmanship of Sir Humphrey Mynors, a former deputy governor of the Bank of England. Maxwell's bid was among the first to be governed by the new code, and Mynors, as referee, had to prove that the City was capable of policing a fair fight.

As a mild-mannered rather uninspired former Bank official, Mynors was 'charming, weak and too much of an insider to be effective'. He was the natural choice of those who hoped that cosmetics would dispose of the political pressure for change. But in the course of two major takeover battles which occurred in the first months of his tenure, Mynors proved incapable of implementing the rules because the new code lacked any penalties which could be used against transgressors. Mynors could only rely upon his own personality, which was no match for the City giants who deigned to sit before him. Maxwell's success would therefore depend upon how ruthlessly both he and his advisers decided to fight Carr's resistance and especially whether they decided to adhere voluntarily to the unenforceable code.

By the first weekend, despite Somerfield's editorial, the omens were favourable. No rival bid seemed to have materialised and Maxwell announced that he was prepared to raise the value of his bid at a later date. For someone who had for the past three years been the butt of an avalanche of vituperative publicity, there was a pleasant surprise. Most press comment was inclined to see the advantages of the marriage. The *Sunday Times*'s cautiously favourable comment was typical: 'there is no doubt that anyone with Maxwell's seemingly bottomless energy and flair can have a remarkably energising effect on the largest of organisations'.

Among the rash of sympathetic profiles, the *Financial Times* described Maxwell's charm, individual talent and care for ordinary workers. Anthony Harris sympathetically quoted Maxwell's own description of his earlier purchase of C. & E. Layton, a loss-making printer: '"Nobody believed in the business anymore. I talked to the workers individually and in groups, about their craft, the quality they had to offer. And I did something I believe that no other take-over bidder has ever done before. I gave a year's guarantee of employment to every man on the books. Then we got down to it." By the end of the year Layton was making profits again.'

There was also a lengthy, endearing interview in *The Times* which suggested that Maxwell, with his 'Frankie Vaughan and Victor Mature' looks, had become a humbled parliamentarian who admitted he had been 'a bit brash' and 'impatient' in the House and had suffered a 'boycott' by other Members. Despite the public image of a 'boastful dictator and a megalomaniac', the profile concluded, he was 'surprisingly mild'. If nothing else, the hefty £200,000 which the bid would cost Maxwell had at least bought him an improved image.

But at the end of Monday 21 October, just five days after the bid had been announced, Maxwell's fortunes abruptly changed. Sporborg's tactics had taken a new, slightly sordid and definitely terminal twist. Soon after the bid was announced, the banker had placed £750,000 of Hambros' money at the disposal of its stockbrokers with instructions to buy every *News of the World* share in the market. Sporborg knew that his tactics were a clear breach of the 'spirit' of the new code, which forbade companies to buy their own shares to frustrate a take-over bid, 'but everyone seemed to be making it up as we went along'. By the end of the week, Hambros owned 10 per cent of its client's shares, which Sporborg unconvincingly claimed was an independent stake. The banker had also cleverly secured contractual pledges of support from other shareholders for a payment of 10s each which guaranteed that the Carrs controlled a formidable 48 per cent of the votes. Robert Clark and Maxwell's other advisers were nonplussed. As one of the code's architect's, Clark could only advise his own client to obey the rules. Maxwell raised his bid to £34 million, while Clark appealed to Mynors for help. In turn, Mynors summoned Hambros. Sporborg's attitude was simply that 'one could drive a coach and horses through the rule book. He'd pop into Mynors and ask whether he could do something. Mynors would just reply: "Why not?" It was a free-for-all.' So at the beginning of the second week Maxwell could expect no help from the City Establishment, but on the Monday that was not of such paramount importance. More fateful was the secret arrival of a man whom Maxwell had recently met for the first time in Australia.

Rupert Murdoch had landed at Heathrow the previous day for the first round of what has since become a regular if unequal bout between two ambitious individuals. Murdoch, then thirty-seven years old, started the competition with advantages which were denied to the forty-eight-year-old Maxwell. The Oxford-educated Australian had inherited from his father money, privileged social status and a small newspaper which he had successfully used to build a sizeable business in Australia. Murdoch was ready to expand into Britain. When he heard that Maxwell's bid was opposed by the Carrs, he dashed to London to propose a deal to Sporborg. In return for Murdoch's purchasing sufficient shares to tip the balance in Carr's favour, Sporborg should convince his client to merge his interests with Murdoch who, as a reliable and junior partner, would sympathise with his interests. The two would be joint managing directors while Carr would remain chairman. Since the investment was well protected and the possible rewards were enormous, Murdoch had everything to gain.

Knowing that after ten-thirty in the morning Carr would be incapable of taking any decision, Sporborg and Murdoch drove on 22 October to Cliveden Place for breakfast in Carr's apartment. Winning his approval was unproblematical. The young Australian and Carr shared friends and acquaintances and both were committed newspapermen. Indeed, with the exception of his new *Australian*, all of Murdoch's own newspapers survived on a diet similar to the *News of the World*'s – sex and scandal. By the following day, Murdoch owned $3\frac{1}{2}$ per cent of the shares. The news that Murdoch was a redeemer leaked quickly, provoking more banner headlines and placing Maxwell back in the centre of the news. Following new complaints from Maxwell to the Panel, dealings in the shares were suspended, but Carr, with Murdoch's help, had already won majority control.

The Cliveden agreement stipulated that Murdoch would obtain a 40 per cent interest in the *News of the World* by purchasing a new issue of shares. In exchange for owning the biggest stake in the newspaper, Murdoch would invest into it 'certain' of his own News Limited interests. Since Murdoch had no intention of investing anywhere near the same amount as the £34 million which Maxwell had bid, Carr was selling his newspaper for considerably less merely to satisfy his prejudice. But as a consequence the other shareholders were being denied the chance of receiving the 50s per share that Maxwell was now offering. Sporborg had masterminded another breach of the code, although in his combined defence with Murdoch's bankers, Morgan Grenfell, he justifiably insisted that Mynors had initially approved his tactics. The spirit, he conceded, might have been broken, but not the letter. Both bankers had just 'popped in' to Mynors and won his agreement, but once the furore broke, Mynors quickly retreated. By then, of course, it was too late for Maxwell, who commented, 'This is a disgraceful affair and it is up to the Takeover Panel to do its proper job.' As a pointed supplementary, Maxwell wondered aloud how embracing an Australian protected the paper's uniquely 'British' ownership. Others waited to see whether Anthony Crosland, the Labour Minister at the Board of Trade, would intervene to help his parliamentary comrade.

At the end of October, the final resolution of the battle depended on the extraordinary shareholders' meeting which was to be called to approve the issue of extra shares to complete the Cliveden agreement. The public outcry was too fierce for the City to allow events to take their course unimpeded. While Carr's advisers pleaded for time to negotiate their deal with Murdoch, Clark, after persuading Maxwell to fulminate in uncharacteristic silence on the sidelines, negotiated a major concession. Mynors, following a meeting summoned by Crosland, secured an agreement from the three merchant banks that they would not use at the decisive shareholders' meeting the 15 per cent of the shares which they had bought after Maxwell's bid. It was a belated attempt to save the Panel's reputation which presented Maxwell with new hope. Of the outstanding 85 per cent of shares, approximately 20 per cent were nominally uncommitted. Maxwell needed the bulk to win control. Overnight, the contest slumped to a new level.

Murdoch had suddenly seen the prize slip just beyond his immediate grasp. A series of stories began appearing in his own Sydney *Daily Mirror* about the tactics of ILSC's encyclopaedia salesmen. Wounded, Maxwell issued the first of scores of writs which, over the next twenty years, he would hurl at newspapers to protect his reputation. In London, Sporborg read Murdoch's files about his rival but was advised that they were too defamatory for publication. That hardly satisfied Carr, who, when approached during the day drinking dry Martinis at the Savoy, only asked his banker, 'What are you doing to keep the foreigner out?' According to one of those present, 'It was an appalling time. Carr insisted on personalising the battle and our lawyers constantly crossed out paragraphs of our publicity as scurrilous.' For Carr, defeating Maxwell was all that counted and even Murdoch's unilateral decision, conveyed in a letter, that Carr could not after all be joint managing director was quietly conceded to secure the Australian's continued support.

Maxwell fought with the same passion but not the same methods. With superhuman energy, his personal publicity machine ceaselessly pushed the advantages of his own bid while he sought from the courts injunctions and damages against every banker, adviser and director connected to the Carr family under every conceivable heading ranging from breach of fiduciary duty to conspiracy. He also sought the support of the trade unions and travelled to Southsea to discuss his plans with Bill Keyes and other SOGAT leaders. His scenario did not appeal to them. 'He didn't understand deadlines,' recalls Keyes, 'he thought it was like a scientific magazine. He wanted to walk in and take over and just cut manning levels among the printers and the journalists. It was a naive bid for power. We told him that he didn't understand newspapers. He packed up his papers and walked out.'

Maxwell felt the pressure tightening. The forecast of ILSC's profits was critical to the price of Pergamon shares, and keeping the price of those shares high was in turn crucial to his bid for the *News of the World*. Between 4 June and 1 November 1968, Pergamon's shares had risen from 34s 6d to 46s 10d, having peaked at 48s. As the takeover battle approached its climax, scattered and unsubstantiated rumours began circulating in the City that ILSC's profits would not be as high as Maxwell had suggested in his circular sent to shareholders on 15 May. In a meeting with Maxwell on 18 September (which was confirmed in writing), Cooper Brothers, ILSC's consultants, who knew the rumours to be true, warned the chairman that ILSC's accounts were 'unreliable'.

That warning was discussed at an ILSC board meeting held on 15 October, the day before the *News of the World* bid was announced. Maxwell and all his fellow directors acknowledged that their company's accounts were in such chaos that they would be unable to comply with their original objective of presenting the normal annual accounts for the year ending 30 June 1968 and would instead organise accounts for the eighteen months ending 31 December 1968. As the weeks passed and the takeover battle progressed, even that target seemed increasingly impossible to meet, fuelling rumours about Pergamon's profits which were naturally encouraged by those acting for Carr.

Since maintaining the price of Pergamon's shares was vital, during the three weeks following Maxwell's bid announcement, one of his private companies, Maxwell Scientific International (Distribution Services) Ltd (MSI(DS)), bought 245,500 Pergamon shares in three transactions through Michael Richardson, who worked at Pergamon's stockbrokers, Panmure Gordon. The purchases, which cost £1,100,000, were properly announced by Panmure and complied with the takeover code. Those purchases clearly had an effect on keeping the share prices at their very high level although Maxwell later explained that it was done as a 'long-term investment' on the advice of his bankers and brokers because 'I was convinced that the bid would go through and that the price would rise very substantially.'

As the battle dragged on, Maxwell was told by his bankers, Hill Samuel and Robert Fleming, that Pergamon's price was weakening. With his agreement and again with proper notifications, the two banks purchased a further 215,500 Pergamon shares in November and December. Maxwell gave undertakings to both banks that he would repurchase the shares at any time up to 31 January 1969.

Even as his chances were waning, Maxwell, unwilling to accept defeat, launched a frantic counter-attack. Michael Richardson was sent to Australia with the brief to launch a bid for Murdoch's own group. The half-hearted attempt, which was dubiously reported as having the support of Roy Thomson, quickly collapsed. Meanwhile in England, Maxwell personally telephoned dozens of shareholders to win their support. His calls revealed that most were antagonistic towards him, despite the press comment running in his favour. In desperation, he sent two thousand telegrams and even personally promised to pay for taxis to bring pensioners to the meeting. Yet on the eve of the final showdown, Maxwell's bid was certainly doomed. To the very last, Sporborg pulled the strings to engineer Maxwell's defeat.

The public venue for the decisive vote was the Connaught Rooms near Covent Garden. On Thursday 2 January 1969, dressed as always in a bright blue suit, Maxwell arrived just before ten-thirty to discover that the hall was packed with hundreds of Carr employees who had arrived in a fleet of company buses. In the front row sat the Carr family dressed in black, but united. Depressingly for Maxwell, that day's newspapers had led with Sporborg's late-night claim that he had collected sufficient proxies to guarantee victory. Visibly nervous in the hostile atmosphere, the outsider watched as Murdoch, smiling and confident, entered the room accompanied by his attractive wife. At a long table in the front sat Carr who, from his right side, would be supplied by Sporborg with an endless stream of prompt cards to answer the prearranged questions from the shareholders. 'Unfortunately, he could not even read what was written,' recalls one banker. Maxwell, by contrast, knew exactly what he wanted to say – that his bid promised shareholders unquestionably a lot more money. Unfortunately for him, the cold logic of the market place was not in issue. The vote was about Maxwell himself.

Others in that predicament, where the glare of television spotlights was certain to seize upon and record every glance of personal antagonism, might at that moment have chosen gracefully to accept the inevitable verdict and treat those who had denigrated him with dignified contempt. Yet it is the very nature of Maxwell to ignore defeat until every possible avenue has been exhausted and then, if possible, to start the fight again. Like a tireless salesman, he would never take no for an answer.

Cheers greeted Carr as he rose to open the meeting, the loudest from his own specially selected employees. Scathingly, he condemned Pergamon's lack of experience in newspapers and was sceptical about Pergamon itself, whose shares had been falling in value despite huge purchases by Maxwell and his friends to support the price. No one mentioned that the price of *News of the World* shares was also tumbling as Carr spoke. Murdoch followed with a succinct statement and was followed in turn by Maxwell. Amid jeers and catcalls, Maxwell launched an unrestrained but fumbling attack on Carr which was punctuated by shouts of 'Go home' and 'Rubbish' before finally ending in uproar. Many of those heckling were identified as 'small men in mackintoshes', the traditional and loyal *News of the World* readers who were delighted to have an opportunity to vent their personal dislike of the publicity-seeking, foreign, socialist millionaire. Sitting just feet away, Murdoch ill-concealed his smile. The outburst of emotion only delayed the inevitable. Once the vote was taken, the hall emptied and only a few waited for the counting to be completed. Untrusting to the end, Maxwell strode into the scrutineers' room, only to be forcefully ejected by Carr. The result was a massive victory for Murdoch.

The final scene as the curtain fell was poignant. The victor embraced his wife. Carr looked on smiling, enjoying his moment, albeit briefly, because shortly afterwards he would be unceremoniously ousted from power by his chosen redeemer. On the side, alone, stood Maxwell, a wet sheen glistening over his eyes, fixedly staring into the distance – an expression which always indicated that Maxwell either felt wounded or understood he had suffered public humiliation. Sportingly, he shook Murdoch's hand and congratulated him on catching 'a big fish with a very small hook'. To a journalist, inquiring about reaction to the City's conduct, he quipped, 'I'm on the side of the angels; it's amazing.' It was the first but also the last time over the next decade.

Days after the defeat, still suffering from the vilification and the abuse, Maxwell flew to New York. 'I felt that the British would never let me succeed,' he told a friend shortly afterwards in a rare display of despair. The events in the Connaught Rooms had been the climax of a disastrous year. His new operation depended upon a constant stream of acquisitions, especially of companies like the *News of the World* whose valuable assets could be exploited more profitably, and throughout 1968 all his major bids had failed. Maintaining the high value of Pergamon's shares depended upon repeatedly improving his profits. In Oxford, his staff were compiling the 1968 accounts but he already knew that it would be impossible to beat the previous year's record. That presented a serious predicament. During the *News of the World* take-over battle, he had issued a forecast that Pergamon would earn around £2 million profit in 1968. If that forecast did not materialise, his future credibility would be harmed.

Whether by the time his plane landed in New York he had actually planned a detailed personal survival plan has always been unclear. But he had already anticipated that there was a fortune to be earned from developing a scientific information retrieval system based on computers and that, because of his poor reputation in Britain, he needed an American partner.

Three years earlier, in Pergamon's annual report, Maxwell had written about the 'decisive importance' of a computer-based retrieval system. Although nowadays that statement seems unexceptional, it was in 1966 a percipient prediction because computer technology was still crude and very few people had even imagined the possibility of personal, desk-top computers. Maxwell had tried to obtain government funding for his ideas and approached Sir Frank Kearton, the chairman of the Labour government's new investment bank, the Industrial Reorganisation

Corporation. Kearton says that he had been 'very impressed' by Maxwell's 'vision and energy' but had rejected his application because 'the technology was simply not yet sufficiently developed'. Nevertheless, Pergamon's 1966 report stated, 'Pergamon is the only company in Europe in information retrieval.'

In January 1969, Maxwell hoped that he would find a partner in America. He had approached several people before telephoning Saul Steinberg, a twenty-nine-year-old American multi-millionaire whose record was by any standards quite phenomenal.

Steinberg was a Jew from Brooklyn, New York who had graduated at the University of Pennsylvania. In the course of writing a precocious thesis entitled 'The Decline and Fall of IBM', he had recognised that IBM was losing potential customers for its computers either because they could not afford the price or because they were reluctant to invest in technology which would soon be redundant. Steinberg's coup was to create an arrangement whereby his company, Leasco, bought IBM computers with finance provided by banks and leased time on the computers to customers.

At the end of 1967, Leasco was worth about $75 million and was earning $1.4 million in profits, which gave it a rating, according to *Fortune* magazine, as one of the fastest-growing companies in the west. In 1968, Leasco's profits rocketed to $27 million and its assets soared to $1,000 million. Steinberg had orchestrated a dazzling display of perpetual corporate restructures amid a blitz of take-overs and mergers. Within one year Leasco had expanded into management consultancy, shipping containers, and engineering and computer service groups in North America and western Europe. His biggest coup was a successful bid for the respectable Reliance Insurance Group worth a massive $740 million. For most of the year, Steinberg's star shone brightly and Leasco's share price trebled but in late summer his ambitions were crushingly halted. He had let slip that he was planning a bid for the prestigious Chemical Bank. Wall Street was aghast and turned with a vengeance to punish the arrogance of a Brooklyn youngster. Leasco's shares plummeted and many of Steinberg's sponsors cringed. Wounded, Steinberg retreated to ponder the predicament of the outsider. 'I always knew there was an Establishment,' he subsequently mused, 'I just used to think I was part of it.'

When destiny brought Maxwell and Steinberg together, the pride of both had therefore recently been shaken by public ostracism. Both were irreverent but wanted to be revered. Inured to criticism, their fantasies continued to flourish inside the bubbles of their own self-promotion.

Both were enigmas since they shared an ambition for power but gave no intelligible explanation about how they would exercise it. Both shared another ambition, to become richer and yet more richer. As footballers are rated by the number of goals they have scored and pilots by the number of hours they have flown, businessmen are evaluated by the number of millions and billions at their disposal. In 1969, as today, Steinberg was much wealthier and therefore in their own terms a more successful man than Maxwell, which must have affected the forty-five-year-old's perception of the American *Wunderkind*.

There are three versions of how Robert Maxwell first met Steinberg. Two are aprocryphal (but they are naturally the most attractive despite their lack of authenticity). Maxwell, it is said, was so keen to meet the man who was even more successful than himself that, from New York, he telephoned his personal secretary Jean Baddeley and asked her to find out which hotel the chubby-faced tycoon would next be breakfasting in. Reliable as always, Baddeley delivered the correct location and reserved the neighbouring table for her boss. In the midst of his meal, Maxwell rose and addressed his neighbour: 'Oi vey, have I got a deal for you,' whereupon, it is said, Maxwell presented Pergamon's latest annual report to the surprised American and suggested that they discuss their joint future.

The second apocryphal version places Steinberg in the Connaught Hotel in London during Maxwell's battle to buy the *News of the World*. A loud conversation at a neighbouring table distracts the American who after a thoughtful stare turns to his guest and whispers, 'Gee, that's the famous Robert Maxwell,' and introduces himself to the great man.

A variation of this version is that Steinberg indeed overheard the conversation about the newspaper battle in the dining room but was more impressed by the protagonist's beautiful blonde escort. He assumed that it was Maxwell but it was in fact Murdoch.

The truth is more prosaic, but only at the very outset. The relationship between the two rags-to-riches Jewish entrepreneurs would progress at a dizzy pace from reality to utter fantasy, in its path bruising the most protected egos, shredding carefully cultivated reputations and culminating in the apparent commercial ruin of Maxwell himself.

The first contact was made on 14 January. Steinberg was working in his office in Great Kneck, Long Island when Maxwell telephoned. Steinberg had heard about Maxwell during his recent visit to London and took the call to hear the Briton explain that he was at Kennedy airport and wanted to discuss a proposition. Within an hour the two met for the first time. Maxwell's proposal was simple but very attractive.

Pergamon had a vast amount of scientific knowledge at its disposal while Leasco possessed enormous expertise in computers. The two should embark on a joint venture, he suggested, initially to compile a world patent index on computer which they would later expand into a scientific library with terminals throughout the world. A small Leasco subsidiary in Washington DC was already transferring some material from Pergamon journals on to computers and Maxwell believed there was scope for considerable expansion. Steinberg was gripped by the idea. Maxwell displayed impressive technical understanding about computers and information-retrieval. Recently, American newspapers had carried a brief report that Maxwell had made a take-over bid for Document Inc., a company which placed NASA's material on computers but the bid had been thwarted by the federal government because of security implications. Maxwell clearly understood the scientific world and was also, by all accounts, a highly successful businessman. His *News of the World* bid had been accompanied by favourable publicity in the British financial press. This seemed to be confirmed as Steinberg glanced through the brochure of Pergamon's 1967 annual accounts which Maxwell had, with a slight theatrical gesture, passed across the desk. After a limited amount of small talk which ended with Maxwell announcing that he would have to dash back to London to attend a debate in the House of Commons, the two parted on the understanding that there might be further exploratory discussions in the future.

But Steinberg quickly lost interest in the patent index because, as he explained in 1973, 'it was unprofitable. I told Maxwell it was premature to discuss any joint venture and I wasn't sure that we needed his particular expertise.' Over the following weeks, Steinberg noticed that Maxwell's name was frequently mentioned in the financial press, in connection either with Craven Insurance or with rumours that he would bid for McCorquodale, a specialised printing company. Maxwell was certainly worth closer attention. In early April, Steinberg was planning a trip to Britain and he telephoned Maxwell to suggest a meeting. Maxwell was on the verge of departing for another world tour but he proposed to delay his trip by one day because, as he told Steinberg, 'I've been studying Leasco and there are many areas where we have a joint interest.' He added, 'Perhaps we can even discuss a merger.' Steinberg was surprised but keen to explore the possibility. On 25 April he arrived in London with his wife and Robert Hodes, his lawyer, 'for a preliminary discussion to see whether it made sense for us to acquire Pergamon'.

In the turbulent and vituperative world of Wall Street corporate lawyers, Hodes was acknowledged as among the most honest and able.

Throughout the turmoil of accusations and emotions that would characterise relations between the two tycoons over the following years, Hodes retained an accurate and relatively objective account of the events as they unfolded. In later statements, Hodes would say that there was confusion when the two sides met at Fitzroy Square. At the outset, their conversation was constantly interrupted by phone calls and visits: 'It's Evelyn de Rothschild,' said Maxwell, 'he's come to see me about a political matter. I'll be right back.' Minutes later, Maxwell was once again seated in the room but was again interrupted. Just after he had left the room, Tom Clark arrived and declared, 'I'm just back from South Africa and the sales of encyclopaedias are fantastic.' Maxwell returned and the telephone calls began: 'It's Moscow; it's Berlin; it's a government matter ...' Awed, the two Americans watched Maxwell's simultaneous management of his political and business affairs. When it was over, Maxwell dropped his first bombshell: he wanted to buy Lesco's international operations. Steinberg was flummoxed. Comparatively, Leasco was a giant and Pergamon a mere minnow. Leasco's international section, worth over $200 million and growing rapidly, alone dwarfed Pergamon. Laughingly Steinberg replied that it was not for sale, but how did Maxwell even intend to pay? 'I haven't worked it out yet,' Maxwell replied, 'but I'm prepared to give Pergamon stock.'

There was a moment's silence broken by Steinberg. The only topic for discussion, he insisted, was whether Leasco would buy Pergamon. Maxwell reflected and then agreed. In principle, Maxwell had undertaken to sell his company for cash and accept a subordinate position under Steinberg within Leasco. His only stipulation was that the preliminary negotiations should be carried out in New York where his associate, Ladislaus Majthenyi, commonly known as 'Martini', could supply all the relevant information about Pergamon's affairs. Steinberg and Maxwell stood up and solemnly shook hands; the visitors left soon afterwards. Outside, Steinberg was visibly excited. Another profitable take-over was under way. Apparently he did not hesitate for a moment to ponder why Maxwell wanted to sell his business. For Steinberg it seemed understandable that even the British politician would want to be hitched to his star. Yet over the following two weeks Steinberg's excitement waxed and then waned. Some mornings, often before 6 a.m., as he travelled around the world, Maxwell called with ideas and even suggested names for their new venture, but Steinberg's staff reported that they had made no progress whatsoever with Majthenyi. At the end of the month, during a call from Maxwell who was by then in Australia, Steinberg sounded distinctly cooler. If there was to be a deal, he told Maxwell, he needed to have a lot of detailed information about Pergamon's business and Majthenyi was being distinctly unhelpful. Maxwell promised immediate action.

Two days later, Leasco's director of corporate planning, Michael Gibbs, who had been delegated to handle the discussions with Majthenyi, arrived at Pergamon's New York headquarters at the Book Center. Majthenyi, a Hungarian-born accountant, was effusive. Pergamon, he explained, was 'very profitable' and its sales in the Americas through the privately owned company Maxwell Scientific International Inc. (MSI Inc.) had topped $2.5 million in the past year. But when Gibbs stepped out again into the Manhattan street his briefcase was strangely empty. Normally, in similar deals, he would leave the corporate headquarters with masses of documents over which he would pore in the days ahead to deliver a detailed report to Steinberg. But Majthenyi had pleaded that he was not authorised to pass on confidential papers. He had muttered something about the privileges of the private and public companies but Gibbs had not completely understood. Indeed, when he returned to Great Kneck he was little wiser, beyond realising that the takeover of Pergamon might be more complicated than he had imagined.

Steinberg was again uneasy and the following day when Maxwell called he complained about the lack of progress. Breezily casting aside the doubts, Maxwell reassured Steinberg that his trip was enhancing both ILSC's and Pergamon's profits and that he would immediately fly to New York. The two met in early May at the Del Monico Hotel. Maxwell was relaxed, charming and confident. Pergamon's sales for 1969, he told Steinberg, would be approximately $25 million with profits of £2 million. ILSC's profits would be about £1 million. 'Pergamon's performance', he promised, was 'right on target'. Steinberg was somewhat reassured, and Maxwell was delighted that a deal, albeit still undefined, was under way. Steinberg's remaining doubts disappeared that evening.

Steinberg had arranged to attend a Democratic Party fund-raising dinner and he apologised to Maxwell that he would be unable to entertain him since a dinner jacket was obligatory. 'Don't worry,' said Maxwell, 'I'll get one.' By the time they had arrived at the Waldorf Hotel, Steinberg was pleased that Maxwell was present because he would have an opportunity to impress the British politician by displaying the scope of his own contacts, especially with the party's leaders, Teddy Kennedy and Hubert Humphrey. No sooner had they walked into the ballroom than Steinberg's vanity was shaken. In his deep resonant voice, Maxwell yelled, 'Hubert!' and Hubert Humphrey turned round in the middle of the crowded room and shouted, 'Bob, what are you doing here?' According to Steinberg, 'Maxwell knew more people there than I did.' Any lingering doubts momentarily vanished.

In the course of the following two weeks, Maxwell sent Steinberg letters, telexes and reports from London with information about Pergamon. But on 17 May the mood abruptly changed. Maxwell telephoned Steinberg and announced that the deal would have to be completed before Pergamon's next annual meeting, which was scheduled for 19 June, just four weeks later. 'Speed is important,' he said. Maxwell explained that he wanted to buy BPC's share of the 'profitable' ILSC but it would be much easier if Pergamon were already a Leasco subsidiary. All the information he needed, Maxwell assured Steinberg, was contained in a letter to Bernard Schwartz, Leasco's president.

Maxwell's letter to Schwartz was unambiguous. After an informative résumé of Pergamon's recent take-overs and its future plans, Maxwell disclosed an eye-opening example of how Pergamon earned its profits: twenty thousand copies of the Pergamon *World Atlas* had been sold at £20 each while the cost of production to Pergamon was a mere £1 10s. But it was ILSC and Maxwell's relationship with BPC which dominated the letter. The joint company, he conceded, had not been as profitable as he had at first imagined. BPC, he wrote, 'is afraid of me and desire to sever the partnership and acquire ILSC'. He added that he wanted to do the reverse and acquire BPC, 'whose sales and profits I know I could double within two years'.

ILSC, he admitted, had run into some trouble and as a result Hedley Le Bas had been fired because, Maxwell alleged, 'he was too fond of liquor', while Jenman was fired 'because of dishonesty'. Both men strongly denied the allegations. Although both dismissals were in May and June 1968, and Pergamon had issued public statements praising ILSC's profits since then, Maxwell nevertheless wrote to Schwartz to say that 'It was not until after the battle for *News of the World*, towards the end of last year, that I realised the inadequacy of the then management.' Harold Moppel, ILSC's financial director, he wrote, had also been fired and he, Maxwell, had taken on the day-to-day management.

Maxwell's compression of the chronology confused the issue, since the *News of the World* battle had only ended in January of that year, 1969, but his assurances about ILSC's current profits were exceptionally explicit: 'I enclose . . . a copy of the first quarter's management accounts and profit forecast prepared on a most conservative basis. These accounts were presented to and accepted by the ILSC board last Thursday; you will see that the company is running well, margins have already improved substantially and will continue to do so as we reduce our administration costs.'

The paragraph which followed was equally unambiguous: 'ILSC made a substantial profit for its first 18 months' trading.' But Maxwell added a critical qualification: 'If the accounts were judged by American standards, the profits for that period would be £800,000, but if British accounting practices were used, then we shall end up making neither a profit nor a loss' although there would be 'enhanced' profits from 1969 onwards. The estimates Maxwell quoted were annual sales of $20 million 'and rising very fast', especially in America.

Steinberg and Schwartz were reassured by Maxwell's letter and, although they realised that ILSC needed further examination, they still could not understand Maxwell's reasons for wanting to complete the deal at breakneck speed. But any doubts were cast aside the following week when Richard Fleming, the chairman of Robert Fleming, Pergamon's merchant bank, arrived in New York.

Fleming's role in the imbroglio which developed over the following months would unintentionally accord with the bank's own description of itself as 'a rather remarkable merchant bank'. The bank had been founded in 1932 and had deliberately retained a rather discreet image, unlike the family's two authors, Ian and Peter Fleming. Until the mid-1960s it had exclusively managed client funds which amounted to an impressive £1,200 million. But when the merger-mania began, Richard Fleming had decided that his bank should expand into corporate affairs and reap the enormous profits available. Richard Fleming's personal misfortune was that he understood little about corporations or their accounts.

Maxwell had approached Fleming in March 1968 (before the *News of the World* bid), to inquire whether the bank would act for Pergamon. Knowing of Maxwell's reputation, Fleming was hesitant but, keen to attract new corporate clients, he sought two guarantees. With Maxwell's agreement, Fleming commissioned the accountants Whinney Murray, who were closely connected to Fleming, to report on Pergamon. Fleming also wrote to Isidore Kerman, Maxwell's solicitor and a Pergamon director, asking for an 'unprejudiced view' of the company. In a personal conversation, he explained to Kerman that the bank would rely on the lawyer's professional assessment. Kerman's written reply stated: 'Mr Maxwell is a man of undoubted integrity and Pergamon Press Ltd is well run.' Pergamon's only problem, added Kerman, was that Maxwell 'took on too much'.

Whinney's report, which was presented on 13 June, had also been reassuring. The adverse rumours in the City, wrote the accountants, were untrue: 'The company has an undoubtedly impressive growth record.... None of this can have been achieved without good management.' Maxwell was given great credit for his 'drive and guidance'. Regarding the state of the accounts, Whinney Murray had also been satisfied, reporting that all the budgets, expenses and sales forecasts 'have been prepared in a proper manner'. There was slight criticism of the 'undoubted difficulties within the accountancy function' but this was to be expected of a company which 'had to struggle in order to keep pace' with its growth. Their only caveat concerned ILSC's accounts, which Whinney had been 'unable' to check, although 'We have however been assured by Pergamon that all indications show ILSC's trading results to be ahead of budget.' Fleming, at that time, possibly did not realise how crucial the encyclopaedia profits were to Pergamon's fortunes.

On the basis of Whinney's report and Kerman's testimonial, Fleming's formal appointment as Pergamon's advisers was confirmed on 21 June 1968. But, less than four weeks later, Fleming told Maxwell that he had had second thoughts and would not be offended if they quietly dissolved their new relationship. Maxwell was disquieted and tried to persuade Fleming to reconsider. Within a few days, the banker told Maxwell that he would after all advise Pergamon but strictly on the condition that, to deflect the Establishment's prejudice, Maxwell should appoint both an independent chairman and a new financial director. Maxwell accepted the conditions but the appointments were not made. As will be seen later, a new group chief accountant, Edward Garside, had recently been hired, and that, Maxwell felt, was sufficient. But Fleming was uneasy during the next year before his departure to New York.

All of Fleming's discussions with Leasco executives were conducted on the basis of what Pergamon's accounts for 1968 would disclose. The New Yorkers, confident that their instincts were finely tuned, remained nevertheless unaware of the tension and drama which had preceded the publication of the twenty-page, purple-covered brochure containing Pergamon's 1968 accounts. Maxwell's business reputation centres on how those accounts were prepared, and what they revealed.

The schedule for preparing Pergamon's 1968 report was tight. The company's annual meeting was set for 19 June 1969 and, to meet the deadline, the printing and circulation of the report had to be completed by 22 May. A company report is generally divided into three parts. The first contains a statement by the chairman describing key events over the past year and setting out his predictions for the future. The second part is the balance sheet as compiled by the company's own accountants to satisfy all the legal requirements. The third part, and probably the most important, is the verification by a reputable firm of accountants who, while paid by the company, are quite independent. Called the auditors, they state that having read the chairman's statement and having scrutinised the balance sheet, they are satisfied of its total veracity. The auditors' report, although normally brief, is the crucial guarantee both to the public and more importantly to all the City and government agencies that the company's officials have produced an honest and accurate statement concerning the company's health. For Maxwell, intent on demonstrating that Pergamon's pattern of growth was unceasing, the 1968 report was more important than ever.

For even the most successful and untroubled company, the compilation of the report produces a hectic period of intense discussion between the directors, accountants, bankers and auditors about how the company's affairs can and should be presented. As Maxwell was rightly fond of saying, accountancy is not a science but an art. With total honesty and strict adherence to the law, it is quite possible for the same accountants to draw up a balance sheet which, using identical basic facts, portrays the same company as highly profitable or as in debt. Simply by deciding whether income should be described as profit, or placed in the reserves column, or carried forward to the following year, or set off against an earlier loss, the image desired may be achieved. There are similar variations in valuing a company's assets – its property, stock and goodwill. But there are three major caveats to what might otherwise suggest controlled chaos. There must be consistency from one year to another; the accounts must comply with the law; and the accounts must also comply with the practices and standards which are agreed by the accountancy profession. There is no dispute that in 1969 the standards and practices of British accountancy were at best variable and at worst wildly misleading.

Maxwell would argue in the years ahead that during those first three weeks of May 1969 while Pergamon's annual report was being discussed and agreed he was the victim of the accountancy profession's lax and outdated habits. His accusers would claim with equal passion that, on the contrary, he exploited those weaknesses to their fullest extent. Both sides, however, agree that those weeks sealed his fate forever.

The heart of the matter was the size of Pergamon's profits: Maxwell wanted them, as usual, to be as high as possible. To achieve that objective depended upon triangular negotiations and agreements between Pergamon's in-house accountants, the company's auditors

Chalmers Impey, and Pergamon's bankers Robert Fleming. With the anticipated sale to Leasco, more depended upon that year's audited profit than previously and there were also more uncertainties to overcome.

In the course of the previous year, some of Pergamon's trading relationships had significantly shifted. The crux of that new pattern was a group of companies, some privately owned by Maxwell and his family trusts and some based in America. To understand the crisis and the accusations which would dominate Maxwell's life in the aftermath of his negotiations with Steinberg, it is necessary to penetrate this constellation of companies established by Maxwell around the publicly owned company Pergamon.

On 24 March 1959, Maxwell's original company, Low-Bell, and Maxwell Limited formally changed its name to Maxwell Scientific International (Distribution Services) Ltd—MSI(DS)—and simultaneously changed the objects clause in its memorandum of association, describing its future activities as general finance and investment. MSI(DS) was owned by Maxwell, his wife and Tom Clark. Maxwell was also associated with two other companies which bore very similar names but whose ownership and legal status were substantially different.

On 1 July 1964, just prior to the public flotation of Pergamon, MSI (1964) Ltd was created as a wholly owned Pergamon subsidiary whose function was to collect Pergamon's debts, a task which had previously been undertaken by MSI(DS).

The third company with a similar name was Maxwell Scientific International Inc. (MSI Inc.), which was a private company, incorporated and based in New York, and owned by two Liechtenstein-based trusts for the benefit of Maxwell's sister, Mrs Brana Natkin, and her children. In law, Maxwell had absolutely no control over MSI Inc. or the Liechtenstein family trusts which owned MSI Inc. The company's main business was the purchase of books and journals from Pergamon in Britain for sale throughout America. MSI Inc. had one noteworthy subsidiary called MSI Publishers Inc. which Maxwell would later claim concentrated exclusively on trading in books rather than journals.

In addition, there were two other companies privately owned by Maxwell which from time to time featured in Pergamon's normal business. The first was Robert Maxwell & Co. Ltd, known as R.M. & Co., which was originally Lange, Maxwell and Springer. In 1955 the company had changed its name to I.R. Maxwell & Co. and in 1963 had changed it again to its current name. R.M. & Co. was granted the sole distribution rights to all Pergamon's publications in Britain and was the company which Maxwell used to establish his bookshops.

The second private company was Pergamon Press Incorporated (PPI), which was also founded in New York in 1952 and was owned by the same family trusts as owned MSI Inc. Indeed, both were housed in two premises, the brownstone at 122 East 55th Street which Maxwell had bought with the British Book Center, and Maxwell House in Elmsford, New York State. Both companies were also managed by the same people: Maxwell, Majthenyi, Tom Clark and Laszlo Straka. Since 1958, PPI had enjoyed the exclusive rights to sell Pergamon's journals and reprints in the western hemisphere. PPI became even more important in Pergamon's overall activities just six weeks after Pergamon was established as a public company in Britain in 1964.

When in August 1964 Maxwell and Macmillan of New York terminated their five-year agreement, PPI had initially bought back Macmillan's stock. Maxwell explained later that he had ended the agreement with Macmillan because, firstly, 'In all the three years that Macmillan purchased books from us, MSI was their biggest customer'; and secondly, the directors of PPI had said that they could earn better profits from the concession: 'They made a good case out to me and I was very happy....' PPI's shareholders at that stage were Majthenyi and R.M. & Co., of which Maxwell was also the principal shareholder. The termination had occurred just six weeks after the publication in London of Pergamon's prospectus for its flotation, but the prospectus did not mention the possibility that the profitable agreement with Macmillan would end prematurely or that Pergamon would sign a new agreement with PPI because, as Maxwell explained, 'I certainly had no knowledge about terminating it.'

Four months later, on 2 December 1964, Pergamon in Britain bought PPI from Maxwell's family trusts in exchange for 276,154 Pergamon shares. The new public shareholders of Pergamon were told about the arrangements in a circular on 18 January 1965. On Pergamon's behalf, Maxwell wrote that he was convinced that an agreement with PPI would be more efficient and more profitable. Then, as another stage of this convoluted series of agreements, on the very same day that Pergamon bought PPI, two further contracts were signed. First, MSI Inc. agreed with PPI to purchase the complete inventory of Pergamon books which PPI had just bought from Macmillan. Secondly, by another agreement signed on that same day, PPI agreed to distribute the same books in the western hemisphere on MSI Inc.'s behalf.

There are two interpretations of that series of agreements. Maxwell's critics claim that the agreement between MSI Inc. and PPI was an important manoeuvre to maintain Pergamon's high profits. If PPI, as a new Pergamon subsidiary, had just taken Macmillan's unsold stock and put it into a warehouse, the original sales to Macmillan could no longer have been counted as profits in Pergamon's accounts. By selling the Macmillan stock to the 'independent' company, MSI Inc., Pergamon's profits were unaffected. Maxwell claimed that MSI Inc. possessed the 'marketing ability' to sell the books while PPI had 'no machinery, no ability and no experience and no know-how in this area'. His justification seemed to contradict Pergamon's circular of January 1969, in which he had praised PPI's organisation as having the capacity to 'effectively ... handle the sales'. Significantly, exactly the same people were managing all these companies and none of these details was fully revealed by Pergamon in Britain during the takeover battles of 1968.

In a Pergamon circular sent by Maxwell in May 1968, he had stated that 'no director had any interest in any asset acquired or disposed of by Pergamon since October 1967'. The following year, the Takeover Panel would accept that the statement was legally true, but others were unhappy because the transactions were conducted by the Maxwell family trusts. Significantly, throughout this year, no one would ever actually read the legal documents which established the trusts or speak to the trustees who administered them. Consequently, there was no possibility of independently scrutinising Maxwell's claim that he had absolutely no control over the trusts or of checking who were the beneficiaries. Nor apparently was Maxwell ever asked to prove his claims.

On 15 August 1968, Pergamon floated PPI as a public company on the New York Stock Exchange. Thirty per cent of its shares were offered for sale. At the time, the flotation seemed a prudent step to establish a firm American base for Pergamon in the future. The £400,000 which was raised was used to improve warehouse facilities and to reduce PPI's debt to Pergamon in Britain. Legally, PPI's relationship with MSI Inc. remained unaffected, yet within one year these otherwise unsensational arrangements exploded the Pergamon empire.

In Britain, the whole pattern of the agreements between Pergamon and the private companies was described in quite general and unrevealing terms by Maxwell before he began the serious negotiations with Leasco. Interested British shareholders and the City would have been hard pressed to glean from Pergamon's annual reports or circulars that PPI, prior to 1964, was a privately owned Maxwell company which had earned approximately $450,000 in each of the previous two years as commission from Pergamon for its sales and services to Macmillan. Shareholders also did not know about the intimate commercial relationship which developed between PPI and MSI Inc. after the break with Macmillan. They were not told that Majthenyi was the managing director of Maxwell's privately owned American company and of the subsidiary of the British public company. Nor were they told that the private and public companies shared common offices, warehouses and personnel for which MSI Inc. paid $600 per month.

Overall, most investors in Britain would have been unaware that Maxwell, in managing the public company of Pergamon, faced a potential conflict of interests. If there was a responsibility for publicising those details, it rested not only on Maxwell but more importantly, as he later pointed out, on his advisers – the lawyers, bankers, accountants and brokers who joined together every year to formulate Pergamon's annual report and upon whose professionalism and independence the public depended.

The first check on any possible irregularities was Pergamon's independent auditors, Chalmers Impey, who were at the time Britain's foremost accountancy experts for the publishing industry. Chalmers Impey understood better than others how to value the various stocks of books and how to assess the profits of an industry whose terms of trade include the unpredictable 'sale or return' agreements. The partner who had been responsible for Pergamon's accounts for nearly fifteen years was John Briggs, a sullen man who much admired Maxwell. Briggs suffered two major disabilities–a paralysing stutter and alcoholism. While his speech impediment was instantly recognisable, he successfully concealed his drinking. The relationship between the very articulate Maxwell and the handicapped Briggs was very relevant to the intense discussions which began at the beginning of 1969 about Pergamon's profits for the previous year.

As early as February 1966, Briggs had written to Pergamon's directors expressing concern about the possible conflict of interests: 'In our view it is undesirable that there should be a trading relationship between a public company and another company which, while not a subsidiary, is subject to any measure of common control, so as to leave room for the suggestion that the profits of the public company might be inflated or deflated as a result of such relationship.' The advice had no effect.

The preparation of Pergamon's 1968 accounts had started in earnest soon after the Christmas holidays. At Headington Hall, three people were directly involved: Edward Garside, the chief accountant, Peter

Bennett, the company secretary and financial director, and Tom Clark, an accountant who was also Pergamon's deputy chairman. Garside had been appointed in April 1968 after Chalmers Impey had complained that Bennett was unable to cope with the enormous workload. Like all new arrivals in the stable block adjacent to the Hall, he would be struck by the revelation that although Bennett was employed by Pergamon he also managed Maxwell's private companies' accounts from the same office. Instead of different accountants located in separate offices handling the potentially conflicting responsibilities, the cash books, wages and invoices for all Maxwell's interests passed across the same desk. Yet under the system of compartmentalisation, only Maxwell really understood the affairs of each of the public and private companies, and that caused further complications.

Chalmers Impey were auditors for Pergamon but not for the private companies. Until 1969, they had accepted without question the terms of any transaction which Pergamon directors stated had been settled with Maxwell's private companies although, as a complicating factor, Pergamon's financial year ended on 31 December while the private companies' financial year ended on 30 June. Briggs's subordinate who personally did all the leg-work to audit Pergamon accounts was Anthony Payne, an accountant with nineteen years' experience. Payne would later describe the reconciliation of Pergamon's accounts with those of the private companies as 'basically impossible', because all the accounts were chaotic.

As he prepared the accounts in consultation with Maxwell and Clark, Bennett endeavoured to meet Maxwell's prevailing commandment – profits were to be maximised to meet Maxwell's publicly announced forecast of over £2 million. There was absolutely nothing illegal or even unethical in that practice, especially since the Companies Act of 1967, by opening new loopholes, had left excessive discretion to the accountants.

At some stage during late 1968, Bennett was told by Maxwell that MSI Inc. and R.M. & Co. had placed orders with Pergamon for two sales of back-issue journals which were worth £708,000. Bennett was also told that in anticipation of a further 'firm' order from MSI Inc., other old journals which were also stored in Pergamon's warehouse in Olney should be recorded as profits to Pergamon. The back issues, which in previous years had been valued by Pergamon itself as nil, were written up as a £266,416 profit. Altogether, the new orders from the private companies added a total of £974,000 (of which approximately £700,000 was profit) to Pergamon's income. Effectively, one-third of Pergamon's total profits in 1968 would be derived from those two sales. Without them, Pergamon's profits would have been approximately £1.4 million, which was £100,000 less than the profits in 1967. Bennett, who claimed that he could never discover the exact terms of credit between Pergamon and MSI Inc., accepted the orders at face value. He insisted that he never saw a written invoice and had acted on Maxwell's oral assurance.

The draft accounts which Bennett therefore sent to Briggs and Payne at Chalmers Impey in March 1969 contained those profits. On the negative side, Bennett had also made two provisions. First, the dividend due from ILSC would be only half the amount expected (£180,000 instead of £350,000) and, disappointingly, could not be counted as profits; therefore there was no dividend from ILSC. Secondly, PPI's profits were lower than expected. In total, however, Pergamon's profits would be over £2 million, a new record which met Maxwell's public forecast.

Payne, a big, bluff Londoner, read the accounts and began his audit. In the normal course of his work, he would expect substantial horse-trading with every client, which would be governed by the law, the interpretation of the 1967 Companies Act by other accountants (which he could copy), and by his professional principles. It was the interpretation of the law which some in the accountancy profession in retrospect criticised at Chalmers Impey. Maxwell, however, was entitled to rely upon the agreement of his accountants and auditors.

By the end of March, Payne had approved the bulk of the accounts. His only concerns were three items: first, a payment of $800,000 from MSI Inc. to Pergamon; secondly, the sale by Pergamon for £100,000 of the Spanish translation rights of its books; and thirdly, MSI Inc.'s order for back issues which Pergamon had recorded as £266,416 profits.

Solving the $800,000 payment proved relatively easy – it had been erroneously entered by a clerk as a credit to Pergamon. It was the opposite. Payne corrected the mistake, so reducing Pergamon's profits, only to be surprised at Maxwell's reaction: Maxwell stated that it had been on his authority that MSI Inc. had been debited with that large amount. Relations between the two did not improve further when Payne requested proof of the sale of the translation rights.

On 21 October 1968, Maxwell had written to Payne to say that he had agreed to establish a joint publishing company with Spanish and Argentinian partners which would be legally watertight 'before the end of the year'. Maxwell estimated that the agreement would produce revenue 'in excess of £100,000' but he was advised to allow only £100,000 to be part of the official profits forecast which at the time was being compiled for the *News of the World* bid. In March 1969, Payne wanted to see the formal agreement with proof of the £100,000 profits which Pergamon had earned the previous year. Payne also told the Pergamon accountants that he wanted to see the evidence of the MSI Inc. purchase worth £266,416.

By the end of the month, the written evidence for neither had been provided and suddenly the Pergamon board meeting which would approve the audited accounts for submission to the Stock Exchange was brought forward by two weeks, to 2 April. Payne immediately reported to Briggs that two outstanding obstacles stood in the way of approval of the accounts. Briggs consulted Maxwell, who promised immediate action to meet his self-imposed deadline.

On 31 March a telex arrived from Dr Edward Gray, MSI Inc.'s president in New York, which confirmed the profitable MSI Inc. order. But the telex ended with a puzzling sentence: 'Our purchases as always in the past are subject to right of exchange if issues still in stock or reprint on a royalty basis if issues no longer available.' Payne did not understand what Gray meant and Bennett would also later claim ignorance. Nevertheless the order seemed 'firm' (although the interpretation would be later disputed). On the following day, two more telexes arrived. The first was also from Gray stating that MSI Inc. had assumed responsibility for the Spanish translation rights' contract, and the second was a confirmatory telex from MSI Inc.'s auditors. Any qualms Payne might have felt about the fate of the Spanish and Argentinian partners disappeared in the frantic rush to complete the accounts for the vital board meeting which was scheduled for 2 p.m. the following day.

During the night, Payne and Briggs discussed how the accounts should reflect the new value placed on the back issues of journals which were reserved for MSI Inc. One possibility was for a formal 'Note', an explanation that would be included with the published accounts, but whether Briggs supported that course before 2 April is unknown; it seems unlikely. Briggs supported Maxwell's interpretation of how MSI Inc.'s order made the previously 'valueless' journals valuable since he was satisfied by Maxwell's assurances that Pergamon had received a 'firm' order. Payne struggled to complete the work and drove at breakneck speed from Oxford to Fitzroy Square – 'I've never driven so fast in my life,' he recalled – to arrive at what would be 'the shortest board meeting I have ever attended'.

Maxwell had barely entered the room before he announced, 'I've got to take the President of Nigeria around the House of Commons. I hope everything is satisfactory.' Whether Briggs had intended to mention his subordinate's concern and was prevented by his stammer from speaking is unknown. But certainly the board approved the accounts without any caveat or agreement for a 'Note', just in time to authorise the Stock Exchange to make its preliminary announcement of 'Pergamon's record profits'. Maxwell swiftly left the meeting. In early May, the accounts were sent to Fleming and Whinney Murray. For both, the status of Maxwell's private companies had assumed great importance.

Fleming had already heard about the high values which Pergamon's accountants wanted to place on the company's stocks and about Pergamon's valuable sales to MSI Inc. Accordingly, in December 1968, he had asked Sir William Carrington of Whinney Murray to undertake a close watching brief on Pergamon's financial management, especially because there had been several resignations from the accounts department. Whinney already had considerable knowledge of Pergamon's affairs because they had written their wide-ranging and reassuring report the previous year. On 9 December Carrington met Maxwell and insisted that he would only accept the new responsibility if Maxwell agreed to allow Whinney's staff full access to Pergamon's employees and if he personally had the right to vet all major schemes. To preclude any misunderstandings, Carrington stipulated that these unusually strict conditions of employment had to be agreed by all of Pergamon's directors and recorded in the company minutes. Carrington's proposals were never put to the Pergamon board. There are conflicting versions of what followed.

There can be no doubt that it is difficult for a merchant bank to establish an intimate relationship with its client while at the same time being totally frank with outsiders. In the course of his work, the banker will inevitably discover adverse facts regarding his client which, if publicised, would often create unnecessary short-term damage. Yet the banker's own interests and those of his other clients demand that on occasion a higher interest must be served which could well harm a client. This, at its most charitable, was Richard Fleming's predicament in early 1969. His relationship with Maxwell was akin to a good stepmother: while he had affection and respect for his 'son', he also recognised his deficiencies, but found it difficult to break the relationship.

During March 1969, Fleming realised that the buoyant profit forecasts for ILSC which Pergamon had announced during the *News of the World* bid were unlikely to materialise. In the course of a lunch in mid-April, Maxwell confessed to Fleming that because of BPC's interference ILSC's profits would be lower than expected. Both men recognised that Pergamon's image as a booming company was endangered. Without evidence of perpetual growth, Pergamon would have difficulty in launching future bids and in raising capital. Maxwell then turned to the approach from Leasco which he had originally mentioned to Fleming in January, soon after his first meeting with Steinberg. He explained that, while he would prefer a joint company with Leasco in Britain, the best solution would be an association with a company like Xerox. When they parted, Fleming was still optimistic about Pergamon's future although he accepted that, in tune with merger-mania, it needed to be part of a bigger group. Hence, when at the end of the month Xerox rejected his feelers, Fleming gave his blessing to Maxwell's talks with Steinberg.

It was at that stage, in early May, that Maxwell flew to New York and met Steinberg at the Hotel Del Monico to allay the American's concerns. Meanwhile, in London, the preliminary accounts for 1968 had been sent to Fleming and his questions had become quite pertinent. Several important new factors had been introduced into the estimate of Pergamon's results for that year.

Fleming felt that the draft was comprehensive but complained that, in the light of their recent conversations, it was too optimistic and lacked precise figures. Carrington, however, was dissatisfied outright and insisted that Maxwell should explain in his chairman's statement the full details of both the unusual relationship between Pergamon and MSI Inc. and the new valuation of the stocks. He told Fleming that although he accepted that MSI Inc. was not a dummy company, it should be sold to avoid any doubts about its independence. In anticipation of his imminent trip to America, Fleming on about 15 May delegated the detailed negotiations to his associate, Burnet Stewart.

According to Fleming's account, by 16 May Stewart had returned to Pergamon a proof copy of the accounts. Enclosed was a list of questions prepared by Whinney Murray which were to be discussed at a meeting arranged for three days later. The most important item was the MSI Inc. contract and the need for what would become known as 'Note 8', an explanation about the valuation of Pergamon's stocks. In the course of those three days, a bitter argument erupted between Maxwell and Briggs on the one side and Fleming and Whinney Murray on the other about that Note. The climax was a telephone call from Stewart, in the course of which the meeting scheduled for 19 May was cancelled and Stewart announced that Flemings was forthwith withdrawing its services. For Maxwell, the row threatened a major crisis with unpalatable consequences. The slightest whisper in the City that his merchant bankers were resigning would threaten calamity. It was in the midst of this row that on 17 May Maxwell telephoned Steinberg and set the deadline for their negotiations – Leasco's take-over would have to be announced prior to Pergamon's annual meeting, which was scheduled just four weeks later.

By 19 May, relations between Maxwell and his advisers had been generally repaired, although George Hazard, ILSC's financial director, had resigned, allegedly because he had disagreed with Maxwell's views of how the accounts should be prepared. On the same or the following day, all the parties met to discuss the Note. Carrington told both Maxwell and Briggs that a full and accurate description of Pergamon's relationship with MSI Inc. and its new methods of valuing its stock should be included as Note 8. Carrington claims that he left under the impression that Maxwell and his adviser had agreed. What remains unclear is whether Carrington also stipulated that there was to be explicit mention that there had been a 'change of practice' in the valuation of stocks. Inclusion of that phrase would have drawn immediate attention to the major source of Pergamon's record 'profits'. On the same day Fleming flew to New York and on 22 May Pergamon's accounts were finally approved by everyone.

When Fleming met Bernard Schwartz, Leasco's president, on 26 May, any disquiet he might have felt was well concealed behind the effete and rather charming self-assurance which at that time so characterised the traditional City gent. Like Steinberg, Schwartz was born in Brooklyn and displayed sophisticated acumen in finance; and like Steinberg, Schwartz had never been exposed to the unaccountable City institutions. Both Americans shared a naive but understandable trust in the supervision of financial affairs in London which dulled their instinctive streetwariness.

Inevitably the accounts of such an important conversation vary. Schwartz reported that Richard Fleming was reassuring about Pergamon and proved his confidence by explaining that his own bank held 13 per cent of Pergamon's stock on behalf of its clients: 'Pergamon is worth more than its share price,' said Fleming, 'and I won't let you steal it.' Fleming later denied saying those words and insisted that the meeting was no more than a chance encounter which covered merely general issues. He specifically recalled warning Schwartz to satisfy himself about Pergamon's financial situation. In view of what followed, Fleming's recollection is unlikely to be accurate since on the same day, over lunch at the fashionable Links Club, he repeated his glowing account to Leasco's lawyer, Robert Hodes. Fleming's account is that he described Maxwell as 'a difficult person to control', but expressed his belief that Pergamon's business was 'sound' although there was 'some' dispute about the balance sheet. Hodes remembers Fleming being much less cautious and can specifically recall that Fleming made no mention of the heated disputes which he had left behind in London.

Indeed, Fleming had been so reassuring that three days later, on 29 May, Steinberg, Schwartz and Leasco's director of corporate planning Michael Gibbs flew to London, more anxious than ever not to let the deal slip out of their grasp. What would later be dubbed 'the SWOT team', referring to an elite American police unit, was well aware that Maxwell had imposed a deadline which expired in less than three weeks. But there was still mystery surrounding the company they were about to buy. Their strategy was single-minded. A list of questions had been drawn up before their departure from New York which needed to be answered if the $60 million deal was to succeed.

Maxwell, the generous host, had prepared a warm reception in Oxford, although Steinberg was not present as his two experts began the detailed discussions. Over drinks and lunch, the Leasco team were introduced to Kerman and Clark; and, while Kerman listened, Maxwell repeated how Pergamon's back-issue business was profitable and expanding. Specifically, the Leasco team claimed that over lunch Maxwell produced a balance sheet which stated that Pergamon would earn $8.4 million profits in 1969 and which included a forecast of $1.4 million profit if Pergamon owned ILSC completely. Afterwards the two were given a tour of Pergamon's headquarters.

Gibbs then disappeared for nearly one week into Pergamon's offices. When he emerged, he had obtained some answers but also had accumulated considerably more questions. Pergamon's profits, he discovered, were falling and Whinney's complaint about the absence of proper internal accounts and inventory control was more serious than he imagined. Once again everyone assured him that ILSC's profits were high, although the final accounts were not yet available. (An earlier assurance that he would be given the accounts for the first eighteen months was not fulfilled.)

But what particularly puzzled Gibbs was the trading relationship between Pergamon and MSI Inc. in New York. Majthenyi had told Gibbs that MSI Inc. was an independent trading company which bought and sold Pergamon's publications. At the time it seemed quite insignificant but his investigation revealed that in the past year no less than $1.1 million of Pergamon's profits had been earned by sales to MSI Inc. To his surprise, Gibbs then discovered that the vast bulk of MSI Inc.'s purchases were still stored, unsold, in Pergamon's warehouse. Gibbs's anxiety was assuaged by Tom Clark. MSI Inc., Clark explained, was in fact owned by Isthmus Trust Inc., which in turn was owned by a secret Maxwell family trust. It was all part of a scheme to avoid Britain's draconian tax laws. The American could only smile at the contortions performed by a socialist politician.

Schwartz had in the meantime become impressed by Maxwell. Despite the warnings, Maxwell seemed always ready to co-operate and proved to be a very important person. Every day, Maxwell invited his guests to a social whirlwind of visits to the House of Commons, Woburn Abbey and the opera while the evenings were filled by sparkling and memorable dinners with the leaders of British society, including the Duke of Bedford, and concluded with dancing at Annabel's night club. According to Peter Stevens, who managed Steinberg's interests in Britain, 'The SWOT team didn't have any time to swot.' Schwartz disagreed, although he was irritated by Maxwell's insistence on the snap deadline. But even that was explicable. Maxwell, he realised, was a 'quick' man who wanted to get things done and he seemed genuinely fearful that BPC would purchase his share of ILSC. Whenever Schwartz pointed out that Leasco needed hard facts, Maxwell promised his personal warranty which could be satisfied by the detailed investigation which would follow the public announcement of the bid. Schwartz left Oxford reassured, and agreed that they would be in contact again within a matter of days.

Travelling back across the Atlantic, the Leasco executives accepted that, although their original questions had been answered, there were many new ones which mere equally pressing 'We couldn't understand', recalled Gibbs, 'all the different company names that kept cropping up. One of our concerns was that Maxwell was undisciplined and had bought a lot of small, unprofitable businesses. There seemed to be no rationale for his buying a lot of this crap.' Schwartz could still not quite understand Maxwell's family trusts which in law were not controlled by Maxwell. They played an important role in both the ownership of Pergamon shares and the ownership of the companies which traded with Pergamon. But Schwartz believed that Maxwell had assured him that he could speak on behalf of the trusts in negotiating the deal. Consequently, their report to Steinberg was positive. The proposed merger was advantageous to Leasco since, although Maxwell had exaggerated Pergamon's computer expertise, he did possess substantial material which could be exploited by Leasco's new data-bank equipment while the books and encyclopaedias had, in Maxwell's phrase, 'synergistic opportunities' for the Americans. However, Gibbs cautioned that everything depended upon Maxwell's complete co-operation after the purchase. Only at the end of the first week of June had the Leasco team recognised the very sharp difference between Leasco's and Pergamon's style of management.

While both Maxwell and Steinberg were ambitious entrepreneurs with an enviably refined ability to exploit the fast-changing and complicated science of accountancy and corporate finance, there were few other similarities. In 1969, Maxwell was an impulsive juggler who disdained the type of cautious financial controls which less flamboyant corporate managers espoused. Many of Maxwell's commercial interests in printing and publishing were gathered as passing targets of opportunity since everything was secondary to his overriding ambition for growth and influence. The notion that Maxwell possessed a master plan was an image cultivated by his public relations. Pergamon *was* Maxwell, and he managed it single-handed. Nothing could be decided without reference to him. Although he spent the week in London and returned to the Oxford headquarters only on Friday afternoons, his staff spent many hours daily on the telephone to Fitzroy Square and were often summoned down to London for consultations which were invariably delayed for hours while Maxwell pursued other business. Throughout the negotiations with Leasco, Maxwell rarely allowed even his outside advisers – the lawyers, bankers and auditors – to discuss Pergamon's affairs if he was not present. If Maxwell was motivated by a commercial strategy during the early part of June 1969, it was definitely not clear then, and it remains bewildering nearly twenty years later. Maxwell himself has never been satisfactorily forthcoming. Some felt that he was bored by Pergamon and wanted the cash to buy the ailing *Sun* newspaper and launch a second career as a newspaper tycoon. Others later arrived at more complicated explanations.

Steinberg's intentions are somewhat clearer. Pergamon was a solid publisher with potential. Leasco, which was then valued at $530 million, could afford to buy Pergamon. Steinberg was and remains a shrewd and thoughtful strategist. 'Every step which Saul takes', said his lawyer, 'is part of a plan and he has very high standards.' Pergamon, as presented in the accounts, fitted into his strategy, but the chance of a successful working relationship with Maxwell was slight. Steinberg believed in delegation. Having hired like-minded and talented staff from similar backgrounds, he relied on their work and judgement. Although his own authority was never questioned, there was a style of rigorous reporting, especially on financial matters, which Maxwell never contemplated. Steinberg, apparently excited by the deal itself, ignored their personality differences.

On 4 June, after he had digested his executives' report, Steinberg called Jacob Rothschild in London. Normally merchant bankers are consulted much earlier than two weeks before a deal is announced and are asked for their advice at every stage. But Rothschild was merely told that a deal was probable and was asked if he would act on Leasco's behalf. He agreed but warned his client that he had grave doubts whether Maxwell was the type who could work as a subordinate. Steinberg's enthusiasm remained undented.

Unbeknown to Steinberg, Sir William Carrington wrote to Maxwell the following day (5 June), acknowledging receipt of Pergamon's accounts, which had been officially signed on 22 May. Carrington stated that he was 'perturbed to find' on reading the report that Note 8 was 'considerably less informative than we had agreed in outline at our meeting'. In the glossy publication, Maxwell had diluted and scattered the information about the relationship and new valuation. Under the heading 'Acquisitions', on page six, the chairman reported that PPI would buy MSI Inc. from his family trust, while on page fifteen Note 8 baldly stated, 'Stocks are valued at the lower of cost and net realisable value and include £266,416 of costs incurred in the year in respect of additional printing and reprinting of journals to meet firm orders.' Carrington believed that the unaware would remain uninformed. He concluded his letter with the news that since Maxwell seemed 'upset' about the questions which Briggs had been asked by Whinney, he had decided it was best that their proposed relationship be 'abandoned'.

On the same day, Fleming also wrote to Maxwell to point out that he shared Carrington's dismay about the accounts, and added that the confidence of the bank's investment staff had been 'shaken' by Pergamon's profits and its prospects even if the new stock valuation was correct. He concluded that the bank should therefore resign its advisory role after the annual meeting two weeks later, but he nevertheless offered to give Maxwell further help if required in his discussions with Leasco. Again Maxwell placated his banker and obtained an assurance that no announcement would be made before the annual meeting, due two weeks later. His attention now switched to Leasco.

Over the following week, Maxwell and Steinberg were in constant communication. Any doubts Steinberg might have felt were swept aside by Maxwell's guarantees and references to the recently audited accounts which had been approved by his independent bankers. By 10 June, Steinberg was satisfied that he should begin detailed negotiations and suggested that Maxwell fly immediately to New York. Maxwell agreed but, just before leaving, dictated letters to both Fleming and Carrington. Maxwell was wounded by their imputations and ultimatums and, after justifying the new and in his view fair valuation of the stocks, he asked them to reconsider their positions, especially their comments about Pergamon's profits.

The very next day Maxwell arrived in New York accompanied by Paul DiBiase, representing Kerman, and Lawrence Banks, representing Fleming. Over the following seven days the teams from both sides met daily. Throughout the weary, continuous negotiations, the major issue was Pergamon's accounts. The queries were always answered by production of the now completed 1968 report, which, as the Pergamon team emphasised, had been officially certified by Chalmers Impey. Two other obstacles were also removed. Since Maxwell's private companies were such an integral part of Pergamon's operations, he agreed to sell an option for their sale on generous terms; and on Schwartz's insistence Maxwell agreed to sign a warranty that 'Maxwell has no knowledge that [Pergamon's] financial statements are inaccurate, taken as a whole.'

Under the agreement, Leasco would bid 37s for each Pergamon share (at the time they were trading at approximately 27s). Maxwell would get a mixture of cash and Leasco stock in return for his own 34 per cent of Pergamon shares. He was to be deputy chairman of the main Leasco company and chairman of Leasco World Trade Company. In total, the bid valued Pergamon at £25.4 million, of which Maxwell and his family would receive over £8 million.

In New York on 17 June, amid considerable excitement, Maxwell and Steinberg signed the agreement that Leasco could launch a formal bid for Pergamon, subject to Maxwell allowing a team of accountants appointed by Leasco to have complete access to every Pergamon file, bank statement, inventory and employee so that all their remaining questions would be satisfactorily answered. Several bottles of champagne were opened and everyone in the room laughed with relief. The impression of those who witnessed the two outsiders clink glasses was that a happy marriage would not easily be achieved but the two protagonists genuinely exuded a desire for a relationship.

The celebration was cut short. Maxwell insisted that they fly immediately to London to announce the deal the following day, just twenty-four hours before his deadline expired. As they dashed to Kennedy airport, phone calls were made to Jacob Rothschild and Richard Fleming asking them to arrange a press conference.

The following morning, instead of driving directly from Heathrow airport to the Rothschild bank, Steinberg first called to see Peter Stevens, his manager in Leasco's Knightsbridge office. 'Baby, do I have a deal for you,' cooed the beaming Steinberg as he walked through the door.

Stevens was appalled when he heard the details. 'I live in Britain,' he told Steinberg, 'and I hear the grass growing here. What I hear about this guy isn't good.' Steinberg was unimpressed, least of all by Stevens's criticism that publishing and computers didn't mix because data banks were a gimmick. Nothing would sway Steinberg. He believed in Maxwell and in Pergamon. There was brilliance and energy which he could harness.

The reception at Rothchilds was warmer. Steinberg was excited by the number of journalists who had crowded into the conference room: 'I was amazed that it was so significant.' The two smiling businessmen sat flanked by their two sullen-faced bankers in a packed room of bemused journalists. Maxwell did most of the talking, which provoked the impression that it was he who was taking over Leasco. As the champion of the 'I'm Backing Britain' campaign, he had to explain the apparent contradiction. Britain, he answered, did not have the finance or know-how to develop a computer-based information-retrieval system. The deal would also benefit Britain's precarious balance of payments. Nearly everyone seemed satisfied.

There was only one slight blot on an otherwise ideal marriage announcement. It was a question from Robert Jones, an authoritative writer on business affairs for *The Times*. 'What is Pergamon's overdraft?' he asked. Maxwell replied, '£500,000.' Jones immediately countered that Pergamon's report coming out the following day showed £1.9 million. Politely but firmly Maxwell insisted that the position had much improved in the previous six months. For Steinberg, sitting nearby, the exchange was 'curious. I didn't understand the significance at the time.' As the journalists left he asked Maxwell for an explanation. 'That man', replied his jubilant partner, 'has been persecuting me for years.' There was a germ of truth in Maxwell's exaggeration. Jones had for long been sceptical about Pergamon's affairs and had some months earlier been contacted by Richard Millett, Butterworths' former chairman, who had not ceased to investigate ILSC's finances. Jones would make only brief mention of his exchange with Maxwell in the following day's newspaper, but Steinberg would seek him out a few weeks later.

The newspaper headlines on 19 June reflected the infectious en-thusiasm and hope portrayed in the photographs, placed alongside the articles, of the two laughing tycoons at their press conference. Everything seemed perfect. The next stage was, in theory, a pure formality. Leasco's bankers, lawyers and accountants would write the document which would spell out the formal offer to Pergamon's shareholders. Heading the taskforce was Rothschilds, who would co-operate with Leasco's accountants Touche Ross to undertake a detailed investigation in London and Oxford.

On that same day, Maxwell was deeply immersed in plans for his next venture, the purchase of the *Sun* newspaper from IPC. He had announced his interest two weeks earlier, in the midst of his negotiations with Steinberg, and had pledged that the paper would be 'loyal to the Labour movement'. He harboured high hopes that his third attempt to win control of a newspaper, financed by the sale of his Pergamon shares, would prove successful. At noon, his negotiations were to be temporarily interrupted as he presented Pergamon's 1968 annual report. The brochure's purple front cover encapsulated his achievement. Under a bold headline 'Profit Growth', the profits for 1967 were shown as £1,541,000 and those for 1968 as £2,182,000. In his personal statement, he credited the 'substantial increase in profits' to 'internal growth', and reaffirmed his confidence in ILSC's 'bright and profitable future'. But when he arrived at the AGM in Belgrave Square he was already troubled.

Just before the meeting, halting and stuttering as always, John Briggs had told Maxwell that he had just been visited by Colin Simpson, a reporter from the *Sunday Times*, who had intimated that he possessed information that the auditing procedures adopted by Chalmers Impey for Pergamon's accounts were questionable. Maxwell was outraged. A few telephone calls confirmed that several other *Sunday Times* reporters had spoken to former Pergamon employees within the last twenty-four hours. After trying unsuccessfully to contact the *Sunday Times* editor, Harold Evans, Maxwell wrote directly to the proprietor of the paper, Lord Thomson. His letter's subheading showed that he feared the worst: 'Maxwell, Crook or Paranoiac. An Insight exposé for publication in the next edition of the *Sunday Times*....' The contents were equally sensational. Reporters on Thomson papers, Maxwell claimed, were intending to 'rely on and repeat' information 'from disgruntled ex-employees' which was 'not only completely false but grossly defamatory'. The information, he continued, was being offered 'at the instigation of Rupert Murdoch' and he called on Thomson to terminate the 'scurrilous attack on me'. Within hours two more letters were hand-delivered to Evans – one from Maxwell and the other from Isidore

Kerman. The politician's language in the letter to Evans seemed particularly intemperate: 'I am reliably told that the team is burning the midnight oil so they can complete their dirty work in time.' In a further letter the following day, he described the Insight team as 'poison weed scribes'. Both the journalists of the Insight team and Evans were stunned. 'Quite honestly, we couldn't understand what he was on about,' recalls Godfrey Hodgson, then editor of Insight.

In 1969, the *Sunday Times* was, in the judgement of many professionals, the best weekly newspaper in the world. Under Evans, the paper consistently set new and original standards in journalism and presentation. Insight was a concept, created by Evans, which would later be dubbed 'investigative journalism'. Essentially, a team of prominent *Sunday Times* journalists and 'stringers' in Britain and throughout the world would, at the request of the Insight editors, either search for original and formerly unpublished information or try to establish the truth behind a major public event. As the individual journalists submitted their stories to London, the editors analysed the combined information and wrote the story which appeared in the newspaper. Expense was rarely an obstacle to a scoop and it was quite normal for a dozen or more highly qualified journalists to contribute to a single story. By 1969, Insight had firmly established itself as the nation's agent to reveal serious scandals in the City, in industry, in government and generally wherever the powerbrokers of society had hitherto trod without fear of exposure. Its successes had already earned its editors quasi-legendary status among their peers. Revelations about the insurance scandals perpetuated by Emil Savundra and the Vehicle and General company, investigations into John Profumo and Kim Philby, and exposés of frauds in the wine and antiques world had all earned the Insight label sterling credibility. The mere mention that an Insight investigation was under way was often sufficient to imply that the subject had committed a wrong and had cause for concern. The corollary, which would be fiercely denied by members of the Insight team themselves, was that they behaved like self-appointed avenging angels whose conceit and arrogance blinded them to any facts, even the truth, if those facts did not suit their preconceived prejudices. This was undoubtedly Maxwell's reaction when he heard that Insight was preparing a profile.

Hodgson, who initiated the idea in the paper, insists that their early inquiries were completely innocent and devoid of any ulterior motives. Hodgson, then thirty-five years old, had been educated at Winchester and Oxford, and had only recently returned to London from Washington where he had reported the 1968 Presidential elections. He had not particularly welcomed his assignment to Insight since he saw himself as a gentle, intellectual analyst rather than the merciless investigator. Yet his interest in Maxwell was not entirely a passing whim.

Millett had not confined his suspicions about ILSC encyclopaedia sales to Jones. Like all professions, the literary world thrives on gossip, and anything new about Maxwell, whose unpopularity repeatedly touched new peaks, was particularly welcome. It was not long before one of London's more eminent literary agents passed on the gossip to Hodgson. With Maxwell so regularly in the news and the contradiction of the socialist millionaire so evident, Hodgson sent out messages to *Sunday Times* correspondents and stringers throughout the world asking them to check the authenticity of Maxwell's claim about his sales of Chambers encyclopaedia during the world tour. By early June, a number of replies tended to support Millett's allegations and Hodgson tried to arrange an appointment with Maxwell. The approach was unsuccessful since Maxwell was immersed in the negotiations with Steinberg. But by coincidence, on 4 June, Maxwell announced his bid for the *Sun* newspaper, which included details of a 'survival plan' involving massive staff cuts and new methods to finance his proposed tabloid *Sun*. Since Fleet Street has always shown an inexhaustible fascination in its own affairs, Hodgson suggested to Bruce Page, the *Sunday Times* managing editor for features, that a profile of the would-be newspaper proprietor was timely. Page, an intelligent and committed investigator, shared Hodgson's enthusiasm. Their instinct seemed doubly rewarded when, two weeks later, on a Wednesday night, Rothschilds announced a press conference concerning Maxwell for the following day. Reporters were rapidly dispatched to collect information for a profile of Maxwell which would appear in that weekend's edition. Twenty-four hours later, Maxwell's aggrieved letters brought their plans to a sudden halt.

Maxwell's explanation in 1973 for his eccentric onslaught against the *Sunday Times* was: 'it seems to be a fashion of journalists in this country that if somebody gets to the top or tries to get there, then it is fair game to try to bring them down.' It is debatable whether Maxwell was 'on top' in June 1969 but indisputably it was the most critical moment in his career. The failure of all his bids in 1968 and his tactless political gaffes had generated a steady stream of abuse from many quarters, much of it unfair and defamatory but nevertheless provoked by what many viewed as irritating self-promotion. His bottomless reservoir of energy and self-confidence had apparently protected him from the wrath of his critics but, if caught unawares, he would concede that the vituperation in the City and in Westminster had exacted its toll. Selling Pergamon and buying the *Sun* offered to him a new and exciting opportunity which he would not allow his enemies to destroy. The *Sunday Times*, he feared, was their new vehicle.

But during the early afternoon of Friday 20 June, Maxwell had second thoughts about his tactics towards the newspaper. In the course of a telephone conversation, Evans reassured him there was not a Murdoch-inspired vendetta and accordingly Maxwell offered to come to the *Sunday Times* building to meet the Insight team for 'some straight talking'. 'They have worked on it', he told Evans, 'and it would only be fair for me to talk to them.'

The exchange which occurred in Evans's office that afternoon would have a profound effect on what became known as the Pergamon/Leasco affair. Both Page and Hodgson claim to have been severely shaken by Maxwell's written onslaught and consequently approached the occasion both indignant and unbenign. In what the two journalists reported as a 'rambling conversation', Maxwell described his conviction that Rupert Murdoch had inspired the *Sunday Times* and others to launch the attack. Indeed, he had sent a letter that day to Murdoch threatening a writ for defamation to prevent further publication of the 'vicious smear material which you caused to be manufactured during the battle for the *News of the World*'. Maxwell explained that he was selling Pergamon because he found it impossible to succeed in Britain.

Turning to Hodgson, Maxwell said, 'I've checked you out with David Astor [then proprietor of the *Observer*] and I'm surprised to discover that you're an honest man.' Hodgson was unimpressed. 'Mr Maxwell,' he retorted, 'you remind me of a chef in the restaurant where I once ate dinner. I tasted the mayonnaise served with my lobster and sent it back because I suspected it wasn't fresh and even possibly from a Heinz bottle. It had barely arrived in the kitchen before the chef rushed into the dining room screaming, "Who's accusing me of lying in here?" ' Maxwell had failed to allay Insight's suspicions and the journalists remained hostile.

Nevertheless, Maxwell agreed with Evans that he would co-operate in a profile. Not only did he genuinely feel that he had nothing to hide but he also probably believed that his very co-operation would enable him to control the journalists. In return, Evans guaranteed by letter that Maxwell would 'see' the text of the profile before publication and, while denied any powers of veto, they would 'discuss' any disagreements. It was a highly unusual concession for a newspaper and would inevitably hinder the *Sunday Times* time-table. On the other hand, Maxwell was a public figure who had suffered a series of wounding defamations and clearly feared that his critics would readily pour out their embittered distortions. Evans calculated that Maxwell's co-operation was worth the risk. On 24 June, Page and Hodgson arrived in Fitzroy Square for their first interview with Maxwell. 'The meeting began', recalls Hodgson, 'with Maxwell offering me a copy of the *Great Soviet Encyclopaedia* and ended with him threatening to hang me from the dome of St Paul's.'

ILSC dominated their discussion. The journalists wanted to know, first, how many sets of Chambers encyclopaedia Maxwell had sold during his world tour and, secondly, when ILSC's accounts would be published. After conceding that his claims for sales in India were possibly mistaken, Maxwell asserted that ILSC's accounts would be published 'at the end of the month'. Both Hodgson and Page knew from other sources the impossibility of meeting that target and pressed the politician to substantiate his optimism. Dismayed that his word was being challenged, Maxwell became agitated and shouted, 'I don't owe you a fucking thing.' The three men parted on a sour note. Hodgson felt particularly insulted: 'From the outset, Maxwell tried to dehumanise and treat me as an object to be bribed and cajoled. I resented it terribly.' The die was set for Insight to embark upon the newspaper's most expensive and time-consuming investigation.

Page and Hodgson were diligent researchers with huge resources at their disposal. Within four days they had obtained detailed and revealing statements from two key ILSC executives about the state of the business, with the reliable promise of more information in the future. Meanwhile, Maxwell again complained to Evans about the two journalists' 'very impertinent questions' and voiced his concern about an affidavit which had been sworn by a former employee of Chalmers Impey who alleged 'irregularities' in Pergamon's accounts. Insight, whose notebooks were being filled with innumerable allegations but few provable facts, began searching for reliable sources. Among their targets were the bankers, brokers, lawyers, government officials and businessmen who were deeply immersed in the Leasco bid.

The take-over process had already lurched into an unconventional pattern. Normally, Pergamon's shares would be purchased after all the investigations had been completed and the formal offer document issued. But on 20 June, just two days after the announcement of the bid, Rothschilds began buying Pergamon shares, on Leasco's orders, on the Stock Exchange. The reason for Steinberg's precipitate action before his accountants had even arrived in Oxford is disputed. Maxwell claims that the first he heard about the purchases was from Rothschilds. Steinberg claims that it was Maxwell who suggested the strategy during a phone call in which Maxwell reported the real possibility of a counter-bid for Pergamon. Leasco, Maxwell is alleged to have urged, should act with haste. In contrast, Steinberg insists, 'I didn't even realise shares could be bought on the open market before the formal offer had been published. It's not allowed in New York. It was Maxwell who encouraged me.' Maxwell vigorously denied that account. In the event, by 11 July, Rothschilds had bought just over 600,000 shares worth over £1 million in the name of nominees at an average price of just over 35s per share. Steinberg was pleased because the price was considerably less than their true worth as estimated by Fleming in New York just six weeks earlier, and it was also less than the bid price of 37s. The American was wholeheartedly committing Leasco to the takeover before he had satisfied himself about Pergamon's accounts.

The investigation of Pergamon's accounts was led by Jack Anderson of Leasco, Paul Thibodeaux of Touche Ross and two bankers from Rothschilds, Rodney Leach and Ivor Kennington. Together they intended to obtain an accurate description of Pergamon's activities and accounts. Full of optimism, Anderson had arrived in Britain on 27 June but Maxwell was too busy to meet him until six days later. Over the following forty-eight hours, Anderson says, 'I put a lot of questions but only got fuzzy answers and even blank copies of bank statements.' Maxwell seemed 'reluctant to divulge hard facts and figures' and when asked about Note 8 in the accounts he gave 'a twenty-minute dissertation in good clear English which I did not understand'. Then for the following two days Maxwell took Anderson on a tour of Pergamon's printing plants, well away from the documents the American wanted to see.

On 8 July, Anderson's patience expired. Puzzled and frustrated, he telephoned Schwartz in New York and revealed that Maxwell had shown him nothing 'in terms of real numbers' and was treating him in an unpleasant way. 'The delivery of information', recalled Steinberg, 'was sluggish. Maxwell was used to bullying people which our people didn't like.' Shortly afterwards, Schwartz telephoned Maxwell and urged him to co-operate. Although Maxwell agreed, Anderson had already decided that he was 'fed up' and would take a short holiday while Thibodeaux 'filled in the blanks'. Ostensibly, at the end of that afternoon in England, there was still no concern about the deal. A letter was sent to Bradford University proposing the establishment of a joint Leasco–Pergamon professorship, and Rothschilds dispatched a telex to New York confirming that Richard Fleming had sold Leasco 2.1 million Pergamon shares worth £3.8 million on behalf of his clients. Some would later criticise the deal as based upon insider information. By the end of that week, Leasco had accumulated a total of four million shares at a price of $17.5 million and had barely started its investigation.

At the end of the same day in New York, midnight in London, Rodney Leach, the Rothschilds banker, telephoned Schwartz. Leach, who had enjoyed a reputation as the cleverest undergraduate of his year in Oxford, had been visited during the day by his old college friend Godfrey Hodgson of the Insight team. The *Sunday Times* investigation had made very limited progress and needed some inside help. As a bait, Hodgson told Leach that they had unearthed a certain Kurt Wallersteiner who was trading in the South of France under the name Rothschild Trust. Leach was grateful for the tip. He was even more interested to hear the gossip about ILSC's finances and the controversial encyclopaedia sales in Australia. It was these rumours which Leach passed on to Schwartz.

In New York the following day, 9 July, Leach's cautionary report was discounted. The Leasco executives still placed great value on the official certification of Pergamon's accounts. Erroneously, they also believed that the same certification included ILSC's sales. By all accounts, everyone realised that the deal had hit some unusual problems but they were overridden by Steinberg's sense of personal commitment to Maxwell. He expected all the queries to be answered on his forthcoming visit to Britain.

Steinberg arrived on or around 10 July, and stayed with Maxwell in Oxford. It was a whirlwind visit during which Steinberg's doubts were repeatedly raised only to be quashed by the succession of glittering social occasions which Maxwell had arranged. Steinberg, the twenty-nine-year-old from Brooklyn, was introduced by his host to an unending procession of Britain's elite from Prime Minister Harold Wilson and other Cabinet ministers including Anthony Crosland and Tony Benn to Isiah Berlin, the Duke of Bedford and Lord Hartwell. Steinberg admitted that he was stunned: 'His scope of relations was incredible to me. I knew that the deal was important for Pergamon and Leasco, but it was amazing that everyone else thought it was so significant to the world.' Their business discussions were affected by the constant introductions: 'Whenever we had a doubt concerning his credibility, he would lay on these marvellous people and his credibility would be restored; and you would say to yourself, "Really, how could I have thought such a thing about this man?"'

Leasco's lawyer Robert Hodes was also persuaded, though not in quite the same way: 'We saw that the British Establishment were snobs and they thought Maxwell was a wog. We felt nothing against him because they condemned him as a noisy upstart – in fact we felt the opposite.'

Others in Leasco were not so easily swayed. Peter Stevens, who managed Leasco's international affairs from London, had told Maxwell just two days after the deal was announced that he was leaving because he did not have confidence in his proposed superior. 'Maxwell said to me,' remembers Stevens, '" Peter, this is a made-in-heaven situation for you. We'll work together tremendously well."' Stevens refused and cleared this desk, although he felt a grudging respect for Maxwell's achievements: 'He came from the wrong side of the track without anything and made it.' But, unknown to Maxwell, Stevens was also a Czech-born Jew who was cynical about his fellow countrymen. 'Czechs', he is fond of saying, 'can never find the easiest way to accomplish anything. They're unable to go in a straight line. The English Establishment never understood what was behind Maxwell's elegant front. He had to cut corners when he could have got to the same destination by the proper route.'

For the remainder of July, Steinberg's sense of affinity and self-confidence assuaged any doubts. Rothschilds had bought on his behalf a total of 5.2 million shares which represented 38 per cent of Pergamon. Leasco owned a 4 per cent bigger stake in Pergamon than Maxwell. But on 28 July, six weeks after the engagement was announced, the suitor felt major, irrepressible and bewildering pangs of doubt. In agonising slow motion, the process for divorce began even before the marriage was properly legalised.

The first source of qualms was a succession of unsolicited telephone calls from disgruntled former Pergamon employees to Rodney Leach at Rothschilds. The callers were only rarely specific, but all hinted that the bank might find 'something interesting' about the rapid turnover of staff in Pergamon's finance department. 'Rothschilds realised that there was something fishy,' says one of those involved, 'but no one could put their finger on what was wrong. All we knew was that we were still denied unimpeded access to Pergamon's files.' The telephone calls did, however, partly corroborate what Leach had heard from the Insight team. By mid-July, no less than six *Sunday Times* journalists in London were devoting their time exclusively to researching Maxwell's life. Their long conversations with Briggs, Wallersteiner, William Curtis (who had managed the Book Center in New York), Alan Back (of MSI Inc.), Hedley Le Bas and Philip Okill had provided them with a hitherto unimagined protrait of the socialist politician and would-be newspaper owner, albeit from Maxwell's arch-critics. Galvanising their interest was the breathtaking speed with which Maxwell seemed always to know whom they had spoken with; he would even anticipate their next call. Regularly, there were heated and acrimonious exchanges between Maxwell and the journalists. These conversations were taped.

Late on 19 July, for example, Maxwell had telephoned the home of John Fielding, who was in the delicate throes of persuading Wallersteiner to co-operate. In the course of a long attack on Fielding, Maxwell said, 'The impression you created in his [Wallersteiner's] mind was that if he did not co-operate to help you to destroy me, then you will destroy Wallersteiner.' Fielding's vigorous denials were eventually accepted by Maxwell but two days later a long letter from Kerman to Evans complained that the *Sunday Times* was still pursuing its 'shameful vendetta of slander and innuendo in search of a "story"'. Accompanying the letter was a writ for defamation, the first of many which would be exchanged between the protagonists.

Maxwell was worried. In the course of his career he had, not unusually, made many enemies and the *Sunday Times* seemed intent on seeking them out. Publicising their distorted versions would, he feared, cause irreparable damage. But while his unique blend of charm and bullying had in the past been a key ingredient to his success, his aggression was now counter-productive. However unjust it might be, there were those who found it difficult to believe that his aggressive protests were simply the cry of an innocent victim. Inevitably, accounts of his exceptional behaviour reached the bankers at Rothschilds.

Leach and his associate Ivor Kennington never revealed in their meetings with Maxwell their awareness of the *Sunday Times* research or of the denunciatory telephone calls, but by the third week of July they were convinced that Pergamon's accounts department and Pergamon's contracts with Maxwell's private companies were the key to the still indefinable mystery. Maxwell sensed their unease and asked the reason. When Leach revealed their concern, the businessman 'exploded'. Maxwell's familiar technique for handling hostile questions now came into play: the employment, first, of a charming, and distracting, story; hen anger; and then, if the questioner persisted for a third time, abrasiveness and sarcasm. He continually misinterpreted his questioners' pliant demeanour as proof of his powers of persuasion. It did not seem to occur to him that his own personality might be generating more suspicions and revealing his own vulnerability.

By the last week of July a new element was added. Leach was puzzled that there was apparently an unstoppable flow of Pergamon shares for sale. The very lynchpin of the 17 June agreement in New York, that Leasco would bid only after the investigation was completed, had been eroded. While maintaining his bland and friendly approach towards

Maxwell – even including a late-night game of chess which ended in disarray when both Maxwell's bishops were found to be on white squares – Leach asked for discreet inquiries to reveal who was actually selling the shares.

Schwartz in New York was also uneasy and on 28 July he decided to fly to London with Anderson. At their meeting with Maxwell the following day, Schwartz made a determined effort to persuade Pergamon's chairman to produce key documents: 'We were always very polite with him – it was a bit like a parlour game – but we told him that he would have to deliver the information about MSI Inc. and ILSC in the end. In particular, we wanted to see the contract between Pergamon and MSI Inc.'

Maxwell countered that he could not understand why the Americans were not satisfied: 'This has all been looked into by my accountants.' Schwartz replied, 'We won't put in a formal offer until we get all the facts.' Maxwell prevaricated and still refused to allow Anderson and Thibodeaux complete access to Pergamon's files. 'It was nearly the end of the line for us,' recalls a former Leasco executive. In New York, Steinberg acknowledged that something was seriously amiss but was as perplexed as everyone else about Maxwell's reluctance to give the accountants access.

On 1 August, Touche Ross sent Tom Clark a list of questions, with an ultimatum requiring an answer within four days. Five days later, the information had still not been delivered and Rothschilds had by then received an astonishing response from the Stock Exchange. Among the Pergamon shares which Rothschilds had bought were 197,000 which had been secretly sold by a Maxwell family trust. The sale had been discovered by Robert Jones of *The Times*, who had dreamed the previous night that he should check Pergamon's register. When he had telephoned Maxwell with his discoveries, the Pergamon chairman had denied all knowledge of the transaction.

By Saturday 9 August, Maxwell realised that Leasco's bid was seriously endangered. The *Financial Times* had reported that ILSC's profits would not be as high as forecast and City pundits were asking why the formal offer document was still not published. Equally worrying, Insight had spread its net throughout the world. Former encyclopaedia sales managers had been approached in the Far East and Australia and some had sworn lengthy affidavits or had recorded conversations with Maxwell at the instigation of journalists. Charles Berger had even been interviewed in New Zealand about the sale of paint to German railways. None of the material, however, produced more than a hint of wrongdoing. For Steinberg, Insight was even losing some of its credibility. 'They told us', he recalled, 'that Maxwell didn't win the MC. But then Maxwell showed us the photo.' Everyone's patience had been exhausted. In a long telephone call, Steinberg told Maxwell that he would call off the deal unless Thibodeaux and Anderson were allowed immediate access to the files in Oxford. Maxwell finally relented.

On 10 August, the following day, the two were finally admitted to the Headington Hall offices. Acting on Schwartz's instructions, they began sifting though files to trace the detailed relationship of the family companies with Pergamon. On each sale to MSI Inc., Anderson wanted to establish exactly when the stock was shipped and to follow the money trail back. Yet, strangely, the two investigators could find very few MSI Inc. orders and those few were for large amounts. Among the invoices was one in particular which struck Anderson as odd. It was for one hundred sets of the *Journal of Inorganic Nuclear Chemistry*, volumes one to twenty-nine, worth $133,000. Anderson wondered whether there were one hundred potential customers for that set in America. Anderson, who had been suspicious on arrival, concluded that it was 'arbitrary ordering, because they were the most expensive and the most unsaleable'. Thibodeaux had in the meantime discovered in another file twelve blanked-out MSI Inc. invoices. Neither he nor Anderson quite appreciated the implications. Nevertheless, three of the blanked-out invoices were discreetly pocketed to show Schwartz. By the end of the day, both understood that MSI Inc. owed Pergamon no less than £800,000 for Pergamon journals and books. This was a huge proportion of Pergamon's £2.1 million profits. They now wanted to see Pergamon's warehouse at Olney.

On Monday 11 August, the two accountants met Tadeusz Kamienski, the Polish warehouseman at Olney. Kamienski, who could barely speak English, showed the visitors Pergamon's valuable assets – the piles of old journals and books stacked on shelves. He had few records, yet it was not difficult to discover that, within the warehouse, no distinction was made in the ownership of the stock between Pergamon, MSI Inc. and Robert Maxwell & Co. Under one roof was the physical evidence of the complete intermingling of the assets of the public and private companies.

Perusing the available records, Anderson saw that Pergamon's major customers for back journals were the two private family companies, yet none of MSI Inc.'s recent orders had even been shipped to America. 'No one is buying the books at the other end,' Anderson realised. That night he reported back to Schwartz: 'Bernie, the situation is worse than we expected.'

Anderson's discoveries, however, were not bad enough to interfere with the big party held at Steinberg's home at Hewlett Bay Park two days later to celebrate the multi-millionaire's thirtieth birthday. Maxwell arrived with his wife and two daughters to enjoy what everyone agrees was 'an amazing and happy party'. If the two fiancés were contemplating estrangement, it was not evident. One memorable comment that the British businessman evoked was that he seemed uninterested in women – 'He just looked straight through them' – a noticeable contrast to his host, whose success with women was, among his friends, legendary.

That same night Jacob Rothschild and Leach arrived in New York. They did not go to the party but travelled direct to Leasco's offices in Manhattan. They had brought the proof that, despite Maxwell's assurances, ILSC's profits would probably be no more than one-tenth of the £500,000 which Maxwell had forecast just four weeks earlier. It had been agreed with Steinberg that, after the party, he would invite Maxwell to meet the bankers the following afternoon.

The meeting in Manhattan turned rapidly into a confrontation, but before he was allowed to return to London Maxwell agreed to a radical and major change in the 17 June agreement. Since the Pergamon profits were now in dispute, a complicated formula was introduced under which the price Leasco paid for Maxwell's shares would be reduced proportionately in accordance with the final independently audited profits. This latest term would be included in the new, fourteenth draft of the offer document. Maxwell agreed this orally and rushed to Kennedy airport to catch a plane for London. The following day, he telephoned Rothschild and cancelled his agreement.

But later the same day Maxwell did agree to see Kennington. Once again the Rothschilds banker pressed him for evidence of the Pergamon/MSI Inc. agreement. To the banker's relief, it was handed over. During that Friday night Kennington studied the contents and, as he said in a midnight phone call, 'It has closed the circle in my mind.'

Until that moment, Leasco's investigators had been searching, as is normal, for evidence that money was being syphoned out of Pergamon. Yet Kennington's search had revealed the exact opposite. The private companies were actually pumping money into Pergamon. But the money did not stay in the company. Kennington had also been handed a crucial document by a Pergamon employee which completely undermined Pergamon's audited 1968 accounts – a twenty-year agreement dated 30 August 1967 under which MSI Inc. had the right to return all the stock it had bought from Pergamon and demand repayment in full. Quite simply, more than one-third of Pergamon's profits could quite legally disappear.

At noon the following day, Saturday 16 August, Steinberg was sitting next to his pool at Hewlett Bay Park watching his children splashing in the water. 'I had the feeling that everything was right in the world. I was rich and my family was wonderful, when Robert, my valet, came with a vodka-martini and said George Bello, my finance director, was on the phone from London.' Steinberg put the handset to his ear, looking forward to a brief conversation.

'Saul,' said Bello, 'we've discovered a major problem ...'

Steinberg's memory of what followed is clear: 'I put Bello on hold, shouted for another vodka-martini, drank it in one, and screamed, "Whaaaat...?"' Steinberg made five phone calls in rapid succession. The first to Hodes, the second to Jacob Rothschild, the third to Maxwell and the fourth to the travel agent for an immediate flight to London. The fifth was to Richard Fleming, to vent his spleen, but the banker was unobtainable – he was grouse-shooting in the Scottish Highlands.

Maxwell's immediate reaction to the allegation of foul play made by Steinberg is not easy to discern. With the exception of the accusation made subsequently to newspapers and television interviewers that 'I was foolish to trust Mr Steinberg and check that he had enough money to complete the deal,' he has been resolutely unwilling to explain his behaviour both between 17 June and 16 August. It is possible that he was agreeable to Steinberg's suggestion on the fateful day that they manoeuvre a quiet separation. Steinberg explained that it was in both their interests – 'no noise, no loss of face, just let's slide out'. There were no secrets about Steinberg's motives. Once Wall Street realised that he had spent $18 million on a possible hype, his rating would nosedive and the price of Leasco shares would tumble. Steinberg was well acquainted with the financial world's caste system and feared ostracism if the highly publicised deal collapsed, revealing that he had made a mistake and perhaps provoking a public brawl. Even worse, he would be liable to a stockholders' suit for failing to exercise due diligence and causing the corporation financial losses. He wanted a cover-up and he had every reason to believe that Maxwell had agreed. But by the time Steinberg landed in London on Sunday morning, Maxwell's attitude had again changed. 'Under British rules,' he told the American, 'once a bid has been announced, it must be carried through.' Technically, he was correct, but Rothschilds had already embarked on an operation to unravel the deal.

Leasco's bid was subject to scrutiny by the Takeover Panel which, in the wake of the *News of the World* debacle, had again been radically changed. Not only were some of the more glaring loopholes sealed, but three months earlier Sir Humphrey Mynors had been demoted and replaced by men whose credentials, the Bank of England believed, would guarantee that the Panel was authoritative, impartial and respected. Its new director was Ian Fraser, who had been recruited from the merchant bank Warburgs. During the previous week, Fraser had heard that the proposed bid was in trouble but he was unaware of the details. He was therefore not completely surprised when Jacob Rothschild telephoned on Sunday morning, soon after Steinberg had landed, and asked for an urgent meeting. The venue that afternoon was Fraser's house in Putney. Present were the banker, Steinberg and Thibodeaux.

Fraser's task was to judge whether or not Leasco had good grounds for withdrawing its bid and how, in either case, the ordinary shareholders' interests could be protected. Fraser had long been acquainted with Maxwell. In 1947, he had been a Reuters correspondent in Berlin and had hazy memories of the boisterous Maxwell enjoying his rank in the officers' bar, surrounded by bizarre rumours about a deal concerning a German scientific publisher. Fraser also knew that Warburgs had declined an approach to act as Maxwell's banker. But his attitude was nearly balanced by an equal lack of sympathy towards Steinberg who, most City gentlemen agreed, was a brash young man in far too much of a hurry. So with fair distaste for both sides, Fraser could judge the case on its merits. On that Sunday, Rothschilds' case – that Pergamon had announced inflated profits for the past three years – seemed irrefutable. When Steinberg reached his hotel that night he called Fleming.

'We've discovered that Pergamon isn't worth what you told us,' said the American.

'How terrible,' replied the banker in a monotone voice.

'We think you owe it to us to buy back all the stock you sold us.'

'That's not possible,' said the banker, replacing the receiver.

Flemings' clients' funds had received £3.8 million for their Pergamon shares, which five days later would become unsaleable and effectively worthless.

Maxwell's predicament was no less awkward when he met Fraser the following day.

'You are accused', said Fraser, 'of inflating the profits.'

'It's outrageous that you accuse me of lying,' retorted Maxwell calmly, and he insisted that the deal should go through. That, of course, was just what Steinberg did not want, but having bought 38 per cent of Pergamon shares, insufficient for total control, he had become more anxious than ever to convince Maxwell that they should seek a private settlement.

The events and chronology of Monday 18 August are too blurred and contentious to permit accurate reconstruction. Leasco was certainly hoping to persuade the Panel to allow the bid to be withdrawn and there is evidence that Maxwell at one stage was also in favour, because late on the Monday afternoon Fleming drafted a press statement announcing the end of the bid. The draft was withdrawn when Maxwell suggested that they seek the help of someone in London who could be relied upon to act as a mutually trustworthy arbitrator – the solicitor Lord Goodman.

Harold Wilson introduced many unusual personalities into the mainstream of British political life during his terms of office and few of them seemed to wield as much influence as his personal lawyer Arnold Goodman. Not many observers outside or even inside Whitehall could understand why the Prime Minister should delegate negotiations with the white rebel regime in Rhodesia to the solicitor. The Leasco team would be similarly bemused when their request for his immediate mediation was rebuffed with the excuse, 'I'm just trying to settle the Ulster problem at the moment. Could we meet later tonight?'

So, just after midnight on 19 August, the two millionaires gathered at Lord Goodman's flat in Portland Place in central London. Poignantly, while Steinberg arrived with Leach and other Leasco executives, Maxwell was alone.

The Leasco team wanted to negotiate a price for Maxwell's shareholding which was dependent upon Pergamon's proven profits. If Maxwell agreed, then the trustees for the family trusts, who owned more than two million shares, would have to sign the agreement. But identifying who actually controlled the trusts was proving frustratingly difficult. When Ian Fraser had asked Maxwell about the sale of the 197,000 Pergamon shares sold by Bahamas Trustee & Executor, one of the family trusts, the businessman had pleaded that he had absolutely no control over the trusts. When a second tranche of 400,000 was sold by another family trust to the unsuspecting Rothschilds, Maxwell again insisted that he was powerless. But ten weeks earlier, on 30 May, when Schwartz had asked about the trusts, Maxwell had said, according to Schwartz, that he could negotiate on their behalf. Yet when the two sides gathered that night at Goodman's flat, Maxwell flatly insisted, 'I cannot speak on behalf of the trustees.' When asked whether they could not be brought to London, Maxwell replied that one was in the Middle East while another was in Majorca and did not have a telephone.

As dawn broke over the London skyline, Steinberg made a final offer and Maxwell suddenly accepted. Steinberg announced that he would hire a private plane to bring the trustees to London to consider the same offer. 'Oh that won't be necessary,' said Maxwell, pulling out some papers from his jacket pocket, 'they gave me signed proxies to negotiate on their behalf.' Everyone was silent until Goodman said, 'There you are. He's quite incorrigible.' Maxwell's last words to the Leasco team as he left would for long ring in their ears: 'I've done nothing wrong. We're all over twenty-one now.'

Throughout Tuesday and again on Wednesday morning, Jacob Rothschild and Richard Fleming continued to negotiate the sale of Maxwell's shares on the basis that the Pergamon accounts were grossly inaccurate. Rothschild was offering 18s 6d per share instead of 37s unless Pergamon's profits exceeded £2.27 million. Relations remained brittle until Wednesday midday, at which point they broke.

The rupture was caused by a draft letter which Maxwell had just sent to Rothschild for inclusion in the formal offer document. It stated that 'The internal management accounts show that ILSC is now trading profitably.' Ostensibly it was an important verification of Pergamon's profits. Rothschild decided to investigate the letter's provenance and discovered that Maxwell was basing it on a statement signed on 13 August by Chalmers Impey and Cooper Brothers which affirmed that ILSC would make a trading profit of just £40,000 at the end of the first eighteen months. But Maxwell had not revealed that, as Pergamon's chairman, he had signed three agreements the day before with ILSC, of which he was also chairman. The first was to buy some of ILSC's stock of outdated encyclopaedias for £200,000, the second was to buy some of ILSC's old debts for £114,895, and the third was to give ILSC £42,000 credit for services it had been charged for the use of the offices at Fitzroy Square. (The transactions only came to light some months later.) Certainly it was not illegal to move £356,895 from one company to another, but it was not what was usually understood by the phrase 'trading profitably'. This was the last straw for Steinberg.

On late Thursday afternoon, Jacob Rothschild issued a terse announcement that the Leasco bid was withdrawn, giving as the reason just the briefest reference to Pergamon's forecast earnings. It was an unprecedented situation involving such a public figure. Since it was August – the 'silly season', when there is normally a dearth of news – and the Labour government's status had fallen to a new low in unpopularity, the politician's crisis was sensational news.

The public's sympathy at first leaned towards Maxwell. While Steinberg, acting under strict orders, was unable even to explain that it was not a sudden decision, Maxwell and Richard Fleming issued a statement expressing 'regret' about the collapse, especially since only the previous Tuesday the two sides had met and had 'reached full agreement on all outstanding points'. The statement continued that Leasco's reasons for withdrawal 'had previously been discussed with full information available and the points were not at issue'. As he stepped out of his maroon Rolls-Royce in Fitzroy Square later that evening, Maxwell beamed at the television cameras. For the ordinary viewer, Maxwell was clearly the innocent victim of an unwelcome American predator. It was an untainted image, which Maxwell felt he deserved.

Among Maxwell's key defences during the ensuing probes into his business activities has been his insistence that he had always relied upon his professional advisers and that they had always endorsed his conduct. A meeting held at Flemings on Friday 22 August, the day after Leasco's public withdrawal, exemplified his justification. Among those gathered to discuss the state of ILSC were representatives of BPC, Hill Samuel, Chalmers Impey, Cooper Brothers and Whinney Murray and Maxwell's solicitor, Isidore Kerman. All of those in Flemings' conference room would have wished to be acknowledged as reputable and skilled professionals. At the end of the meeting, they unanimously agreed to a statement, to be circulated to all Pergamon shareholders the following day, which declared that 'The management accounts of ILSC show that it is now trading profitably.' The amount specified was just £40,000. There was no mention of their previous forecasts (the most recent had been four weeks earlier) that ILSC would earn 'pre-tax profits of £500,000 per annum' or of Pergamon's recent purchases from ILSC worth £356,895. Many of those present would later claim that they left that meeting with qualms; but that was only in retrospect, once the accounts were proven to be in shambles.

On Friday morning, in the wake of Rothschild's announcement, dealings in Pergamon shares were suspended. Maxwell, Briggs and David Pearson of Flemings were interviewed on the same day by Ian Fraser. The Panel's director left his audience in no doubt where his sympathies lay. In his view, the 1968 accounts were inaccurate. Maxwell was outraged and excited, claiming that Fraser was raising 'unjust and unfair allegations'. As Pearson attempted to soothe his client, Fraser went through Leasco's allegations until he reached Pergamon's sales to

MSI Inc. 'That's a reputable company,' said Maxwell. 'Who is the owner?' asked Fraser. 'A trust,' replied Maxwell. 'Who is the beneficiary of the trust?' 'I don't know.' 'I can tell you,' interjected Fraser, 'your sister.' Both Briggs and Pearson claimed to have been surprised by the revelation. What probably shocked them more was the realisation that their conduct was being questioned by their peers. The following day, Fraser announced that he was prepared to allow Leasco to withdraw its bid; Maxwell immediately appealed.

During that Saturday, Maxwell gave several interviews. There was nothing wrong with Pergamon, he insisted. The bid had collapsed, he said, 'because Leasco did not have the cash to complete the deal'. Both the *Sunday Times* and the *Sunday Telegraph* were assured by Maxwell personally that 'I and my financial advisers are completely at a loss to understand why Leasco acted the way it did.' When Richard Fleming read the newspapers on Sunday morning he instantly resigned as Maxwell's adviser, claiming that the statement had been made 'without [my] knowledge or consent'. Both Fleming and Rothschild disputed Maxwell's claim that Leasco lacked the funds. Nevertheless, Maxwell perpetuates that claim to his day. For it would be his style in the months ahead solemnly to issue statements which he no doubt believed to be true but which the others involved condemned as wholly incorrect. Such a statement was Maxwell's explanation that Richard Fleming had resigned to avoid involvement in the legal proceedings which he, Maxwell, was threatening to launch against Leasco. Maxwell's bravado was impressive. 'I shall ask the Panel,' he told BBC radio news at Sunday lunchtime, 'to investigate the real reasons as to why Leasco was unable go to through with the offer.'

But even if the press that day reported Maxwell's comments in full, there was unanimity that his commercial fortunes were waning by the hour, possibly beyond the point of recovery. In fact, quoting his comments verbatim confirmed the gravity of his plight. He had been too arrogant in the past for most commentators not to reflect the prevailing sentiment in both the City and Parliament that Britain was witnessing his approach to the first station on the Via Dolorosa. Naturally, drawing on the information collected over the previous two months, the *Sunday Times* published the best analysis about the real cause of the collapse – ILSC and MSI Inc.

Maxwell was convinced that the newspaper and Rothschilds were conspiring to hasten his crucifixion. In a public statement, he attacked the 'highly inaccurate and grossly defamatory article' which among many mistakes wrongly suggested that 'Leasco and its advisers were

[not] freely given all information required on ILSC, MSI Inc. and Robert Maxwell & Co.' His comments were sufficient for his brokers Panmure Gordon also to resign and even Chalmers Impey sent a long letter containing twenty-five questions and qualifications to their previous statement on Pergamon's accounts. Within two days, Maxwell found himself practically alone, firmly on the outside as he faced the first of the series of bruising investigations into his business conduct.

At 11 a.m. on Monday morning he arrived at the Bank of England's office in New Change, near St Paul's Cathedral, to attend a meeting of the full Takeover Panel, which had to adjudicate on whether Leasco was entitled to withdraw the bid. Presiding over the ten panelists (all of them heads of City institutions) was Lord Shawcross, who had hurriedly returned during the weekend from his summer holiday in Yugoslavia. The former Labour Attorney-General enjoyed a reputation as one of Britain's most skilled courtroom interrogators who, with a minimum of words, could demolish the most reluctant witnesses. His appointment as chairman of the Panel in the wake of the *News of the World* bid was interpreted as the City's last chance to prove that it was able to regulate itself. The Pergamon bid was the new Panel's first major opportunity to prove its mettle – 'to show we weren't going to pull our punches' – and it would not be an exaggeration to suggest that the City especially relished the prospect because of the subject himself.

Shawcross's ostensible style was to introduce a measure of informality into the proceedings. When Maxwell suggested that he wanted to be represented by John Silkin, his fellow Labour MP and friend, Shawcross looked through his half-moon glasses and said gently, 'Come, Mr Maxwell, you are perfectly eloquent to argue your own case.' The first day was to be gentle. While the Leasco team waited in an adjoining room, Fraser put the case for the prosecution, displaying, it was noted by some, great confidence. Maxwell followed, speaking without notes and at great length. 'I know nothing about accountancy and relied entirely upon Chalmers Impey,' he pleaded, and everyone noticed that Briggs was absent, uncontactable on a fishing holiday in Scotland. Then, while Maxwell waited, Shawcross heard the Leasco case. 'At that stage it was felt that the Americans had gone into it with their eyes wide open,' recalls a panelist. 'As far as we were concerned, both sides were mavericks who deserved each other. Later it became a joke that, for the first time in his life, Steinberg was the "good guy".'

It was on the second day that Shawcross applied the pressure. Probing and reasonable, but never aggressive, the lawyer cut through Maxwell's defence, forcing him first to admit that Leasco was not short of funds and then to concede that Leasco had not intended to depress the price of Pergamon shares to buy the company at a discount. 'Everyone was impressed how Shawcross just pulled Maxwell's contradictions apart,' remarked Ian Fraser at the time. Others were critical. 'He was too aloof. You don't get the best out of professionals by treating them like Hermann Goering at Nuremberg.' Nevertheless, by the end of the second day Shawcross's rapier questioning had exposed the questionable profits of the Spanish translation rights, the MSI sales and the ILSC profit forecasts. The ground was cleared, while the Panel adjourned, for some hard negotiations between Maxwell and Leasco.

Jacob Rothschild had been severely mauled by Shawcross and, although some believed that it was just for 'form', Rothschild himself realised that the affair had not embellished his bank's reputation despite his initial cautionary advice to Steinberg. Whatever the Panel's decision, it was in the interests of Pergamon, in which Steinberg had invested £9 million, that a settlement should be reached. Late on Tuesday night, Leach had secretly asked Michael Richardson, Maxwell's friend and broker at Panmure Gordon, to act as an intermediary and persuade Maxwell of the advantages of urgent talks about a settlement. Richardson, who has always been faithful to Maxwell's interests, succeeded.

At Wednesday lunchtime, Maxwell, Kerman, Leach, Hodes and Fraser sat down for lunch at Rothschilds' headquarters to hammer out an agreement. By the end, Hodes believed that he had successfully extracted from Maxwell his near-complete surrender in a seven-point plan. Maxwell agreed that five Leasco nominees and two directors nominated by Rothschild would sit on Pergamon's board; that he would relinquish his own proposed position in Leasco and, while remaining chairman, would cease to be the managing director of Pergamon; and that, when Leasco's bid was relaunched, the amount paid for the outstanding shares would be proportional to the true profits, which would be determined by independent accountants. Maxwell's only victory was that his family trusts would keep the proceeds of the sale of their shares – effectively over £1 million. Those funds would be a vital ingredient in his eventual recovery.

On Thursday, the Panel reconvened. The first business was the previous day's agreement, which deprived Maxwell of any control over Pergamon. Shawcross approved the deal. Hodes asked that the agreement be properly signed and witnessed. Shawcross gave him an icy stare and in a most judicial voice replied, 'The City, Mr Hodes, operates on trust.' Hodes had no chance to protest that it was precisely the collapse of that trust which had brought them all together. Shawcross had started to deliver the Panel's verdict, which according to Fraser was 'expressed in the most memorable, beautiful English': 'The Panel is satisfied that Leasco's decision to withdraw from the proposed offer was the result . . . of a series of difficulties and doubts which eventually destroyed their confidence. . . . In all the circumstances, the Panel accepts Leasco's explanation for its withdrawal from the proposed offer.' Couched in the most prudent form, Shawcross then listed the Panel's concern about ILSC and Pergamon's failure to disclose the trading links with the family companies.

When Maxwell and Silkin read the proposed statement, they became alarmed and urged its modification. Officially and unofficially, the Panel was concerned only with the takeover and it had never been suggested that there would be any mention about the internal affairs of Pergamon. Maxwell felt that he had not been given a proper opportunity to defend himself. The Panel's bias, he argued, was plain. Their statement was exclusively about Maxwell. There was no mention of Flemings, Chalmers Impey, Whinney Murray or Cooper Brothers, upon whom he had expressly relied. Even Flemings' hugely profitable sale of Pergamon shares was only referred to as requiring the Panel 'to contemplate studying the general principles which should apply in circumstances where possible conflicts of interest may be . . .'. But, worst of all, the Panel called for a full Board of Trade inquiry. This was totally unprecedented as regards a profitable company. Maxwell demanded that Shawcross modify his statement.

Once again, Maxwell saw that the City would protect its own kind and damn the foreigner. It was the second station on the Via Dolorosa. But he had no intention of either playing the game or keeping a stiff upper lip. He demanded changes and then additions. As the night developed, everyone became hungry and thirsty. The only source of drinks was a vending machine and, appropriately, only the Rothschilds had the correct coins. Just three packets of biscuits were divided between twenty-nine men. By 2 a.m. Maxwell had secured the inclusion of an important caveat which would both precede and follow the criticism: 'Nothing in the information before it casts doubt on the standing or future prospects of Pergamon, a company which under the energetic leadership of Mr Maxwell has made notable progress. Nor is there any suggestion at all of personal misconduct on Mr Maxwell's part.' But Maxwell could not prevent the Panel recommending a full Board of Trade inquiry. His only course was for an appeal on the grounds that the Panel had gone beyond its terms of reference.

The public reaction to the report satisfied the Panel. 'There can be no possible doubt that we now have a watchdog with teeth,' commented *The Times* under the headline 'Discipline Arrives in the Takeover World'. Publicly, Maxwell did not dissent from the overwhelming praise. 'A much better Panel than before,' he declared on BBC television that night and pledged full co-operation with the Board of Trade inquiry. There was no suggestion from his side that he had been censured after four days inside a Star Chamber, that he had been abandoned by his advisers or that he would lose control of Pergamon. Instead, he acted as the champion. He naturally endorsed *The Times* editorial: 'It has to be said that Mr Maxwell has shown himself to be a man of quite remarkable energy and initiative and has conducted himself with courage throughout the proceedings.'

The following day Maxwell posed, smiling, outside Rothschilds bank, shaking Steinberg's hand. The American had flown overnight from New York to approve the details which would incorporate Pergamon within Leasco, without Maxwell.

CHAPTER 9

Steinberg's takeover of Pergamon was timed for Tuesday 2 September. At 9.35 a.m., two Leasco executives arrived at Fitzroy Square. Peter Stevens had been designated managing director and George Bello finance director. Neither was enthusiastic about his task. Stevens had always been critical of the venture and had since become depressed by the particularly widespread *Schadenfreude* which the row had sparked in London. Too many had sniggered, 'Let the two Jews fight it out.' The Czech-born American had no illusions that managing Pergamon with Maxwell as chairman would be easy, but the heads of agreement as approved by Shawcross and the Panel seemed cast-iron.

As the Americans walked into the building, they were told that the Pergamon directors were meeting in the board room. Stevens asked for an office to make a brief telephone call. While he was speaking, Jean Baddeley told him that Maxwell was waiting. Stevens intimated that he would just finish his call. Two minutes later another telephone on the desk rang. 'If you don't come immediately,' snapped an unmistakable voice, 'you can pack up and go home.'

Stevens and Bello rushed into the board room. 'He was furious,' recalls Stevens, 'almost incoherent, stabbing at that day's copy of *The Times*, which had my photograph and a caption describing me as the new managing director. He said that there was too much publicity, too many new directors and too many leaks to the press. It took me some time to calm him down.'

Stevens suggested that Maxwell might introduce him to the directors. When this had been done, Stevens asked everyone to submit by the end of the morning a description 'on one side of paper' of their duties and the relevant financial data in the individual departments. As he spoke, Maxwell became noticeably agitated: 'We're not having all this stuff. It's too early. Your appointment hasn't been made official yet.' Stevens had expected some tension and possibly some aggravation, but no one had anticipated what Maxwell said next: 'You know, Peter, there's no agreement in writing about your appointment and no special board meeting is planned, so I suggest that both you and George return on the next flight to New York.' After a brief pause, there was a roar: 'Get out!' Startled, George Bello looked at Stevens as, sweeping some papers into his briefcase, the former declared, 'I've got four kids and I'm leaving.'

Just before noon, the Americans were back in Knightsbridge reporting the latest twist in the saga to bankers, lawyers and Leasco executives on both sides of the Atlantic. By mid-afternoon, many highly paid and supposedly shrewd professionals were exasperated. Once more, they had been smartly outwitted. The 'seven heads of agreement' which had been negotiated at Rothschilds six days earlier, and then approved by the Panel, had not, because of Shawcross's insistence that in the City it was customary to abide by oral undertakings, been formally recorded and signed.

Everyone knew, of course, that the cliché 'My word is my bond' was a sanctimonious bromide contrived for public relations. The Panel's recent history was littered with examples of broken promises and avoidance of the rules which had passed unpunished, and none more so than during the battle for the *News of the World*. Twelve months earlier, the City herd had not been overly troubled by the anguish which the outsider had suffered yet they still expected him to obey their club rules. But since the children of peasants do not become multi-millionaires unless they challenge those rules, it was not surprising that Maxwell saw no advantage in meekly complying.

In Maxwell's view, the City and Leasco were either intentionally or by default destroying his company. The so-called 'well-informed' stories over the weekend in the *Sunday Times* and *The Times* were undermining both his own and Pergamon's credibility. He blamed the Leasco side for inspiring speculation that Pergamon's bank overdraft had risen from £1.9 million to £4 million while he knew that it had actually been reduced. Pergamon was his business and only he understood scientific journals. Respectable City institutions had endorsed all his accounts but they, protected by their own kind, had seemingly escaped blame. Yet he was expected to lose everything without a murmur. For Maxwell that was unacceptable. He would not be taken to the next station on the Via Dolorosa without a fight. His counter-attack started with a detailed letter to *The Times* which ignored the Rothschilds agreement and raised a raft of new and complicated demands. He had left the corner and was back in the centre of the ring.

Subconsciously, Rodney Leach had anticipated that Maxwell would not go quietly. During the Panel's last, late-night session, he had thrust a letter of resignation drafted by a Rothschilds lawyer in front of Maxwell for signature, but it was deemed to be legally valueless. Soon after Stevens had telephoned him and reported his ejection from Fitzroy Square, Leach had appealed to Fraser, requesting that the 'unconditional' agreement should be implemented. Fraser was naturally sympathetic but urged patience while Shawcross was again recalled from his holiday. Fraser also telephoned Maxwell.

Brazenly, Maxwell disputed Leach's and Fraser's interpretation of the agreement and insisted that Shawcross would support his version. The impasse was complete and he might have waited. Instead, a few days later, he issued a hazardous challenge. In a press release, he announced that because 'Leasco and Pergamon cannot work together', and because the Pergamon directors would not surrender the company's management until Leasco had secured a majority of the shares, he was calling an extraordinary general meeting (EGM) of all shareholders on 9 October to decide whether Leasco was entitled to sole management. Maxwell the gambler had pushed aside the businessman and bargain-hunter. The player had committed his future to be determined at a public meeting.

After the sales by his family trusts, Maxwell controlled only 28 per cent of the shares against Steinberg's 38 per cent. His future depended upon the City institutions, who held 17 per cent of the stock. For Maxwell to have expected their support was to take an uneven risk. Regardless of the flattering newspaper comments in the previous week, the City was abuzz with rumours and defamatory allegations which made those circulating in the past seem tame by comparison. But Maxwell, who was always genuinely surprised that others did not share his high self-esteem, had spoken to the fund managers and calculated that he could count on their support because they agreed that, without him, Pergamon would collapse. There was also another motive. By then, one of the reasons for selling Pergamon had disappeared and his major ambition had again been thwarted.

Soon after he had expelled the Americans from Fitzroy Square, SOGAT had announced its 'loss of confidence in Mr Maxwell' as a possible proprietor of the *Sun*. Preoccupied by the fight to save Pergamon and deprived of the anticipated finance from the sale of his shares, Maxwell unemotionally conceded victory to Rupert Murdoch for the second time within twelve months. Thrice he had played by the rules and had pledged to support a Labour newspaper and each time he had failed. Maxwell did not ponder for long about the paradox that Murdoch without any social status in Britain could succeed while he, a Member of Parliament with a fine wartime record, should constantly fall flat on his face. His explanation was simply that he was the victim of the Establishment's prejudice. His own style was not a factor worth contemplating. This time, Fleet Street wrote off his ambitions forever. 'This is obviously the end of Mr Maxwell's dream of being the proprietor of a national newspaper,' pronounced Hugh Cudlipp, the chairman of IPC, which owned the *Sun*. Many now predicted the same fate in the world of business.

Leasco placed a great deal of faith in Shawcross and in the City's much vaunted self-regulation to enforce the agreement made on 28 August. Steinberg and Hodes flew from New York to be present when Shawcross returned from Yugoslavia. Maxwell had consented, in the event of any disagreements, to be bound by any new ruling which Shawcross might make. Maxwell was summoned to attend on 9 September at the Panel's office to explain why he had not relinquished management control.

Accompanied by his new merchant bankers William Brandt, Maxwell told Shawcross that the lawyers' interpretation of the agreement was 'wrong' and later denied that he had ever agreed to abide by any further rulings. His icy, impenetrable sense of righteousness disconcerted Shawcross but endowed Maxwell with increased courage. The next to arrive in Shawcross's room was Hodes, who asked what decisive remedy the Panel now proposed. He was answered by a deafening silence. Maxwell had not obeyed the ritual and had paralysed his accusers. Despite his status, Shawcross was powerless and even humiliated.

Outside in the City streets Hodes and Steinberg assessed Leasco's dilemma. In New York, the Securities and Exchange Commission would have wiped Maxwell off the floor. But in London, while the City patricians smugly pretended that their behaviour was impeccable, they condoned any malpractice so long as it was invisible; and when it burst out, they ignored their impotence. They were standing in the middle of a market which was nourished on a cracked ethic and managed, in Leasco's view, by amateurs who were not equipped with the technical expertise to understand a balance sheet. They heaped the blame upon Maxwell to protect themselves. There was no alternative but to remain and fight to recover their $18 million. 'We shall gain control of Pergamon whatever happens,' said Steinberg before flying back to New York.

Steinberg left a disaster and returned to an earthquake. Since the debacle, the price of Leasco shares had collapsed from $33 to $10 and there was serious unrest among his staff, who were uncertain about his company's very survival. His stake in Pergamon was also in doubt. If he

(Above) Maxwell as Private Du Maurier (back row, right), the keen footballer, with the Sixth Battalion of the North Staffs Regiment in Cliftonville in 1944.

(Left) Second Lieutenant Maxwell receiving the Military Cross from General Montgomery in March 1945.

(Below) Maxwell as an officer with the 1/5th Battalion of the Queen's Royal Regiment (West Surrey) before the crossing of the Rhine in late March 1945. Maxwell is in the back row, eighth from the left.

(Left) Maxwell and his wife Elizabeth in London in 1947.

(Below left) Maxwell with his eldest daughter Anne. There were nine children in the Maxwell family.

(Below right) Peter Orton, Maxwell's partner at Lange, Maxwell & Springer, was an intellectual who did not always appreciate Maxwell's style of business.

(Left) Maxwell with Tönjes Lange, the Springer executive who taught him about the profitability of publishing scientific journals. Maxwell called him 'Onkel'.

(Below left) Gunther Heyden, recruited to LMS in Berlin, sitting on Maxwell's first Cadillac, in London in 1950. Ownership of foreign cars for British subjects was forbidden, so the car was not registered in Maxwell's name.

(Below right) Kurt Wallersteiner, Maxwell's partner in the hectic barter trade, an investor in Simpkin Marshall and later a convicted fraudster.

(Above left) Ambitious to become Britain's prime minister, Maxwell valued his friendship with Hugh Gaitskell; but his closeness to Labour leaders failed to win him the high office he felt he deserved.

(Above right) Maxwell's energetic election campaigns won him decisive votes in a marginal constituency, but by 1974 his style alienated some of his supporters and denied him the crucial support needed to win back his seat.

(Below) In 1968, Maxwell was prepared to give up politics to own the News of the World, but his bid was defeated by an alliance between Sir William 'Pissing Billy' Carr, the newspaper's owner, and the then unknown Rupert Murdoch. Afterwards, Maxwell was convinced that the Establishment would deny him the success he sought.

(Right) On 18 June 1969, Maxwell announced the sale of Pergamon to the American, Saul Steinberg, who described their agreement as 'perfect'.

(Below) At the press conference on 18 June, Maxwell's banker Richard Fleming was less enthusiastic than his client, whom he had privately informed that he wanted to sever their relationship because he was dissatisfied with Pergamon's accounts.

(Bottom) On 15 August 1969, Steinberg's banker, Jacob Rothschild, announced that the American would not buy Pergamon. It took Maxwell more than a decade to recover from the scandal and investigations which followed.

Mr Robert Maxwell

(Below) The first investigation
was conducted by Lord
Shawcross, the chairman of the
Takeover Panel. While some
praised Shawcross's ability to
destroy Maxwell's explanations,
Maxwell complained that he had
been unfairly victimised.

(Above) Even at the shareholders' meeting, on
11 October 1969, when he was deposed from the
board of Pergamon, Maxwell's bitterness was
interrupted by some good humour.

(Above) After more than a decade in the
wilderness, Maxwell astonished his critics
when in April 1981 he bought the British
Printing Corporation and, with the support of
Lord Kearton, saved the company from
bankruptcy and earned himself new
respectability in the City.

(Right) His most important ally in the
resurrection was Sir Robert Clark, of the
merchant bank Hill Samuel.

At 7pm on 13 July 1984, Leslie Carpenter *(above left)* and Sir Alex Jarratt *(above right)* of Reed International reluctantly agreed to sell Maxwell the Mirror Group of newspapers, transferring Northcliffe's former empire to the son of a Czech peasant.

(Above) Clive Thornton, the chairman of the Mirror Group, arrived at 7am on 14 July in his office. 'I couldn't miss Mr Maxwell,' he told reporters later, 'because he was sitting behind my desk.'

(*Above*) Maxwell's long cherished dream was to own a London evening newspaper — which was finally launched in February 1987. Just as the headline 'Labour victory' was a disastrous prediction (the SDP candidate won), so too the newspaper failed, after a series of commercial mistakes.

(*Below left*) Maxwell, a keen footballer during the War, has ever since wanted to own a club. By 1988, his family owned interests in three clubs, but he was deeply disapproving of the game's management.

(*Above*) Throughout his turbulent career, Max has usually ignored his critics and just enjoyed life.

completely eliminated any connection with Maxwell, the publisher might set up a competitive business or interfere with customers. He could cause unlimited damage especially if there were more unknown agreements with the family companies. Steinberg was frankly incredulous about the mistakes he had made. The only glimmer of hope was the announcement that Anthony Crosland had appointed a Board of Trade inquiry into Pergamon. The two inspectors, Owen Stable QC and Sir Ronald Leach, an accountant, were expected to deliver an interim report within three months. Their activities might persuade the City institutions to favour Leasco's bid.

For Maxwell, Crosland's decision was calamitous. Despite welcoming the announcement in public, he had lobbied his fellow politicians intensively to support him against the appointment of an inquiry, pleading that he was the victim of a vendetta. But pressure from the City, especially from Shawcross, and the oblique references to Simpkin Marshall, compelled Crosland to approve the investigation. When Maxwell heard that he had lost, he told David Pearson of Fleming that he would fight 'tooth and nail'.

Perhaps it was the realisation that, unlike so many other setbacks, this one could not be lightly shrugged off that caused the first crack in Maxwell's hitherto resolute image. The occasion was his appeal against the Panel's decision. Hearing his case was a senior judge, Lord Pearce, who sat with three representatives of the City. The grounds of the appeal were restricted to procedure; the facts could not be re-argued. Maxwell claimed that he had been denied natural justice at the original hearing because Shawcross, without notice, had considered and commented on Pergamon's internal affairs, which were beyond the issue of the bid. Paying no heed to the restrictions of the appeal, Maxwell began to re-argue his case. Pearce continuously interrupted. Eventually, when Maxwell still persisted, Pearce said firmly, 'I really can't understand your defence, Mr Maxwell.'

Large tears began to roll down Maxwell's cheeks; he blew his nose several times and in a cracking voice said, 'I was born poor in a tiny village in a part of eastern Czechoslovakia which you have never heard of —' Pearce interrupted, 'Oh yes I do, Mr Maxwell. It's called "Klein Russland". I travelled there before the war.' Maxwell continued, 'All my family was lost in concentration camps. I fled the Nazis and joined and fought with the British army because I believed in Britain's justice and law and fair play, but I am now being denied it. . . .' Pearce was moved but unsympathetic to his plea. The appeal was rejected on 18 September.

There were no lingering doubts that Maxwell was fighting for his very survival. The next arena was the EGM on Friday 10 October (it had been postponed by one day). Except for a brief lull when he disappeared on a brief trip to America, Maxwell maintained a barrage of publicity to secure the institutions' support, arguing that Pergamon's past success was synonymous with his personal management and that, until Leasco made an outright bid, it should be denied 'ownership on the cheap'. His only concession was that Leasco would be allowed to nominate three directors. During the early days, he was reasonably sure of success, especially after Norman Freeman, the manager of the ICI pension fund, intimated that he might offer his full support.

Steinberg, in contrast, had never enjoyed much support in the City and few believed that the unknown American could successfully manage a specialised publishing company based in Oxford. After Maxwell's refusal to implement the Rothschilds agreement, Steinberg had insisted on his complete removal. The Leasco package which was to be put to the shareholders would be to elect a new board of directors comprising independents and Leasco executives under an independent chairman. It was not an attractive package for the City fund managers who had lost money and disliked any interference with their quiet life. Leasco's refusal to bid for the remaining shares until the completion of an independent audit was considered to be irksome and its detailed explanations were too difficult to read and understand.

During the days before the EGM, the national newspapers, radio and television overflowed with pronouncements by commentators. None would have a more profound effect than the first part of the *Sunday Times*'s 'intimate profile' published four days before the EGM, analysing the 'astonishing businessman' whose record 'shows an uncanny capacity for rising from the ashes'. Maxwell fought hard to prevent the article appearing.

Harold Evans had promised Maxwell in June that he could read and comment on the profile before publication. The draft of part one had been delivered at the end of August. Maxwell was appalled, since it confirmed his original fears that the *Sunday Times*, having interviewed disgruntled ex-employees, was going so far as to suggest that he was not an honest businessman. The journalists had been unwilling to accept his word and were, he believed, unenlightened about normal practices in the world of commerce. Evans believed that both he and his staff were trying to be fair while Maxwell was, to say the least, being disingenuous. On 11 September, Evans wrote to Maxwell regarding a series of 'corrections' the publisher had provided about the Book Center in New York, the 'special exchange rate' in post-war Germany and Simpkin Marshall. After exhaustively re-researching their facts, Evans wrote, none of Maxwell's 'corrections' had been substantiated: 'I am certainly still very willing to consider carefully any comments you make, but on this experience I am also somewhat discouraged from taking assertions as fact.' Maxwell's reply was the delivery of a writ, the second since June, seeking to prohibit publication. The tension increased.

Maxwell had heard that denunciatory affidavits from many of his enemies had been obtained by the *Sunday Times*. Documents which they supplied had been forensically tested, and they were deliberately telephoning him to tape conversations. Frantically, he cross-checked from country to country to unearth what was being said. In one instance, he heard that Paul Hövel of Springer had been tracked down to his holiday hotel in the Black Forest by the intrepid Anthony Terry in the hope that he would reveal some skullduggery about Maxwell's original 1947 deal. Hövel insisted that their agreement had been perfectly legal but Maxwell was convinced that the German had said the contrary. Yet remarkably, amid all the chasing and the checking, Page and Hodgson still visited Maxwell at Fitzroy Square to obtain material for the profile, albeit in fraught circumstances, while Maxwell and Evans regularly discussed their content on the telephone – on one occasion, nine times in a single day. 'It was an exhausting psychological battle,' recalls Hodgson.

On 1 October, after Maxwell had read a newly revised version of the profile, he issued a fourth writ against the *Sunday Times* for defamation and, late at night, telephoned Evans at home. 'This is worse, much worse than the first [draft],' he complained. 'Let's meet.' They met, but Evans insisted on publication, despite the objections, on 5 October.

The profile began by stressing 'the boldness of his courage and the poverty of his beginnings' and traced the foundations of Maxwell's fortunes as a turbulent and controversial entrepreneur whose business ethics were questionable. Few subjects on the eve of a fateful public meeting would have enjoyed a profile which, after mentioning the award of the Military Cross, concluded, 'The boy from Slatinske Doly had definitely arrived,' or, concerning his optimism about his recovery after the Simpkins crash, alluded to his nickname as 'the bouncing Czech'. But for once Maxwell was practically defenceless, and the topicality guaranteed a very wide readership. His only riposte was a long circular sent to all Pergamon shareholders denouncing the paper's allegations and its violation of Evans's original undertaking. Later he condemned the *Sunday Times* journalists to their face as 'the forces of evil'.

The opposition to Maxwell, undoubtedly influenced by the article, solidified over that last weekend. The institutions, on the advice of their newly appointed merchant bankers, Schroeder Wagg, decided unanimously on Maxwell's removal. Maxwell tried, on Tuesday 7 October, to win a reprieve during a heated meeting with Schroeders' representatives. But he failed, and news began to trickle out during the next day of an unforeseen twist in his tactics.

Small batches of Pergamon shares were being issued to over one hundred Pergamon employees, which would enable them to attend and vote at the EGM. Leasco's lawyers scrambled to scrutinise Pergamon's rules and saw that on a mere show of hands Maxwell would have sufficient support to adjourn the meeting, delay his removal and remain in control of the company. Suspecting the worst, Leasco attempted to transfer some of its shares to one hundred supporters but, late in the afternoon on 9 October, their request was refused by the company secretary.

The only solution, said Peter Curry, Leasco's lawyer in England, was an injunction from the High Court to prevent Maxwell adjourning the meeting. Three Rolls-Royces filled with bankers, lawyers and their clients from New York roared from the City towards the Strand. Impatiently they waited outside a courtroom for a judge to become available. At five o'clock, as the building closed, they were told that they had come to the wrong court. The bankers and the businessmen were struck with horror. 'Don't worry,' said Curry, 'I know a judge who will help.' In the early evening, the retinue crammed into the small chambers of the much needed friend, Mr Justice Shaw. 'Hello, Peter, how's your wife?' asked the judge, who then warned, 'I've got a train to catch and you've got a few minutes to convince me. It won't be easy.' Speaking in very blunt terms, the lawyers described Maxwell's alleged sins. The judge raised his eyebrows and Curry wrote on lined paper in long hand the required order. Mr Justice Shaw signed, and there was a collective sigh. The injunction was formally served on Maxwell at ten o'clock the following morning, two hours before the meeting was due to start.

The Connaught Rooms had few happy memories for Maxwell but they were nevertheless the venue for the EGM. Dressed as usual in his bright blue suit, he arrived with Betty, understandably tense. There had been no respite over the past weeks from the unrelenting pincer movement which would so unjustly destroy his own creation. 'I and my family have been through hell,' he would later reveal to the meeting. Some chairs on the podium were noticeably empty. Briggs and Payne from Chalmers Impey had refused to sit alongside their client. The remainder were occupied by Pergamon's directors shifting uneasily in anticipation of the embarrassments to come. A few had urged Maxwell to make the meeting as short as possible but they knew that their advice had been ignored. Earlier that morning, Maxwell had overridden their wishes by instructing Kerman to appeal for the injunctions to be set aside. He would fight to the last even if the outcome was a foregone conclusion. Just as Sir William Carr had packed the hall nine months earlier with his employees, now among the five hundred who had crowded into the hall were many Pergamon employees and sympathetic small shareholders who had cheered him when he entered. In the back stood Steinberg, relaxed and smiling, obviously enjoying life in London. The American had arrived arm-in-arm with two glamorous young women, both dressed in white, wearing large Ascot-type hats. Strangely, Maxwell felt no hostility towards his estranged partner and respected his business acumen. Overwhelmingly, his venom was directed at Jacob Rothschild.

The meeting began at noon. Maxwell spoke first into the microphone: 'My Lord, ladies and gentlemen, at ten o'clock this morning I was served with an injunction by Messrs Rothschild, without any notice,' and a tirade against the bankers ensued. 'This arrogant and stupid action by Rothschild is but the final chapter in the sorry way in which they have conducted the affairs of Leasco in this long-drawn-out battle.' Maxwell thereupon did exactly what he was forbidden to do and adjourned the meeting, 'because of this incredible and unbelievable behaviour of Rothschild's', claiming that he wanted to await the outcome of his own appeal against the injunction.

Uproar and bedlam followed his words. Amid shouts of 'Sit down!', 'Stand up!', 'This meeting is commenced and should proceed!', and 'Shut up!', the directors slowly filed down from the platform. Curry made a dash for the microphone and had just began to speak when Maxwell's hand snatched it from him: 'This is a meeting of Pergamon representatives, not Leasco. Would you mind leaving this floor.' Curry grabbed the microphone back, began speaking and was suddenly mute. The power had been switched off and his voice was drowned by slow handclapping. Maxwell beamed and after reconnecting the microphone announced that the meeting was not adjourned but 'delayed' and would remain so. The chaos rose to a new crescendo as dozens of soberly suited men stood waving their arms in the air, sat down in frustration, only to rise again, their crouched bodies suspended in the air, their faces contorted in fury, their shouts inaudible.

Maxwell returned to the microphone and, pointing at Curry and Jacob Rothschild, said, 'These men are obviously proposing to wreck this meeting. Maybe they are providing good entertainment. . . . I propose to withdraw from the meeting and I invite you to deal with these gentlemen as you deem fit.' Again there was uproar and again the microphone was switched off after Maxwell had threatened to call guards to remove those who gave 'stupid advice' to their clients.

Inside the hall, Lord Aldington, formerly Toby Low, a Conservative Member of Parliament, watched in discomfort. His bank, William Brandt, had agreed to represent Pergamon, and he now feared that his reputation might suffer by association with the turmoil he was witnessing. During a five-minute discussion with his client he insisted that the meeting must continue and be 'conducted according to the Queensberry Rules'. Maxwell agreed and returned to the podium holding the microphone. 'Ladies and gentlemen,' he said, 'let us forget all about that, shall we? I hope none of us will get unruly and disorderly. Particularly that is directed towards Rothschild lawyers.' The meeting started.

Uninterrupted, Maxwell now launched a bid to reconvert the converted, namely the institutions: 'Who are the brains that will run this business ...? a leading educational institution ... cannot be run by experts only in financial affairs.' After twenty minutes, he stopped and then started again. No one doubted that he was delaying the inevitable. Perhaps he was waiting for a divine spirit miraculously to sweep away the hostile faces before him and deliver Pergamon firmly back into his control. There were more attacks on Rothschilds – 'I received many impertinent letters from Rothschild' – followed by several mournful appeals to Rothschilds to 'withdraw their hostile, harmful and most damaging resolution to the company'. Jacob Rothschild rose to give his reply. Perhaps Maxwell hoped against hope that this was the deliverance. 'I propose', announced the tall banker, 'that Mr E.J. Buckley be and he is hereby removed as a director of the Pergamon Press Limited.' There was a cry of 'Shame!' and it was nearly all over. Each vote would take ten embarrassing minutes as Maxwell sought to prevaricate and appeal to the institutions to reconsider. When Rothschild stood to propose Maxwell's own removal, the chairman uttered what seemed like his last words before the executioner's axe fell: 'My record in peace or war is open and published in spite of the slander and innuendo in the story by the *Sunday Times*.' But despite being deposed, Maxwell remained firmly in the chair to continue the proceedings.

Once the board had been dismissed, Maxwell momentarily relaxed and even cracked a joke. But as the elections for the new board progressed – and on Maxwell's recommendation Steinberg and Hodes would be elected unopposed – the deposed chairman once again began imploring the institutions to reconsider. When his pleas were answered by stony stares, his anger returned: 'It is well known in the Square Mile of the City that the arrogance of Rothschild knows no bounds.'

After four hours, Leasco was declared the victor with 61 per cent of the vote. No one claimed to emerge from the bear garden with any credit, although Maxwell delivered one final surprise. Ever anxious to retain the initiative, he announced that, with the Takeover Panel's agreement, he would make a cash offer of 25s for all non-Leasco shares. Everyone, including his own bankers, was stunned but too exhausted to ask where Maxwell could hope to raise £5 million. Maxwell refused to be drawn, although he believed that Leasco had only won a Pyrrhic victory. 'I wish to thank you all for coming and God speed to you on your way out.' After a burst of applause, it was all over. Standing alone in the emptying hall, humiliated and defeated, he admitted, 'You can't expect me to be other than very, very sad.' The men from Leasco looked at their tormentor. 'Somehow,' recalls Stevens, 'Bob looked a lot more lovable in defeat.'

The new managers of Pergamon did not open any champagne bottles when they met later that night at Rothschilds for a board meeting to consider their strategy. No one was sufficiently tactless to speculate about just why they found themselves managing a company which employed over 2,500 people, which had just lost its key personnel, and whose financial status was in dispute, although it definitely had no money in the bank. As Hodes silently mused, 'We've been through the engagement and the divorce. Now it's the marriage.' Briskly, they agreed that their priority was to establish exactly what they had purchased for £9 million and to invite Buckley, Gilbert Richards, who managed Pergamon's journals, and Anthony Wheaton, who managed a printing company, to rejoin the board. Then Steinberg, Hodes and Schwartz formally resigned from the Pergamon board to which they had been elected just two hours earlier. For the moment they were replaced by just one new director and chairman, Sir Henry d'Avigdor-Goldsmid. The need for an independent chairman had surprised Leasco but it was the price which the institutions exacted in return for their support. 'The institutions were terribly stuffy,' recalls one of the bankers, 'and decided that they wouldn't trust the Americans.'

Finding a suitable nominee had not been easy. After two other men had refused, Sir Henry, a Conservative Member of Parliament, a banker and a leader of British Jewry, was approached. When Rothschild rang, Sir Henry was out hunting, which at least provided reassurance that the candidate was still active. Lady d'Avigdor-Goldsmid had answered and Rothschild explained why Sir Henry was needed. 'He should accept', implored the banker, 'for England.' It was an appeal which Sir Henry eventually could not resist. Stevens wished later that his reluctance had been backed by stronger will-power: 'He was so senile that he couldn't negotiate his way out of a paper bag.'

The following day, Stevens drove with d'Avigdor-Goldsmid to Oxford.

The politician's joints were stiff and heavily bandaged following falls from his horse. Stevens's concern about Sir Henry's capabilities had been placated by the bankers. 'You'll really like him,' he had been assured. 'He'll never come to meetings.' During the journey, Stevens started to discuss his objectives and tactics they might adopt when they arrived at Headington Hall. D'Avigdor-Goldsmid hearteningly replied that he too had priorities. Thereupon, to Stevens's dismay, he produced a list of recommended restaurants in the Oxford area. As Stevens swallowed his reaction, d'Avigdor-Goldsmid turned knowingly and said, 'I've been appointed to make sure that neither side fouls the pavement.'

Their entry into Pergamon's offices was an anticlimax. Sir Henry asked the secretary who welcomed them for 'the papers'. When she queried, 'From which file?', he replied, 'No, no, the newspapers.' Stevens was dumbfounded: 'I gawked and said nothing.' Over a three-hour lunch, d'Avigdor-Goldsmid expounded his view: 'I'm not allowing you to dig a tunnel into the company.' As he spoke, the American was reassessing his plans. Leasco had no choice but to withdraw from any direct management and rely on the long-serving employees. Approaches were already under way to three of the deposed directors. Within four weeks, with Maxwell's encouragement, they would return to the company.

But the hands-off strategy was fraught with difficulty: Pergamon's editorial offices were built in the same grounds, approximately fifty yards distant from the house where the Maxwell family lived. Although the Hall was owned by Pergamon, it had been leased to Maxwell and he curtly refused even to consider leaving his low-rent 'council house', which also served as the offices of his private companies. His constant physical presence, he told inquirers, was 'my guarantee that I know the status of my shareholding'. The extent of his supervision quickly became apparent.

Soon after the American takeover, Maxwell was seen at night prowling through the editorial offices. D'Avigdor-Goldsmid ordered guards to be posted around the building but, considering the enormous loyalty which so many Pergamon employees felt towards Maxwell, especially after the reappointment of the three directors, the guards were token symbols. The tension between the two sides – they were divided by a finely manicured lawn – broke into open warfare, often manifested in childish spite. The two buildings shared light and heating. Whenever their disputes intensified, Maxwell turned off their common boiler. In retaliation, d'Avigdor-Goldsmid ordered the Hall's electricity to be disconnected. 'We froze and they sat in darkness,' recalls Stevens. That the hiatus would continue was predictable, but no one had anticipated that the crisis would arise so quickly.

Leasco was intent on quickly establishing control over the Pergamon subsidiary in America, Pergamon Press Inc. (PPI), since 50 per cent of Pergamon's sales were exported to America and all the American journals were supervised from PPI's premises. PPI was the generator of Pergamon's future profits and growth. Pergamon in Britain owned 70 per cent of PPI, which was a public company. The remaining 30 per cent was owned by the American public. Under American law, Maxwell was president and chairman of PPI's board of directors. Prominent among those directors were his old freinds – Laszlo Straka, Sigmund Wahrsager and Ladislaus 'Martini' Majthenyi. Two days after removing Maxwell in London, Leasco's lawyers wrote to the secretary of PPI in New York requesting a special shareholders' meeting. They intended to remove Maxwell and his friends and appoint a new board of directors. Simultaneously, d'Avigdor-Goldsmid wrote to Maxwell asking for his resignation. Maxwell's rejection was carried by hand across the lawn. After criticising d'Avigdor-Goldsmid's 'crude attempt to go behind my back', Maxwell 'deplored' the new chairman's lack of 'courtesy and consideration' because 'good manners cost nothing'. The crux was that he refused to resign and 'as the second-largest shareholder' defiantly insisted that he could not be ignored. By 20 October, Pergamon's new management realised just how smartly they had been outwitted by Maxwell. Stevens's admits his amazement: 'We hadn't focused on the subsidiary and our own vulnerability until after Max had covered his arse.' In fact, Maxwell had protected his position during the same week in June that he was in New York negotiating the original sale with Steinberg.

Unknown to the Pergamon directors other than Tom Clark, Maxwell had on 12 June 1969 approved a resolution at PPI's annual general meeting which stipulated that PPI's secretary was not obliged to call a special meeting at the request of a majority of the shareholders. In effect, under the new rules, Pergamon in Britain was deprived of its powers over its own company except at the annual meeting and the next meeting was not due until June 1970. The new rule was approved while Maxwell was in New York negotiating to sell Pergamon to Leasco. He would later produce affidavits to prove that the initiative for the change had been taken by his American lawyers, who believed that the previous rules were outdated, and it is possible that under any circumstances Leasco would have had difficulty in establishing control over PPI. Whatever the reason, Maxwell had cause to be confident at the end of the day in the Connaught Rooms that, because he retained total control over PPI, Leasco's victory was hollow.

In the second half of October, Leasco's accountants began sifting through the files in Oxford looking for the section concerning PPI. The revelation that MSI Inc. owed Pergamon $1.6 million and enjoyed a favourable 'sale or return' contract with Pergamon suggested the real possibility of other unknown agreements. Yet the accountants found that Pergamon's files contained practically nothing relevant to PPI. There were no copies of bank statements, hardly any copies of correspondence or other contracts with MSI Inc., no list of assets and only sparse details of PPI's contracts with authors and customers. It was a textbook example of Maxwell's compartmentalisation.

At Maxwell's disposal in New York was Detlev Raymond, who had worked for Pergamon since 1950. Maxwell could expect, with Raymond's loyalty and his long experience at PPI, to establish a rival company which would be a direct competitor with Pergamon in Britain. The risk was the more pertinent because the files in Oxford did not reveal whether Pergamon even owned the copyright of the articles in its own journals. Steinberg agreed that it was imperative to end Maxwell's control of PPI. The fight, which began in the last week of October, was ferocious and unrelenting.

Under PPI's new rules, a director of the company did have the power to call a special shareholders' meeting, and Leasco discovered that James B. Ross, a vice-president responsible for commissioning publications, was sympathetic towards their cause. Leasco's misfortune was that they contacted Ross two weeks after he had submitted his resignation although it had still not been formally accepted by Maxwell. At Leasco's behest, Ross withdrew his resignation.

Ross's next move was to reinstate himself in his office. It was an attempt which was forcibly opposed. Guards from the Burns security agency cut off his telephone, destroyed his mail and eventually manhandled him off the premises. Maxwell had by then accepted his resignation. To confirm Ross's impotence, PPI's rules were again amended on 30 October, to empower only the president, that is Maxwell, to call a special share-holders' meeting. By then, Ross had appealed to the courts. What followed was a succession of Keystone Kops-type contests between Leasco and Maxwell through the courts of New York, as Ross, financed by Leasco, attempted to call a special shareholders' meeting.

Throughout the contests which followed in New York's courts, Maxwell was represented by Maurice Nessen, a small, charming but brutally aggressive lawyer who had defended Clifford Irving, the 'biographer' of the recluse Howard Hughes, against criminal charges. Nessen's tactic on Maxwell's behalf was to exploit every legitimate device in the lawyers' arsenal to delay and obfuscate Leasco's claims. Nessen's first riposte to Ross was to plead that Maxwell could not attend any court hearing due to a series of 'mandatory votes' in the House of Commons over the following six weeks which needed his constant attendance. This excuse was dismissed by Quintin Hogg MP, QC (later Lord Hailsham) as 'incredible' because 'pairing' allowed MPs to travel. Nessen's next ploy was to deliver an affidavit in which Maxwell swore that d'Avigdor-Goldsmid had requested that he stay as chairman of PPI. Nessen was successfully frustrating Leasco's plans.

In the meantime, Ross formally announced a shareholders' meeting for the end of November. In reply, Maxwell, claiming to be the protector of PPI, sent the same shareholders a letter condemning the 'reckless' Ross for his 'unauthorised and illegal' action. Within three weeks the contest had sped through the judicial process up to the New York Supreme Court, and there Maxwell won. Leasco had no option but to wait until June 1970. For Maxwell, the victory was fundamental to his recovery. He gained a vital break which he would use to persuade d'Avigdor-Goldsmid to recognise his indispensability in the management and survival of Pergamon, while psychologically it boosted his will to fight against the avalanche of writs and investigations which, by the beginning of November, had enveloped him.

The first writs were delivered in New York on 2 November by Leasco alleging conspiracy for 'fraud and deceit' and a claim for damages of $22 million. Those receiving the writs were Maxwell, Isidore Kerman, Robert Fleming, Chalmers Impey and the Maxwell family trusts. The writs alleged that Maxwell and his advisers had conspired to mislead Leasco about Pergamon's real financial status. Initially, Hodes had expected to sue Maxwell in Britain, but was advised that under British law the chances of success were extremely slim because neither Flemings nor Chalmers Impey owed a special duty of care to Leasco and so could not be liable even if they negligently endorsed false statements in the annual report. There was also, the British lawyers told Hodes, no claim whatsoever against Maxwell since his assurances had always been oral and therefore difficult to prove. He had not signed any documents which showed more than possible irresponsibility and anything else was based upon the certified accounts. Maxwell's only commitment in writing had been his letter to Schwartz on 17 May, but that was ambiguous. Because American financial laws were much stricter and because, according to Leasco, the takeover agreement was negotiated and signed in New York at Maxwell's request, the writs were issued in New York.

Maxwell's defence and counter-claim was that Leasco had deliberately sought to depress the value of Pergamon shares in order to buy the company cheap, that he had never encouraged Leasco to buy Pergamon shares before the formal offer was accepted, that Leasco misrepresented its own financial position, and that, as a result of Leasco's mismanagement of Pergamon, the value of Maxwell's own shares had fallen.

John Briggs's defence was that he had acted in good faith and that, since he did not even know about Maxwell's negotiations with Leasco, he could not have been party to any conspiracy. Richard Fleming filed a defence claiming that he was only on the periphery of the deal, that he had not made any detailed representations and that he was present during the New York negotiations not as a representative of Maxwell but to protect the interests of the bank's unit trusts. Leasco's case against Kerman was eventually dropped.

But the first argument which Nessen deployed, and which would keep the dispute simmering for the following four years, was that the American courts had no jurisdiction because the dispute involved a British company and all the pertinent documents and witnesses were in Britain. That argument would be finally heard in the state Supreme Court.

Meanwhile, Maxwell was under investigation by two inquiries in Britain, both of which had begun formal hearings in late September. The first was mounted by the Board of Trade and the second was the independent audit by Price Waterhouse which would determine Pergamon's 1968 accounts. His attitudes to the two were sharply different.

Still suffering from the injustice he felt Shawcross had meted out at the Takeover Panel hearings, Maxwell feared that the Board of Trade inquiry might similarly maul his reputation without allowing him the opportunity to defend himself adequately. Therefore, before agreeing to appear, he asked the two inspectors to explain the procedures they would adopt and to assure him that he would enjoy the normal protections of a British court of law. Owen Stable QC and Ronald Leach were unwilling to give those guarantees. They argued that the efficient conduct of the inquiry depended upon informality and flexibility, which would be suffocated if they were to be 'bound hand and foot' by legalisms and procedures. On 22 September, Maxwell arrived for the first session. He gave his name and address, stated that he was the holder of the Military Cross and a Member of Parliament. Then he refused to answer any further questions. Instead, he applied to the High Court for an order requiring the inspectors to adopt a more formal procedure.

Since the Court would not hear the case for some months, the inspectors started their inquiry. Their first witness was Ian Fraser, followed in succession by Godfrey Hodgson, Jacob Rothschild, Rupert

Murdoch and Richard Millett. Maxwell's fear that the inspectors were giving a platform to his enemies seemed to him to be fully justified.

Maxwell's attitude towards the Price Waterhouse inquiry was quite different. If he was to retain his credibility, both commercial and moral, he had no choice but to co-operate since he had staked his reputation upon his company's profitability. Moreover, Steinberg had agreed to bid for the remaining shares within two months of the accountants' report and, as Maxwell had announced that he would make a counter-bid, it was vital for Maxwell to persuade Price Waterhouse to accept his version of the 1968 accounts.

Martin Harris, a mild-mannered senior partner of Price Waterhouse, led the investigation, which the firm had initially been reluctant to carry out on account of the fear of endless litigation. Only after Maxwell sent written confirmation that both he and his family trusts would un-conditionally co-operate, including the provision of any necessary documents, had Price Waterhouse committed itself. Within weeks that undertaking would be thwarted. MSI Inc. claimed that, on legal advice, it could not disclose any documents which would prejudice its defence against Leasco's suits. For the moment, the legal distinction between the trusts and Maxwell defeated the accountants.

Price Waterhouse adopted a textbook approach to its investigation. Maxwell, accompanied by Nessen, answered the accountant's questions for more than forty full days. Eight accountants divided into four teams worked through the files in Oxford. By the end of November, they had prepared a thick 'summary of the facts' which was presented for comment to everyone who had been involved in preparing Pergamon's accounts. Over the following three weeks, daily from 9 a.m. until 7 p.m. in Price Waterhouse's Cheapside offices, there were four simultaneous interviewing sessions where the Pergamon directors and their auditors were invited to 'indicate our errors'. Questions were asked and answers written down in long hand. Voices were never raised and suspicions were never mentioned. But every night, when the team gathered for debriefing sessions whch often continued until the early hours, the day's revelations swept aside their professional taciturnity. 'Accountants are professional cynics,' recalls one of the investigators, 'and there was pure joy in unravelling the complex paper trail.'

The questioning of Maxwell personally was 'a poker game. We had to treat him gently to make sure that he stayed.' It was characteristic of Maxwell when difficult questions were posed that he rambled into tangential areas. Whether it was intended to confuse the questioners or just, as Peter Stevens surmised, the common Czech inability to stay on a straight line, is debatable. The result was that Maxwell spoke at great length, giving an uninterrupted explanation, filled with facts and figures, which was all faithfully recorded. A couple of days later, the same question would be posed. Very often, Maxwell could not recall the identical facts and figures which he had so authoritatively cited just forty-eight hours earlier. 'We quoted back to him what he had said earlier and it unnerved him,' recalls one of the accountants.

At the end of the year, Harris handed Maxwell his preliminary conclusions. As he read though the thick folder, Maxwell recognised that it consisted of remorseless censure. Price Waterhouse had decided that Pergamon's audited 1968 profits of £2.1 million should be reduced by £1.6 million and that the remaining half million pounds would be swallowed up by the ILSC losses. According to Price Waterhouse, Pergamon had actually made a loss in 1968. 'Maxwell was furious when he read our interim report,' says a witness of the occasion, 'so we offered him a cup of tea and spoke about the weather.' To the accountants it seemed that Maxwell had placed himself inside a straitjacket.

Among the papers which they had discovered in Oxford was a contract, signed by Maxwell, for the resale of the Spanish translation rights from MSI Inc. back to PPI. The contract was dated 6 October 1969, just four days before the EGM. Maxwell had little choice but to agree that Pergamon could not claim the £104,000 as profit. Similarly, R.M. & Co. had in August returned to Pergamon books worth £149,000 from its warehouse in Wolverton. Finally, Pergamon's massive £1,250,000 'sale or return' deal for back issues signed on 30 August 1967 with MSI Inc. was clearly revocable and therefore had to be removed from Pergamon's income. In effect, the accountants had discovered that in the weeks before Maxwell's removal from Pergamon, Pergamon's profits had been depressed.

The beleaguered executive could count on few sympathetic ears for his explanations. In the era of Emil Savundra, Bernie Cornfeld's IOS and the sudden demise of the washing-machine salesman John Bloom, a certain seediness had infected the image of British business. Maxwell was afraid that he was being tarnished by the same brush, especially since his reputation had been severely damaged by newspaper and television coverage of Pergamon's tribulations. Again, none was more wounding than the accounts which appeared in Lord Thomson's newspapers.

The second part of the *Sunday Times* profile had appeared on 12 October, two days after his epic defeat at the Connaught Rooms. According to the newspaper's heading, 'Robert Maxwell Has Lost His Empire'. In the centre of the article was a photograph of Maxwell and

Gaitskell laughing together in 1962, the caption stating that the Labour leader had been a 'friend since the fifties', the era which was associated with Simpkin Marshall and so on. Maxwell was still a Member of Parliament and, with a general election due within two years, the article questioned his suitability.

By 1969, Maxwell's parliamentary career had barely progressed. His appearances and interventions in the chamber had sharply declined in number compared to earlier years and only his management of the House of Commons Catering Committee had been rated a success. The *Sunday Times* suspected that even that success was a mirage and approached Richard Crossman, who had originally nominated Maxwell. Crossman praised Maxwell's 'staggering success'. He continued, 'He took over a department totally demoralised, whose staff included a number of prostitutes and thieves, all of whom he sacked without a strike.... He purged the gross abuse and pilfering; legs of mutton and rounds of beef were being regularly removed under their raincoats by members of the staff. All that is now stopped.... He took over a restaurant which was incurring gigantic losses in order to provide excellent food and drink....' The published article ignored Crossman's favourable comment and dwelt on the accounts, which the journalists believed were controversial. Described as the 'ballet of Robert Maxwell, caterer extraordinary', it lampooned his management technique and questioned his accountancy methods: 'It displays all the classic movements in the Maxwell repertoire – the Amazing Leap from the wings with Loud Promises of Modern Efficiency; the Masterly Treatment of Accounts; and the Rapid Disappearance, just before the audience starts to throw things.'

That cameo, in Maxwell's view, proved that the *Sunday Times* was determined to destroy his career, and he complained to the House of Commons Committee of Privileges. After thirteen meetings, his complaint was rejected, although the committee stated that there was no evidence that his conduct was 'in any way improper or departed from normal procedures in compiling the accounts'. The issue, and Maxwell's reputation, were left dangling.

Political life irked Maxwell. He was perplexed and frustrated that despite his ideas, energy and abilities, he had not won the Prime Minister's admiration. Equally, he was disillusioned by the government's policies. Despite the noble promises, British science and industry had not fared well; the government's tax policies and especially the Selective Employment Tax had been disastrous; the perpetual lurch through a succession of apparently insoluble financial crises had opened the door to the International Monetary Fund to act as sole arbiter of Britain's financial management; while the Labour movement lamentably persisted with a wave of suicidal strikes in the face of an unenforceable prices and incomes policy. Even Maxwell's own efforts to reform the inept management of the party headquarters at Transport House had been spurned. Within the Labour Party and inside the House, Maxwell was an awkward misfit who, though pleading for enterprise and for the rapid dismantling of Britain's pretensions to world-power status, had not managed to create an identifiable political cause for himself. His only success was to pilot through the Commons with the flamboyant Conservative Member, Sir Gerald Nabarro, an extension of the Clean Air Acts.

Yet in his constituency his efficient organisation and his apparent relish for looking after his constituents' interests had earned him considerable popularity – not an easy achievement for a Labour MP representing a Home Counties constituency. Much of his success was owed to his political secretary, Judith Ennals, who managed and executed the bulk of the parliamentarian's routine and time-consuming chores. Constituents were encouraged to write with their problems, which Ennals researched and settled before obtaining Maxwell's endorsement and signature. Although this was an unusual arrangement for a Labour MP, the arrangement was common practice in the Conservative ranks. Under Ennals, Maxwell's political office scoured the announcements columns in the local newspapers and automatically sent congratulations or condolences to those advertising births, marriages or deaths. Even the victims of road accidents would receive a 'get well' card from their MP. His motives were realistic. Every vote in the next election would count.

To describe his approach as squirarchical is not to be critical but merely acknowledges that, in the context of a hunting and shooting constituency, the Labour Member of Parliament's unorthodox lifestyle was not incongruous. Receptions, tea parties and meetings in his large mansion endeared him and his wife to most of his party workers. His constituency never suffered from a common Labour Party malaise of poor organisation. On the contrary, his machine was so well oiled that it aroused, among the traditionalists, irritation and eventually outright anger.

Soon after his re-election in 1966, Maxwell had revamped the party organisation. At the grass roots, so-called Polling District Committees were established in every village where no party group had previously existed. Like the branches, these 'committees', even if they represented no more than two people, had the right according to the constituency's recently revised rules to send delegates to the all-powerful General Management Committee meetings, the constituency's governing body, to which Maxwell was answerable. Within a short time, Maxwell's support on the GMC was overwhelming and had aroused resentment among the working-class members who lived in the railway town of Wolverton.

Frank Atter, who had been a Labour Party supporter effectively since birth, was one of those who had become uneasy about the effects of the MP's organisational reforms. Atter, who had sat on the original selection committee in 1959 and was impressed by Maxwell, had gradually become disillusioned: 'We began to get the feeling that unless you were a one hundred per cent Maxwell man, you were side-stepped. Ordinary party members were losing control to his own staff and that wasn't healthy.' Maxwell, complained Atter, was not sympathetic to the democracy which was natural to the Labour Party. It was said that he just did not like opponents or critics. Party meetings rarely debated the government's performance or policies and never questioned their own Member's opinions.

Jim Lyons, Maxwell's agent in the constituency, suffered more than others his MP's reluctance to consult but he suffered in silence, even when he was severely embarrassed. One such case was Maxwell's announcement that he would resign if his bid for the *News of the World* was successful. Lyons had been neither forewarned nor consulted. He concealed his surprise and spoke for many in saying that he hoped his bid would fail because 'We would not like to lose him.' But, by election time, Maxwell was uneasy about his agent. Lyons was not as attentive to the party organisation as Barnard had been and had not maintained the vital canvass of all the electorate. Although he had been warned by the regional agent, Geoff Foster, about his performance, Lyons had not worked as hard as Maxwell expected. Irritated, he had excluded Lyons from most decision-taking and had reduced his responsibilities. Headington Hill Hall had gradually become the *de facto* party headquarters where important meetings, often summoned without Lyons's knowledge, were held, and where official papers were stored. Even the constituency's budget was beyond Lyons's control. Most Labour members agree with Bryan Barnard that in the approach to the election the constituency was not 'as well organised as before'.

By spring 1970, the tide had turned for the Labour government. The appalling succession of economic crises which had cost the government its popularity, suddenly seemed to have been overcome. Exports were rising and Britain was for the moment no longer the sick man of Europe. In mid-May, the opinion polls swung in Labour's favour. The Conservatives seemed vulnerable to Wilson's derision as heartless and incompetent politicians who could be mercilessly lampooned as 'Yesterday's Men' or the 'Selsdon Man'. The Prime Minister decided to make a dash for victory and announced a general election for 18 June. The party's slogan, 'Now Britain's strong – let's make it great to live in', was not to every candidate's taste, but it satisfied Maxwell.

Maxwell might have expected his task to have been made more difficult by the adverse publicity about Pergamon. Yet party workers reported that his troubles in the City were barely mentioned during the three-week campaign. Voters were impressed by his constituency record and were not influenced by his apparent failure to win promotion. That he could cite as parliamentary achievements only his membership of 'UK parliamentary delegation to the Council of Europe' and the vice-chairmanship of its Committee on Science and Technology was irrelevant. His management of the Catering Committee was not mentioned. Some did notice that no senior government minister was prepared to speak on his behalf in the constituency, a surprising omission for a marginal.

The campaign, organised by Betty, his sons and his secretaries, did not differ from those of previous years. Charging around the constituency, his head sticking out of the top of a bright red Land Rover like a commander leading the assault, Maxwell's energy, oratory and charm won him warm ovations. The highlight of his speeches was his condemnation of the Conservatives' proposed legislation to prevent wild-cat strikes. 'This is not the way to run a country,' he said about Tory leader Edward Heath's ideas. 'This is one of the stupidest things anyone has tried to foist on this country.' Fifteen years later, he would praise Mrs Thatcher's anti-union legislation as a godsend and admit that it was the basis of his revived fortunes.

But after the first week of the campaign he recognised his difficulties. His new Conservative opponent, William Benyon, was superior to his predecessor, and the Conservative Party machine had been successfully overhauled. In comparison, Lyons had, he felt, failed dismally.

In the light of the unexpected national swing towards the Conservatives, Maxwell had perhaps only an even chance of holding his seat. Benyon won by 2,521 votes but the swing was less than half the national average. Although that was some consolation, the result was nevertheless a bitter blow for Maxwell. The television pictures showed a fallen face and glistening eyes, but he was gracious in defeat.

Away from the cameras, both Maxwell and his wife were, like most defeated politicians, desolate that their mammoth efforts and unswerving dedication could so easily and so ungratefully be disposed of. In all of Maxwell's other defeats, it had been possible to launch an immediate counter-attack. The democratic vote could not, however, be challenged. Instead, the Maxwells sought a scapegoat. On 4 July, three weeks after the election, the GMC set in motion the censure of Jim Lyons. In ten days, no less than six resolutions expressing no confidence in the agent were passed. Lyons says that he was not notified that any of the branch meetings were discussing his conduct and was not even invited to attend his own branch meeting. Frank Atter is rueful: 'If they win, they say it was a marvellous candidate; if they lose, they blame the agent. Maxwell just went too far.'

With members of the legal profession Maxwell maintains an uneasy, bitter-sweet relationship. Lawyers thrive on interpreting, redefining and bending rules to suit their cause, but will always resort, when in doubt, to the law's preference for certainty. In contrast, if aspiring tycoons diligently obeyed every rule, their ambitions would be stymied. They normally choose to avoid the courts as unmanageable, unpredictable and therefore dangerous. Maxwell is the exception. By 1970, he had earned a contrary reputation as a breathless challenger of rules, but also as a most litigious person who would readily appeal to the courts to assert his rights. Paradoxically, he found the intellectual frisson of the lawyer's craft exciting, but he was also frustrated since his very reliance upon their expertise denied him total mastery of his fate. Nevertheless, until 1970, his combination of energetic determination and unique bravado usually cowed many defendants into reluctant submission. To the interested observer, Maxwell seemed positively to enjoy his appearances in the witness box and when sitting with his lawyers in the well of the courtroom. That changed during the Board of Trade inquiry.

Until 1970, Maxwell normally relied upon his confidant and business partner Isidore Kerman for legal advice. But once the inquiries into Pergamon began, Kerman was precluded from acting because, as a director, he was required by the inspectors to be a witness. The exposure of Maxwell's relationship with other lawyers therefore coincided with his intensive recourse to the courts to defend himself. Maxwell first consulted the solicitor David Freeman, a Labour supporter who had built a successful commercial practice in London's West End. Freeman selected as their advocate Morris Finer QC, who had earned a glowing reputation among his profession as the master of reducing the most complicated facts to a digestible and persuasive argument. Finer's supreme credential for arguing Maxwell's case was that he had recently investigated on behalf of the Board of Trade the collapse of John Bloom's washing-machine company, Rolls Razor. Freeman believed that Maxwell's greatest obstacle would be to secure a fair hearing, and there was no one better suited to argue that Leach and Stable were bound by what are known as the 'rules of natural justice' than a former inspector himself. Maxwell was fortunate that his representatives were skilled and sympathetic and had also grown up in humble circumstances, but he was unable to desist from interference. Many of the conferences at the Temple became tetchy debates between Maxwell and the eminent barrister who, with grisly foreboding, could anticipate a judge's unsympathetic reaction. 'Maxwell was always barking orders,' recalls one of those present. 'He was very clever, very intelligent, very hard-working, but utterly impossible.'

The two inspectors, Owen Stable QC and Ronald Leach, both enjoyed redoubtable reputations. Stable was rated a high-flyer at the commercial Bar who had a good chance of appointment as a High Court judge once the inquiry was completed. As the lawyer, it was Stable's duty to ensure that the proper legal procedures were observed. Leach was an accountant and a senior partner of Peat Marwick Mitchell. Although he was considered to be among the nation's most senior practitioners, his appointment was not without its critics. As president of the Institute of Chartered Accountants, he was open to the charge that he might seek to deflect the widespread disillusion with his profession which the Pergamon affair had provoked. Yet these were common and inevitable vulnerabilities which would not ordinarily have affected his impartiality. Notionally, their appointment and the rules of procedure they would follow were no different from those of any previous departmental inquiry: the hearings would be in private and, while each person would receive a transcript of his own evidence, Maxwell would not have access to the transcripts of other witnesses. The inspectors' report would be confidential except for the portion which the government decided to publish. The core of their task was to undertake an investigation into Pergamon and to report on whether the shareholders 'had been given all the information they might have expected'. They were not adjudicating as in a trial.

Maxwell, however, believed that his circumstances were exceptional: Pergamon was still trading apparently profitably; the Leasco bid had provoked enormous controversial publicity; the past eighteen months had convincingly proven the City's and Fleet Street's antagonism towards him; an interim inspectors' report could be used by Leasco in pursuit of its claims in New York; and the inquiry would hamper any bid for Pergamon once the Price Waterhouse report was published. Among his unpublicised concerns was the inspectors' determination to investigate his private companies. That, he felt, was a sensitive area which should be barred to a government inquiry ostensibly concerned with a public company. He therefore sought, as a condition of his co-operation with the inquiry, guarantees that he would have the customary protection of natural justice afforded by a court of law – namely, that he could be accompanied by his lawyers, that his lawyers could cross-examine all the witnesses and that they would have full access to all the evidence which the inspectors were considering and make submissions about all that evidence. Lastly, he demanded that, if the inspectors came to any conclusions unfavourable to himself, they would be bound to offer him a chance to answer those criticisms.

The inspectors disagreed. On 1 December they wrote to Maxwell to explain that while they were 'most anxious that no one affected by our inquiries should feel that he has been unjustly treated at our hands' they could not agree to unrestricted access to the transcripts of what were quite intentionally private meetings. The negotiations made no further progress and Maxwell threw down the gauntlet: he would only answer questions if ordered to do so by a court.

In early April 1970, the inspectors appealed to the High Court to order the Labour politician to answer their questions without further guarantees. On Maxwell's behalf, Finer appeared before Mr Justice Plowman and argued that, as Maxwell was 'under suspicion', he had the right to demand that the 'freedoms and safeguards woven into the fabric of life in this country' as in a judicial inquiry would be observed.

In reply, the inspectors made a concession. They were not bound, they argued, by the rules of natural justice because they were undertaking an investigation and submitting a report whose publication was by no means a foregone conclusion. However, they assured the Court that they would not submit a critical report without giving Maxwell an opportunity to answer any points which they raised, although they would provide only a broad description of their complaints. Plowman supported the inspectors' argument and ordered that Maxwell answer their questions. Maxwell appealed.

Maxwell's strategy now led to his first break with a legal adviser, his solicitor David Freeman. There was a clash of personalities and a sharp disagreement about whether they could refuse to co-operate with the inspectors. Since Maxwell was committed to fight the inquiry 'tooth and nail', he rejected any hint of concession and transferred to his friend John Silkin, the Labour Member of Parliament.

In July, Morris Finer re-argued his case in the Court of Appeal. Lord

Denning agreed that the inspectors had to be fair and abide by the rules of natural justice because reputations and careers could be affected by their findings. Quite explicitly, Denning said that the inspectors had to give Maxwell an outline of any charge against him, so allowing a fair opportunity for correction or contradiction. But he rejected Finer's argument that the inspectors were bound to allow Maxwell the opportunity to rebut any adverse evidence and to cross-examine witnesses. The crux, according to Denning, was that the inspectors were investigators and needed flexibility. In the public interest, speed was essential and Maxwell was bound to help. If he refused, he would be in contempt of court and he could 'expect no further mercy'.

On 4 September 1970, Maxwell appeared for the first session of questioning at 11 Ironmonger Lane in the City. Displaying no apprehension, Maxwell treated the inquiry over the following months as a regrettably unavoidable chore to be slotted into his increasingly hectic schedule. He was energetically relaunching his business activities, a relaunch neatly coinciding with Denning's judgement.

In a four-page circular to shareholders, he announced that, supported by a major publisher who was still undecided, he would announce a bid for Pergamon once the Price Waterhouse report was published. Were he to win control, Maxwell also promised that he would assume the management for 'up to two years ... until the company was on its feet again', and then hand over to a younger man. He postulated that he would offer 25s per share for a further 23 per cent of the shares which, combined with his own 28 per cent holding, would leave Leasco stranded.

Maxwell prided himself on the timing of the announcement. Steinberg was once again fighting for survival as Leasco's fortunes tottered. Its share price, after slumping from $33 to $10, had dropped another $5. As a consequence, under a complicated series of warranties which had financed its purchase of the Reliance Insurance Group, the fall of its share price had triggered demands for Leasco to repay loans worth $31.9 million, an enormous burden. For the Americans, arranging the re-scheduling of those loans in New York was infinitely more important than the time-consuming management of Pergamon.

The board meetings in Oxford, Schwartz and Stevens had discovered, were taken up by interminable discussions about finances and accounts and rarely about the business itself. The Americans decided that their attendance was a waste of time and selected Dr Felix Kalinski to replace Bello on the board as a full-time appointment. Kalinski, who had been recruited from the CBS television network in New York by a firm of headhunters, was a former West Point graduate and a decorated combat pilot who demanded and received the then enormous annual salary of $80,000. Leasco hoped that Kalinski, as a full-time director, would monitor Pergamon's recovery pending delivery of the Price Waterhouse report and would protect their interests from the ever-ubiquitous presence of Maxwell.

On several occasions during the year, Maxwell had attempted to effect a reconciliation, either by approachng intermediaries or on one notable occasion by booking every available trans-Atlantic flight in order to be on the same plane as Steinberg. Having finally trapped the American in the first-class cabin at 39,000 feet, he unsuccessfully attempted to discuss a settlement of their differences. 'I think he just took the next flight out of Kennedy back to London,' recalled Steinberg.

More sober negotiations had started between Maxwell and d'Avigdor-Goldsmid in June under the chairmanship of Lord Aldington. Maxwell offered, in return for his reappointment as a Pergamon director and the cessation of the litigation against PPI in New York, to merge his family companies and PPI into Pergamon while both Leasco's and his own shareholdings would be committed to a trust pledged to support the board. Pressured by the Americans, who vetoed any proposal which included Maxwell's return, d'Avigdor-Goldsmid initially rejected the peace offer but after the middle of 1970 had become resentful of the New Yorkers' antagonism. Quite simply, d'Avigdor-Goldsmid disliked disagreements and was insulted by the Americans' dismissive criticisms of his role as an independent intermediary.

The Americans could not hide their disdain for the Colonel Blimp who lived in a huge, depressing house in Tonbridge where they had to wait until precisely twelve noon before they were offered a drink. 'The house was so cold', recalled Steinberg, 'that we had to go outside to warm up.' Steinberg commuted regularly to London to persuade d'Avigdor-Goldsmid to break Maxwell's grip over Pergamon while Stevens shuttled across the Atlantic, sometimes three times weekly, to report on the problems which d'Avigdor-Goldsmid's stubbornness was causing. Their personal dislike of d'Avigdor-Goldsmid mirrored their contempt for the decayed British financial system but their undisguised irritation reinforced the chairman's obstinate refusal to manage Pergamon as they wished.

Maxwell in contrast had by the autumn charmed Sir Henry into believing that the two could work quite well together. Consequently d'Avigdor-Goldsmid had become unwilling, on Pergamon's behalf and at Steinberg's behest, to pursue Maxwell aggressively in the courts. In June 1970, Maxwell knew that he was safe in refusing outright to call the statutory PPI annual meeting in New York because d'Avigdor-Goldsmid would not enforce Pergamon's rights. Effectively, nine months after his humiliation at the Connaught Rooms, he still retained control of PPI and, negatively, of Pergamon.

In August, the Price Waterhouse report was finally published. The accountants explained that they had adopted 'material changes' in preparing the 1968 accounts and accordingly had reduced the pre-tax profits from £2.1 million to £140,000, which did not take into account ILSC's accumulated losses of £2.1 million.

The report confirmed, in Leasco's view, that it was the innocent victim. Maxwell robustly argued that it proved the whimsy of accountants and absolved him from any blame. 'I note', he wrote in a circular, 'that hindsight has been employed,' and blamed the new board for causing all the losses. The transactions with his family companies which had amounted to £2.5 million had, he claimed, 'been fully disclosed and have been beneficial to your company'. But he did not explain why those same transactions had all been cancelled just prior to his removal from the board. 'Shareholders', he continued, 'need not be perturbed. The suggested scaling down of profits is well within the margins when reporting accountants apply different accounting principles.'

Price Waterhouse had also prepared Pergamon's accounts for the first nine months of 1969. In the heyday of the negotiations with Leasco, Maxwell had forecast that Pergamon's profits would be £2.5 million. In New York in August 1969, he had agreed that they should be revised downwards to £2 million. Price Waterhouse, however, calculated that Pergamon had actually made a profit of just £29,000 which was turned into a gigantic loss of nearly £2 million if the ILSC's losses and the revocation of MSI Inc.'s contract were also taken into account. It was an indictment, not least of the accountancy profession. Their report contained no outright blame for the discrepancies but Chalmers Impey were replaced by Cooper Brothers as the company's auditors.

Pergamon's annual report published in September 1970 reflected the gloom. 'Ghastly' was the epithet which d'Avigdor-Goldsmid voiced to journalists. All the board's efforts, he said, 'were concentrated on keeping [the] Company going'. His admission was not an understatement. Investigation of Pergamon's files was continually revealing more unforeseen and costly anomalies. There was, for example, the European Printing Corporation (EPC), a firm of specialist printers in Dublin. EPC had been bought by Maxwell from Lord Thomson in 1967 and had never earned a profit. By 1970, EPC's total losses amounted to the substantial sum of £214,000. Pergamon's new managers were perplexed because EPC was owned by R.M. & Co. but Maxwell insisted that Pergamon had agreed to underwrite its massive debts. In pursuit of that money, Maxwell had written to d'Avigdor-Goldsmid on 23 June 1970 claiming that there existed a binding obligation upon Pergamon to buy EPC from R.M. & Co. which would cause R.M. & Co. to bear 'neither profit nor loss'. A search through the Pergamon files revealed unsatisfactory evidence of that liability, but in his annual report d'Avigdor-Goldsmid conceded that Pergamon would bear those losses.

D'Avigdor-Goldsmid also reported that Maxwell's continued control over PPI was proving costly. The British company was not receiving any funds from America, and Maxwell had actually sold two subsidiaries of PPI without any consultation. D'Avigdor-Goldsmid's summary was doom-laden. The threat of litigation, he said, 'hangs over the company like the mushroom cloud at Hiroshima'.

Maxwell, whose omnipresence also hovered like a cloud, was ebullient despite the unqualified censure of his company. Price Waterhouse, he felt, had been determined to paint the worst picture. Accounting, he commented cryptically, 'is not the exact science which some of us thought it was'. He blamed Price Waterhouse for denigrating the 'substantial' profits which he claimed Pergamon earned from its trade with his private companies and attacked their 'tortuous' compilation of unrecoverable debts which he could have collected. 'In all things and at all times,' he concluded, 'I have acted in good faith and tried to serve both sides with fairness and equity.' Maxwell's stout defence of himself and Chalmers Impey was par for the course, but the principles of accountancy in Britain and in the profession's textbooks were quietly and substantially overhauled to prevent similar mistakes.

The delivery of the Price Waterhouse report set a two-month deadline for Leasco to publish details of its bid for the remaining 62 per cent of the shares. In New York, there was little enthusiasm for any further connection with Britain. Pergamon was plagued by uncertainties and owed more than £3 million, including £2.3 million to the National Westminster Bank. There seemed little reason to bid for a near-bankrupt company. Leasco had written down its $22 million investment to just one dollar in a rescue package which included writing off $44 million of its debts. But Rothschilds, who now valued Pergamon at just £3.6 million, urged their clients to make a bid of 3s 6d per share. The bankers feared that their reputation would suffer if Leasco withdrew, but sentiment and status were at a discount in the equation. On 3 November, Leasco announced that 'we do not wish to shoulder the burden of owning Pergamon', and both Schwartz and Stevens resigned from the board.

Maxwell was jubilant. Keeping PPI had paid rich dividends and he was now poised for his comeback. 'I could hardly have dealt the cards better myself,' he told the *Daily Telegraph* after he returned from a negotiating session with d'Avigdor-Goldsmid. But speculation of a bid soon petered out. There were doubts whether he possessed enough money and whether the institutions approved of his conduct regarding PPI. But there was already a hint of victory.

During that winter, Maxwell executed another masterstroke. After winning the sympathy of d'Avigdor-Goldsmid, he also secured the allegiance of Leasco's appointee, Felix Kalinski, who abruptly deserted his patrons. Steinberg was incensed but powerless. The balance now depended upon a newcomer to the board, Sir Walter Coutts, a former governor of Uganda and later an assistant vice-chancellor for administration at Warwick University. 'We were all fed up with the arguing,' recalls Coutts, 'but I was particularly antagonistic towards Maxwell.' That would change, as Maxwell continued to exercise his charm, albeit from a distance. He took a six-month Kennedy fellowship at Harvard University to study a favourite theme: how to encourage industry to apply the results of scientific research and how governments could shape industry through their purchasing power. The fellowship was financed by an anonymous fund which the University was reluctant to reveal. From afar Maxwell watched as Pergamon's fortunes stumbled and sank. Then he seized his opportunity.

In April 1971, d'Avigdor-Goldsmid was receptive to Maxwell's appeal that their differences should be buried. Pergamon's losses in 1970 had risen to £2.3 million (due mainly to reducing the valuation of the stock of journals and books) and the value of its assets had been reduced by a further £1.2 million to £6.1 million. D'Avigdor-Goldsmid was exhausted by the fight and he was convinced that the company needed calm and its founder's expertise if it were to survive. Unanimously Pergamon's directors, including Kalinski, agreed to forgive and forget everything. Effectively, all the disputes about the loans and all the litigation between Pergamon and Maxwell's private companies were to be dropped; MSI Inc. was to pay $1.5 million to Pergamon for all the rights in the back issues; and PPI was to be placed again under British control. In return, d'Avigdor-Goldsmid supported Maxwell's re-election to the board as a non-executive director. As a gesture of goodwill, Pergamon also granted Maxwell a lease on the Hall until 1999 for an annual rent of £1,100 exclusive of overheads. In return, Maxwell offered d'Avigdor-Goldsmid some PPI shares for his personal ownership. After remonstration from Coutts, who complained that it was inappropriate, d'Avigdor-Goldsmid tore up the offer. 'D'Avigdor-Goldsmid's conduct was sometimes difficult to understand,' says Coutts. The DTI inspectors concluded that Maxwell had negotiated a very favourable settlement.

D'Avigdor-Goldsmid, who flew to New York to finalise the deal with the American board of PPI, was honest about his capitulation. Schwartz was outraged: 'It was astonishing that Harry surrendered his only leverage against Maxwell.' Both Schwartz and Steinberg flew to Britain to persuade the pension funds to block Maxwell's formal election to the board at the annual meeting in July. Their arguments were greeted with the same stony looks which had glared at Maxwell when he had pleaded to the institutions in the Connaught Rooms 18 months earlier. Maxwell was on the verge of a victorious return. Just one final blemish needed to be cleared: his writs alleging defamation against the *Sunday Times*.

No publicity had been so permanently wounding to Maxwell as the Insight profiles. On the eve of his return to the board, Maxwell needed to prove publicly that the *Sunday Times* had retracted its allegations. To wait for a trial in court was unsatisfactory since it would not start for at least three years and would be both expensive and unpleasant. There were, he believed, more efficacious methods. On 2 January 1970, he had met Roy Thomson to propose that the Canadian become a partner in Maxwell's future bid for the outstanding Pergamon shares. Thomson had rejected the idea but Maxwell took the opportunity to discuss the possibility of settling the libel writs, although the newspaper's proprietor had a reputation for not interfering with his editorial staff. What Thomson told Maxwell is uncertain but Thomson did ask his lawyers to 'examine the idea from all angles, although I am not urging any kind of climb-down by the *Sunday Times*'. Two weeks later, Maxwell wrote to Thomson's son Kenneth, suggesting that since his father had agreed to a settlement it was surprising that the *Sunday Times* lawyers had not yet submitted their proposals. Was there, he wondered, 'some slip-up'? The executives of the Thomson organisation were puzzled. Their firm understanding was that the initiative had been taken by Maxwell and that his solicitors would send their proposals. No, said Maxwell, Lord Thomson had personally said that he would initiate the apology. On reference back, Kenneth Thomson denied Maxwell's interpretation. There was again stalemate, although the official announcement that ILSC (which had been sold by d'Avigdor-Goldsmid to BPC in February 1970) had lost £3 million was gratifying confirmation for the Insight team that their initial allegations seemed well founded and that they would be totally vindicated in court. But, unknown to them, by July their editor Harold Evans was prepared to compromise. In return for Maxwell withdrawing the writs, he was ready to publish a long 'question and answer' interview in which Maxwell would be permitted a free hand to make his case. Evans, it seems, had lost both belief and interest in the investigation. For the next nine months, Maxwell insisted that he wanted the article also to contain an official withdrawal and an apology, but that was refused. Nothing changed until on 1 December, Maxwell telephoned Evans and urged a settlement 'because I want to get my company back. Let's settle it. No money, no crawling.' Evans recorded in a minute that Maxwell, 'went on for some time about how important it was for him to get an early settlement and couldn't I as a reasonable man work something out, etc.'

Evans suggested again an interview to put the record straght but by the beginning of February their agreement was stumbling on Maxwell's insistence that the *Sunday Times* make a contribution to his costs. 'He wants £5,000,' minuted the *Sunday Times* lawyer, James Evans, 'as the *sine qua non* of settlement.' Both the lawyer and the editor rejected the condition because they feared the interpretation which Maxwell might publicly place upon any payment. On the eve of his return to the Pergamon board Maxwell compromised, because timing had become important.

At the end of April 1971, the journalists Hodgson and Page were both on holiday. Unknown to them, on 2 May, their newspaper published an interview with Maxwell. The headline was bold: 'The Week Robert Maxwell Bounced Back'. The introduction explained that Maxwell, who had just rejoined the Pergamon board, had withdrawn his writs and in return the newspaper 'has offered this remarkably resilient businessman the opportunity to express his point of view and describe his plans for Pergamon in the future'.

Maxwell recounted that Pergamon had suffered without the benefit of his intimate relations with the journals' editors. Concerning his bid for the company, he was quoted as saying that, although he had sufficient personal finance, he would wait until the annual profits were at least £1 million: 'I am not prepared to risk the accusation that I am trying to buy Pergamon back on the cheap.' His immediate task, he said, was to relaunch the company's sales and reinvigorate its one thousand editorial advisers around the world. 'Now I am back,' he said, 'we are out of the period of crisis ... we are a force to be reckoned with.' Besides the ebullience, there was also a dose of contrition. Maxwell conceded the validity of the criticism that Pergamon was 'largely a one-man band ... and the one man was spread pretty thin'. He also admitted the mistake of selling encyclopaedias, although only partially, with a familiar hint that others were really to blame: 'I.L.S.C. was a real whopper – the one element in Pergamon that I really regret. I trusted people and I was let down. But as chairman I must and do accept full responsibility.'

The article then permitted Maxwell to 'correct' four allegations which he described as 'of crucial importance, on which I am deeply concerned to set the record straight'. In an answer which must reflect some confusion within the newspaper at the time, Maxwell said this about the relationship between Pergamon and MSI Inc.:

These [relationships] were investigated in great detail by Price Waterhouse & Co., the leading accountants, and although their report described certain parts of the agreements between Pergamon and MSI Inc. as 'contradictory to some extent' and ambiguous to a degree where their 'precise legal effect is uncertain', it concluded by affirming that 'in all the circumstances we consider that the accounting treatment adopted by the Group accounts at September 30, 1969 is fair'. In the light of this, the business relationships between the Maxwell family companies and Pergamon have continued during the split, and will continue in the future, virtually as before.

This was an unusual interpretation of the Price Waterhouse report. The accountants in reporting that the treatment of the 1969 accounts was 'fair' were referring to their *own* treatment, since they, Price Waterhouse, had compiled the 1969 accounts. The accountants were *not* referring to the trading relationship which Maxwell had cultivated between Pergamon and his own companies. On that issue, they had criticised and substantially changed the 1968 accounts because of the hitherto undisclosed agreements between Pergamon and MSI Inc.

The article ended with Maxwell buoyantly demanding the restoration of the Stock Exchange quotation since there was by then no chance of new revelations. 'The [DTI] inspectors', he said, 'would have been impelled to take action immediately if they found any evidence of serious offences.' If Maxwell was hoping that the article would aid his rehabilitation, he was not disappointed. It was so effective that the DTI deliberately timed the release of its first report to coincide with his anticipated return to Pergamon's board.

During the previous ten months, Maxwell had appeared before the inspectors, accompanied by John Silkin and occasionally by Morris Finer. Maxwell and his lawyers claim that the procedure adopted by the inspectors disarmed them completely. Questions would be asked, documents were either requested or proffered, but there were no allegations, criticisms or direct accusations. According to one of those at the hearings, 'The inspectors never showed that they believed his critics or disbelieved Maxwell.' The inspectors prided themselves on the fact that they never sprang any surprises upon him but gave clear notice of the areas of questioning. Regularly, he left the sessions content that the inspectors had accepted his explanations: 'It was terribly chatty and chummy. The worst might be Stable saying, "Oh, come, come, Mr Maxwell," but nothing more.' Stable had after all said in the Court of Appeal that he would recall any individual if he was to be criticised and 'ask them if there is an explanation. I think that natural justice requires that.' In Maxwell's view, Stable's smokescreen was so effective that at one point, which they would quote in the report as an example of the 'casual and unbusinesslike manner' in which ILSC was managed, Maxwell was even seduced to reply, 'I can see the value of these enquiries.'

On 4 June 1971, Maxwell was travelling by car with Silkin to the twelfth questioning session when he mentioned rumours that a first, interim report which concentrated exclusively upon ILSC had been completed. Maxwell suggested that Silkin should ask the two inspectors for confirmation. Silkin refused. At the end of the session, Maxwell, to Silkin's fury, asked Stable, 'I have heard that the report is finished and it is damaging. I'm surprised because I thought that you were bound to requestion me if there was any criticism.' Stable's reply, which was recorded in the official transcript, was to the effect that the report had not yet been submitted and that nothing critical would appear without first 'fairly and squarely' informing Maxwell.

The report had in fact been completed and signed by the inspectors two days earlier although it was presented to the Conservative Minister, John Davies, only five days later. The decision whether to publish depended entirely upon Davies. Some time after the exchange between Maxwell and Stable, the inspector wrote to Silkin announcing that the report had been formally completed. On 10 July Davies, as required by law, had allowed the Pergamon board, including Maxwell, to read a copy of the report. Maxwell was appalled. Silkin, who knew that the courts had no power to prevent the government publishing, urged the DTI to desist because all the undertakings made by the inspectors had been broken.

Within days, the report's existence was widely known, and pressure intensified, especially from the City, for its immediate release. Lord Shawcross even allowed himself to be named as one of those lobbying the Minister. On 13 July, the Minister agreed. The report was published, sweeping aside Maxwell's imminent re-election to the Pergamon board and changing his life forever.

Stable and Leach had adopted a style which would do credit to the author of a pot-boiling thriller. Under headings such as 'A False Statement', 'Another False Statement', 'More Misleading Statements' and 'Still More Misleading Statements' they wove a gripping narrative which suggested that ILSC was negligently and deceitfully managed. None of the revelations in their 209-page report would attract more attention than the chapter entitled 'A Remarkable Sale'.

The date of the 'remarkable sale' was 30 June 1968, the day on which Pergamon, under certain circumstances, became liable to compensate BPC if ILSC's profits did not total £500,000. The sale was for no less than five thousand complete sets of New Caxton encyclopaedias at $70 per set. ILSC's customer was Pergamon's own subsidiary, PPI in New York. At ILSC's board meeting the following day to review the company's profits, Maxwell, according to the inspectors, made no mention of that crucial sale. The inspectors also claimed that on that day ILSC neither had a written order for that sale nor even possessed that number of sets 'in a deliverable state'. The sale, they believed, was arranged in autumn 1968 and 'deliberately ante-dated so that the profit on the so-called sale could be credited to ILSC in the warranty period which ended on the 30th June 1968'. It amounted to a charge that Maxwell was guilty of deception. (Maxwell vigorously denies that the sale was ever credited to ILSC's profits and insists that the inspectors ignored his evidence that ILSC did not make a profit on the transaction, and that he had notified the ILSC board. He has repeatedly criticised the correctness of the inspectors' finding.)

The report's examination of Maxwell's management of the ency-clopaedia business was critical, especially of his dictatorial methods and his utterance of unsupported statements. The inspectors alleged that he had sent a crucial letter regarding the creation of ILSC which was 'misleading and untrue'; that he allowed important documents to be destroyed; that proper records were not kept; that he must have known that the letter to Bernard Schwartz was not true; that his letter of 23 August 1969 that ILSC 'is now trading profitably' was 'calculated to mislead', and that 'the history of ILSC, with regard to what was disclosed, is a series of suppressions of information and of optimism verging on recklessness with the occasional statement which was untrue and calculated to mislead'.

According to the inspectors' account, Maxwell compounded his wrongdoing while giving his formal evidence on oath. They quote the example of the bid document for Butterworths which contained his reassuring statement that ILSC had 'informed Pergamon that sales and profits for the first three months of operations are running at the level forecast'. During the questioning Maxwell had insisted that the statement had been approved both by his advisers and by the BPC directors at a meeting in Fitzroy Square. In contradiction, Stable and Leach pointed out to Maxwell that not only did the BPC directors deny having seen the draft but they also denied there ever was a meeting in Fitzroy Square. Maxwell replied: 'I am amazed. That is all I can say. It is incomprehensible to me,' and he added that the circulars were given a wide distribution. Later he said, 'I can recollect clearing the document with the BPC directors of ILSC.' In their report, the inspectors state that they had requested searches in the files of eight separate principals and advisers – the merchant banks, solicitors, stockbrokers, at BPC and at Pergamon – and not a single original or carbon copy was found of the draft document. On a later occasion, the inspectors asked Maxwell if he himself had yet found a copy of a letter signed by an ILSC director which gave that memorable forecast. Maxwell replied, 'Not yet.' The inspectors therefore concluded, 'Mr Maxwell's assertion . . . is inaccurate.' They also pointed out that neither Maxwell nor Kerman had ever, throughout the questioning, sought to 'justify the statement'.

Among several other deals questioned was the sale of Pictorial Knowledge for £200,000 from ILSC to Pergamon on 12 August 1969 which according to the inspectors betrayed 'an element of desperation' to boost ILSC's profits. Concerning that alleged contract, stated the report, 'Not a single director of Pergamon [other than Mr Maxwell] admitted ever having seen [the contract] or been aware that Pergamon had made this purchase.'

But the report was also, in some instances, unfairly biased against Maxwell. In the case of Hedley Le Bas and Rod Jenman, the two Caxton encyclopaedia executives who bore tarnished reputations within the encyclopaedia trade, the inspectors sided absolutely with Maxwell's critics although both had been dismissed for alleged dishonesty. Both Robert Fleming and Chalmers Impey were gently chided in the report but then seemingly excused by statements such as 'Flemings too had lost faith in Mr Maxwell and his integrity,' or 'Mr Briggs, due to a severe impediment in his speech, is at a great disadvantage.' Although other personalities involved, like Kerman, Ormrod and Clark, were criticised, the overwhelming preponderance of blame for the sins committed was placed on Maxwell. BPC's directors, who in many instances were also to blame, were censured but with considerably less emphasis. As Maxwell retorted, 'I am constantly being amazed by the evidence from the BPC side.' But whenever contradictions of evidence were cited, the inspectors invariably concluded that Maxwell's version was to be disbelieved.

Probably the inspectors best revealed their standpoint by their emotive explanation about how Maxwell recruited the Caxton sales team in South

Africa. Describing what is normally called 'headhunting', the inspectors stated, 'Poaching is a polite [description]: sabotaging is a more robust description, but the complaint is sabotaging by poaching.' The inspectors conceded that some might say that the poaching was 'a perfectly standard commercial tug of war' but they felt that 'such a standard leaves much to be desired'. The inspectors were prim and naive about common business practices and demonstrated clear bias against Maxwell. Overall, the report revealed a lack of balance and a propensity to exaggerate where the bald facts appeared sufficiently discreditable.

The report's conclusions concentrated exclusively upon Maxwell. The catastrophic mismanagement of ILSC, the inspectors claimed, was principally due to Maxwell, of whom they said:

He is a man of great energy, drive and imagination, but unfortunately an apparent fixation as to his own abilities causes him to ignore the views of others if these are not compatible. This is very evident in the recurrent (and frequent) changes of personnel in ILSC which were one of the factors which contributed to the disaster. Neither his fellow directors, his professional advisers, nor his employees were able to sway his views and actions. The concept of a Board being responsible for policy was alien to him.

We are also convinced that Mr Maxwell regarded his stewardship duties fulfilled by showing the maximum profits which any transaction could be devised to show. Furthermore, in reporting to shareholders and investors he had a reckless and unjustified optimism which enabled him on some occasions to disregard unpalatable facts and on others to state what he must have known to be untrue....

We regret having to conclude that, notwithstanding Mr Maxwell's acknowledged abilities and energy, he is not in our opinion a person who can be relied on to exercise proper stewardship of a publicly quoted company.

The publication of the last paragraph on 13 July 1971 was unprecedented, unmerciful and devastating. It amounted to nothing less, as a judge later said, than his 'business murder'. Maxwell had finally been crucified and, beyond his family and his closest advisers, there were few who expected or even willed a resurrection. At a press conference, Maxwell denounced the 'so-called City Establishment' who had been let off very lightly. The report, he said, was 'a smear and a witch-hunt'. The inspectors had gone beyond their powers in what was a Star Chamber procedure and their unwarranted conclusion had virtually barred him from the possibility of making a living. Overnight, all Maxwell's hopes of election to the Pergamon board were utterly crushed. The inspector's indictment, which was so warmly welcomed in the City, had intentionally made him a leper within the business community.

The publication was timed to coincide with Maxwell's return to the

Pergamon board. That was no longer possible. Maxwell withdrew to Headington Hall. The Establishment, he felt, knew how to keep outsiders firmly beyond the pale.

If Maxwell has ever suffered a trauma, it was reflected on his face when he read for the first time the inspectors' report published in July 1971. Indelibly engraved on Maxwell's brow is the inspectors' damning judgement about his management of Pergamon. Ever since, he has insisted that his fight through the courts to reverse their indictment was successful. That is not true, but understanding his persistent and erroneous insistence helps to explain both the inner dilemmas of Maxwell and the environment in Britain in which he desperately sought to succeed. Whether he would ever have been satisfied by any inspectors' report is most unlikely, but his initial apprehension about the inspectors' conduct of that inquiry, the realisation of those suspicions and the attitude of Britain's judges towards both Maxwell and the inspectors confirmed for Maxwell the Establishment's prejudice, dishonesty and vindictiveness.

On the day of publication, Silkin issued a writ seeking a court declaration that the inspectors had failed in their obligation to be fair and accurate as required by the rules of natural justice. At the court hearing in September, Silkin asked Mr Justice Forbes to prevent two further reports being published – the first on Pergamon itself and the second on MSI Inc. – until the trial concerning the inspectors had been completed.

Mr Justice Forbes was sympathetic. In his view, Maxwell should have been given the opportunity to defend himself: 'Surely, before they started making their swingeing criticisms they should have said to Mr Maxwell, "Now look, we are minded to say this. You tell us why we should not."' Counsel for the DTI insisted that the inspectors had said those words but Maxwell had failed to grasp the opportunities to defend himself. Forbes was unconvinced, especially after the inspectors admitted that they had not repeated every tentative accusation to Maxwell because it would be 'unnecessarily burdensome'. All they needed to do, they claimed, was to make sure that Maxwell realised that his 'conduct was open to question'. Forbes disagreed. The inspectors' failure, he judged, to allow Maxwell a proper opportunity to rebut their criticisms amounted to a denial of natural justice. He cited what Lord Denning had said in 1970: 'Before they condemn or criticize a man they must give him a fair opportunity for correcting or contradicting what is said against him.' That requirement, said Forbes, had not been followed and he criticised the inspectors for intentionally adopting a standard substantially below that set by Denning and very different to the procedure which they had originally pledged themselves to observe.

Although Forbes had given valuable ammunition to Maxwell, he emphasised that the inspectors had not been unfair but had simply not followed the correct procedure. On a technicality he refused to grant Maxwell's application for an injunction but urged a speedy trial on the substantial issue, which, he speculated, Maxwell would probably win and as a consequence there would have to be a new inquiry. This was welcome but nevertheless cold comfort. A single judge could not eradicate the damnation inflicted by the inspectors' concluding paragraph.

Maxwell did not appeal against the Forbes judgement but instead waited months for the trial to be heard. John Silkin was allowed to represent his interests on the Pergamon board while he remained as an unpaid consultant and still controlled PPI. But his opportunities of management were strictly limited.

On 11 April 1972, the DTI published the inspectors' second report, which concentrated upon his original entry into the encyclopaedia business in 1965 with the purchase of Newnes and upon his subsequent highly publicised world tour to sell Chambers encyclopaedias. In some respects, the report was more mellow, which suggested that the Forbes judgement might have caused the inspectors some concern. Greater allowances were made for the possibility of genuine accounting errors, but the overall effect, based on the evidence, was a severe criticism of Maxwell's management and his deliberate overstating of profits.

Quoting Maxwell's own oral evidence, the inspectors showed that while Maxwell had claimed that he had relied upon his experts, Briggs and Bennett, the accountants had testified that Maxwell bullied them into recording profits which they disputed. 'I think', Bennett told the inspectors, 'there is a limit how far one can argue when one is an employee.' The inspectors accepted Bennett's evidence that Maxwell had forced him to record unrealistic profits but at times also accepted that Maxwell had support for his creative accounting from Chalmers Impey. The inspectors also suggested that Maxwell had submitted to them as evidence phony documents and had used 'bogus' invoices to justify his claims of record profits. Concerning the press conference at the Dorchester on his return from the world tour, the inspectors stated, 'We are firmly of the opinion that the claims which Mr Maxwell made were exaggerated and that he knew that they were.' His management, they reported, fell below the standards one should expect of the director of a public company.

At the end of this report, the two inspectors sought to defend themselves against the charges that they had breached the rules of natural justice, but by default they partially demonstrated the truth of Maxwell's complaints. 'When we came to write this report', they stated, 'and following our normal practice of checking we realised that we had not put to Mr Maxwell the effect of the evidence which we had heard on the question of his world tour and the press conference which he is alleged to have held shortly after his return to the U.K. In order to remedy this oversight on our part Mr Stable wrote to Mr Maxwell's solicitor, Mr Silkin, a letter dated 14 July 1971. . . .'

The coincidence that the letter should arrive the day following the publication of the first report was unfortunate. Stable had suggested that Maxwell give his answers within fourteen days but Silkin replied that they needed time for research, and suggested a session after 18 August. Amid quibbling over dates and a refusal by the inspectors to guarantee that Maxwell's answer would be included in their final report, the dispute escalated. Silkin insisted that Maxwell's only recourse was to reapply to the courts. This the inspectors interpreted as a deliberate tactic to delay the completion of their reports. 'Our own conviction', they stated, 'is that Mr Maxwell was given by us a fair and reasonable opportunity to deal with and comment on the matters raised. . . .'

The report's publication passed virtually unnoticed. For most, Maxwell was already commercially 'dead' and the inspectors' findings served only to place another layer of cement over his grave. Maxwell, however, had become determined to avenge the injustice and was spending many hours every week with John Silkin and his assistant, John Levy, to prepare their arguments for the initial court case; namely a declaration that the inspectors were bound by the rules of natural justice which they had ignored.

The task for his lawyers was arduous. Only the publication of the first report, they would later explain, had caused Maxwell fully to understand the gravity of the charges against him and had spurred him to produce the documentary evidence which rebutted the inspectors' report. Even so, their endless consultations in his office would be repeatedly interrupted by his telephone calls to brokers, bankers, lawyers or editors occupied in producing Pergamon's scientific journals. His ability to glide apparently without a moment's pause from one complicated subject to another, often switching languages between simultaneous telephone conversations, was impressive. But, above all, they appreciated that as they worked amid a shower of curses and loud exhortations, his resilence was impenetrable. In one particularly difficult all-night session where two lawyers and three secretaries were editing one hundred pages of a closely argued legal submission, Maxwell was urged: 'Do us a favour, Bob. Just go away and let us get on with it.' To the lawyers' surprise, their client for once obeyed. At 6.00 a.m. he returned. Everyone assumed he had been asleep but he was dressed in the same clothes. 'I didn't go to bed,' he roared, 'I've been earning your fees.' Maxwell had been to the Les Ambassadeurs gaming club and had won over five thousand pounds. Winning the case against the government inspectors before Mr Justice Wien which started on 20 November 1972 was not as easy.

Sam Silkin QC MP, John's older brother, appeared for Maxwell and ran into difficulties immediately. Speaking in slow and measured terms which invited interruption, Silkin opened his argument by suggesting that, had the inspectors properly heard Maxwell's case, they would have written a different report. Even before lunch on that first day, Wien seemed to be fidgeting. By the end of the afternoon, he displayed unmistakable signs of impatience and interjected that he would not hear any arguments about facts or about the quality of the evidence. It was, he said, a case about procedure. An unedifying skirmishing started as Silkin persisted and Wien reprimanded him.

As they looked up at the judge, Maxwell's lawyers did not need the powers of clairvoyance to realise that there was no sympathy for the client or his cause on the bench above. Despondently they accepted that the odds were irrecoverably against them. The bias, they believed, was not only against their case but directed against them personally. The prejudice was unpleasant to mention but was, in their view, a reality. Like their client, all the barristers and solicitors were Jewish. 'Before that day,' recalls one of those lawyers, 'I disbelieved the possibility of anti-semitism, but I realised the truth at the end.' The sentiment was unanimous among Maxwell's lawyers, who had after all appeared before so many other judges, so one may conclude that their suspicions must have had some validity despite one circumstance which could also explain so much – namely, that Sir Phillip Wien was a Welsh Jew. (A less emotional view would be that Wien simply did not believe Maxwell's case.) That night, Maxwell refused to be infected by their despondency and belligerently urged them to fight on regardless.

For three days Silkin sought to weave the arguments about the merits of Maxwell's unargued case into the constraints that Wien had established. At the end of the third day, Maxwell demanded a change of tactics. Sitting cramped with his four lawyers in Silkin's room in the House of Commons, Maxwell was aggressive. 'I must have my third leg,' he shouted, implying that his lawyer should attack the inspectors themselves. Quietly, Silkin refused because Wien had emphatically forbidden that argument. Eventually, Maxwell seemed persuaded, climbed into his Rolls-Royce and drove off. Early the following morning, Maxwell telephoned his friend and said, 'You're fired. I'll argue the case myself.' His lawyers were amazed. 'You're like a Christian going into the arena,' said one but he was ignored. Silkin made his apologies to Wien and departed.

Dismissing the barristers was a doubly perilous act for a man who had defended himself in front of the DTI inspectors as a hapless innocent who relied in matters of accountancy and finance upon his experts. How would Wien interpret Maxwell's impetuosity other than as confirming the inspectors' conclusions about Maxwell 'ignoring the views of others if these are not compatible.' It was also a perfect example of Maxwell's inability to understand the impression he was creating. Anxious not to suffer the same accusations as the inspectors, Wien allowed Maxwell four days to prepare his case.

Working with his solicitor through the night in a suite at the Savoy Hotel, Maxwell prepared his presentation. On Monday morning, he rose with solemnity from the silk's bench in the courtroom. The result was an embarrassing shambles. Unable spontaneously to fashion a speech to build an argument, he presented a woolly monologue which ignored his prepared brief. In cross-examination of witnesses, he could not ask questions to support his case. At every stage, Wien was indignant about the submissions which Maxwell thrust towards him. With jarring repetition, Wien interjected: 'What is the point of this, Mr Maxwell?' Had Wien sat in Maxwell's board room with as limited an experience of finance as Maxwell displayed in the art of advocacy, Maxwell would have been equally impatient. After six days, Maxwell finally conceded that even he could not override the will of a British judge and selected a new barrister to represent him. Michael Ogden QC, an Establishment figure with a fruity voice, was deemed the most suitable. It was naturally to no avail.

In his judgement, Wien pulverised the plaintiff. The inspectors, he said, had acted 'eminently fairly' despite Maxwell's deliberate obstruction, by giving him 'chapter and verse' of the case he was expected to answer. They did not have to show Maxwell their draft conclusions before publication. It was sufficient, he judged, that they gave him 'a fair opportunity of replying to what is said against him'. Clearly irritated by Maxwell, Wien ended by echoing the inspectors' own conclusions: 'He regarded professional advisers as tools to achieve his own ends and if they gave him advice not to his own liking he simply brushed it aside.' Maxwell was not in court on 20 December to hear the judgement although the costs were estimated at £50,000. He announced that he would appeal. With absolute certainty, he would again be judged by Lord Denning.

One of Maxwell's great weaknesses and a source of irritation to others is his unwillingness to believe or even care that his behaviour has left a bad taste in someone's mouth. His insensitivity is of course also a source of strength; but while that doggedness might have provided the finance to open the doors to the Court of Appeal, it did not help much further. In January 1974, Lord Denning might have surmised that he was in a slight quandary. After all, he had set the guidelines for the observance of natural justice in 1970 and both Forbes and Wien, in contradiction of each other, had claimed to implement them. It would be, however, to underestimate the potent virtue of the common law not to accept that each judge fashions the law to suit the case. If Lord Denning were to accept that the inspectors had not followed his requirements as rigorously enunciated four years earlier, they would have been obliged to reopen the whole inquiry. Maxwell, it was commonly agreed, had committed too many sins to be granted that victory. Hence a not unusual ritual was performed.

In his judgement, Lord Denning emphatically rejected Maxwell's appeal, citing from the original inquiry's transcript that in the case of each criticism the inspectors had indisputably put the facts 'fairly and squarely to Mr Maxwell'. Wien was right, said Denning: 'This is nothing more or less than an attempt by Mr Maxwell to appeal from the findings of the inspectors to the courts. But Parliament has given no appeal. So Mr Maxwell has tried to get round it by attacking the conduct of the inspectors themselves. In this he has failed utterly.'

But Maxwell had not completely failed. Just as the accountancy profession changed their practices in the wake of the Pergamon revelations, so were the procedures for future DTI inquiries changed. Quietly, a procedural order was introduced spelling out how the rules of natural justice had to be followed; it included a provision that those who would be criticised in a report had to be given the opportunity to comment before publication. It was, some felt, an implicit criticism of Owen Stable's management of the inquiry.

Maxwell was naturally determined to have the last word. In November 1973, the third and final DTI report, concentrating upon the private companies, was published. It was a voluminous and once again damning indictment with accusations of phoney and back-dated invoices and of rewritten board minutes; examples of Maxwell presenting documents allegedly to support his case which failed completely to live up to their promise; and repeated examples of how Maxwell sowed unusual confusion between his private companies and Pergamon. The inspectors encapsulated that confusion perfectly in paragraph 916: 'On the 30th June 1969, the debt of £104,166 was paid by MSI(DS) on behalf of MSI Inc. to MSI (1964) on behalf of Pergamon with money received from

R.M. & Co. as trustee of MSI Inc. out of the proceeds of sale of the warehouse property at Wolverton, which is . . .'.

An example of Maxwell's compartmentalisation suggesting the intentional injection of a conflict of interests into his commercial affairs which caused the inspectors to be so distrustful was cited in another exchange. Leach asked Maxwell why, in June 1966, there had been a sudden need for an agreement between Pergamon and MSI Inc. Maxwell replied: 'Because MSI Inc. continuously feared the competition of R.M. & Co. . . . and R.M. & Co. refused to be bound by this arrangement.' Both private companies were owned and effectively managed by Maxwell, yet he was suggesting that he was in genuine competition with himself.

The third report was tarnished by the inspectors' admission at the beginning that the text contained an error. Although it was not serious, and only affected 9 out of 1,254 paragraphs in the report, their embarrassment was perfect ammunition for Maxwell's counter-attack. Contemporaneous to the publication of the third DTI report, he issued a thick press release entitled. 'They Must Be Fair', which charged the inspectors with damaging his reputation and going out of their way 'to whitewash everyone else'.

Maxwell's document succinctly reflected the problem which the inspectors themselves found difficult to overcome. Every explanation provoked more questions and confusion. His own defence document proves that, even at the risk of possible unfairness, he was criticised on a balance of probabilities. Yet Maxwell's publication and the inspectors' own mistake sowed real seeds of doubt.

The publication of the third report in November 1973 coincided with another attempt by Maxwell to return to the Pergamon board. Few could believe it possible that after all the revelations he still possessed the sheer energy and courage to attempt a comeback. The inspectors did not hide their own dismay that despite their massive indictments he gave no appearance of being crippled. In their final report they stated: 'to outward appearances, [the criticisms have not] abashed him or affected his fixation as to his own abilities'. After more than three years' hard toil, they had failed to suppress the businessman. At last, Maxwell was on the verge of resurrecting himself.

CHAPTER 11

The national newspaper headlines were succinct: 'Maxwell Rides Again', 'The Second Coming of Mr Maxwell'. He shared the belief that he was about to stage a triumphant return from the wilderness to become once again the chairman of Pergamon and a Member of Parliament. Just as he had never relinquished complete control of Pergamon, he had similarly struggled to retain his position in his Bucks constituency, although in the aftermath of his election defeat his relations with some important party members had soured. Even from his entrenched position, his bid to return was fraught.

Soon after the 1970 election, the Maxwells had organised votes of censure in several branches in the constituency against Jim Lyons, the election agent, whom they blamed for allowing the party organisation to deteriorate to the extent that crucial votes had been lost. As the emotional accusations and critical reports materialised, Lyons requested that the party's National Executive Committee undertake a proper investigation. Reg Underhill, the assistant national agent, arrived in the constituency on a Friday morning in early January 1971 expecting to leave at the end of the day. Instead, the inquiry lasted until 2.45 on Sunday morning. The drama in the New Bradwell Labour Hall as both Maxwells set out the indictment against Lyons epitomised all the circumstances which had frustrated his political ambitions. On one side of the room was Underhill, formerly a junior insurance clerk, born in Leyton, east London, whose life's credo was steeped in the traditional strengths and weaknesses of the British working class – loyal, decent but for some too blinkered. Underhill was dedicated to the party and Transport House, whose inefficiency and petty politics were criticised even by Harold Wilson. On the other side of the room were two millionaires born in Czechoslovakia and France who had joined the party a mere eleven years earlier, and they were telling Underhill over and over again how the British working class should be organised. 'I didn't want to crush him,' sighed Underhill sixteen years later, 'but he kept on repeating himself. He did go on.' The rightness of the Maxwells' pleas was irrelevant. The Labour Party's representative was not in the mood to take lessons from their ilk.

Paradoxically, in view of Maxwell's complaints against the DTI inspectors, Lyons was not told beforehand what charges he was expected to answer, but he was not slow to argue that there had been no complaints, only praise, until the election defeat. That was not quite true but the official report issued by Transport House was prepared to accept Lyons's defence and condemned the Maxwells for having distorted the evidence and 'exaggerated [the complaints] beyond limits that could be substantiated'. Underhill's report illuminated a distasteful relationship between the family and the agent and criticised the manipulations of Maxwell's supporters to increase their representation in party meetings. Officially, Transport House 'severely censured' Maxwell, his wife and 'others associated with him' for interfering with Lyons's work and for denying the agent absolute control over the election funds. Further, it ordered the constituency's rules to be amended to prevent the packing of the General Management Committee. Maxwell was personally 'warned as to his future conduct'. There was little precedent for such a sweeping condemnation of a former MP and his wife. 'I told the constituency', recalls Underhill, 'to look for a new candidate.'

Maxwell was in America when the report was publicised. If either he or Betty were embarrassed, it never showed. Both let it be known that they were still attached to the constituency and expected to fight the next election. In most parts of Buckinghamshire, there was little overt reaction to the prospect but in the working-class area of Wolverton there was positive dismay.

The Bucks Labour Party had been founded in Wolverton in 1917 and dedicated activists like Frank Atter, a party member for twenty-one years, saw themselves as the rock of socialism. To those members, loyalty to the party is as precious as loyalty to a school or a cricket club for those of another class. The Transport House inquiry and the censure were personally hurtful. During the summer, following the publication of the first DTI report, Atter and others in his branch were struck by the similarity in criticisms expressed by the inspectors and Transport House. From their limited and narrowly focused experiences, they had not realised that Maxwell's treatment of Lyons and his cavalier treatment of themselves as councillors reflected his behaviour in business. They were angry that Maxwell's oft repeated promises of future employment on the land he had bought from British Rail in Wolverton had failed to materialise and they more than ever resented his critical lectures about their allegedly parochial attitudes towards the new town in Milton Keynes. Compared to Maxwell they were inarticulate and even mute. To his face, they were unable adequately to express their disenchantment about his stranglehold over the party organisation which prevented them openly debating with him their views about political events. He interpreted their passivity as acquiescence and prided himself on his qualities of leadership especially of the workers. Unfortunately, he failed to make the distinction that these were not his employees. 'He just didn't think that the common man had any common sense,' according to Geoff Foster, the regional organiser. The first to protest against the grip of pro-Maxwellites over the constituency had been Ray Bellchambers in 1960.

Bellchambers, who was employed at the Wolverton railway works and had been a member of the party since the age of fifteen, criticised Maxwell at a ward meeting. Without his knowledge, weeks later, Bellchambers was formally suspended from the party as the first step towards expulsion. 'The first I heard was when a friend telephoned,' he recalls. Bellchambers appealed to the party's National Executive at Transport House who ordered the pro-Maxwellites to reinstate the member because their act was unconstitutional. Reluctantly, the constituency complied but it did not hide its irritation.

The working-class unease about Maxwell after the 1970 election defeat was articulated by new members who had recently taken jobs at the Open University at Milton Keynes. Young men like Geoffrey Edge, a lecturer, did not believe that Maxwell was a natural socialist. They were ambitious, irreverent newcomers who expressed, in Maxwell's opinion, a lack of respect for the status quo. Like Atter and Bellchambers, Edge and the other lecturers joined and worked for the Labour Party not because of the candidate, but for the cause. In their minds, the party exists to change society, and the evenings spent in political debate were important to their lives. Edge says that they joined the party with the best intentions but gradually resented the stifling of opportunities for their brand of political debate, although it was unlikely that university socialism would find many converts in the old rural constituency. 'If you didn't agree with him,' says Edge, 'you had to go. When the government inspectors said the same about him, we realised that our feelings weren't misplaced. We just didn't like the lack of freedom of speech in the constituency.' Maxwell's belief that he would continue as their candidate provoked their ire. In the autumn of 1971, although there was no liaison between the two dissenting groups (the workers had little in common with the lecturers), they felt individually predisposed to demand a new candidate.

At the end of October, the Wolverton branch passed and publicised a motion of 'no confidence' in Maxwell and warned that they would not work for him in future campaigns. The resolution, proposed by Frank Atter, stated that Maxwell's candidature 'would result in a humiliating defeat at the next election, with a corresponding and lasting erosion of Labour morale and support'. Within twenty-four hours the constituency Labour Party was deeply split. Wolverton's refusal to work for a candidate would be a serious impediment to any campaign. The question was whether the candidate was more important than party unity. Maxwell had no doubt about the answer. Confident that he still retained the support of the majority, he responded forcefully. Atter, he claimed, was unrepresentative, undemocratic and irresponsible. It was, he announced, 'an unprovoked personal attack which was made without notice and without giving me the courtesy of an opportunity to reply'. Atter's comment was harsh: 'What notice did he give Jim Lyons or Ray Bellchambers?'

Throughout 1972 the local party was plunged into a frustrating, fratricidal conflict. Public rows are not uncommon in the Labour Party, but the effect on a marginal constituency is more damaging than most. At the end of the year, Lyons retired and Transport House refused to sanction the appointment of a new agent. The party's organisation in the constituency began quickly to disintegrate as Geoff Foster paid repeated visits to 'make sure we had no more shenanigans about membership'. Fifteen years later, the scars had still not disappeared. 'It was rugged and unpleasant,' according to Atter, and 'Absolutely unremitting,' according to Edge. The pro-Maxwellites led by Jim Cassidy, the constituency's president, were equally hurt: 'It was ugly.' Although outsiders would attempt to characterise the battle as ideological, the issues of left and right were not strictly relevant. Cassidy and Atter never disagreed that the floating voter ruled in Bucks and only a centrist candidate could win the seat for Labour. The issue was Maxwell himself and for the majority like Cassidy, who described himself as a Gaitskellite, their former candidate was ideal: 'He succeeded from nothing. The other side could never dream of the poverties and personal tragedies which Bob suffered. Yet he's a giver, not a taker.'

By 1973, what had previously been confined to arguments hardened into an outright struggle for power. Under Betty Maxwell's chairmanship, a meeting approved a motion proposed by Robert Maxwell that Edge was 'guilty of anti-party activities' and voted to expel him. Other anti-Maxwellites were not voted on to committees, and councillors who were critics of Maxwell lost their party's sponsorship for the local elections. Transport House was powerless other than to forbid the constituency to begin the process for selecting a parliamentary candidate. London's hope that another candidate would somehow appear to heal the divisions ignored the reality that the executive committee was firmly pro-Maxwell. In summer, the probability of a general election meant that a decision could no longer be delayed. Maxwell was summoned to Transport House for a private conversation about Underhill's report, while Cassidy was allowed to call a selection conference for 29 September. Maxwell now tried to mend his relations with Wolverton.

On 9 July he politely wrote to Atter outlining their joint achievements since 1959 and asking that he be allowed to address the Wolverton party to win their support for the nomination as the candidate. By return, Atter curtly rejected the peace-feeler and Maxwell's request. Their feud was reopened and Maxwell replied that Atter's letter demonstrated 'the latest shocking example of your continued unfairness to me and dictatorial behaviour in matters concerning the Wolverton Local Labour Party which is so harmful to Party unity'. There were, said Maxwell, many in Wolverton, and they represented the majority, who had pledged their support for him. Instead of leaving Wolverton to its fate, Betty Maxwell organised a petition to overrule the ward's decision. Unfortunately, she chose as her envoy someone who neither lived in Wolverton nor was a member of the Labour Party. Worse still, four days after launching the petition, the representative was tried in a local court for theft. The names on the final petition were a motley collection of non-Labour Party members, non-residents and people who eventually denied that they had signed. When Maxwell failed to win the nomination, he launched a public attack on Atter and the ward, who had nominated a left-wing academic, Stuart Holland, as their candidate.

Gratifyingly, the selection committee under Cassidy did not choose any other well-known centrist candidates for consideration. Holland, Maxwell's only other opponent, would hold little attraction for Buckinghamshire's voters. On the day of the selection conference, puffing a large cigar outside the Labour Hall in Bletchley, Maxwell showed some nervousness as he waited for the outcome. Inside, carefully supervised by Foster, who checked every delegate's credentials, Cassidy ran meticulously through the procedures, knowing that the result was a foregone conclusion. In the weeks before, Maxwell had successfully obtained sufficient nominations to guarantee the result – 82 votes in his favour and 33 against. Maxwell and Betty were thrilled. It was proof, said Maxwell, of the strength of his support. Some leaving the hall claimed that the vote showed the strength of the opposition. In an appeal for unity, Foster asked the majority not to 'hammer the dissidents' and told the latter, 'Although I do not expect everyone to retract their attitudes towards the candidate, we must work to return a Labour MP from this constituency.' Cassidy was confident: 'With Bob, we've got a winner.' Delighted, Maxwell boarded a chartered plane to fly to Blackpool for the party conference, certain of his return to Parliament. Hours after his arrival, he stepped ahead of dozens of other applicants on to the rostrum to address his comrades. On that occasion it was to advise the party organisers not to pay the rental fees for the hall unless the wages of its employees were improved. 'Bob', it was muttered, 'was true to form. He never makes the right speech. For him, just to have spoken is counted as a success.' In retrospect, Maxwell would admit that, in the glow of reselection, he had been foolishly shortsighted.

Atter and Edge were simmering about their defeat but Maxwell made little attempt to placate his enemies. In Wolverton, eight weeks later, Atter seized upon the third DTI report as justification for the criticisms. The report disclosed that the fifteen acres of railway land at Wolverton which Maxwell had purchased in 1966 for £355,000 had been resold three years later for over £1 million. For the workers in the locality, his enormous profits seemed incompatible with socialism. Disgruntled, they predicted that Maxwell could now definitely not count upon their help and consequently he would never win the seat. He dismissed the dissenters as irrelevant. They had been defeated and now there was more good news. His triumph in politics coincided with his return to the board of Pergamon. After a hard year, his other enemies, in the City, had also been trounced.

During 1972, Pergamon, whose staff had shrunk to just over eight hundred, struggled to survive on the core of its scientific journals. Its profits of just £315,000 were dwarfed by debts of nearly £5 million. Sir Henry d'Avigdor-Goldsmid had resigned at the end of 1971 because he was unwilling to mediate in the continuing feud between Maxwell and Steinberg. He was replaced by Walter Coutts, who had inherited a board of directors which was, with one exception, totally pro-Maxwell. As a former colonial officer in East Africa with no commercial experience, Coutts had been appointed by his friend Toby Aldington to fill up the necessary quota of independent directors. If anything, Coutts was less suited to the task than d'Avigdor-Goldsmid, and he was equally uncomfortable in the chair. 'I didn't like Maxwell,' says Coutts, 'and I had no time for Steinberg.' His discomfort with both men was probably aggravated because during the year he needed to understand Pergamon's business, he became reluctantly convinced that Pergamon's survival depended upon its founder.

Soon after his appointment, Maxwell sought to impress Coutts with the support he enjoyed among the journals' editors, especially in America, and to explain how Pergamon's viability was endangered by their growing dissatisfaction. Coutts agreed to visit New York, Boston, Chicago and Los Angeles to meet groups of editors who had been preselected by Maxwell. He set out intending to explain that until the DTI's reports were all published and the government had signalled that there would be no criminal charges, Maxwell's reinstatement as Pergamon's manager was untenable. But by Chicago, the third stop, Coutts felt the noose tightening. 'The strong undercurrent was that if Maxwell wasn't put back, we would lose their services,' says Coutts. In Chicago, the discussion degenerated into a brawl: 'I was violently attacked as an interloper and I was furious. I told them that the City would never let him return but they just abused me. I spat blood at Maxwell for that.'

Nevertheless, after meeting thirty-one editors, Coutts returned impressed by Maxwell's indispensability, although those he had met represented only a minority of Pergamon's 128 editors. He was anxious to break the impasse. Steinberg was showing only negative interest in the company – 'All he wanted was to keep Maxwell out,' says Coutts; the Stock Exchange still blocked any chance of trading Pergamon shares; and the DTI inspectors, whom Coutts labelled 'dodderers', had still not completed their reports, which until then had, in his view, resulted in 'Nothing firm or positive.' A shadow lay across the company which the authorities were deliberately unwilling to lift.

Stalemate is not a condition which Maxwell can endure for long. At the end of April 1973, he forced the issue by threatening to refuse to renew his consultancy contract in October unless he was voted on to the board. Coutts, fearing the prospect of Maxwell establishing a rival publishing house, summoned an extraordinary meeting for 18 June. Pro-Maxwell editors were flown from America and introduced by Coutts to Norman Freeman, the ICI pension fund manager who co-ordinated the institutions' policy, to urge Maxwell's election. Freeman, who represented the balance of power, was unimpressed. Reluctantly, Coutts adjourned the extraordinary meeting and Maxwell's bravado seemed doomed. But Maxwell was unwilling to succumb. During July, when he realised that publication of the final report was imminent and could possibly again delay his return to the board, he gave Coutts another ultimatum. The chairman, whose several abilities did not include a willingness to stand between Maxwell and his opponents, felt vulnerable to Maxwell's renewed threat of resignation and agreed to reconvene the extraordinary meeting in November. Maxwell set about marshalling his supporters and telephoned Brian Spalding, a professor of heat transfer at Imperial College in London. Spalding, more than any other editor, tipped the balance firmly in Maxwell's favour.

The two had met in the mid-1960s at one of the multitude of scientific conferences which Maxwell attended, seeking new ideas. Among those new ventures was a journal on heat transfer under Spalding's editorship. Like most of Maxwell's editors, Spalding was sincerely grateful for the opportunity of controlling a journal and, like most of his colleagues, he had been frankly uninterested in the City squabbles and the DTI's criticism of Maxwell. But Spalding was particularly grateful to Maxwell because the publisher had offered to assist his campaign for a Soviet academician, Ben Levitch, to be allowed to emigrate to the west. 'Maxwell said that he was going to Moscow and would speak with Brezhnev,' recalls Spalding. Once in Russia, Maxwell visited Levitch's home and the Russian was eventually released. Spalding was touched that Maxwell had 'gone out of his way to help'.

In early 1973, Spalding was on the Yugoslav Adriatic, chairing the annual meeting of his journal's editorial board, to which scientists had travelled from Japan, Russia and France. He was surprised when Maxwell telephoned to say that he would be joining them. Maxwell was charming and generous, hosting two fine dinners, and made no bones that he wanted in return their support. Spalding was receptive and warmed to Maxwell's comparison of his plight with Levitch's. 'Both had suffered from an unfair system,' explains Spalding, 'of faceless men in a Star Chamber court allowing no opportunity for a defence.' Spalding admits that he has never read the DTI report and is quite candid that Maxwell's initial approach was 'very subtle. He correctly assessed me that I felt this was something I wanted to do.'

On his return to London, Spalding met Coutts who in turn confided to the professor that Pergamon had not a penny in the bank and was possibly bankrupt. 'Coutts', says Spalding, 'gave the impression that he was out of his depth and uncomfortable.' By the end of the second meeting with Coutts, after many calls from Maxwell and visits to Oxford, Spalding was convinced that he was important to the company's survival: 'I hadn't realised before that we had so much power, but I decided to use it.'

Coutts, at Maxwell's suggestion, arranged a series of meetings between the scientist and Freeman. Their undisguised hope was that the institutions would bow to the pressure and switch their vote at the November extraordinary general meeting. As an afterthought, it was decided that Spalding should also meet Steinberg. The American had been aware of Maxwell's tactics and had organised a number of testimonials from American scientists to be delivered to Freeman pledging that there would not be mass defections from Pergamon if Maxwell was not on the board. Among them was Professor Bruce Chalmers of Harvard who wrote, 'I specifically refute the implication that my continuing as editor of materials published by Pergamon Press is conditional on the reinstatement of Robert Maxwell.' The battle for the hearts and minds of the editors and their influence upon Freeman was to be resolved in a conference room on the seventh floor of Imperial College, starting at 9 a.m. at the end of October.

Spalding was visibly surprised by the number of 'City men' who had appeared, outnumbering the delegation of scientists. Maxwell, an uninvited guest, sat one floor below in Spalding's office. Steinberg meanwhile was 27,000 feet above London, stuck in a jumbo circling the capital and waiting for the weather to clear before his plane could land. Spalding, accompanied by Maxwell's faithful ally Professor Harold Thompson, used the time to tell Freeman that the scientists' loyalty was to Maxwell, 'the devil that we know', and that they would withdraw if Maxwell were not put back in control. 'Maxwell is indispensable,' said Spalding, 'because only he understands and encourages us while we have never heard a squeak from the Americans.' Freeman interjected that Maxwell might face criminal charges, so forcing the editors to accept a change. Spalding was unmoved. Freeman's evident antagonism towards Maxwell had an adverse effect upon Spalding. 'It's not our task', said the editor, to the fund manager's ill-concealed irritation, 'to judge guilt. We are scientists who base our actions on what we know, not on value judgements which masquerade as statements of fact.' There was little answer to such pious oratory, which ignored nearly one thousand pages of evidence to support the condemnation of Maxwell, as Steinberg discovered when he finally arrived in the afternoon. The American's offer of more money, new editors and a bid for the institutions' shares pleased Freeman but not Spalding, who announced that, after hearing the arguments, he would definitely speak on Maxwell's behalf at the extraordinary general meeting. 'We want Maxwell back,' he said as he offered his guests a glass of whisky before they left. He would never be rewarded for his support and would be surprised that Maxwell's promise to 'rationalise' the journals, to reduce the costs for libraries, was not

completely fulfilled. But he is pleased that Maxwell, despite its unprofita-
bility, has protected Levitch's own journal on chemical-hydronamics.

Steinberg left Imperial College resolved to renew his campaign against
Maxwell and now also against Coutts. 'I am fed up with your confusion of
our position,' he told Coutts after he had read the chairman's letter to
shareholders which condemned 'eternal squabbles between contesting
parties'. Once again, the independent chairman with no financial stake in
the company was siding with Maxwell. He had little choice. Four years
after the debacle, Maxwell still controlled PPI and his family companies
were still deeply intermingled in Pergamon's business because they had
retained the exclusive worldwide rights to sell the journals. Pergamon's
meagre trading profits were still falling and there was the suggestion that,
according to a secret agreement, in the event of Pergamon's bankruptcy
the ownership of the journals reverted immediately to MSI Inc. More
than ever, Maxwell had successfully frozen Steinberg on the sidelines.

In a pre-meeting circular, Coutts resolutely told shareholders that
Maxwell would be brought on to the board regardless of any condemnation by the DTI. 'The company', Coutts explained, 'needs his entrepreneurial flair for recognising the publishing opportunities in the international scientific world and I am unaware that the DTI inspectors have
criticised that part of his work.' Naively he asked Steinberg to abstain in
the vote because 'Maxwell has promised' not to interfere in the company's
financial management. Steinberg thought the idea was preposterous but
Coutts, urged on by Maxwell and the board, was set on the strategy.
Notice was given that the extraordinary general meeting would be
reconvened at the Connaught Rooms on 20 November. When Steinberg
protested, Coutts threatened that the board would just ignore the
majority of shareholders and co-opt Maxwell.

Steinberg might fume, but other than making a bid and taking over
Pergamon, or forcing the company into receivership, he was powerless.
On Rothschilds' and his lawyers' advice, he had deliberately adopted a
low profile and had not even given evidence to the DTI inspectors.
Pergamon's problems had been ignored as he guided Reliance towards a
remarkable recovery. His company was now rated by *Fortune* magazine
as America's twenty-fourth largest with annual revenues of over $700
million and it was growing fast. But the American's strength could not
neutralise Maxwell's single-minded strategy. Maxwell had skilfully
convinced Freeman and the institutions about his own indispensability,
and the City's disinclination to involve themselves directly in Pergamon's
management by an alliance with Leasco had grown. Steinberg was
therefore unable to extract anything from Coutts and could only threaten

to vote against Maxwell's return. During the day before the meeting, Peter Stevens telephoned Coutts several times but he did not sense that a coup had been planned.

On the day itself, at precisely 8 a.m., the DTI released the third report describing the relationship between Pergamon and the private companies. Its timing was interpreted as an attempt to sabotage Maxwell's return. At 11.05, once again in the Connaught Rooms, the meeting was formally opened. Coutts announced that, since the report had just been released, the meeting would have to be adjourned until the board had given it proper consideration. Coutts and the board including Maxwell had been given copies four days earlier and some inspired leaks had already appeared in the newspapers about the inspectors' 'blunder' of admitting a mistake although the error did only affect 9 out of the report's 1,254 paragraphs. But Coutts realised that the publication removed any hope that the institutions would support his proposal for Maxwell's return. But, just as the vote for the adjournment was to be taken, Spalding rose and urged the chairman, on behalf of the editors, to co-opt Maxwell on to the board. Coutts nodded and called for the vote which, on a show of hands, was approved. Puzzled, Stevens neither voted nor protested. It was just after the adjournment that Coutts delivered the bombshell. The board, he announced, had decided, considering the views which were expressed at the meeting, that Maxwell should be invited to return as a temporary measure until a proper extraordinary general meeting could be reconvened in January. The artifice, despite the failure to obtain approval, was engineered in Coutts's words by the generous agreement of John Silkin, who, 'at his own risk', would allow Maxwell to sit as an 'alternate director' in his place on the board.

In the afternoon, Stevens telephoned Coutts and demanded an explanation for his 'outrageous capitulation'. Coutts was unapologetic. There had just been 'no time' to inform Stevens about the change of plan. 'I had given Stevens nothing more than an undertaking that we would not co-opt Maxwell without further consultation,' says Coutts. 'If we were to continue to govern Pergamon, and keep the editors with us, we had to act immediately. Maxwell threatened the night before to vote against the adjournment because he would resign his consultancy if he wasn't allowed back on to the board. I had no alternative but to allow him back. There was no time to ask for Leasco's opinion. The question was whether Leasco would make a bid for the company or shut up.'

Maxwell had no doubt that Steinberg was outwitted. In March he had strengthened his control over PPI by changing its certificate of incorporation. The British company would no longer be able to prevent Maxwell stripping PPI of its assets and could not even force PPI to repay its debts of nearly £1 million. To prove his point, Maxwell had sold Vieweg, a printing company in Brunswick, West Germany, which was wholly owned by PPI, for £400,000. The transaction perfectly symbolised Maxwell's control.

Throughout December and early January, all the actors in the drama frantically and wearily negotiated the terms of possible bids. In the background was Coutt's reminder that the whole board would resign and Pergamon be made bankrupt if the Americans did not make a final decision by the end of January. Six months earlier, Leasco had valued the company at 10p a share. Maxwell therefore lowered his bid to 11p a share and promised that, if successful, he would commit all the shares to an independent voting trust for two years. Cynics noted that four years earlier Maxwell and his advisers had suggested that Pergamon shares were worth 185p each. By 20 January, Steinberg conceded that he would not take the risk. Maxwell had won back his company. Steinberg sold his 38 per cent holding for 12p a share to Maxwell, receiving just over £600,000 in return for his original £9 million investment. Freeman, for the institutions, negotiated the same deal. Maxwell was jubilant. For under £1 million, his new American company, Microforms International Marketing Corporation, owned 90 per cent of Pergamon. The sum was considerably less than his family trusts had received when they secretly sold their 600,000 shares in 1969. 'Even with your huge fees,' he laughingly told a lawyer, 'I've come out of this with a big profit.' Not quite.

In New York, in February 1974, the Supreme Court considered Leasco's suits against Maxwell and Flemings for violations of the anti-fraud provisions of the securities and exchange legislation. The judges ruled that the New York courts did have jurisdiction over the case. The trial was set to start in July 1974. In May, Flemings intimated their willingness to settle and their lawyers began negotiating. Maurice Nessen, on Maxwell's behalf, made his approach soon after. Their joint capitulation was announced in the *New York Times* on 29 July under the headline 'Reliance Group Collect $6,250,000 from Robert Fleming Co Ltd and Maxwell Family in Pergamon Fraud Settlement'. The details were never revealed but it is believed that Maxwell paid $5 million and the bank paid $1.5 million in instalments. By then, Maxwell had purchased the remaining 10 per cent of Pergamon shares and was set to rebuild the company's fortunes beyond the public's gaze and the City's control. Three year later, the Director of Public Prosecutions announced that criminal charges were no longer under consideration. The DPP's decision would pass unnoticed. By 1974, many other British politicians had been exposed for their murky dealings with the world of secondary banks, building corporations and company perks. Duncan Sandys, John Stonehouse, Reginald Maudling, Jeremy Thorpe and Edward Du Cann were all former ministers or privy councillors who were involved in business controversies. Even Edward Heath and one of his own ministers had enjoyed a close connection with a famous falling star called Jim Slater. None of them had attracted the opprobrium attached to Maxwell's complex affair and, among his colleagues in the parliamentary Labour Party, many had become very dubious about the provenance of the stigma which he had attracted.

Labour politicians are unique in criticising capitalism while not really understanding the sophisticated banking, broking and market mechanisms upon which the system relies. Those furthest to the left, whose distrust of capitalism is greatest, know the least about business and finance. In the Commons, Maxwell's millions had lost him a lot of sympathy but he had won grudging respect, possibly even envy, for understanding the system. Amid that mixture of ignorance and jealousy, the overwhelming view in the Labour ranks about the DTI reports was that 'they' had come down deliberately hard on a Labour supporter. 'He was set up by the Tories,' was a common sentiment among the party's hierarchy who vaguely recalled the report's damning conclusion and believed that the treatment of Maxwell had been exceptionally harsh whatever the reasons. Merlyn Rees, who does not believe that Maxwell was more than a man 'who tried to cut corners', probably represents the views of most. 'The DTI reports', he says, 'did not convince me that he was dishonest.' Michael Foot, the left-winger, agrees: 'I was suspicious of the reports.' For his friends like Tam Dalyell, 'It was all very complicated.' None, it must be said, had actually read the three volumes or probably even cared to understand the details. By January 1974, it had also become totally unimportant.

Maxwell's resumption of control over Pergamon was as dramatic as his removal, although there were few eyewitnesses. Three weeks after his bid had been accepted, Coutts was chairing a regular board meeting in Oxford. Suddenly the board-room doors burst open and Maxwell marched in with Elisabeth Maxwell, Tom Clark and other supporters running close behind. 'Right, we're taking over now,' said Maxwell with a grin. 'You can all go.' Coutts was startled: 'I quickly picked up a few personal things and left. I didn't remember him saying thank-you or even goodbye. I was just glad to go.'

After recovering his business, the next goal was to return to Parliament.

Edward Heath's government had been flawed by U-turns in policy, an economic boom fuelled by property speculation and major industrial bankruptcies. In the midst of the 1973/4 winter, Heath and the miners declared war against each other and Britain became gradually paralysed when the government restricted industry to a three-day week. In February, the Prime Minister appealed to the electorate for support against the unions, confident of success. But after the first week of the election campaign, the government's support began drifting away. In a marginal constituency, Maxwell had grounds for optimism.

Election to Parliament and ministerial office had always been foremost in Maxwell's ambitions but in 1974 his bid was especially important. The repeated defeats he had suffered in the courts about the DTI reports would become so much history if his fifth appeal to the electorate were successful. Buckinghamshire's positive verdict would embarrass the Establishment and give him an impregnable platform from which to wreak his revenge. The realisation of his hopes depended much upon Bryan Barnard, his former agent and admirer who had returned to organise Labour's dispirited supporters. 'It was worse than in 1959. There were no records, no canvass returns and we had the troubles in Wolverton,' Barnard recalls. 'But Bob was very optimistic and I thought in the circumstances of Heath's disasters that we had a good chance.'

In normal circumstances, Maxwell would have expected support for his campaign from the party leadership. His constituency was, as always, an obvious target if Labour was to win a majority and even fleeting visits of national politicians would at least arouse enthusiasm among the party workers. In the event, only James Callaghan passed through. Others are still too wily to explain their absence. Maxwell therefore fought a solitary campaign, ignored even by the national media, which, had he been a lesser man not engulfed by passion and energy, he might have noticed.

Glimpses of the red Land Rover charging through Buckinghamshire's villages preceded by the familiar booming voice were soon reported in the local press. Maxwell on the campaign trail, appealing for support from the fold, was as always an impressive sight. The reception he won was polite, but also mixed. In the rural areas, the sensational rows and inquiries of the past five years had made slight impact on farmhands and villagers. Maxwell had been a warm friend to them and he quickly recovered any lost ground. 'The reception was,' says Barnard, '"Poor old Bob, he's had a rough deal." They couldn't understand what the fuss was all about.' But in the towns he encountered a different reception. The rows had left an irreconcilable gulf. 'We were let down by Wolverton,' recalls Barnard, 'where some people just refused to work for us.' In Milton

Keynes and Newport Pagnell it was worse. Not only did the anti-Maxwell faction withhold their help, but in the absence of a party organisation the undecided voters, especially among the newcomers, had not been pinpointed. As Barnard ruefully admits, 'Bob's troubles didn't help us among those people and the Tories were well organised.' But Maxwell enjoyed two major advantages. In the reorganisation of the electoral boundaries, a solid Tory ward had been relocated to a neighbouring constituency, and in the election itself there was an 0.8 per cent swing to Labour which allowed Harold Wilson to form a minority government. Labour won fourteen new seats, but Maxwell's was not among them.

The Tory candidate in Buckinghamshire did not so much win the election with his 3,123 majority, the biggest since 1945; rather it was lost against the national trend by Labour. The votes which Maxwell could have expected were won by the Liberals. The recriminations were inevitable and predictable. A certain Labour gain was lost, said many party stalwarts, because of the candidate. There was the familiar sheen over Maxwell's eyes as the accusations were made in the streets but he had no intention of surrendering. There were no comforts other than the expectation of another election within months to capitalise on the disarray in the Tory ranks. With a little time, his organisation would improve and he would benefit from any national swing to Labour. Barnard and Cassidy were urged to hold the selection conference rapidly. In April, one hundred delegates crowded into the Labour club for an acrimonious four-hour meeting. They emerged with the same candidate, who had little chance and showed less willingness to heal the divisions. Instead, Maxwell publicly attacked Atter and his working-class critics, making it harder to persuade them to work for his re-election.

By the second election in October 1974, Barnard's hopes were limited. His candidate had become lacklustre and the historic trend of the Home Counties in turning away from Labour had already begun. The second defeat was particularly painful because, while Maxwell's personal vote barely improved, the Labour Party won an overall majority. Barnard watched his candidate 'collapse emotionally' when he was declared a loser for the fourth time. 'He'd done his best and failed. He was ill for days afterwards.' In their post-mortem, Maxwell finally admitted to his agent that Pergamon and the rows with his opponents had cost him the election. 'He looked like a beaten man,' recalls Barnard. When Maxwell emerged six days later from the shock, he announced that he would not stand for election in the constituency again. But his appetite for power and influence had not diminished.

After twenty years in the power game, his opportunities seemed exhausted. (Two later attempts to win nominations for Labour seats in fact failed.) Politically he was discredited and his commercial obituary was, it seemed, already written. As his friend the financial journalist William Davis said, 'You don't get many second chances from the City. In order to succeed on the scale that he did before, you need millions. And you need the goodwill of the big institutions, and somehow I doubt if he'll ever get there again.' Philip Okill, the encyclopaedia salesman, knew differently. In 1973 he said, 'I think that Mr Maxwell will attempt to climb up the slippery pole as long as he's alive. Because he's that type of man. For tenacity of purpose, for determination, one can only admire him. It's the methods he uses that a lot of us don't like.' Okill's perception was correct. Maxwell was set on a permanent resurrection which would, if successful, rank with Lazarus'. At that time his only concession to any fault was: 'I was a bit too sure of myself and accused of trying a bit too hard, which is a characteristic the British Establishment didn't like. I should have been less brash and more tolerant of others than I have been. I have undoubtedly made many mistakes and certainly accept part of the blame for the difficulties that the company got into.' But, he added, 'I was not guilty of any misdemeanour. I had done nothing to be ashamed of.' Few believed him when he claimed that his future was 'very bright': no one could imagine a route out of the wilderness.

CHAPTER 12

An unsolicited telephone call in April 1975 offered Maxwell the serious opportunity he sought for his rehabilitation. Two Scottish newspaper printers, Nathan Goldberg and Charlie Armstrong, were trawling through the rich of London to find a saviour for their jobs in Glasgow. Both were former employees of the *Scottish Daily Express*, which Beaverbrook Newspapers had closed a year earlier to stem the company's financial haemorrhage. The two printers explained to Maxwell that about five hundred of the redundant workers had established an Action Committee which hoped to buy from Beaverbrook the site on Albion Street where the *Express* had been printed and establish a workers' co-operative to produce a new newspaper called the *Scottish Daily News*. To their surprise, Maxwell, with the best of intentions, invited them to come immediately to Fitzroy Square.

Maxwell in the flesh is always impressive but for the two Scotsmen, who were unemployed and desperate, he personified a divine omen. In their presence he telephoned Sir Hugh Fraser, the owner of Glasgow's competitor newspaper, and spoke jocularly in the shorthand most mortals only witness on glossy television dramas: 'Let's take it away from this boy-scout outfit and give it a bit of credibility, give the boys a break.' After a few calculations, Maxwell told his incredulous visitors that he would contribute fifty pence for every pound invested by the workers up to a limit of £100,000. Maxwell did not disguise his motives as pure philanthropy. Under Tony Benn's aegis, workers' co-operatives had become synonymous with the socialist cause and the regeneration of British industry, and Maxwell could hope to win prestige in the party by aiding the venture.

The two printers returned to Glasgow euphoric. To have found someone who pledged support for a cause which invariably attracted cynical disdain was a success. To have ensnared Maxwell seemed particularly fortunate since he was a socialist. Others would see his offer as a characteristically flamboyant gesture which could be withdrawn later, similar to his recently abortive bid to save Aston Martin. But this venture had a particular attraction – it was a newspaper which he had twice failed to buy. The imponderable is whether he understood that a co-operative was a transient political opportunity and not a business proposition.

In its heyday, the *Scottish Daily Express* had become synonymous with the most outrageous excesses of Fleet Street – an extravagant style of tabloid journalism which thrived upon exorbitant expense claims and incredible overmanning among both the printers and the journalists. Beaverbrook's willing indulgence was reflected in the wildly misconceived redundancy programme which had encouraged the most productive employees to leave at the highest rates only to require others to be hired as replacements. It was a madhouse with inevitable consequences. By 1974, Albion Street represented a legend with a falling circulation, an awesome reputation for industrial strife and a series of unsuccessful editors. The employees were nevertheless shocked when Beaverbrook finally declared that the salad days were over. Amid scenes of emotion, on 28 March 1974, the last edition appeared and 1,800 employees were unemployed. By then a caucus had formed who were committed to the political ideal of a newspaper owned and managed by the employees. With the support of Beaverbrook and Benn, the workers had one year in which to find £2.5 million to purchase the site on Albion Street and have sufficient working capital.

The inspiration and leader of the Action Committee was Allister Mackie, a forty-four-year-old compositor who enjoyed a reputation in his local community as a responsible politician, wily trade unionist and justice of the peace. Those who supported Mackie and awaited the realisation of the *Scottish Daily News* were not the best and the brightest of the old *Express*. Generally, they were a mixture of idealists and those who had been unable to find alternative jobs. Among the best were the printers whose talents were becoming redundant with the introduction of new technology, while the least able were the journalists who lacked either the talent or the initiative to move elsewhere.

Maxwell recognised all those weaknesses and especially their ignorance of financial management. Soon after his introduction, he advised Mackie that he should seek the services of a professor of accountancy, Richard Briston. In September 1973, Briston, on his own initiative, had written an article in *Accountancy* magazine suggesting that Maxwell had been unfairly victimised by the DTI inspectors. The two later met for a pleasant and non-committal encounter which was followed by an urgent summons by Maxwell for the academic to undertake a critical analysis of the second DTI report. After an exhaustive session – 'It was a lot of work and he wanted it yesterday,' says Briston – the accountant delivered his critique personally to Maxwell at the Blackpool party conference. 'After reading it,' recalls Briston, 'his mood changed completely. He started shouting, "This isn't what I wanted!" and became very rude. He had expected me to defend him on every count and that wasn't possible.' Briston's fee of one thousand pounds remained, despite repeated reminders, unpaid and was effectively written off when Maxwell telephoned from Glasgow and suggested that Briston come immediately to Glasgow to advise the Action Committee, who were 'financially naive', about their negotiations with the government and Beaverbrook Newspapers. Briston undertook the task 'because I thought it was worthwhile, but not for Maxwell'.

Professor Briston quickly achieved results. Beaverbrook reduced the price for Albion Street from £2.4 million to £1.6 million and also agreed to a £725,000 loan to the co-operative. The source of most of the money, £1.2 million, was to be the DTI's Industrial Development Unit, which under Tony Benn's initiative was championing workers' co-operatives throughout the country. But Briston discovered that, despite the political directive, Benn's civil servants were reluctant to hand over the money. 'They didn't hide their scepticism about Benn's policies or about the newspaper's chances of success,' says Briston, who was handicapped by a pessimistic feasibility survey produced by a team of management consultants. 'The civil servants', he says, 'set impossible terms which they hoped the workers couldn't meet.' Those 'impossible terms' included the stipulation that part of the finance had to be raised from other sources besides Beaverbrook Newspapers. The casualty of that condition, Briston claims, was a secret agreement he negotiated with Jocelyn Stevens, Beaverbrook's managing director, that the latter would loan to the co-operative whatever amount was still outstanding after they had tried every other source. 'Our deal meant', says Briston, 'that the workers would never have needed Maxwell. Unfortunately, the DTI was tipped off about our arrangement.' The alternative sources of finance were limited.

A deadline, 28 March 1975, had been set for the workers to raise the £475,000 needed to qualify for the government loan. By that date, the Action Committee had collected £350,000 in addition to Maxwell's £100,000. Just hours before the cut-off, Mackie and the committee were collected inside a stuffy hut, adjacent to Albion Street, awaiting Maxwell's arrival from London desperate for £25,000 to meet their target. They all, including Mackie, who was inimicably suspicious of Maxwell, acknowledged that he was their only hope if their dream were to be realised. Exuding confidence and wealth in his camelhair coat, Maxwell quickly removed their qualms and promised the extra money but only if some new conditions were accepted. He wanted a twenty-four-hour paper, a commitment by the workforce to unlimited overtime and an assurance that he would be appointed publisher of the newspaper and co-chairman of the co-operative. With expert brinkmanship, he eventually won the committee's acceptance although a last-minute contribution from two journalists reduced Maxwell's extra payment to £14,000. In unison, the Action Committee and Maxwell marched to the City Hall where the workers gave their saviour a thunderous reception. When the cheering died down, Maxwell repeated the three conditions on which he was giving his money. 'For 5 per cent of the finance,' says Briston, 'Maxwell won disproportionate influence. The DTI pushed the workers into Maxwell's arms.'

Neither then nor in the aftermath would anyone take responsibility for the irony that, within just one year, the same government department which had published the unprecedented condemnation of the business-man had also officially committed taxpayers' money to a venture whose very birth was dependent upon his participation. Some suspected the DTI officials of a devious plot to use Maxwell's presence to destroy future co-operative schemes. But Tony Benn, who harboured serious misgivings that his officials were sabotaging his socialistic policies, was more intent on realising his political ambitions than listening to any conspiracy theories. By all accounts, Benn could also be counted among those in the Labour Party who were sceptical of the inspectors' conclusions about his colleague. The Minister publicly told the members of the co-operative that they were fortunate to have Maxwell's help.

Once the Action Committee had bought Albion Street, tremendous efforts were made to organise the newspaper's launch, commercially and editorially. Maxwell volunteered his help and, without formally consult-ing the co-operative, negotiated during the first days for telephones, newsprint, the supply of news agency wire services and the hire of an advertising executive. Briston, Mackie and the renamed Workers' Council were irate. Maxwell, they felt, did not understand that he was not the boss but just one member of a team. Among his negotiations was a reduced rate for the use of the Press Association's wire services. But when he informed the council of his coup, it was instantly disavowed. The council wanted to pay an additional £16,000, nearly double Maxwell's deal, to prove that the workers would pay the 'going commercial rate'. For them, it was a question of ethics, since they were intent on ridding themselves of employers, profiteers and the purveyors of capitalist abuses. Consequently, two weeks after his welcome, Mackie sensed that he could count on substantial support for a coup against Maxwell.

On 17 April, at a mass meeting, Mackie proposed that Maxwell should lose his executive powers. In a heated session, Maxwell recited his commercial achievements on the co-operative's behalf. Briston, who by then half-regretted his original defence of Maxwell, had become strongly critical and cited a deal for newsprint negotiated by Maxwell which he described as excessively expensive. Maxwell fumed while Briston read out the damning conclusions of the DTI's report before commending Mackie's motion for the removal of a self-styled boss. 'There'll be a writ in the post!' shouted Maxwell as his erstwhile defender left the hall and the workers voted on his removal from the council. Ostensibly, Maxwell accepted his demise in good heart and returned to Oxford, sharing the doubts of others who were not politically committed that a newspaper whose *raison d'être* was not to make profits but to keep five hundred people at work was doomed.

By definition, in a co-operative no single person becomes a leader to inspire the remainder. In a collective, there is either communal inspiration or nothing at all. But many would regard that idealism as incompatible with the realities of establishing the firm editorial leadership which a newspaper requires. The *News*'s editor was Fred Sillitto, a sixty-year-old former deputy editor of the defunct *Express* who was a compromise choice. Under his guidance, the paper lurched towards its unveiling without agreeing its strategy, its political point of view, its editorial style, how to attract sufficient advertising or even a purpose. Neither Sillitto nor the council had targeted who would buy the paper nor had they decided what type of stories they would want to read. A similar malaise affected the advertising and circulation departments who were organising a launch during the traditionally lean summer months in the depths of an economic recession without an adequate brief to present to potential customers. Only the production section was well manned, and the printers were already anticipating the journalists' failures.

But there was only a passing hint of those shortcomings when the first edition of the newspaper came off the presses at midnight on Sunday 4 May. On the production floor, there was genuine euphoria as television cameras, journalists from other newspapers and well-wishers jostled Tony Benn and Maxwell, who stood reading the lead story about a successful model who, after 'dying' in a car crash, had been resuscitated.

If the headline, 'It's Great to be Alive' was pedestrian or clichéd, that was not reflected in the first week's sales, which zoomed from 260,000 to 330,000 copies. As the novelty disappeared, a partial decline was inevitable. Every new newspaper suffers a jolting curve of expectation and sales at its birth but professionals can distinguish between the struggle for life and the inexorable decline to extinction. In the case of the *Scottish Daily News*, the circulation, in the second week, began to free-fall down towards 200,000 copies and the awful reality dawned. Even the most favourably prejudiced agreed that the newspaper was confused and dull. There was still a chance of survival if the Workers' Council would take swift remedial action but, to one outsider, they seemed fixated and paralysed.

On 19 May, Maxwell struck. In a telex to Mackie, Maxwell appealed to him to 'sink our differences and work together' by lifting the ban on Maxwell selling advertising as the only way to 'save the *Scottish Daily News*'. Mackie did not reply and the following day Maxwell sent another much longer telex to the council predicting that the *News* would collapse by 31 October if its editorial and commercial policies were not changed. The paper, he reminded his readers, had started its life with £950,000 cash in the bank. Sixteen days after its first publication, £500,000 remained and the losses, assuming circulation fell no further, were accumulating at £30,000 per week. On the existing pattern, there was, he said, no chance of redemption. 'I know that your immediate reaction will be to accuse me of panic-mongering. The accusation would be as untrue as it is undeserved.... In view of the grave danger which our enterprise finds itself in, I hope that you will cease your stubborn refusal to comply with the letter and spirit of the workforce [*sic*] ... and save 500 jobs.' Considering the criticism which he would later attract for his role in the newspaper, his message is a model of moderation and sanity.

Over a long period I gave you a considerable amount of my time free and unstintingly and many of my suggestions which the Action Committee followed were certainly instrumental as you yourself have admitted in getting the project off the ground. I was therefore surprised, to say the least, by your attempting to remove me from the co-chairmanship so soon after I had been instrumental in helping you raise the necessary money to get the project launched.

However, I decided that this was your show and that you should be allowed to run things the way you liked. Several times I pointed out that without me or somebody like me you would find it difficult to launch the paper successfully, to maintain its high circulation and get quickly the necessary advertising. You insisted that you could do all this by yourself and 'in any case you should be allowed to make your own mistakes'. As unanimously desired by our workforce I agreed to keep my peace and not rock the boat and I have adhered to this decision.

Maxwell then pointed out that, with falling circulation and low advertising, 'our workers' co-operative is literally heading for the rocks.' The political and human cost, he warned, would be 'ghastly' and offered the council some 'concrete proposals which may just save the situation'; these involved 'improving the journalism, increasing circulation and selling more advertising'.

The following day, the Workers' Council rebutted Maxwell's accounts and shrugged off their responsibility. Instead of losing £30,000 per week, the meeting agreed, the paper was at worst breaking even, but that was optimistic. When the riposte reached Maxwell, he was outraged. Albion Street suddenly represented everything he hated most: inefficiency, blinkered trade unionism and, worst of all, insubordination. The philanthropist launched a bid to take control of the newspaper's commercial transactions. The annual elections to the Workers' Council were due on 4 June. By then, the circulation had fallen to 80,000 and the paper was attracting less than half the required advertising. Maxwell was proposed as a candidate by the journalists and, in an emotional speech which prophesied imminent ruin, he recommended himself, the socialist entrepreneur, as the redeemer. Mackie opposed his election but nevertheless, by seven votes, Maxwell was elected to the council which by then had become disillusioned and divided. His return brought a new, if controversial spirit.

Maxwell pledged himself to work exclusively for the *News* for three months and appealed to everyone not to be 'cavalier . . . when dealing with public funds . . . and save our paper from extinction'. But he did not hide his frustration that he controlled only the advertising and circulation departments. He wanted to be the newspaper's publisher, manager and editor and to thrust himself boisterously forward as the incomparable saviour of the whole enterprise. In anticipation of victory, a Glasgow public relations company, Donald and Partner Ltd, was asked to conceive a campaign which would identify the newspapers under Maxwell's command. Their proposal was revealing of his intentions: 'Since Maxwell is pivotal to all the changes taking place, he must unequivocally be seen to be taking the helm and setting the pace.' Again Mackie opposed Maxwell's bid but on 30 July, as the newspaper veered towards total collapse, Maxwell was granted full executive powers, although his control was subject to the votes of the council and the workforce. The collective had a boss.

In classic style, as 'chief executive', Maxwell moved a bed into an office, fried his food in the canteen and walked around the building exhorting everyone to work harder. The next stage was a survival plan. Most were by then agreed that the paper should be relaunched as a tabloid, but Maxwell also argued that the cover price should be reduced by one penny. Mackie disputed the economics and asked him to prove that the newspaper's circulation would increase sufficiently to cover the fall in revenue. Maxwell brushed the detractor aside as someone ignorant about business and with a mixture of ultimatums and exhortations won the committee's support. The relaunched tabloid, published on 17 August, was an immense improvement and sales soared. Had Maxwell patiently allowed his creation to develop gradually and not insisted on the counter-productive price cut, he might have reaped enormous praise. Instead, unwilling to suffer further the chaos of democracy, he sought to remove those who challenged his decisions, especially Allister Mackie, and he adopted controversial methods.

Mackie was anathema to Maxwell. His ardent Ulster Protestantism was matched by a philosophical disdain for commercial realities. His idealism had fertilised the concept of the *News* but he wanted to prove a principle, not to make a profit. For Mackie, Maxwell represented the archetypal press baron and everything which was wrong in the industry. The new tabloid even contained a daily column written by Maxwell containing his thoughts, which Mackie noted was not blessed by sparkling prose or pithy insight. A showdown was inevitable and came in late August. It centred on a demand from Beaverbrook for a final payment of £59,000.

Maxwell had astutely discovered that Beaverbrook's negotiators had carelessly omitted to define the price for Albion Street as 'exclusive of VAT'. Accordingly, the price was inclusive and Beaverbrook would be expected to pay the £59,000 tax from the money already received. For Maxwell it was natural that Beaverbrook should suffer its own folly but for Mackie the notion was outrageous. Integrity was important to him, so he signed a cheque and sent it to London. To Maxwell, who believes that survival in business depends upon extolling virtues, even those which are non-existent, and concealing glaring inadequacies, Mackie's behaviour was inexplicable. Only a fool, he felt, would be charitable on his way to oblivion, and he ordered the bank to stop payment.

That confrontation confirmed Mackie's sentiment that the co-operative was dead. His view was shared by William Wolfe, the chairman of the Scottish Nationalist Party who was also the *News*'s company secretary. On about 1 September, Wolfe handed the DTI a summary of the accounts which were compiled as if the paper were going into liquidation. 'It was bankrupt, so what else could I do?' says Wolfe. Maxwell was irate and condemned both men as 'irresponsible elements'. To Wolfe in particular, he wrote describing his 'disgust at your unprofessional conduct' because the company, he said, was definitely solvent. Hitherto, their dispute had been contained within the Workers' Council, but Maxwell decided to gather support among the workforce and began regularly using the tannoy system to denounce Mackie and his supporters as 'fools', 'knaves', 'the enemy in our midst' and 'terrible people'. Ironically, it was the type of language which, when used by critics to describe Maxwell, would be answered with an avalanche of writs.

On 3 September, just after 6 p.m., Maxwell's message over the tannoy presaged the climax: 'Attention. This is Robert Maxwell speaking. We have doubled our circulation. What a time to pick by these terrible people, the enemy in our midst, to destroy our courage and reputation. I want you to reflect carefully on what I have said. Now is the time when you have got to stand up and make up your mind – either you want the management and leadership I have provided, or else you can take the situation which Mackie and Russell and their ilk have brought about.' After outlining their disagreement about the cheque and suggesting that Mackie and Wolfe wanted to call in the liquidators, Maxwell delivered his ultimatum: 'Now is the time to let your feelings be known. . . . I want to hear from your chapel representatives what you want to do to save your jobs. Thank you and goodnight.' The following week, he apologised. But the demoralisation had spread rapidly and, after more confrontations, Maxwell appealed again to the workers.

On 14 September at a mass meeting, Maxwell promised to arrange new finance to stave off bankruptcy if a vote of no confidence was passed on Mackie and Wolfe. In Mackie's absence, Maxwell won, and both Wolfe and Mackie resigned the following day to be joined by the company's lawyers and accountants, including Briston. The newspaper's future now depended entirely upon Maxwell. At a press conference called soon after, which was filmed by BBC Television, Maxwell impatiently but authoritatively asserted, 'We are very solvent; we have no financial problems. . . . if every business in the United Kingdom was as well off for cash and paid its bills as promptly as this company, there would be no crisis.' It is the very enigma of Maxwell: whether he believed that assurance to be accurate or whether, unwilling to accept defeat, he was putting on a brave face to buy time for a rescue.

The following day, on 15 September, Maxwell informed the council that the newspaper would be bankrupt within one week but he showed no signs of panic. With a circulation of 150,000 and a revaluation of the assets by a new firm of accountants, he was optimistic that he could raise more loans from the major banks. Goldberg and Sillitto supported Maxwell and got down to improving the paper in a period of calm. Six days later their hopes were completely dashed. Mackie's departure had aroused curiosity in Fleet Street. The industry's trade paper, *Campaign*, quoted him as saying that the *News* was 'finished' and then the *Sunday Times* decided to investigate Mr Maxwell's latest enterprise.

The mastermind of the *Sunday Times*'s new venture was Bruce Page, who six years earlier had been one of the executive editors responsible for the Insight profiles. In the intervening years, he had observed that the DTI's reports had exposed Maxwell's commercial reputation as worse than the paper had imagined. Yet by 1975 the DTI's investigation had been practically forgotten and Maxwell had emerged apparently unscathed. The news of Mackie's resignation and the troubles in Glasgow were therefore a good 'peg' to summarise the DTI's devastating reports and query just why the same department had committed taxpayers' money to that individual. Prior to embarking upon the story, Page naturally consulted Harold Evans, the editor, and won the assurance that under no circumstances would the *Sunday Times* capitulate to Maxwell's inevitable barrage of writs as on the previous encounter. Two journalists were dispatched to Scotland while Page remained in London. The result was a major article which appeared on 21 September under the sensational headline 'How Maxwell Sabotaged the Workers' Dream'. Breathless and blistering, it opened by alleging that Maxwell, 'having cut a unique swathe through British capitalism, has now succeeded in turning the latest manifestation of British socialism – the workers' control movement – into an instrument of his own ambitions'. The article's style lacked any pretence of neutrality in its summary of Maxwell's past. But in putting all the blame for the *News*'s collapse upon Maxwell's stewardship, its bias was evident: 'Without Maxwell, the socio-economic experiment would have been carried through to the end, the results observed, the lessons learned . . . For the lack of the last £114,000 that dream of the co-operative was sacrificed.' The newspaper's editorial blamed the collapse on Maxwell's 'insatiable appetite for control' although he had wielded complete power for a mere week and it omitted even to hint at the contribution made to the collapse by any additional factors. If the condemnation was harsh, it nevertheless reflected the feeling that Maxwell's past and personality made him an unacceptable recipient of public funds.

Maxwell was too vulnerable to withstand the onslaught. On 1 October he resigned despite the workforce's resolution that 'We wish to put on record that our co-operative has benefited from Maxwell's consultation and his administration to further our project,' and despite their overwhelming vote, 248 to 18, urging him to stay. He blamed Page for pursuing a vendetta and issued writs for defamation. The workforce was similarly outraged.

Kenneth Grant, a union official in Albion Street, protested to Page about his description of Maxwell: 'Like everyone else he has his blemishes. Yet even his antagonists must concede that he is a courageous and brilliant entrepreneur. He can be aggressive but he can also be wounded to the moist-eyed stage by unmerited calumny.... His unorthodoxy can be very upsetting to the conventional mentality. And his few aberrations appear to be his impulsive generosity and his desire to publish another newspaper.' The Workers' Council also protested to Harold Evans that the allegations about the paper were 'unfounded, cruel and irresponsible' and that he had endangered five hundred jobs. Evans printed their complaint but the *News* perished by the end of the month, precisely as Maxwell had predicted.

The wilderness neither intimidated nor frightened Maxwell. It was the natural habitat for someone who in the 1960s had confessed to being 'a jungle man'. The Teflon coating upon those who had passed through the school of Slatinske Doly and survived frontline warfare could easily shrug off the brickbats aimed by men who were deemed to be vindictive and prejudiced. Maxwell retreated to his family, his reservoir of strength and support which few who have spent so much time away from home can possess. His relationship with Betty and his seven children galvanised his single-minded search for yet another opportunity to stage a recovery. At that moment the only testament to his record and ambitions were a series of huge, leather-bound scrapbooks which Betty had meticulously collated. Every newspaper article and every significant piece of memorabilia had been diligently stuck on to the thick pages awaiting the needs of the future biographer. But first he needed to climb out of the bunker after 1975 and it was more than ever made difficult by his past. Only money could liberate him. The sole available source was Pergamon. Maxwell devoted his entire energies to rebuilding its fortunes.

Sir Walter Coutts had relinquished his chairmanship in 1974 when Maxwell had bought all the outstanding Pergamon shares. Three years later, under Maxwell's tight control. Pergamon's traditional business had been rebuilt. In 1977, the company employed a record three thousand personnel and was publishing 360 scientific journals and one thousand books a year. Its sales had increased from £7 million to £20 million and its net annual profits zoomed from £27,000 to £3.3 million. Out of the public glare, the legal ownership had been transferred to Pergamon Holding Corporation, registered in the United States. The move was consistent with Maxwell's policy of minimising his liability for taxes and cloaking his activities in as much secrecy as legally possible.

But since Pergamon was a private company and Maxwell was for most a forgotten and discredited figure, the recovery passed unnoticed by those whose profession involves an interest in corporate affairs. There were no City reports that for three consecutive years Pergamon had paid its single shareholder, Maxwell and the family trusts in New York, £1.3 million as a dividend. Even in January 1978, when fire destroyed most of head office in Oxford, the dividend was maintained.

By 1979, Pergamon had hit the same suffocating plateau which ten years earlier had provoked Maxwell's bid for the *News of the World* and the deal with Leasco. The sale of Pergamon journals was static and the printing subsidiaries were losing money. Once again Maxwell was frustrated and anxious to find new horizons. Over the previous five years the company had paid off its debts and amassed more than £5 million in its reserves. But since Maxwell could not expect financial support in the City, he needed more cash if he was to launch a bid. In 1979, Maxwell sought a new and potentially major source of income – dealings in shares. In the previous two years, he had speculated annually about £2 million in gilts in London and bonds in New York. The profits had been modest. In 1979, his speculation spiralled to £60 million but went sour in New York. He lost £1.5 million in that year's deals, which halved Pergamon's annual profits.

In 1980, his fifty-seventh year, an age when most men think about their retirement, Maxwell was sure that he had found an escape from oblivion. In preparation, the figures on Pergamon's balance sheet dramatically increased. The turnover in share deals expanded to £79.9 million and produced profits of £1 million. Pergamon's subscription income doubled, pouring no less than £11 million into the company. On paper, Pergamon's assets had increased fourfold in five years to £24 million. His personal fortune in the same period, from accumulated dividend payments and profits from the sale in the USA of scientific journals, can be conservatively estimated at a further £10 million. Maxwell was flush with money at the moment of his nemesis.

During 1980, Maxwell quietly began buying shares in the British Printing Corporation. By July, he had accumulated a stake just below the limit where he would be required to reveal his interest. There was at least £15 million of his own money to finance a gamble which he hoped would transform him from an outcast into a welcome visitor at places which were previously out of bounds.

Jonathan 'Johnny' Bevan is a big man in stature, ambition and lifestyle – a prototype Yuppie long before any slick observer had imagined that those making money in the City could enjoy the glamour and power normally associated with a Hollywood studio boss. In Bevan's life, a 'dawn raid' could be a breakneck race down the Cresta Run or the highly publicised seduction of a society belle. But Bevan has rarely been as thrilled as when he dispatched his dealers to the centre of the Stock Exchange floor at precisely 9.30 a.m. on Friday 18 July 1980, to hold up their arms and offer to buy eleven and a half million shares of British Printing Corporation for 25p each, 7p more than their market price. Ten minutes later, as the waves of excitement still reverberated around the hall, Bevan was certain that his first dawn raid would earn a mention in history. His client had paid £2.9 million for 29.5 per cent of his estranged, erstwhile partner. By any yardstick – timing, price and strategy – it was an innovative coup which, on Maxwell's part, reflected the accumulation of thirty-five aggravated years of experience. That day, the Maxwell presented to the world was unbellicose, mellow and thoughtful. His public comments were unusually guarded; he suggested that BPC's management had nothing to fear from their new 'constructive shareholder'. The opposite, of course, was the truth. For Maxwell, his dawn raid was akin to the Normandy landings in June 1944: a bridgehead had been established and the ultimate goal was Berlin – to take the City by storm. After the smoke had cleared and the initial euphoria had waned, the real battle commenced.

No one was more surprised by the raid than Peter Robinson, BPC's chairman and managing director. As in a Hollywood 'B' movie, the news had been delivered melodramatically, by Maxwell himself. A 9.30 in the morning, as Bevan's dealers stood on the floor of the Stock Exchange, Robinson's secretary had announced that Maxwell was on the telephone. The chief executive of Europe's largest printers assumed that it was just another of the regular business calls which he was compelled to take from a man for whom no one in BPC had any affection. Relations with Maxwell had been strained ever since the collapse of ILSC, and their conversations were never amicable. But, on this occasion, the announcement by the voice on the telephone that he had just become a major shareholder foretold disaster.

'I want a meeting,' said Maxwell.

'I'm busy,' replied Robinson, who feared that Maxwell would demand a seat on the board.

'What about over the weekend?'

'I'll be in Sevenoaks.'

'I'll come down.'

'Sorry, it will have to wait until Monday.'

When he replaced the receiver, Robinson's stomach was cramped and his head was spinning. Maxwell's timing had been impeccable. BPC, despite annual sales of £200 million, was losing a lot of money; its board of management was in disarray, grappling to steer their company away from bankruptcy. If Maxwell was set on realising his ambition to control BPC, Robinson would fight back, not just for the company, but also on his own behalf. For a decade he had worked so hard to rescue the monster, and he was not about to open the door to the likes of Maxwell.

Robinson's promotion to manage BPC in 1969 had represented an acknowledgement that his technical abilities in the packaging division might heal the wounds which had bedevilled the company since its creation four years earlier. BPC had never fully recovered from the revelation that its megalomaniac founder, Wilfred Harvey, had perpetuated a succession of costly frauds. In the wake of his resignation, the new management had grappled with a disparate collection of printing companies and a legacy of massive debts which were augmented by the £5 million losses from ILSC and the publication of unsaleable encyclopaedias. BPC's debts had accumulated just as a succession of new disasters hit its core activity, printing.

During the 1950s, Britain's three major printers – Sun, Odhams and Bemrose – had individually expanded to capitalise on the boom in colour women's magazines. Flush with orders and money, the managements bowed to most trade union demands for higher wages and more restrictive practices. By the late 1960s the boom was history. Television had cut deeply into magazine circulations but the print unions refused to acknowledge the new reality and accept any redundancies. At BPC's Sun Printers in Watford, as in Fleet Street, the weak management recoiled from confronting their nightmare until 1969. The resulting strike cost Sun Printers its most lucrative magazine contracts and cost BPC its total annual profits.

Throughout the 1970s, buffeted by postal strikes, power cuts and a gyrating economy, Robinson struggled to save the company although he was handicapped by his limited understanding of finance and by persistent industrial disputes. If pressed, Robinson would admit that his personality and character were ill equipped to confront Tony Dubbins and Joe Wade, the obdurate leaders of the NGA, the print union concerned. According to Robinson, neither man was willing to discuss the company's survival or agree productivity deals. As Robinson's stance alternated between politeness and desperation, the union leaders gained the impression that he was an appeaser who, after accusing them to their faces of blackmail, would always bow before their intransigence. They blame Robinson for 'never moving into our century'.

To stem the losses, Robinson sold some printing plants and closed others, but lucrative customers, among them the *Economist* and *Newsweek*, were lost forever. The tilt towards bankruptcy was delivered in October 1978 at the Savoy Grill by Marmaduke Hussey, then the managing director of Thomson Newspapers. Robinson had been relieved that Thomson's contract to print the *Sunday Times* colour magazine had been renewed. But, during the meal, to his consternation, the 'Duke' briefed him that Thomson newspapers were going to 'discipline' the Fleet Street workers by closing down their newspapers. 'In one month,' the 'Duke' told the incredulous BPC chairman, 'We'll have them in retreat.' Hussey failed, but for Robinson the cancellation of the magazine's contract for one year caused a ruinous £2 million loss which was aggravated by more NGA strikes and the loss of more customers to foreign printers. As the abyss loomed, Robinson thought that he had snatched a lifeline by winning a seven-year contract to print the *TV Times*. Although BPC would lose £12 million that year and there was no money to pay for the new printing machinery which he had just ordered, Robinson was dreaming about deliverance by a miracle when Robert Maxwell telephoned.

The two came face to face on Monday morning, 21 July 1980, in Robinson's office. Maxwell's initial charm was offset by Robinson's frostiness. As Maxwell spoke about placing his talents at BPC's disposal to save the company from bankruptcy, Robinson reminded him of the DTI's conclusion that he could not be relied upon to be a steward of a publicly quoted company; an opinion which, over the weekend, all of BPC's bankers, brokers and major customers had repeated to each other.

'I want a position on the board,' said Maxwell.

'I haven't decided,' replied Robinson as the acrimony intensified.

'I demand it,' hissed Maxwell as he left the room, 'and I will expect the appointment by the time I return from Moscow.'

Robinson was thunderstruck and could not conceal his emotions. After so many years struggling to manage BPC, he could barely perceive his own weaknesses but consoled himself with the reflection that his pleas about the very unsuitability of the predator would be heard sympathetically in the City and Whitehall. He ordered that BPC's defence should rest entirely on regurgitating Maxwell's record.

Compiling the indictment was assigned to a fellow director, Montague 'Monty' Alfred, who set about plundering the DTI reports and newspaper cuttings. The character of Maxwell which Alfred chose to draw for submission to the Office of Fair Trading was of an evil genius who had been so persuasive that decent men would do and say things which they knew were wrong. But after three weeks Alfred acknowledged that for the board to rely uniquely upon such a negative argument was demoralising and he decided as an afterthought to telephone a former colleague, Lord Kearton, with whom he had worked at Courtaulds, to seek his advice and help.

Kearton's career had won him prestige as a skilled and independent industrialist who was critical of what some called the City's traditions but which he condemned as incompetence. He had just retired as manager of the Labour government's agency which controlled North Sea oil but he was still a non-executive director of BPC's merchant bankers, Hill Samuel. To Alfred's relief, Kearton agreed to help the beleaguered board despite the company's tense relations with their bank who, it was inevitably but wrongly suspected, had 'failed' to anticipate the dawn raid because of the close relationship between Maxwell and Hill Samuel's director, Sir Robert Clark.

Acting as the honest broker, Kearton called first on Henry Benson, who had a special responsibility for Britain's 'sick industries' at the Bank of England. Kearton was surprised by his old friend's attitude. 'His view was simply that BPC should be liquidated as quickly and quietly as possible,' says Kearton, 'and without a public row about Maxwell.' At the DTI, Kearton found that Peter Carey, the permanent secretary, was similarly uninterested in BPC's fate. 'Peter believed that it was beyond redemption and he wasn't keen on Maxwell.' Kearton concluded that BPC, which was losing £1 million every month, was not only heading towards the rocks but was also friendless. By November, Robinson had discovered the same unpalatable truth but was desperate to deny Maxwell the prize he anxiously sought.

Robinson's relations with Hill Samuel had by then deteriorated and he sought the help of Hambros, who had enjoyed such a mixed relationship with Maxwell. Antony Beevor's brief was to produce any rescue package which was predicated first to exclude Maxwell and only secondly to save BPC. In the meantime, Robinson appealed to BPC's major creditor, the National Westminster Bank, with a formula which included the appointment of a new chairman. The response of Peter Dodds, the manager of NatWest's London District, was decidedly unsympathetic. He told Robinson that the only appointment he would consider was of a receiver and said further, 'We are not neutral and we don't want a battle.' The bank stood to lose £17 million if BPC collapsed and as far as Dodds was concerned, 'We'd looked at so many of Robinson's schemes and none of them were attractive. Mr Maxwell's ideas were the best to save our money and the company.' Dodds insisted that Maxwell be given a seat on the board because he was offering to invest £10 million in the company. When Robinson queried whether Maxwell had that sort of money, Dodds was surprisingly well informed. Unknown to Robinson, Dodds was also Maxwell's banker. In fact, Maxwell was a very special client who had opened an account in Fitzroy Square in the early 1950s: 'He had an excellent track record with us,' recalls Dodds, 'and had always fulfilled his undertakings. We never had any reason to doubt him. That counts for a lot with bankers.' In lengthy sessions after the July raid, Maxwell had persuaded Dodds that the bank could depend upon Maxwell to recover its money and it should therefore grant him exceptionally favourable terms for the huge loans which he still required. The DTI reports, says Dodds, were 'irrelevant'. 'A far-seeing man,' is Kearton's judgement about Dodds.

By Christmas, Kearton's role had changed: he became the mediator between Maxwell, BPC and the City. 'Maxwell had bombarded me with ideas on how to save the company,' recalls Kearton, 'and no one else was interested. I thought his survival plan might work, despite the unions and board saying it was "impossible".' Kearton had also shrugged off the many warnings from those who had been employed or had negotiated with Maxwell. Kearton could not understand their antagonism although he had never occupied either position. 'He's just a hard taskmaster,' says Kearton, later adding, 'I'll concede that the one way to cease having any influence over him is to work for him.' Kearton had also no sympathy with Robinson's references to the DTI reports: 'I read them carefully and decided that Maxwell was the victim of his own exuberance, verbosity and optimism, but he wasn't wicked. I felt that his wrongdoings were small change compared to a lot of happenings in the City and the inspectors had been unfair on him.' Kearton's conclusion stunned Robinson and Alfred: 'I told them that they had no choice but to let Maxwell see the accounts and decide if he wanted to invest his money.' Robinson resisted until Dodds issued a firm veto on a public battle with Maxwell, and Hambros' overly complicated rescue had to be jettisoned along with the bank. BPC's survival depended on Maxwell. In trepidation, Robinson returned to Hill Samuel and the unpalatable cure of Maxwell's 'survival plan'.

In Maxwell's life, it was a historic moment, similar to the award of the

Military Cross, and on this occasion there could be no suggestion of reckless bravado. Deserted by all his bankers, Robinson had no choice by the end of January but to agree that Maxwell should effectively take over the company, which was on the verge of bankruptcy. 'I feel pretty sick,' Robinson told a friend.

Formally, on 17 February 1981, Maxwell was voted on to the board as deputy chairman and chief executive. Kearton was appointed chairman with Robinson as managing director. The next stage was for Maxwell to convince the print unions to dismantle their restrictive work practices since his personal investment and the National Westminster Bank's funds were available to save BPC only if the unions made enormous concessions. Maxwell was now on public trial not only to save a major British company but also to prove that he was a reformed man. Kearton sat as the judge.

Under Kearton's scrutiny, for sixteen hours, seven days a week, Maxwell negotiated with the unions about the details of his 'survival plan'. Although it would cause 2,500 redundancies (one-quarter of the workforce), the closure of five printing plants, the wholesale removal of restrictive practices and the effective reduction of wages, Maxwell called it a 'rebuilding exercise'. Five years before Rupert Murdoch sabotaged trade union power in his British empire by a midnight flight to Wapping, Maxwell sought to unclasp the union's stranglehold at BPC by releasing an irresistible series of demands.

Representatives from each BPC factory were brought daily to the Queen Street headquarters in London where Maxwell had installed a bed in an office. With a rigid deadline of six weeks, the trade unionists were 'locked' in a room to negotiate a survival plan. Fresh from their triumph over Thomson newspapers, and after a decade of unparalleled union aggrandisement, they greeted Maxwell's unique brand of haggling with truculent disdain. 'I watched with fascination', recalls Kearton, 'how, moving from room to room, he gradually played off the rivalries between the chapels, and then between the chapels and the national organisations. They abused him but he never lost his temper, he never gave the impression of being under pressure and he was always the master of his facts. Above all, he left no one in any doubt that, without him, they'd all be unemployed.' The recollections of the union representatives are less generous. Dumbfounded by the long hours and the unprecedented *diktat* of a deadline, they gradually retreated, deflated and perplexed to be dealing with a workaholic whose first offer had been the best. In one tense moment, as they argued to recover lost ground, Bill Miles, a SOGAT official, blurted out to the menacing publisher, 'You've got so many balls in the air, Mr Maxwell, but don't forget, two of them are mine.' Maxwell roared with laughter, satisfied that his tactics were being rewarded.

But his growing success was also due to a consistent display of charm. For someone who is so notoriously impatient with lesser men, his performance over those six weeks was of a compassionate man anxious to understand the most mundane objection from the most inarticulate machine-minder. Forever darting in and out of those twenty rooms, Maxwell identified which local officials were presenting the obstacles. Either late that night or early the next morning, the intransigent union member would receive a phone call: 'Hello, Robert Maxwell here. I just want to say...', and then would follow a conversation which was 'a secret between the two of us. Not even the general secretary must know about this. But you and I can settle this because you are so important to our plans...' At their next meeting, Maxwell's giant arms were wrapped around the printer. 'My friend and I', Maxwell said to the bewilderment of the other negotiators, 'have settled this problem.' Bill Keyes was repeatedly amazed: 'The greatest wheeler-dealer we'd ever met. He wasn't out to destroy the unions, but just to promote Bob, and also to be loved.' Those very contradictions unnerved the blinkered union negotiators. The charisma, the complexity and the charm of a man who spoke their language so fluently was baffling. 'He always had to prove himself,' says Keyes, recalling how the 'nice-guy act' was selective and rarely genuine, especially towards the BPC board: 'They were treated with contempt.'

The apparent cause of that contempt was Maxwell's anger about the abuses and profligacy which had been cultivated under Robinson's regime. At the Park Royal plant, which printed the *Radio Times*, the average pay was £15,000 a year for four days' work per week, and the car park, says Kearton, 'was packed with Mercedes cars earned from second jobs'. Inside Park Royal, six men instead of one were 'minding' machines and if one of those six were absent through illness, the management were compelled to hire a temporary replacement with enormous penalty costs. Even seventy-year-olds were still on the payroll, although they were not working. Maxwell seized on these symbols to undermine the unions and humiliate Robinson's record. Under his regime, he told Robinson in front of Kearton, there would be no frills. Executives would follow his example and fly economy class. Expenses would be slashed. He had even noticed, he scolded Robinson, that excessive bottles of milk were ordered at several warehouses. Robinson was ashen-faced and Kearton was impressed. Any man who promised to eradicate the obesity and caprice of executive life appealed to Kearton, although there were not many who today would recognise the image of the self-denying millionaire which Maxwell portrayed for the *Bookseller* in August 1980: 'I come from a farm-labouring family,' he said, 'and I don't go in for owning yachts or going to big parties.'

Kearton had also paved the way in the City for Maxwell's return. 'I assured everyone that, having seen Maxwell at close quarters, he was a genius. I even insured him for £15 million because of his importance.' If in retrospect it seems that in BPC Maxwell had shrewdly chosen the firmest foundations for his latest relaunch, that was not the common opinion at the time. Maxwell, it was felt, was taking a major risk to buy his way back to respectability and his chances were slim. He would have agreed that his initial investment was a gamble, but it was of a different complexion from what others imagined. In all his years, other than the barter trade, he rarely invested in a business without anticipating or inventing a profitable exit. In BPC's case, his initial £2.9 million investment was certainly a risk, but it was also carefully calculated to lead to the next stage. For £10 million, Pergamon would own assets worth £70 million, a huge tax loss and a guaranteed income in the future because, even before committing his money to BPC, Maxwell had secured support and new orders from his future customers, among them the Thomson Organisation.

Despite their differences over the years, Roy's son Kenneth Thomson had sympathy for the irascible Maxwell. The impulsive, unpredictable salesman and trader possessed qualities which might destroy the same trade unions who had recently driven Thomson from Fleet Street. Like other customers for BPC's colour magazines, Thomson saw no advantage if the choice of possible suppliers diminished. In Thomson's view, Maxwell was BPC's only hope, but was being harmed by carping criticisms which suggested that BPC's customers, including Thomson, would refuse to deal with Maxwell. In an unusual gesture of support, Gordon Brunton, Thomson's managing director in Britain, therefore issued a letter for circulation to both the unions and the City which promised that his group would place as many orders as possible with BPC if Maxwell were successful. The pledge would be honoured for one year but ended when Maxwell tried, slyly in Thomson's view, to renegotiate the contracts.

Maxwell's potential losses were accordingly less than those extracted from BPC's employees, since his money was committed only when every chapel had succumbed and signed a binding and publishable agreement. Bill Keyes was present when the last chapel signed the agreement and as Maxwell theatrically wrote out the cheque for £10 million. 'Do you want to come with me to the bank?' he asked the union leader. 'You must be joking,' Keyes replied, 'I've just lost a lot of members.' Among the assets which Pergamon now owned was ILSC and Caxton encyclopaedias. The wheel of fortune had turned full circle.

A special shareholders' meeting was summoned for 24 April to approve the reconstruction of the company. The alternative, spelt out in bold, dark type on the memorandum, was that BPC would be placed in liquidation. Overwhelmingly, the proposals were supported, and Maxwell was rehabilitated. Appropriately, the meeting (held in the Connaught Rooms, the venue of so many past humiliations) was followed by a champagne celebration at BPC's headquarters. The star was jubilant, applauded and feted by men who six months earlier would have looked askance at him. This was a perfect moment to judge his character for, as Kearton would write on Maxwell's sixtieth birthday, 'The best is still to come.' Until then, in Maxwell's business life, the trait most frequently perceived was his indomitable will to recover from defeat. Repeatedly, Maxwell could be heard appealing for fairness and justice. Without precedent for a businessman who had so often tumbled and fallen, he had miraculously won another chance.

Peter Robinson did not arrive at the champagne celebration. During the shareholders' meeting he had collapsed from pneumonia caused by an untended gallstone in his kidney. Maxwell had said little as the former chairman staggered from the hall. Understandably, Robinson had no future in BPC but nothing had prepared either Robinson or others for the scathing contempt felt for him by his successor. As Robinson lay in the operating theatre, Maxwell showed that those who have no power to exert over him, whether employees or competitors, can expect neither respect nor their due. Robinson's office was occupied by Maxwell, his name was removed from the door, his papers sealed, and he was told by Maxwell that, despite years of service, his performance at BPC disqualified him from receiving a pension. It was a telling omen which Kearton, with effort, rectified. Others, over the following years, would often fail to find a similar agent of mercy to give them protection. Few outside Maxwell's immediate employment, which until then had been so limited, had realised that a man who had personally suffered such scorn would himself seek to humiliate others. But Robinson's misery was long forgotten in the frantic schedule which Maxwell undertook in the weeks after the takeover.

Travelling incessantly by helicopter to BPC factories around the country, Maxwell appeared before all the BPC employees in the role he would come to adore. 'Gentlemen,' the giant would say, often standing astride a table in the canteen, 'I am Robert Maxwell and this company has been grossly mismanaged. I am going to put it right. We must make more money. I am looking for job cuts, but I'll save the rest.' As patches of hostility appeared, the voice rose slightly: 'Gentlemen, you must remember that I am now the proprietor of this business.' Few would be more impressed than his new employees at Taylous, near Maidenhead. So roused was his audience by the performance and by the promise of a bright future that they clapped and cheered, oblivious of the fact that their new hero had just announced that, to create the new Jerusalem, the majority were about to lose their jobs.

But in Queen Street, soon to be renamed Maxwell House, few observed that charm. Instead, his new staff experienced unprecedented scrutiny, especially of every penny's expenditure. Only Maxwell could sanction the purchase of a new car or the hire of a temporary secretary, or sign a cheque for over £500. On one memorable occasion, an assistant pushed a chit in front of him.

'What's this?' growled the great man.

'Approval for a new car for a rep,' replied the humbled employee.

'Why does he need a new car?' asked the employer as his voice rose to a roar. 'Why do we need this man? Fire him.'

But not only reps were dismissed. In the first five years of Maxwell's reign, very few of the company's directors, even those whom he appointed, survived for more than one year. Few could satisfy his demands or cope with the stress. 'It was annoying and mentally tiring', recalls David Perry, a former English rugby captain and the manager of BPC's factory at Taylous, 'that he acted without consulting anyone.'

Daily, after seven every morning, Perry and all the managers rang Maxwell for instructions. 'Take this down,' said the chairman, dictating the orders of the day before banging down the receiver. What emerged was not always pursued and indeed was often contradicted by Maxwell himself. Behind the bluster and the bullying there was a drastic strategy to reduce costs. The strategy was successful but the qualities of leadership and vision demanded by some were lacking. Overheads tumbled as the closures and redundancies were implemented. After one year the monthly £1 million loss was transformed into a £1 million profit. But those whom he admitted that he needed most – managers like Perry, the financial director David Harbut and the innovators like Peter Hassell – had decided to leave. They were weary and wary of an instant decision-maker, 'shooting from the hip', who rejected the conventional organisation of management and who seemed to thrive on creating rather than settling uncertainty. Perry calls it 'motivation by fear' and, among other reasons, left because 'I couldn't stand wondering when the stab would come.'

Monty Alfred was among the many who was embarrassed in front of other employees before leaving the corporation. It was a settling of scores.

By the end of 1981, BPC's survival was described even by Maxwell's most bitter critics as a miracle. Despite a major recession, the company's profits could finance a £100 million investment plan for new machinery. Yet, as his visibility grew, the apparent patience and understanding shown towards trade unionists, which won Kearton's blessing during those six weeks of negotiations, disappeared.

Throughout the 1960s, Maxwell had combined the role of buccaneer businessman with his pledge to socialism. In the House of Commons, he had been an outspoken if ineffectual critic of the suicidal Luddism which imbued both British management and unions. In the 1970s, he had observed his predictions come true and had eagerly awaited the opportunity to effect his draconian solutions. The BPC agreement which sliced trade union power was just a foretaste of 'Maxwell's law'. He realised that challenging trade unions where previous, supine managements had failed was a profitable strategy and one which, for him, was politically acceptable. Although the cause was also popular among the Conservatives, in his own ranks, where he became renowned as anti-trade unionist, he provoked bitter opposition.

The first to protest were the unions at Pergamon's headquarters in Oxford. Maxwell's attitude towards his own employees had hardened since the days in Neal Street and Maxwell House in Marylebone. There were, he felt, to be no free meal tickets and he had ordered the installation of an electronic recording system which monitored the hours each employee worked. Maxwell still enjoyed using a tannoy system to address his workers, always prefacing his monologue, 'Attention, attention, this is your chairman speaking....'. Some found the atmosphere unpalatable.

In a memorandum dated 14 September 1979, Maxwell had acknowledged that labour relations in his own publishing house were bad and cited as evidence the awkward fact that 'during the past few months there has been a turnover of more than 50% within the Department. This high staff turnover is harmful....' Feelings about working for Maxwell were mixed. Some were content, but a minority criticised the atmosphere as reminiscent of school. Throughout the 1970s, Maxwell had only reluctantly improved wages, which by 1980 ranked fifty-fourth in the NUJ's list of fifty-seven publishers. Similarly, fringe conditions such as maternity benefits had not improved since 1972 despite the company's new profitability. Patrick Tickell, who was employed as joint managing director for eight months in 1977, was among those who disliked the atmosphere and was deemed unable to cope with the exacting demands.

'The reason for the level of turnover', says Tickell, 'was simply that people did not like the conditions of work. They were expected to work extremely hard and never make mistakes. Yet their duties were never really explained to them. Instant dismissal without substantial justification was common, but I recall people being hastily reinstated after having been summarily fired by Mr Maxwell.'

After 1979, serious disagreements erupted between Maxwell and the unions concerning the further employment of two probationers. On reasonable grounds, Pergamon had not renewed their contracts, but the manner of their treatment prompted the NUJ in March 1981 to call for an official strike because, after two years, Maxwell had refused to negotiate a new wage settlement. Nine employees were summarily dismissed two days after they went on strike. Maxwell described the strikers as having 'sacked themselves' and defamed them as 'politically motivated musketeers' and even as 'Trotskyites'. Since the strikers were poorly supported, the dispute would not have escalated into a test of Maxwell's principles had a feeling not spread among many socialists that, although he was a member of both the Labour Party and the Association of Scientific, Technical and Managerial Staffs, he was bullying the union. Maxwell, who was operating in a goldfish bowl where every gesture was scrutinised, was sensitive to any coverage of his troubles, especially when it appeared on 6 June 1981 in the *Bookseller*. 'I took a call from Maxwell,' recalls David Whitaker, the publisher of the magazine, 'and he demanded a retraction of the report. He said it was a libel. I told him we had just reported facts. He threatened a writ for defamation if I didn't apologise.' The conversation ended dramatically.

'Rubbish,' said Whitaker.

'Are you calling me a liar?' said Maxwell.

'No, I just think that you are very mistaken'.

'I want a retraction.'

'Balls,' shouted Whitaker.

'I beg your pardon?'

'Balls,' repeated Whitaker as the phone went dead.

In reply, Maxwell issued a writ and spent the following two years engaged in all ill-tempered struggle.

The magazine had reported that Maxwell's terms of employment and style of labour relations were not quite perfect. For more than one year, during the Pergamon dispute, Maxwell had either refused to meet union officials or cancelled meetings. Often, he uttered exaggerated allegations about union officials and then, when national union officers answered his claims by substantiated and detailed rebuttals, he not only ignored their refutation but repeated the same unfounded allegations. For those with memories about Maxwell's speeches on the tannoy at the *Scottish Daily News*, the pattern was familiar: namely, any opponent or critic was deemed to be a subversive. By 1981, Maxwell was becoming estranged from his political allies. As Jonathan Hammond of the National Union of Journalists said, 'Mr Maxwell frequently boasts about his commitment to trade unionism and socialism ... [but] is Mr Maxwell's behaviour at Pergamon consistent with the standards recognised by membership of those organisations?'

Hammond and the NUJ leaders were particularly irritated that Maxwell excused his refusal to negotiate by pleading travel abroad on business. On subsequent occasions, similar excuses were proven to be untrue. Twice in March 1982, Maxwell's lawyers had told industrial tribunals that their client was travelling in South Africa and Japan, while in fact he was in London and Oxford. Maxwell claimed that those trips were cancelled 'at the last moment' and blamed his subordinates for failing to remind him of his appointment in court. The unions threatened to escalate the anti-Maxwell campaign just as he was anxious for rehabilitation. Their ability to cause damage was undoubted and persuaded him to reinstate the Pergamon strikers and improve their conditions of employment. He also withdrew his writ against the *Bookseller* and paid a record £30,000 towards the publisher's costs.

The Pergamon dispute, literally on his own doorstep, was mild compared to his struggle with the typesetters and machine-minders at BPC's presses at Park Royal where the *Radio Times* was set and printed. Despite their written undertaking, the local union leaders, who were members of the NGA, had reneged on their agreement and, ignoring the orders of their national leaders, began two years of vituperative and disruptive strikes. Production was sabotaged by interfering with machinery, paper runs and the electricity supply, while the printers extracted agreements for double manning levels and pay increases which were three times higher than those of other BPC employees. It was a trial of strength which Maxwell could not afford to lose, either commercially or, more importantly, personally after the militants had doused him in oil and insulted him to his face.

If the original purchase of the BPC shares in the dawn raid three years earlier had been his Normandy landings, Park Royal was his Battle for Berlin. The ground had been carefully prepared. BPC workers at East Kilbride in Scotland and Leeds had been promised a glowing future if they agreed to print the *Radio Times*, and the national union leaders had been carefully manoeuvred into dissociating themselves from their rebellious membership. On 14 November 1983, after sixteen million copies of the magazine had been lost, a group of large men with 14lb sledge hammers entered the premises and smashed the fifty-year-old presses to pieces. The printers watched with amazement as their sword of Damocles disintegrated before their eyes. Their reaction was unprintable. 'Jungle man' was victorious. 'If Britain had six more Maxwells,' commented Lord Kearton, 'the country would have no more worries.' Maxwell beamed. This was a talent which he could capitalise on. After all the years in the wilderness, the emerging chrysalis was very confident: 'If I can run BPC, then I can do so much more.'

At the end of 1982, Maxwell admitted that he felt 'slightly bored' and needed new challenges. That year, BPC boasted £20 million profits, 'the highest in its history', and although the accounts concealed its enormous debts, no one doubted that its salvation was secure. Maxwell's ambitions were signalled by the change of name to the British Printing and Communications Corporation, which encompassed his target of spreading into cable and satellite television, into computers and data banks, into electronic printing and every communications technology that was invented. Like a revolving door, 'experts' passed through BPCC to satisfy the chairman's restless urge to develop his company to 'rank among the world's ten largest communications corporations'.The vision he extolled to Saul Steinberg in January 1969 would finally come to fruition. No one else in Britain could boast his foresight, which had been fed by an insatiable appetite to learn during his travelling. But he was sixty years old with at best a decade to achieve the everlasting fame which had for three decades so unfairly eluded him. BPCC needed more money and he wanted more activities to occupy himself. The solution was to return to what he could do so well, the mixed recipe of juggling and trading which had earned his fortune in Maxwell House on the Marylebone Road.

In rapid succession in 1983, Maxwell sought to rescue Oxford United football club from bankruptcy for £120,000, bought a 13.8 per cent stake in Central Television, and purchased a rash of companies with terminal financial problems. Most of the investments earned him headlines but only limited profits. At the end of 1981 Oxford United was in the Football League's Third Division losing £2,000 a week, when a Pergamon employee approached Maxwell and asked whether he would be interested in saving his local club from bankruptcy. During the 1960s Oxford United had enjoyed a mercurial revival but in the mid-1970s its fortunes began declining. According to Bill Reeves, then club chairman, 'There was a crisis in football generally because the gate figures were dropping. There just wasn't any commercial input in the game.' In Maxwell's view, the game was suffering the same malaise as BPC and so much else of British industry. It was managed by parochial, short-sighted and sometimes uncommercial men who had allowed their industry to degenerate in filthy stadiums plagued by hooliganism. In America, by contrast, the sport was beginning to thrive. Here was another chance for Maxwell the reformer to change another British institution. Despite his accountants' advice that the club was a bad investment, Maxwell agreed, on 6 January 1982, to pay off the club's debts of £128,000 in return for taking control. Since there were no evident business reasons for the investment (which was in any event a relatively insignificant amount), there can be no doubt that, despite the incredulity of the football world, he was solely motivated by philanthropy. 'I'm doing it as a service to the community,' he would say later about becoming involved in a new sphere. Two days after the acquisition he began looking for a new manager, and demanded that the local council should agree to moving the club to a new and larger stadium while granting permission for its old ground to be redeveloped. The council instantly rejected his demand and was rewarded by the traditional bombardment of criticisms and epithets. 'When I became chairman,' he later said, 'I was promised by the City Council that we would get the Marston site for a new ground. Then they changed their minds.' The Council denied his claims. As his row with football's establishment intensified, in April 1983 he proposed a radical new solution – to merge Oxford United with Reading FC. The idea collapsed one month later. But by then, his survival plan and the appointment of Jim Smith as manager had transformed the club's finances from debt into profit. More spectators were watching a winning side, yet his presence had caused endless controversy. The sport was perplexed by an overweight club owner running across the pitch, appearing on the terraces and basking in the applause of the fans demanding his autograph. The high profile earned him opprobrium and death threats as he waded into the terraces to stop fighting and threatened to close the club unless the Council co-operated with his efforts.

Three years later, when the club had won its way into the First Division, the Council agreed to invest in the club. Jim Smith, the star manager, however, resigned, claiming that he could no longer work with Maxwell. Smith had been surprised that his employer, who was involved in so many other businesses, still required to be regularly consulted about the weekly selection of the team, transfers of players and every aspect of the business. Maxwell easily shrugged off Smith's departure; but his difficulties in business were not so easily ignored.

In June 1983, he embarked upon a take-over bid which rebounded upon him and revealed, to his discomfort, that his past was still an albatross.

His new target was John Waddington, a small but important firm of printers and packagers whose expertise fitted in well with BPCC's aspirations. They were also the manufacturers of 'Monopoly', the world's most famous game for aspiring capitalists. The bid started at 7.30 a.m. on 17 June. Victor Watson, Waddington's impish chairman, had been at his desk for fifteen minutes when Maxwell telephoned. Later that morning, said the caller from London, he would be making a bid for the company. Watson was already fighting off another bid and Maxwell presented himself as a 'white knight' who would save the beleaguered damsel.

'Waddington is not for sale,' replied Watson, 'and I won't meet you.'

'I always win,' snapped Maxwell. 'So there's no point in fighting.'

'We will fight you every inch of the way,' said Watson.

But Maxwell's timing was perfect. Waddington had barely recovered from huge losses on video-games and was vulnerable to a bid. 'He was like a shark, who smells blood and chases the prey,' says Watson.

In the three years since he had bought BPC, Maxwell had assumed that rejection was something of the past. He had after all become the printing industry's self-styled great hope. Over the following six weeks, as the two men engaged in a hectic battle to secure the support of Waddington's institutional shareholders, Maxwell was convinced of victory because he had secured acceptance in the City. But according to Watson, 'I was going to use any tactics to give him a nasty shock.' Maxwell, however, possessed the initiative and his tactics were unnerving. There were regular telephone calls to both Watson and his managing director David Perry, who had recently resigned from BPC, to persuade them to surrender. Perry recalls particularly the calls early on Sunday mornings:

'Bob Maxwell here. I just want you to understand that we can work together.'

'The business is not for sale,' replied Perry.

'You know that I'm going to win. It's inevitable,' concluded Maxwell with intimidating certainty.

Maxwell also persistently telephoned Watson in attempts to arrange a meeting. 'I always refused,' recalls Watson, 'because I feared giving the wrong impression.' Finally, on Maxwell's promise that he would never reveal the encounter, the two met to discuss Maxwell's offer of a better price for the company and a seat for Watson on BPCC's main board as the vice-chairman. This, Watson realised, was Maxwell's classic ploy which had so often evaporated. The story of Donald Davies, who had been offered the post as BPCC's managing director by Maxwell in 1982, was already legendary. At lunchtime, Davies had excitedly confided the offer to two friends in a pub, only to be hear that they had received identical approaches. Watson thought of the Yorkshire maxim, 'He talks as he warms.' All Maxwell's offers were refused and Watson returned to Wakefield. The next day's newspapers carried reports that the two men had met. Watson was shocked and called in experts to check Waddington's offices for bugs. 'He established an atmosphere of paranoia,' recalls Perry, 'and it seemed to be successful.'

Towards the end of August, Maxwell was heading towards a slender majority. Watson was as desperate as Robinson had been three years earlier: 'I wasn't going to let him win.' His defences included the use of private detectives. One of their tasks was to check the truth of a claim by BPCC that it had sold a large property in Watford for £20 million with planning permission for development as a shopping centre. If true, BPCC's profits would be higher than predicted, so enhancing the value of the BPCC shares which were offered in the bid for Waddington. The detective reported to Watson that planning permission had not yet been granted since the local council was still hostile. BPCC's announcement had been premature.

Watson seized upon that mistake as an example of the 'optimism' which characterised Maxwell's past transgressions. His targets for the message were Waddington's shareholders, among them the Norwich Union, whose holding was 5 per cent. Their stake had already been pledged to Maxwell. 'I appealed to the fund manager to change his allegiance,' says Watson. 'I told him it was his duty to see me on a moral issue.' Take-over bids have rarely been perceived as moral issues but Watson transformed the bid for his small company into a test of Maxwell's character.

Unaccustomed in his recent past to such resistance, Maxwell was distressed by the unusual blitz of antagonistic propaganda which Watson had inspired. 'I have had several Waddington shareholders complaining they had up to eight telephone calls urging them to withdraw their acceptances,' he complained. 'This borders on harassment.' Maxwell had clearly forgotten his own tactics during his bid for the *News of the World*. But when the Norwich Union switched sides, Maxwell tersely conceded defeat: 'Mr Watson threw a googly at me.' 'When he said that,' Watson remarks, 'he betrayed himself as a foreigner because every Englishman knows you "bowl" a googly.' When prejudice and prospective profits compete in a contested bid, Maxwell would always be the loser. His opportunities lay only where the unique talents of the 'jungle man' could be applied.

In 1982, Sir Alexander Jarratt, the chairman of Reed International, was seeking an opportunity to save the conglomerate from the legacy of merger mania and bankruptcy. Among its loss-makers was Odhams Press in Watford, an inheritance from the International Publishing Corporation, which was sited near BPC's Sun Printers. Odhams, which printed *Woman* and *Woman's Realm* magazines, would lose £5.5 million that year and had accumulated losses over the previous ten years of £30 million. Odham's plight could only worsen. Magazine circulations were still declining, there was chronic overmanning and there was no money to buy new printing machinery. Both Jarratt and the chairman of IPC, Leslie Carpenter, identified the only potential customer for their liability in Robert Maxwell. 'Although Maxwell was helped by the change of environment introduced by the Thatcher government,' says Jarratt, 'he had also changed the environment. But also, we lacked Maxwell's temperament and style to confront the unions.' Jarratt was soon to discover that he was a less effective negotiator than Maxwell.

'Negotiating with Bob', testify both Reed executives, 'is not a pleasure. We agreed to the terms of the sale within ninety minutes and then he began haggling and spent days and weeks renegotiating and rewriting the deal we thought had been settled. He's a born haggler.' When they finally did sign, Maxwell had obtained for a mere £1.5 million the Odhams factory, its twenty-three acres of land, a print order worth £30 million for IPC magazines plus a £7.5 million interest-free loan from Reeds for two years. It was a brilliant deal if he could cower the unions into agreeing to mass redundancies. His scheme was to sack 1,500 Odhams employees and transfer the printing to BPC plants. He would then sell the Odhams estate. If the unions protested, he would threaten to close not only Odhams but also BPC's own Sun Printers on the grounds that only one factory could be profitable. As always, there would be a deadline. 'Maxwell can say and do things', says Carpenter, 'which would stick in the gullet of traditional British owners. He is hard, skilful and persuasive.' All those qualities were exploited on the day the deal was signed. It ended, Jarratt recalls with amazement, 'in true Maxwellian style'.

Carpenter had travelled to Southend to brief SOGAT about the deal. Meanwhile in London, Jarratt, surrounded by lawyers, was signing the raft of documents which such agreements entail. Maxwell sat impatiently until he announced that he was flying by helicopter to Watford. Jarratt was still signing when one hour later Maxwell telephoned:

'I addressed all the workers in the canteen and told them that at least half of them would be made redundant but I would save the rest of their jobs.'

'Yes,' replied Jarratt in trepidation.

'And do you know, they cheered me . . .'

'Well done,' interrupted Jarratt with relief.

'Yes, I'm rather good at that sort of thing,' swooned the man in Watford with pride.

After financing the 1,400 redundancies, the remaining profits of the Odhams site saved BPC from losses in 1984. Without that property sale, and the purchase and asset-stripping of the Bishopsgate Trust in the same year, BPCC's spectacular growth of profits, which plays such a vital role in Maxwell's self-promotion, would not have occurred. Combined with Pergamon's record profits from sales of journals and his share deals, Maxwell started 1984 with substantial funds.

In contrast, Carpenter and Jarratt were still pondering how they would rid themselves of their last commitment to Reed's printing legacy – the *Daily Mirror* group.

CHAPTER 13

'I only want to be of service to my fellow man' is a phrase which Maxwell fondly professes whenever he is asked to justify the apparent contradictions of his politics, lifestyle and business career. To many listeners, it strikes the same chord as the superlatives which pepper his companies' annual reports. Invariably, they contain a surfeit of phrases such as 'excellent results', 'valuable source', 'record level', 'outstanding contribution', 'significant profit increase', 'very substantial', 'world leader', 'dramatic profit growth', etc. Throughout Maxwell's life, his chosen words have conveyed meanings to his audience very different from those he intended. Accordingly, while the phrase 'service to my fellow man' implies the performance of a charitable or beneficial act, used by Maxwell in 1984 it meant, besides much else, his intention to purchase the *Daily Mirror*.

Soon after Odhams was sold, Alex Jarratt and the Reed board agreed that they also wanted to be rid of the *Daily Mirror* and the grinding struggle with Fleet Street's print unions which was sapping managerial energy in return for paltry profits – just £1 million on a turnover of £200 million. Jarratt is a former civil servant but with a distinctly non-Whitehall ability to take initiatives. He harboured no sentimental reservations about selling the *Mirror*, and had no wish to play the power game as the chairman of Britain's largest newspaper group whose six titles (*Daily Mirror, Sunday Mirror, Sunday People, Daily Record, Sunday Mail* and *Sporting Life*) sold thirty-one million copies every week. Jarratt was nevertheless mindful of the *Mirror*'s historic traditions.

Formerly owned by Lords Rothermere and Northcliffe, it had in recent memory been controlled by similar giants, Cecil King and Hugh Cudlipp. The paper's radical editor, Guy Bartholomew, who in fifteen years had pushed the newspaper's circulation from 720,000 to $4\frac{1}{2}$ million, had secured for the *Mirror* a mention in history as the western world's largest-selling daily newspaper. Its soaring popularity was based upon a mixture of sensationalism, original journalism and easily digested but intelligent reporting. The newspaper's heady success bolstered its executives' image of themselves as godlike figures who could stride the world without care about censorship or cost. The first major casualty was Cecil King in 1968, after he wrote and published a signed editorial 'Enough is Enough', demanding the removal of Harold Wilson, the Labour Prime Minister. Two years after his well-publicised dismissal, IPC merged with the Reed group, its glamour and prestige still intact, but its profitability declining fast.

Reed placed most of the blame for its losses on the thirteen trade unions in the Mirror Group. The machine room in the *Mirror* building had by 1970 become an unendearing model of anarchy and villainy. During the nights, especially Saturdays, large numbers of highly paid but unneeded printers sat in the basement of the ugly red-topped building watching blue movies or playing high-stake poker. Depending upon their seniority and muscle, many had even clocked in under two names and were receiving double wages for no work. Others had registered but were working or sleeping elsewhere. It was not unknown at the end of a shift for wage packets to remain unclaimed because the printers were too drunk to recall which phony names they had registered under on arrival. By any standards, their wages were phenomenally high, ample to provide luxurious homes, several foreign holidays every year and even funds to set up private businesses. It was an abuse whose roots could be traced back four centuries to the introduction of Gutenberg's presses. Although after 1970 technology had rendered their ancient crafts long redundant, the printers' jobs and privileges were protected by their mere threat to stop production if management dared to interfere.

At the *Mirror*, in common with all Fleet Street newspapers, the printers were paid not only to perform their task but also extra sums as 'compensation' if work was contracted to outsiders. Whenever the management attempted to interfere with this notorious catalogue of 'old Spanish customs', the consequences were predictable. A flick of a knife on a paper run or an inspired malfunction of a machine would sabotage that night's production, causing irrecoverable losses. Anxious to keep their papers on the street, the *Mirror*'s management paid their printers' demands and suffered in as much silence as their self-interest determined.

The management's tolerance of those abuses would have been surprising had they not enjoyed similar privileges. In the floors above the printing presses, the Mirror Group's executives and journalists enjoyed a lush all-expenses-paid lifestyle which their talents would not have earned in pastures outside journalism. Both Tony Miles, the chairman of the Mirror Group, and Douglas Long, the deputy chairman, were grateful that Reed's granting of total editorial independence allowed them considerable freedom over expenditure. New arrivals at the newspapers were always pleasantly astonished by gargantuan meals, constant high-cost celebrations on the smallest pretext and profligate foreign travel in the style which few could defend as vital for journalism. There was constant ribaldry that the Mirror management's introduction of new technology had actually increased costs while similar machinery installed in Lagos, Nigeria, was functioning perfectly and saving money.

Throughout the 1970s, Jarratt and Carpenter hardly interfered with the abuses in High Holborn and did not even appoint a representative to the Mirror board. Deliberately, they made High Holborn into a no-go area. The sole overt sign of their control was a monthly dinner which Jarratt hosted at the Savoy for the senior editors. Jarratt rarely complained that the *Mirror*'s circulation of 3.3 million had fallen behind the *Sun*'s or that the newspaper's profits were declining despite his editors' down-market chase in the nipple stakes. But by 1983 the excesses were infecting expectations of other employees throughout the group and Reed's share price was suffering by association with its unwholesome subsidiary. Nearly all the traditional newspaper families had been driven out of Fleet Street because of the abuses and Reed wanted to join the exodus, especially since its shares in the Reuters news agency had become unexpectedly valuable and boosted the price it might expect.

During the summer of 1983, Jarratt and Leslie Carpenter put out what are known as 'discreet feelers' intimating that the newspaper group might be for sale. To their disappointment, there was absolutely no interest. 'The papers' profits had fallen badly and the reputation for excesses was so bad that no one would risk their money,' says Carpenter. Even Maxwell declined the offer, because, it was believed, he did not have the £100 million in cash which Carpenter mentioned as the price. Reed's problem was how to dispose of its costly asset. After brainstorming with its advisers, an unusual formula emerged which would make a virtue of their failure to find one individual who was prepared to buy the whole group.

In October 1983, Jarratt announced that Mirror Group newspapers would be floated as a separate company on the Stock Exchange and there would be a special provision in the conditions of the sale to prevent one individual winning total control. Ironically, since no one knew that he had privately rejected the chance to purchase the group, Jarratt's public announcement was interpreted as a deliberate snub to Maxwell's known ambitions. Jarratt mentioned two further conditions which would be included in the prospectus for the sale. The first was the tradition that the Mirror Group's editors had enjoyed unfettered freedom from the newspaper's owners. The second was the support for the Labour Party which the paper had espoused for decades. Reed's announcement was therefore greeted by the *Mirror*'s staff with some regret but no foreboding. It fell to Leslie Carpenter to supervise this unusual transaction.

Carpenter, who was educated at Hackney Technical College, had worked in the print industry all his life and was well acquainted with its problems and personalities. Unlike Jarratt, he was a technician but he shared the lack of sentiment about the proprietorship and power of newspapers. His first task was to select the chairman of the new company. Significantly, his ideal candidate was not expected to know anything about the newspaper industry; instead he was to be an expert in management and finance, since his function was to present a glowing prospectus of the independent Mirror Group to City institutions and persuade them to buy shares prior to the flotation. Since Jarratt's announcement had stressed that Reed intended that the paper should retain its pro-Labour bias, Carpenter's candidate needed also, for the sake of credibility, to be at least not an obvious Conservative, who might also keep the unions quiet 'for the duration'. Consistent with Reed's benevolence, Carpenter asked Tony Miles and the Mirror board to suggest their ideal candidate.

Their choice was Clive Thornton, the stocky, fifty-four-year-old chairman of the Abbey National Building Society. Over the previous four years, Thornton had become nationally recognised for transforming the dowdy savings and loan agency into an active cartel-buster, pushing the number of depositors up from four to nearly ten million in four years. Thornton, a solicitor, had enjoyed the glow of media attention which his success as a 'people's maverick' had attracted and he responded swiftly and positively to Carpenter's approach. When, at their short introductory meeting, Carpenter suggested that Thornton might remain at the Abbey and take the Mirror chairmanship part-time, Thornton replied that he envisaged the chairmanship as a full-time job. Carpenter shrugged, pleased at least that there was someone who would take the responsibility. 'Everyone thought that we had a credible and popular man who might become a super-hero,' recalls one of Reed's advisers. 'He had successfully turned an old-fashioned business around and we thought he would just run the business successfully until the float.' A press release was issued which stated that, under Thornton's management, shares in the new

Mirror company would be offered during 1984. The secret target date was January. The new chairman threw himself into the job with relish. 'We thought that very unusual,' says Jarratt.

Thornton is candid: 'I am ambitious and I'm not everyone's cup of tea.' Within weeks, relations between Carpenter and Thornton became uneasy. There were reports that Thornton was dictatorial and difficult towards the Mirror's executives, who had known their business for years. The cause was the new chairman's discovery of Fleet Street's debauched style of life. 'It was the expenses of the executives which really hit me,' recalls Thornton. 'Everyone was spending thousands of pounds taking each other out for entertainment.' He had heard about the Street of Shame but these antics were beyond his imagination, and on top of that were the intransigent print unions. As Thornton raged, Jarratt advised him to 'ride your troops a little more gently'. Thornton ignored the suggestion and in October handed Carpenter a poison pill: the flotation was impossible unless the union problems were resolved. 'I told Carpenter and Jarratt that we needed a package agreement with the unions of no-strikes and non-automatic replacement of printers.' At first the Reed executives were bemused. Thornton's aspiration had eluded the managers of Fleet Street for generations. Ennobled families like the Thomsons, Berrys and Beaverbrooks had been humbled to near ruin, unable to persuade the unions to agree to that simple formula. Thornton, the Reed executives signalled to each other, was naive. 'Just float it first and worry about the union negotiations later,' advised Jarratt. Thornton disagreed. He would not accept that trade unionists could behave so insanely and for the next months he intensively sought to reorganise the Mirror Group's industrial relations. The unions were decidedly unsympathetic. According to Bill Miles, the SOGAT representative in Fleet Street, 'Thornton thought industrial relations was having cups of tea with the workers in the canteen.' Bill Keyes was equally sceptical: 'He spoke visions and not nuts and bolts. We couldn't lock into his proposals.' Consequently, the flotation was repeatedly postponed.

By April 1984, Jarratt and Carpenter were seriously worried. Thornton had adopted a very high profile, eagerly giving press interviews about worker participation and the need for massive investments where he outlined his undiscussed plans to build a new printing plant costing £20 million in Manchester and to launch a range of new daily and evening newspapers once the *Mirror* was independent. Thornton, it was clear to the two Reed executives, was no longer just floating the company but apparently launching himself as a nascent newspaper baron. Of equal concern was Thornton's speculation in the interviews about worker participation and the need for massive investments by the unions and the Labour Party in the new group to protect it from capitalist predators, especially Maxwell. Carpenter feared that if reports of Thornton's arguments with the unions and the Mirror managers did not dissuade potential investors' interest, then his populism would certainly deter the conservative elements in the City. In Thornton's view, if he did not find a formula for industrial peace and a reduction of expenses, there would never be a float. 'It was my open-mouth policy,' he says, 'because I was the ham in the sandwich between Reed, the unions and the potential investors.'

By June 1984, Reed and its advisers had become decidedly unsympathetic towards their nominee, who they believed was becoming an unwelcome liability: 'We wanted a sale, not a lot of socialist rubbish which was damaging the chances of the sale.' In the third week of June, they set 19 July as the irrevocable date for the float. For the countdown, Thornton's office in the Mirror building was turned into a battle headquarters, housing up to twenty advisers to write the prospectus for potential investors. Among those advisers was Derek Higgs of Warburgs, Reed's merchant bankers, who had unexpectedly delivered some very gloomy news.

Twelve months earlier, Higgs had estimated the Mirror Group to be worth £100 million and had hailed Thornton's appointment as 'a masterstroke', but he was fast revising his opinion. Price Waterhouse, the accountants, had been asked to undertake an independent survey to produce the 'short form' report for the prospectus which would give investors an informed idea about the company's true value. Unknown to the unions or many managers, the accountants had surreptitiously visited the Mirror building at sensitive moments and noted the excesses. Among their revelations was that 'James Bond' and 'Mickey Mouse' had signed on as printers, and the discovery of horrendous facts about the petty cash, the car pool, drinks and women. The group was more out of control than anyone had realised. Everyone's fears seemed confirmed by a short SOGAT strike in the spring. Considering that there was also a possible liability for large redundancy payments, the bankers told Reed on 27 June that they would be lucky to receive £60 million and it might fall as low as £40 million. Thornton was furious: 'They completely undervalued their assets and the pension fund,' he says, but Warburgs insist that their assessment was fair.

Jarratt and Carpenter were also shaken by the sudden diminution of their potential prize. Their options suddenly seemed to be quite limited because of their public assurance that no dominant shareholder would be permitted to buy control and because employees were to be encouraged to buy shares. However, they decided that there was no alternative other than to proceed and, after much discussion, the mechanism to implement that assurance was agreed at the end of June. The articles of the new company would forbid the registration of one person's share ownership if it exceeded 15 per cent. Just four days after agreeing that clause, the very person whom it was intended to obstruct made an anticipatory move. Maxwell once again fulfilled his notable reputation as a master of timing.

How Maxwell discovered about the 15 per cent rule and that the flotation was becoming stymied by disarray among the personalities involved has been a matter of conjecture ever since. Thornton is certain that Maxwell had an informant among his own staff on the ninth floor: 'How else would he have known?' Jarratt implies the same: 'Mr Maxwell was certainly well informed.' Traces of paranoia often afflict Maxwell's victims since it is an element of his tactics. Part of the explanation may well be that, metaphorically and physically, Maxwell is always awake when others are asleep and he undoubtedly did have good contacts among the senior *Sunday Mirror* executives. Alternatively, he might have read about the Mirror Group's problems in the *Financial Times*.

Maxwell's lust to own a national newspaper had been an unfulfilled ambition for fifteen years. In the previous three years there had two other opportunities. The first was the *Times* group which Thomson offered for sale in October 1980. Maxwell was the first to show an interest but since he was still in the midst of battling to win control of BPC he was dismissed as having neither the money nor the reputation as a candidate for the Top People's newspaper. His second and more serious bid was launched in April 1984 for the *Observer*. Tiny Rowland, the newspaper's owner, was in the midst of a public row with the newspaper's editor, Donald Trelford. Their disagreement concerned a story, written by Trelford about atrocities allegedly committed in Zimbabwe, which greatly embarrassed Rowland, who prides himself on affectionate relations with Africa's leaders. Rowland, like many tycoons, was unaccustomed to being defied by his employees, especially those who were not earning any profits. But Rowland's arsenal of threats was limited since Trelford had won the decisive support of the independent directors whose authority had been guaranteed by Rowland as a condition of his original purchase. Rowland's only course was either to accept defeat or to sell the newspaper. He hinted that he was 'fed up' and considering the latter option and released the news the day before the independent directors and their editor were due to meet. Trelford, who was already concerned because Britain's oldest newspaper had barely recovered from a succession of ownerships, became alarmed when Rowland also leaked that the new owner could be Maxwell, whom he described as a 'super leader' for the paper. That was of course exactly what Trelford was resisting. 'I'd want the same guarantees of independence,' he said, thinking aloud about Maxwell's condemnation of his recent report that Mark Thatcher, the Prime Minister's son, had been engaged in doubtful business exploits in the Oman.

The *Observer*'s directors were due to meet at midday on 23 April and Maxwell was the bogeyman whom Rowland had introduced to upset their discussions. Normally, Rowland is the most discreet of businessmen who eschews personal publicity and deals only with a few trusted journalists who can be gently controlled. Yet on this occasion every newsroom was informed that, at 9 a.m. on the day the directors were meeting, Rowland had invited Maxwell to breakfast at Claridge's Hotel in Mayfair. Not surprisingly a large crowd of journalists and cameras were waiting on the pavement as the German and Czech multi-millionaires, who both delight in speaking with impeccable English accents, stepped on to the street. Rowland stood slightly back smiling as Maxwell went to the cameras. The talks, Maxwell said, were 'productive, positive and pleasurable', and 'I am keen to buy' the paper, although there were still a few obstacles. Everything could be settled within a day. Rowland then stepped forward: 'We had a good long chat and Bob tells me that he is very keen to buy.' It seemed to confirm that morning's *Daily Mirror* headline, 'Maxwell set to buy *Observer*'. Still smiling, Rowland stepped into his Rolls and sped off to meet the independent directors. Maxwell went back inside the hotel, his temporary headquarters since striking printers were in the second week of occupying Maxwell House in protest against his policies. By the following day, it was all over. Rowland had accepted a reprimand from the *Observer*'s independent directors for his attempt to censure Trelford, and talk about selling the newspaper fizzled out as fast as it had arisen. Using Maxwell as a threat had been unproductive and he was soon forgotten by Rowland. If Maxwell felt exploited, it barely showed. Players in the big league expect to be treated in the same way as they treat others.

Yet Maxwell's fortunes had rocketed during that year. The price of BPCC shares had risen from 12p to 160p since his takeover and Pergamon was reporting 'record' profits. Maxwell had both money and a reputation and now he wanted the power and influence which he believed came automatically with ownership of a newspaper. In May, Maxwell had telephoned Carpenter about the sale of the *Daily Mirror*: 'I'm about to invest in the *Express*,' he confided to a man whom he had known since the

1950s, 'but I won't if there's a chance that I can buy the *Mirror*. Can you give me any encouragement that I might?' Carpenter replied that he could not. On 22 June Maxwell paid approximately £16 million for 10 per cent of Fleet, the owners of the *Express*, who were known to be unhappy owners of the fading Beaverbrook empire. It was, Maxwell said, 'a stake for the future'. Over the following week, everything changed. Maxwell heard from a senior Mirror executive that there was strife among those planning the group's flotation, especially between the Reed executives and Thornton. The suspected presence of Maxwell's mole inside the Mirror camp would become part of the saga's folklore.

On the ninth floor of the Mirror building, Thornton was disputing Warburgs' low assessment of the group's potential value and insisted that the company be sold for £100 million. Higgs advised Jarratt and Carpenter that both the high price and the 15 per cent limit would endanger a flotation, and with the additional union problems they could not expect any serious investment. 'Warburgs told us to pull back. We were going to flop,' recalls one of the Reed executives. Maxwell heard about that terminal warning and on Sunday morning, 1 July, telephoned Carpenter at home: 'I am going to make a bid for the *Mirror*. Can we meet?' To stall Maxwell, Carpenter resorted to a well-used excuse: 'I'm sorry, I don't discuss business on Sundays.' Early on Monday morning, Maxwell telephoned again. Carpenter told Maxwell that the group was not for sale to a single bidder and that they could not meet. Just to be in his presence, Carpenter knew, would start the slide into his clutches. But the rejection was too polite to have any effect. The following day, Tuesday, Maxwell sent a letter to Jarratt outlining his offer and ending with the assurance that Jarratt had ample time for consideration. There was, however, no advantage for Maxwell in uncharacteristically restraining himself. The very next day, 4 July, he called a press conference and issued a public statement that Pergamon had made 'a formal offer of not less than £80 million cash for Mirror Group Newspapers. If justified by the financial and other information on the group, Pergamon will increase its offer to a sum not exceeding £100 million.' After adding that he had given assurances about the papers' future 'prosperity and ... political line', Maxwell concluded:

Some people may call me a predator but it is the proposed public flotation which will expose the group to the laws of the jungle. I regard myself as the saviour of the group against the heavy commercial advantages of its rivals. Mr Molloy, Editor of the *Daily Mirror*, has said in a recent article in the *Guardian* that 'The Mirror Group has lacked the kind of autocratic player who can take his seat in the Fleet Street poker game.' If Pergamon succeeds, then, as Mr Molloy and all his colleagues must wish, power will once again truly return to the ninth floor at Holborn Circus.

Jarratt and Carpenter were not surprised, but Thornton was afraid and arranged to meet Carpenter that night. Thornton had always suspected Maxwell as a potential buyer and, on his second meeting with Carpenter a year earlier, had asked why Reed did not sell the *Mirror* to the publisher. Carpenter had explained that Maxwell had shown no interest. Three times during that last year, Maxwell had contacted Thornton with offers to print the *Mirror* but had been brusquely rejected. An element of paranoia had entered Thornton's feelings after Charles Williams, the chairman of Ansbachers, who were Maxwell's original merchant bankers, had visited Thornton to discuss the flotation. Williams had claimed he was representing the Labour Party's interests, but Thornton feared otherwise, though Williams denies that those fears had any justification. But on 4 July the threat of Maxwell had become a reality and Thornton was afraid that Carpenter would be attracted by a guarantee of £80 million instead of risking the flotation. The only obstacle to taking the money immediately was Jarratt's public pledge not to sell to a single bidder. 'I was sure that Carpenter wanted to sell to Maxwell immediately,' says Thornton, 'but Jarratt felt bound by his honour.'

Over the next four days, while Thornton laboured under intense pressure to finalise the prospectus, Maxwell bombarded the Reed board with phone calls, letters and telexes demanding meetings and issuing ultimatums. He was met by silence. 'We refused to take any of his phone calls,' says one Reed executive, 'but you could feel his presence everywhere.' As connoisseurs of Maxwell's style, Jarratt and Carpenter knew that it was precisely the effect which he intended. On 8 July, Maxwell sent Jarratt another telex, except that on this occasion Jarratt had already read the message on a news agency tape. The $80 million cash offer, said Maxwell, was completely unconditional and could be increased to £100 million. More phone calls and telexes with deadlines followed – 'It felt like a bombardment' – but Jarratt and Carpenter refused to be drawn. Two days later, Jarratt read on the agency tapes the contents of another letter which Maxwell had sent. The offer had been raised to an unconditional £100 million cash with another £20 million available. Jarratt once again rejected the offer, but Maxwell refused to take no for an answer. 'They've not turned down my offer; they can't turn down my offer,' he told Channel 4 News. Inside Reed House in Piccadilly, Jarratt was perplexed: 'He just won't go away.'

Thornton felt more intimidated then most. His *Daily Mirror* horoscope for 9 July read: 'Unless you have written guarantees and solid promises, then leave financial matters alone for a while. Others may seems plausible and reliable, but the chances are that you are being manipulated in some way or worse.' Clearly the ninth-floor mole, he felt, was telling him something.

To exert more pressure, Maxwell had revealed as an aside in his letter to Jarratt, which was released to the press, that Derek Higgs of Warburgs had spoken to Maxwell's banker at Hill Samuel. He went so far as to accuse Warburgs of failing in their duty to represent Reed in a proper fashion. To the casual reader that mention would be unimportant but on the City grapevine everyone knew the significance. Warburgs had never hidden their distaste for Maxwell, whom they dubbed a despot, and would have preferred to have no dealings with him whatsoever. Even if his accusation were untrue, everyone inside Reed's barricade realised that it was a valid ploy to compel them talk to Maxwell; once the discussions began, it would be difficult to withdraw. Thornton became alarmed about his employers' growing instability. 'Both of them looked nervous but again assured me that they would never sell to Maxwell. What could I do other than believe them?'

Warburgs' doubts were influencing the two Reed executives. They were worried about Thornton's failure to control the unions, whom the City universally regarded as gangsters and a risk to their investment. To counter that sentiment, Thornton summoned the unions on Wednesday 11 July. For three hours he explained that he needed a non-strike guarantee or else Maxwell would be their new employer. Both Bill Miles and Keyes suddenly forgot their disdain for Thornton and agreed. Only the NGA withheld their support, because ironically they could not believe that Jarratt would break his pledge. Without a unanimous guarantee, Thornton had nothing new to offer when he telephoned Carpenter late that afternoon and was told that Maxwell was tightening the screws.

In their Piccadilly headquarters, the two Reed executives had just heard that they had a new neighbour. Across the street, in the Ritz Hotel, Maxwell had rented a suite, 'so that I can be closer to be of assistance to you', he told them. Both men felt the noose tightening and had reluctantly agreed that Warburgs could send Maxwell some draft agreements but strictly 'without commitment'. Like a Don Juan seducing a woman, Maxwell knew, as the first resistance disappeared, that it was just a matter of delicate tactics before all the defences began to crumble. He was on the verge of becoming a press baron. Only Jarratt and his conscience blocked his way.

Neil Kinnock, the Labour Party's leader, was delighted by Jarratt's conscience. The Mirror Group's traditionally pro-left position is considered crucial to the party's very survival, since its millions of readers are the bedrock of its electoral support. During every election, the *Mirror*'s coverage is scrutinised for the slightest hint of criticism. Kinnock was convinced that Thornton's plan was the best guarantee for the continuation of that heritage and that Maxwell's bid was not in the party's interests. Convincing the Labour Party that they could trust him was vital for Maxwell if he was to persuade Jarratt to break his undertaking.

On Wednesday 11 July, Maxwell drove to Hampstead in north-west London. He had telephoned Michael Foot, the former Labour Party leader, and invited himself to lunch at the left-winger's home. Maxwell was politically estranged from Foot and the two had spoken only rarely over the past twenty-five years. But Foot was grateful to Maxwell for contributing £38,000 in 1983 towards the legal fees for a High Court action against the Boundary Commission's recommendations for the redrawing of constituency borders which would deprive the party of thirty seats in the House of Commons. More recently, Foot had hosted a lunch for Maxwell at the Gay Hussar restaurant in Soho to discuss the possibility of a new left-wing paper. Maxwell, whose mind in such matters resembles a ledger – 'I owe you, you owe me' – wanted Foot's support for his bid.

Foot was sympathetic. By the Wednesday, the newspaper reports suggested that the flotation was endangered and Foot feared that if Maxwell did not secure the *Mirror*, it might fall into the hands of the Conservatives. 'Maxwell had been a Labour MP and a long-serving member of the party,' recalls Foot. 'He promised that the papers would continue to support the party and I felt that we could trust him. The *Mirror* would be in safe hands.' Maxwell left satisfied and communicated Foot's approval to others.

On Thursday morning, 12 July, Jarratt was painfully facing his dilemma. Infuriatingly Maxwell had interfered in the flotation and his public negotiations with Reed through the media had irritated the former civil servant. One could not deny Maxwell's financial astuteness – his success at Odhams had been awesome, and with hindsight Jarratt realised that they had sold it far too cheaply. He feared the man. Would the country thank Reed for allowing Maxwell to become a press baron who might one day even bid for Reed itself? By the end of the morning, closeted with Carpenter and Higgs, Jarratt accepted that he owed a higher duty to his shareholders. Maxwell's offer was too good to reject.

One mile away in Holborn, the *Mirror* journalists were waking up to the possibility of Reed's capitulation. Hitherto, they had been remarkably docile, relying on information about their fate from newspaper coverage which repeated Reed's assurances. Some wags would later carp that the alcohol level was so high in their favourite hostelry, the Wig and Pen, that those who heard the rumours were too drunk to understand. The truth was nevertheless harsh. The *Mirror*'s own management had lost its way and could offer no leadership. Miles and Long had allowed the newspaper to go down-market to compete with the *Sun*, and every night their staff nervously anticipated what new angle the *Sun* would invent on the same regurgitated stories. The group's managers lacked innovative vision and their disagreements with Thornton did not suggest that the flotation would greatly improve the company's management.

On the Thursday morning, however, rumours were flying around the Mirror building and the third floor became the location of a continuous meeting. No fiction writer could ever conjure up a more pitiful image. Dozens of highly paid men and women who prided themselves on their ability to embarrass the powerful and to fashion the views of millions were flapping to find an answer to a plight which they had so often witnessed others suffering. Initially, their feelings about Maxwell were evenly divided. Many felt that he might give the paper a new sense of direction, even self-respect, especially since tabloids seemed to flourish better under the shadow of a giant than under that of an anonymous conglomerate. Among those supporting Maxwell were Bob Edwards, editor of the *Sunday Mirror*, and Terence Lancaster, the *Mirror*'s political editor.

But the mood changed markedly once Joe Haines, the *Mirror*'s esteemed columnist, began speaking. Haines, a small, spikey figure born in Rotherhithe, east London, had been Harold Wilson's press secretary between 1969 and 1976 and knew both the Labour Party and its leading luminaries intimately. Inside 10 Downing Street, Haines had been renowned for what some of Wilson's kitchen cabinet called the 'Bermondsey Dockers' Syndrome' – an antagonism towards the elite, especially the educated, the wealthy and the City. Firmly etched in the memory of those close to Wilson was Haines's advice to the Prime Minister whenever Maxwell's name surfaced: 'Don't touch that man with a bargepole.' Most of the *Mirror* staff had come to share Wilson's appreciation for Haines's flair with words.

At the meeting on the third floor, Haines rose to a pitch of eloquence well suited to the heated occasion. Standing next to Haines as he spoke was Geoffrey Goodman, the *Mirror*'s respected industrial editor. He and others heard Haines say, using the most graphic words, that Maxwell could not be trusted and should be opposed. Most of his audience, who knew very little about the details of Maxwell's past, were impressed with Haines's vehement denunciation of Maxwell's character and personality. The meeting voted in favour of a motion condemning Maxwell and urging Reed to stand by its assurances. For professional cynics, especially self-proclaimed critics of capitalism, they were surprisingly trusting that Reed would place its honour above profits.

At about 10 a.m. on Friday morning, Roy Hattersley, the Labour Party's deputy leader, received a call at his home from his friend Charles Williams. 'Don't let anyone know I've phoned you,' said Maxwell's banker, 'but Bob will be buying the *Mirror* today. Jarratt cannot afford to keep his promise.' Hattersley, despite rumours to the contrary, had little affection for Maxwell, but as a shrewd political animal he understood the implications for the party. Immediately after Williams's call, Maxwell had also phoned and asked Hattersley to tell Kinnock. Thirty minutes later, Hattersley walked into Kinnock's office in the House of Commons to find the leader drafting a public statement supporting the flotation and criticising any proposal which allowed Maxwell or a single proprietor to take control.

'He's going to buy the *Mirror* whatever you write,' said Hattersley.

'What do you think about that?' asked Kinnock.

'In my opinion, any man who can afford to buy a newspaper should not be allowed to own one. But there's nothing we can do.'

Kinnock's proposed statement, advised Hattersley, would be injudicious, since Reed's decision would not be influenced by the party's attitude, and if Maxwell won, the relationship between the party and the newspaper would be imperilled: 'It's a risk we cannot afford.' Unlike his predecessors as leader, Kinnock was neither cosmopolitan nor impressed by self-made businessmen. Maxwell had provided the party with a lot of financial support which would probably increase in the future. He therefore accepted Hattersley's warning that an outright condemnation would be folly. A mild statement would be issued instead.

By lunchtime in Piccadilly, no one dared look out across the street to the Ritz in case they glimpsed Maxwell standing by the window staring back. Carpenter had finished outlining his final opinion to Jarratt. The advice about the flotation upon which they had relied, he said, was flawed. Reed might raise no more than £45 million, perhaps even less, and that was indefensible to the shareholders. Thornton had been the Mirror executives' own choice and they would have to bear the consequences of their error. Maxwell's offer was too good to refuse. When the board arrived at 2 p.m., they would recommend acceptance. Jarratt's conscience was overridden by his legal duty to the shareholders. By 4 p.m., the board had agreed that Carpenter should negotiate and return with an outline of Maxwell's best offer. The meeting was adjourned while Carpenter walked across the street to meet Maxwell in his suite. Tea and cucumber sandwiches were already prepared. Maxwell could not hide his excitement as the cups were filled.

Carpenter had one goal – if there was a deal, Maxwell would not be given an opportunity to haggle. Maxwell's style was always to make an agreement and then start wearing everyone down by renegotiating everything. That was why the Odhams sale had been so painful. To avoid a repetition, Warburgs, before allowing Carpenter to cross the street, had extracted an agreement that Maxwell not only would pay cash, but would pay every penny the same day. It was a very unusual demand. Maxwell was to be held to his word that his £100 million offer was unconditional and he would pay on the spot.

The £100 million, however, contained provision for £23 million which Reed owed to the Mirror Group. Therefore, when Carpenter arrived, Maxwell's offer stood at £77 million. Carpenter believed that Maxwell was buying blind since they had forbidden him sight of the Mirror accounts but he nevertheless insisted that the Reed board wanted more. After some discussion, Maxwell slowly raised his offer to £84 million – 'That's it, my final offer.' Compared with the £45 million which the float would raise, Carpenter had every reason to feel pleased, but instead he said, 'I want ninety.'

'No,' said Maxwell.

Carpenter rose and walked towards the door: 'It's ninety or nothing.'

'I just don't have that last £6 million,' Maxwell said.

Carpenter pondered: 'I'll lend it to you for six months at the bank's rate of interest.'

Maxwell sighed and agreed. 'It's a deal.'

At 5.30, they shook hands. Carpenter felt elated. He had extracted blood from a stone. The board would approve. Maxwell was doubly pleased. On his sixth attempt, he was on the verge of becoming a press baron, and the price was low. Fortunately, he thought, Reed had been unwise. The value of the Mirror building had been underestimated and they had not realised that there was a surplus in the pension fund. Probably neither knew that the Reuters shares would become even more valuable. But both sides accepted there was a premium on Maxwell's inimitable style with the unions. His threats would carry conviction. 'The assets', Maxwell later boasted, 'are equal to what I paid. The newspapers are in for free.' His grandfather, Yaacov Schlomovitch, would have been proud of his strategy.

As he recrossed Piccadilly, Carpenter's private telephone was ringing. It was Thornton to report that all the union leaders who had rushed to his office that morning had now agreed to a no-strike deal. A secretary took a note of the details. 'Has anything happened with Maxwell?' he asked. 'No, nothing,' was the reply. 'The board is still meeting.'

Carpenter was reporting to the board the £90 million cash offer. By 6.30 p.m., they were agreed. The sale should proceed. Outside, the telephone was ringing again. It was Thornton. Carpenter took the call.

'Has there been a deal?' asked Thornton.

'No,' replied Carpenter, which was technically still correct.

'You know about the unions' undertaking?'

'Yes.'

'Does Jarratt's pledge still stand?'

'Yes,' said Carpenter.

As he spoke, dark-suited lawyers and bankers began filing into the board room to complete the mammoth legal transaction. Dozens of thick documents whose contents had been unofficially discussed over the previous days appeared from briefcases and were passed around. An exuberant Maxwell arrived at 7 p.m., and was greeted with polite resignation by Jarratt and Carpenter. 'I haven't sold the *Mirror* to Maxwell,' mused Jarratt as he watched the huge man lumber around his board room. 'He's bought it off me.' Around the polished table, their experts were scrutinising phrases and figures, and feeding an endless stream of amendments into a battery of word processors to produce a contract which would transfer Northcliffe's former empire to the son of a peasant.

Maxwell and Carpenter began talking about why Reed had sold the papers. 'Our share price will substantially improve,' said Carpenter.

'I doubt it,' said Maxwell.

'A £10 bet?'

'Done,' said Maxwell. Carpenter would win the bet.

Outside, Carpenter's phone was again ringing. It was Thornton again. He was told that the board was still meeting. There was no news.

Inside, as the rewriting and signings continued, Higgs asked Leslie Goodman of Hill Samuel whether he had the money. Goodman showed the banker a document which guaranteed that Hill Samuel would pay the entire £90 million if Maxwell's cheque did not arrive the following day.

Higgs, who feared anarchy at the *Mirror* when the news finally leaked out, folded it carefully.

There were no celebrations as the signing ended at midnight. Higgs turned to Maxwell: 'Are you going home now?'

'Yes, off to bed,' he replied.

Carpenter intervened: 'Bob, do me a favour. Don't go to the *Mirror* tonight. Let's be tactful and break it in the morning, or else you'll have a stoppage.'

'Yes, you're quite right,' said Maxwell.

Maxwell walked out into Piccadilly and got into his Rolls. 'To the Mirror building,' he told Les Williams, his long-suffering chauffeur.

The journey from Piccadilly to Holborn lasted just five minutes. As the Rolls raced towards his latest acquisition, Maxwell was preoccupied, an informed guess suggests, by his image as the new Beaverbrook. He would become a great newspaper tycoon. leading from the front, inspiring great feats of reportage. The *Mirror* would once again become a great newspaper with unbridled influence. He, Robert Maxwell, would be the modern colossus, bestriding Fleet Street, Westminster and the City. Like the 'Beaver', his counsel would be sought by politicians, financiers and even trade unionists. All would seek his advice and help, and eagerly await his judicious opinions on solving Britain's major problems. Daily, his newspapers would disseminate his views to the world in what he would publicly describe as 'a small contribution'. Then, preferably sooner rather than later, as his influence increased, governments would entrust him, as the Beaver had been entrusted, with the tasks which only the recognised talents of a tycoon could accomplish; and then the honours would follow. As the limousine silently drew up outside the grotesque glass tower, a monument to modern philistinism, there might, as he stepped out, have been a subconscious, transient flash: 'The *Daily Maxwell*'.

Daydreams are normal. Actually realising them is a joy denied to most, even to the rich. Aged sixty-one years, this was a new climax to his career and who would deny any man the pleasure at that joyous moment as he walked through the glass door and replied to an innocent inquirer about his business in the building: 'I've just bought it. I'm the new proprietor.' But as he travelled up to the ninth floor in the leather-lined executive's lift ('inside Cecil King's wallet' was the old joke), there were no thoughts about telephoning his cronies to come for a celebration as Beaverbrook would have done. Maxwell had no cronies in London to summon at that time, only employees and contacts. That was his lifestyle and it had never troubled him. As he walked into the chairman's empty office, he had fulfilled his dreams to avenge Murdoch, and that was sufficient. But his pride in his self-education had deluded him about the subtle difference between image and substance. His only similarities with Beaverbrook were the ownership of newspapers and a burning ambition to influence history. Their major difference was that, unlike Maxwell, Beaverbrook understood both newspapers and history.

The Beaver had understood that those who desire to make history must also be students of their predecessors. Beaverbrook may have been a tyrant, but he was highly educated and could hold his own in discussion with H.G. Wells and Arnold Bennett. For him, making his millions was a means to an end, and the end was managing newspapers. Finance and industrial management occupied only minutes of his day. He was an intellectual who boorishly injected his prejudice into his daily newspapers but also knew how to cultivate an atmosphere for great stars to develop within his firmament. This, above all, won him recognition, even by his political opponents. To his most distinguished employees like the *Daily Express* editor Arthur Christiansen, the *Evening Standard* editor Michael Foot and the historian A.J.P. Taylor, he was a great journalist who possessed both that instinctive genius for identifying 'news' and the art of reporting.

Since Maxwell has read few books and forgot long ago the art of instinctive learning, the delicate relationship between dictator and creator was elusive. Fixed in his mind was a confused impression of the pre-war newspaper giants and television image of Murdoch supervising the smallest details of his own newspapers just as Arno Scholz had done forty years earlier in Berlin. Maxwell's moment had finally arrived: now he was to perform the same task. Without any self-doubts, he would control everything because he knew best how to defeat Murdoch and rank alongside Beaverbrook. In his view, the quality of a leader depended upon a display of despotism. Exactly twenty years earlier he had entered the Commons because he wanted power; in Richard Crossman's words, 'he wanted to shine'. But those closest to him also say that he wanted to be loved. The paradox of a bulldozer seeking affection is not an unusual one. Ownership of the *Mirror* would be a passport to all of that and more. Maxwell truly believed that the world revolved around himself. His being was the news and his thoughts would sell newspapers. And if it didn't, so what? The newspapers belonged to him and he was intent on enjoying the rewards of his exceptional struggle. If ever an aspiring Citizen Kane was incarnated in London, it was on 13 July 1984.

Seated behind the desk in the chairman's office, looking out at the dark and sleeping capital, this was the *Mirror*'s new proprietor. He would seek fulfilment and pleasure but not confrontation. The arguments came naturally as a condition of leadership. During that night, the first article of Lex Maxwelliana was imposed on the fallen citadal: Who works for Maxwell, jumps to his command. 'When Maxwell shouts "jump!"', a long-forgotten employee had explained years earlier, 'my only response is, "How high?"' So, members of the Mirror Group board were woken and told that they were expected to attend an immediate meeting with their new proprietor. The executives emerged from their introductory meeting as daylight broke, nervous but reassured. Maxwell had been firm but charming, and a courtship had been established. Only a few believed that the future was rosy. 'Maxwell's assurances are nice,' someone later told the *Daily Mail*. 'But I went to bed last night on a long-standing assurance that the paper would never belong to one man.'

Thornton was not invited to that meeting. He had heard the news finally from Carpenter just after midnight and arrived at his office at 7.30 that morning. 'I couldn't miss Mr Maxwell because he was sitting behind my desk,' he said as he left the building. 'I congratulated him and packed my things.'

The new captain of a faltering ship can choose between two methods of introducing himself to those for whom he is newly responsible. Roy Thomson chose the gentle approach when he bought the *Sunday Times* in 1959. Walking around the machine room, he was introduced to a printer. 'How do you do,' he said, 'I'm Roy Thomson, the new owner of this paper.' 'You may own it,' replied the man, 'but I run it.' That unrectified truism cost the Thomson family approximately £70 million.

Maxwell chose a different style. At midday, on 14 July, he summoned the *Mirror*'s union leaders, the Fathers of the Chapel, to a meeting in the Rotunda, on the third floor. His speech started jovially. After explaining that he wanted to restore the *Mirror* to 'its former glory', he admitted that his ambition was to topple Murdoch's *Sun* as Britain's 'Number One Paper' and earn the same high profits which News International, owner of the *Sun*, was reaping – £23 million as opposed to the *Daily Mirror*'s £1.6 million. It need an extra million sales, and while there would be no compulsory redundancies he would be negotiating a reduction of printers with the unions. He added that he would also be launching a London evening newspaper 'in the autumn' and would want to introduce colour.

The atmosphere began to turn sour soon after his introduction. Referring to the rumours that some printers had considered stopping the previous night's production in protest at his take-over, he said in a soft but deliberately menacing tone: 'If you would have stopped the paper, it would have stayed shut and if you don't believe me, ask the people at Park Royal.' As the audience became sullen, Maxwell began using swear words, but, after protests, apologised. 'Do you think that I am on an ego-trip?'

'Yes,' shouted the audience in near-unison.

'I have invested £90 million in this business and I don't belong to the Salvation Army. . . . I am the proprietor. I am the boss. And I want that to be understood very clearly. There can only be one boss and that is me.' It was an honest riposte. For £90 million, he was entitled to create a profit-making business by removing those managers who had so badly failed and simultaneously to indulge himself, if he cared to do so.

Only four people applauded as he sat down. Many were too fearful to move. Later that day, the same four provided the only votes against a motion condemning Reed for breaking its promise and insisting that Maxwell adhere to his guarantees of non-interference in editorial content. Maxwell had in the meantime dictated the following day's front page, a bold statement to the readers. 'The Mirror Group newspapers have changed ownership,' it read. 'Their policies will not change. I am proud to be the proprietor of this group of publications.' (One week later, after urgent calls from his lawyers, he angrily denied that he was the proprietor of the group, and insisted that he was only the publisher.)

That afternoon, Maxwell held a press conference. His carefully phrased statement was a pledge of intent, repeating the very assurances which he had given to both Jarratt and Foot and, more importantly, to his senior editors and staff:

I am very proud to be associated with Mirror Group Newspapers. . . . It is my intention to restore the *Daily Mirror* to its rightful place as Britain's biggest-circulation popular newspaper without sacrificing any of its influence or tone. . . . I shall ensure that the Mirror Group becomes more efficient and more competitive and more attractive and exciting so that it can attract readers from other tabloids which seem to me to pursue policies which are against the best interest of many, many millions of our citizens in these islands. Under my management, editors in the group will be free to produce their newspapers without interference, with their journalistic skills and judgement.

I shall place only two strictures on those who have editorial responsibility for newspapers that are members of the Mirror Group. One, the papers must retain their broadly sympathetic approach to the labour movement. . . . Two, the papers must and will have a 'Britain first' policy. I want them to inform Britain, entertain Britain and boost Britain. Morale in Britain is low at present, but there is much in our country that is good and I want that to find a voice in the Mirror Group papers, on an even better and larger scale than is the case at present. We can and must revive our fortunes for our own sake and for our young people, so many of whom are being thrown on the scrapheap before they've even begun to live their lives.

His critics readily noted his promises in order to compare them with his performance over the following twelve months. The comparison would, they felt, reveal a lot about Maxwell's attitudes, his character and above all his veracity. Although he had successfully compartmentalised his activities, his behaviour at the *Daily Mirror* would determine whether the allegations and criticisms about his business career were valid or whether he had, as he claimed, been unfairly maligned. The commercial world is complicated and shadowy, and Maxwell, like all other entrepreneurs, operated within a ghetto. Whatever had been revealed was a mere glimpse compared to what remained hidden behind the walls. In sharp contrast, at the *Mirror*, all his performances would be witnessed by professionals whose only motive when something of interest occurs is to publicise the deed as quickly as possible. Inside the Mirror building, Maxwell had established his own ground rules by which he could be judged. Intentionally, he exposed himself more than any other present-day publisher. He had forsaken the ghetto for a goldfish bowl and could be held to account by his critics without redress against accusations of distortion.

On Sunday morning, Joe Haines arrived at his desk to begin collecting his belongings. Like most *Mirror* staff, he had heard the news of the take-over on Friday's early-morning news. His forceful speech against Maxwell at the union meeting had undoubtedly been reported to the new proprietor. He had meant every word he had uttered. Maxwell was unfit to own the newspaper and much worse. The day previously, he had told a friend, 'I'll be cashing in my railcard on Monday morning.' Minutes later his telephone rang. It was Maxwell. 'Joe, come up please.' Haines expected to be dismissed and told his trusting colleagues later, 'I didn't want to work for Maxwell.' But Maxwell had decided that he needed Haines. He had not calculated how long he needed his talents, but it was wise to juggle the options and forestall any headline about hacks leaving the sinking ship. Pinpointing an enemy's price and winning his sympathy lies at the heart of Maxwell's technique, and to Haines's surprise, he was offered promotion and a glowing future. If Haines was torn, his dilemma was soon resolved; he agreed to stay on two conditions: a guarantee of non-interference with his work and a promise that the *Mirror* would continue to support the Labour Party. 'What could I do?' he asked his colleagues dejectedly when he explained his acceptance, but it did not stop one observer rattling some coins as he walked past. Another of the *Mirror*'s star columnists who expected dismissal was the investigative reporter Paul Foot. To his surprise, after he had insisted that he would stay only if he could write without interference, Maxwell agreed to his terms.

A third who was offered similar conditions was Geoffrey Goodman. Maxwell asked him to 'help me revive the *Mirror* and join my Politburo to steer the paper', and promised that there would be 'no interference in your writing'.

For Haines, Foot and Goodman, those guarantees were vital to their self-respect. All three also believed that the *Mirror*'s readers, to whom they felt a responsibility, would cease buying the paper if, instead of proper reporting, they read the proprietor's opinionated articles. But they were the exceptions. Few of their senior colleagues stipulated similar conditions for remaining.

The day following the takeover, Maxwell wrote a front-page article re-explaining his policies and aspirations. It was forceful and pungent. Within two weeks it was clear that, as many suspected, his self-introduction was not an isolated appearance.

July was the fourth month of the miners' strike, which many already suspected was no longer an industrial dispute but had evolved into a clear-cut political battle between the Prime Minister and the miners' leader, Arthur Scargill. Many Conservatives believed that Scargill was intent on repeating his 1974 victory over Edward Heath. In their view, the very survival of both the government and the nation was at stake and the compromises which were customarily engineered to settle strikes should be ignored. Their priority was finally and utterly to rout the miners and deal the trade unions' hegemony a mortal blow.

The *Mirror* was in an awkward predicament. Normally, it would be sympathetic to the miners but, like the Labour Party leadership, the newspapers' editors and senior staff were disturbed by Scargill's extremism, by the violence around the pits, and most of all by the union's refusal to ballot its members. Nevertheless, many socialists felt that the government had deliberately cut off any chances of negotiation and that the long-term damage caused to the Labour movement would be grave.

One of the *Mirror*'s voices on these issues was their well-informed and distinguished industrial editor Geoffrey Goodman. Goodman was politically left-wing and had often found himself, during more than 30 years on the staff, in opposition to the newspaper's editorials especially about the common market, unilateral disarmament and governments' economic policies. On several occasions, the disagreements had ended in emotional rows. On 26 July, Goodman wrote a column about the strike entitled 'Digging into a Vendetta'. Writing in the *Mirror*'s colloquial style, Goodman alleged that during the miners' strike in 1974, Margaret Thatcher had been, with one other, a lone voice in the Heath Cabinet urging her Prime Minister to 'Take on the miners, fight 'em to a finish and win. . . .' The present strike, claimed Goodman, was the delayed 'vast political test of will and strength' which the present Prime Minister had urged one decade earlier. In the emotion generated by the strike it was a distinctly anti-government story.

That night, Goodman left his office believing that the article would work its way through the editorial machine and appear the following day. Instead, in his absence, Maxwell seized his piece, personally crossed out all references to a 'vendetta' and headed the revised and now rather confused column, 'The Enemy Within'. As the rumours of Maxwell's interference, executed without consulting Goodman, spread through the Mirror building during the morning of 27 July, the reality of Lex Maxwelliana dawned and questions began to be asked: Had Goodman protested? Had Joe Haines, promoted to assistant editor, raged? Had the editor Mike Molloy himself threatened to resign in defence of his staff? In fact, none of these had happened.

Goodman had been telephoned at 11 p.m. and told about Maxwell's changes. Minutes later he had threatened Molloy that he would resign if his own article were not resuscitated but he was persuaded to wait until the morning. When he met Maxwell at 10 a.m., the proprietor 'put his arms around me and said, "How can you ever forgive me for such a thing? I should never have done it."' Goodman did forgive his employer, agreeing that in future he would send his articles in advance to Maxwell to read, and the proprietor insisted, 'I promise that I won't interfere.' The proprietor had struck and, despite the overwhelming might which the opposition could have brought to bear against him, he encountered only appeasement. 'I fooled myself', says Goodman, 'that he'd keep to his promise.' Maxwell, many would discover, respects only those who resist his cajolery.

That same morning, after settling the local difficulty, Maxwell summoned his senior staff and enthusiastically outlined his next foray. There would be a special issue three days later about the strike. Goodman was detailed to arrange a secret meeting between Maxwell and Scargill at the Hallam Tower Hotel outside Sheffield. When they met, Goodman observed, the two 'got on very well together. They were practically interchangeable. Maxwell was very impressed by Scargill and especially by his complaints about police violence.' Yet, as the special issue was being prepared, Maxwell's animosity towards the miners seemed to wax. An opinion piece was commissioned whose line was to be critical of the miners. Reluctantly, Goodman and Terry Lancaster wrote the article for Maxwell's approval but refused to allow their names to be printed above it. Since Maxwell demurred placing his own name as the by-line, Molloy suggested that they use the alias 'Charles Wilberforce', which had previously been used by Cudlipp. Maxwell was satisfied and particularly approved the splash headline: 'The Pigheaded Identical Twins'. The journalists left his office dejected. 'We had become accomplices to his destruction of editorial independence,' says Goodman. In the lift going down from Maxwell's office, he confessed his fears to Molloy. 'There's no point going on, Mike,' he said.

'Let's fight it out. Don't hand it over to him,' replied Molloy, who was afraid that any opposition would be greeted by dismissal. 'It's his paper.'

Molloy's pragmatism was born of long experience. In his view the ritualistic worship of editorial independence was a myth, especially on the *Mirror*, because he could well recall how both King and Cudlipp would constantly interfere. If Goodman did not like the new owner, he had the simple but effective option of resigning.

Seated in his ninth-floor office, Maxwell warmed to the notion that he, using the *Mirror* as a platform, could solve the strike. Among those who were summoned to serve that purpose was David Seymour, the newspaper's second-ranking leader writer beneath Joe Haines. Seymour is a committed and professional journalist of the sort which newspapers need if they are to innovate and thrive. During his thirteen years with the *Mirror*, Seymour had earned a reputation for writing '*Mirror* Comment' pieces which evoked the spirit of both the newspaper and its readers. Seymour had been surprised when Maxwell, soon after his arrival, had asked to see his 'Comment' pieces and had begun changing occasional words. Since none of his superiors objected, he was left with no alternative but to wait most days with crowds of other journalists in the ante-room to Maxwell's office to submit his articles.

'I want you to use all your Jewish chutzpah to write the following . . .' would often be the introduction to the proprietor's command. The editor Mike Molloy was rarely by Maxwell's side. Over the next weeks, Seymour regularly wrote the '*Mirror* Comment' about the strike, consciously distorting what he felt to be the truth to suit Maxwell's views. 'The whole strike became a blur for me,' he recalls, 'because I was being battered the whole time by Maxwell, who was jumping up and down on my head telling me what was happening, which I knew was wrong.' Regularly, Seymour sat in Maxwell's office, negotiating the following day's 'Comment' amid constant telephone calls to the proprietor from stockbrokers, property dealers, the manager of Oxford United football club, other City tycoons and an endless stream of unidentifiable foreigners to whom Maxwell spoke in one of his eight languages. All these conversations about take-over deals, transfers of soccer players and currency movements, a testament to an unusually agile mind, took place while Seymour sat worrying about the advancing deadline, watching Jean Baddeley scurrying in and out of the office to feed the revised copy into the Wang computer, and pondering with others about the consequences for the newspaper's reputation.

For the *Mirror* men who had prided themselves on their accuracy about industrial matters, the opprobrium they were gradually receiving from their readers was disquieting. The process reached a zenith on 10 September. The *Mirror*'s headline was dramatic: 'Scargill to Ballot Members on Final Offer'. The report explained that the miners would be allowed to vote on the coal board's final offer. Alongside the article was an anonymous 'Comment' entitled 'A Vote For Sanity'. The story, which followed strenuous efforts by Maxwell to act as a peacemaker, was untrue. For the *Mirror* to publish an error on such a major issue further undermined the newspaper's credibility.

Maxwell was unperturbed. At both the TUC and Labour Party conferences, as the *Mirror*'s proprietor he had become the centre of attention, wielding the political power which he had sought for so long. According to Seymour, 'He just didn't seem to care that we were wrong.' He was also unconcerned about contradicting the assurances he had given at the 14 July press conference when he was asked how he could achieve the editorial changes without interference. His reply had been, '(a) I haven't got the time and (b) if you've got the talent of the kind that we have on these newspapers, what the hell are you going to do – tell them how to do their job? Come off it.' That statement was, he later said, a 'guarantee of editorial integrity' because the editors were not 'just a bunch of lackies and zombies [who] will do what I bid them'.

Days after making that statement, Maxwell was filmed by BBC Television inside the Mirror building asking why a photographer was being sent to a James Bond set – why couldn't the film's producers provide a photograph free?; telling Peter Thompson, the *Sunday Mirror* editor, that he would not tolerate the newspaper following Liz Taylor to Richard Burton's grave, and later explaining, 'I refused to allow any of our photographers or reporters to go and invade [her] privacy'; and declaring that he was 'shocked' by the Press Council's condoning the *Sunday Times*'s exposure of suspicious transactions as evidenced by Denis Thatcher's bank accounts. There was, said Maxwell, to be no 'cheque-book journalism' and 'no nipples'. Gloom spread among the *Mirror*'s staff. Everything they feared about Maxwell seemed to be true, especially in the one area where his arrival might have promised improvements.

Maxwell brought two great strengths to Holborn. He understood printing and the print unions, which he could reorganise efficiently, and he claimed that he was a superb salesman. Once those talents were utilised, he said, the *Mirror* would be profitable. Since the Fleet Street chapels were more powerful than those he had confronted at BPC, their subjugation would take time. The salesman's promise of 'One million extra readers within one year' could, he believed, be realised without delay. After waiting so many years, Maxwell was more impatient than usual to confront his arch-rival and overtake the *Sun*. In his first press conference on 14 July Maxwell had said, referring to the daily prize games which newspapers were using to attract readers, 'I am not very keen on Bingo,' because it was a considerable expense which the *Mirror* had been compelled to undertake to match Murdoch. He wanted it to end.

Three days later, Maxwell telephoned John Banks, the chairman and chief executive of the advertising agency Young and Rubicam, who had handled the Mirror Group account for many years. According to Banks, the instructions were 'to invent the most sensational game for his group of newspapers'. The brief was to produce a campaign within three days to 'beat the Bingo sensation of the *Sun*' which would be 'the most exciting game of the decade'. This time Banks's agency could not automatically expect to launch the new campaign because Maxwell had asked other agencies also to offer presentations. So when Banks arrived at Headington Hall on the Sunday morning, he needed to present a concept which was even more audacious than his client could have imagined. Banks was unusually excited with his agency's idea. Called 'Who Dares Wins', a play on the motto of the crack SAS regiment, Banks presented a campaign which he calculated would endear itself to the architect of a 'Forward with Britain posture'. The game itself was nothing more than a variation of bingo but Banks added two major innovations. The prize would be £1 million cash and Maxwell would appear on television in person to introduce the new game with the immortal phrase, 'I'll make you a millionaire.'

Banks pitched his presentation to appeal to his client's vanity: 'You epitomise the new spirit and change in the *Mirror* and you have a vision for the paper. We think that your presence on screen would enhance the paper and yourself.' Maxwell did not commit himself immediately. His reluctance was purely about his own appearance. He apparently had no qualms about the game, thus contradicting his earlier distaste for selling papers by means of bingo instead of journalism.

After reflection, he telephoned Banks and agreed to the package and to his appearance. It seems he did not take into account the fact that Murdoch had earned his fortune and phenomenal success without appearing on television and was in fact beginning to eschew publicity. Maxwell adopted the contrary view and warmed to Banks's notion that his appearance to promote bingo-fever could sell his newspaper. He explained his conversion later: 'Since I arrived at Fleet Street and everybody is playing the game, I've decided to play the game for real.' The justification for the game was that his newspaper, rather than making rash promises like its competitors, was actually paying a million pounds, proving 'the integrity of the *Mirror*'. If ever Maxwell exposed himself as a player and not as a strategist, this was the moment. The filming was to take place in his office in the Mirror building.

Maxwell was of course no stranger to television performances and he can be surprisingly patient with its tiresome demands, but on this occasion Banks was expecting him to behave like an actor whose words and movements had been carefully scripted. To begin with, when filming started at 2 p.m. in his office, everything looked easy:

When I bought Mirror Group Newspapers, I asked our people to come up with the most spectacular free game ever. They've done it. It's not bingo. It's the 'Win a million game'. I'm writing the cheque for a million pounds now. It's not made out to anyone, but for the first time in Britain I guarantee one of you will win it. So buy the *Daily Mirror*, *Sunday Mirror* or *Sunday People* and play the 'Win a Million' game. I could be writing your name in here very soon. It's fun, instant and free. There are thousands of cash prizes to be won, and I'm waiting to make one of you a millionaire.

By the third attempt of filming the thirty-second speech, the proprietor was becoming weary. It was, he complained, too complicated. Not the words, but everything else. He was expected not only to speak, but also to sit at the desk, write the cheque, put the cheque-book into a drawer and the signed cheque into his pocket, get up, and walk across to a logo saying, 'Who Dares Wins'. Meanwhile he would be smiling and speaking and being careful not to trip over anything.

There was a printing empire to manage, deals on the stock and currency exchanges to consider and there were constant telephone calls from all around the world to handle. His office was crowded with people and cumbersome equipment, and the lights were hot. Lines were fluffed, lights fused and, infuriatingly, he completed his walk and talk in either twenty-nine or thirty-one seconds whereas he was required to take precisely thirty seconds. Yet by 7 p.m. one take was judged suitable enough for transmission. Maxwell was thrilled with the results but by then the gimmick was no longer a secret. The *Mirror*'s competitors had heard the news and made hasty plans to launch an identical campaign. 'There's no better form of flattery than copying,' said Maxwell, basking in the success of his own 'scoop', which was aired on ITV on 17 August.

The following day, Maxwell's photograph and message covered the *Mirror*'s front page. The game was explained over three more pages and similar mass coverage reappeared in the newspaper on each of the following three days. The miners' strike, which days earlier had been described as 'terribly damaging', was relegated while pages and pages of the *Mirror* were devoted to the game and its beaming proprietor who had warmed to Banks's pitch that he personally 'epitomises the new spirit'. Joyfully, he felt that he was beating Murdoch. Not only had he launched the biggest bingo game in history but he had also resisted following the *Sun*'s price increase despite the higher cost of newsprint. 'We have won hands down,' he said to his editorial conference. '[Murdoch] spends most of his time in America. I think he'll seriously have to consider coming home.' As always in his career, his optimism blinded him to so many awkward truths, not least of which was that Murdoch trusted his staff in Britain to handle the challenge. Delegation was a management style which Maxwell could not accept, despite his frequent assertion that 'I am a very efficient manager of men and assets.'

Just five days after the hugely expensive campaign to boost the *Mirror* was launched, it was scooped by its rival. On 23 August, the *Sun* announced the first bingo millionaire. The television pictures showed Maxwell gritting his teeth. Murdoch had beaten him, again. Churlishly, he directed the paper to make the best of his defeat by proclaiming all over the *Mirror*'s front page, the '*Sun*'s millionaire can thank the *Mirror*'. But Banks had unwittingly released an irrepressible genie.

Maxwell enjoyed appearing on television. The day following his first appearance, he telephoned Banks: 'John, I've arranged it all. Get your cameras round there immediately.' Coutts Bank, at Maxwell's behest, had agreed to provide one million pounds in notes on a trolley for a new commercial in which he would star. In the meantime, he resorted to his other favourite to stimulate sales. The *Mirror*'s price was cut by one penny – a tactic he had unsuccessfully employed nine years earlier at the *Scottish Daily News*. Every day for three weeks, the *Mirror*'s front page was dominated by news of its price cut and the 'million pound game'. At the end, he gave away his million pounds and surreptitiously increased the price. The enormous impact which Banks had promised had rebounded. The readers had become unsettled. The gyrations in price reflected the newspaper's variations in content. Molloy and his staff knew the cause.

Their newspaper was less spicy and less fun to read. If they tried to intervene, Maxwell ignored them. He was enjoying the publicity and it was fun running newspapers. His contribution, he felt, was satisfying and should increase even if the *Mirror*'s circulation, after a slight increase, was beginning to fall. All that was needed, he believed, was a greater contribution from himself.

In October, Britain became aware of a dreadful famine in Ethiopia. The television news pictures were dramatic and Maxwell saw a chance to help the starving and the *Mirror*. In line with its great tradition, the *Mirror* would save the unfortunates with Maxwell in charge of the operation. Few journalists travelling with him on the specially chartered 'mercy mission' to Addis Ababa were convinced that this was a normal venture, since Maxwell featured so heavily in the *Mirror*'s coverage of the victims' plight. He and his retinue were omni-present, a trait which few outside his organisation had yet witnessed. The personal attendants, the battery of telephones, the huge consumption of food and his sheer need to place himself, rather than the victims, at the centre of attention contrasted strangely with the images of famine. Back in London, David Seymour, Goodman and other *Mirror* staff were startled when the proprietor, having commandeered the Hilton Hotel in Addis, sent messages dictating what action the newspaper should demand to solve the latest crisis in the miners' strike: 'He was completely out of touch but still sending us his "action memos" as if we were a business not a newspaper and his judgements were contradicted by the facts.' Like so many others, Seymour and Goodman would eventually leave in despair.

On Maxwell's return, the escapades increasingly promoted Maxwell rather than the newspaper. On 4 March, *Mirror* readers were entertained by a flattering profile of the President of Bulgaria who is believed to have organised the murder in London of the dissident Georgi Markov with a poisoned umbrella and to have sanctioned the attempted murder of the Pope. At the end of the gushy eulogy about a country which few *Mirror* readers would appreciate, the article mentioned the President's 'special guest across the table, Robert Maxwell', who apparently 'had just struck a huge deal with the Bulgarian Government to help update the country's printing and packaging industries'. Tucked away elsewhere, the paper reported that the miners' strike had ended on the previous day.

After the end of May, Maxwell was presented in the *Mirror* as a roving ambassador. Photographs would appear of Maxwell with Soviet and Chinese leaders exchanging views about the world situation. There was also a footnote mentioning that a lucrative business deal had been concluded. During a trip to Poland, Maxwell visited General Jaruzelski, the Polish military leader who had organised the first military coup against a civilian Communist government in the Soviet bloc but had failed to squash the Solidarity movement. In a radio interview recorded after his dinner with Jaruzelski, Maxwell said that the Solidarity problem was 'solved' and that his newspapers would be 'devoting less space' to the dissenters. The accurate reporting of his comments in London caused an outcry. He countered that he had been distorted, especially by a 'mendacious' *Times* article. Nevertheless he found that he was defending himself against accusations that he was promoting not just himself but also his business interests.

The *Mirror*, it was said, had become a family photograph album which reflected the family business. No fewer than five of the seven children were now employed by their father's companies, which silenced any suggestion that on his death there would be no inheritance. His sons Kevin and Ian had become key executives in the management team. The three would meet at 8 a.m. for private discussions, before Maxwell encountered other executives. The *Mirror's* front-page story on 10 June 1985 confirmed the trend. It reported that Maxwell would rescue Britain's technical wizard, Sir Clive Sinclair, whose company was bankrupt. Maxwell, according to the report, had paid £12 million to save Britain's famed inventor. Like his earlier bid to rescue Aston Martin, it was described as an act of patriotism. Production of that night's newspaper was delayed while the announcement was dispatched from Headington Hall to the Mirror building. Maxwell was subsequently asked why he had ordered the editor to carry the Sinclair story on the front page. He replied: 'The fact that I was involved in it is incidental. . . . I'm certainly not aware [of holding up the front page]. The matter of the front page is a decision for the editor.' Asked if a rescue bid mounted by someone else would have appeared so prominently, Maxwell replied, 'I never answer hypothetical questions.' In August, he quietly pulled out of the deal. Profits, he decided, were more important than patriotism.

After one year, despite spending £5 million in promotion, the *Mirror* had lost 350,000 sales. Six months later the circulation would fall to 2.9 million, a massive half a million less than when he bought it. It confounded the new proprietor's commitment to achieve daily sales of four million copies. The combined daily loss for the whole group was one million sales. It was an unprecedented collapse in the history of Fleet Street. *Marketing Week* commented, 'It takes something close to genius to lose so much circulation so quickly.' His target of overtaking the *Sun* within one year had withered.

Maxwell, understandably worried, consulted Molloy. Molloy's advice was to return to the old formula of cheque-book journalism and heavy advertising. In April, Maxwell announced a £10 million promotion campaign, sanctioned the use of 'dolly birds' and approved the invasion of privacy. *Mirror* executives were authorised to buy the titillating memoirs of Peter Bogdanovich, a film director whose beautiful girlfriend, a model called Dorothy Stratten, had been brutally murdered. Bogdanovich claimed that she had been the victim of sexual perverts associated with Hugh Hefner's Playboy empire. It was an averagely intrusive and voyeuristic sex saga.

In normal circumstances, the serialisation would have passed off unnoticed but since it was Maxwell's latest stratagem against Murdoch, there was an opportunity for his competitors to lampoon the challenger. By that time, Maxwell's energetic self-promotion in his newspapers and on television chat shows was a major topic of conversation. While Maxwell assumed that all the requests for interviews and appearances were recognition of his importance, the invitations were in fact often motivated by the search for good entertainment, especially to expose any glaring inconsistencies. So, when Fleet Street heard that he had strayed into areas beyond his experience, the incentive to embarrass 'Cap'n Bob', as he had unaffectionately been dubbed, was irresistible. The *Sun* decided to run the identical story about the model's murder but culled from contemporaneous newspaper accounts. In the industry it is called 'a spoiler' and can be deflected by time-honoured methods. Maxwell naturally was ignorant of those devices and resorted once again to asking the courts for an injunction against the *Sun*. In the process, the owner of the *Mirror* was boosting his competitor's circulation.

Standing outside the High Court in the Strand, Maxwell condemned the *Sun* as a 'lying, cheating, thieving paper' for regurgitating an old interview with the model and dressing it up as a scoop. There was even talk of demanding the imprisonment of the *Sun*'s editor. Inside the courtroom, the judge rejected Maxwell's case and ordered that he pay the £50,000 costs. Outside in the streets again, Maxwell said, 'Spoiling may be legal, but it's not nice.' Fleet Street, he said, needed to be 'cleaned up'. The cleansing would no longer concern the coverage of lurid sex scandals but would be designed to prevent competition. 'Everything's got a moral, if you can only find it,' as the Duchess said to Alice.

On the first anniversary of his purchase Maxwell was asked about his interference: 'I don't think that has any effect on the sales of the paper except to improve the adrenalin throughout the building.... Whether I appear in the paper or not, that's a matter for them to decide, not for me.' When pressed to explain whether those stories would have received such prominence or even coverage if Maxwell had not featured, he replied, 'You'll have to ask the editor, not me. . . . It's the editors who interfere in the publisher's prerogative, not the other way round.'

In August 1985, Maxwell was finally persuaded that his enjoyment was too expensive. His financial staff forecast that the group's paltry £1 million profit would be replaced during that year by a £6 million loss. His salesmanship had failed and he had made no progress in reducing the *Mirror*'s printing costs, which were approximately three times higher than the *Sun*'s. His flamboyance had disillusioned his editorial staff and, worse, had undermined his credibility with the unions. His warning, issued in April, that all the newspapers would close if there were not 'massive cost reductions' had been ignored. Although he spoke about the 'People inside Mirror newspapers [who] know that I do not bluff. I will close the newspapers if they are ever brought to a halt by the unions,' the unions had not shifted their ground. Reasoned negotiations had failed and the papers' future was overshadowed by the threat posed by Eddie Shah's proposed *Today*. With the latest German presses and free of all union restrictions, Shah promised to produce a national colour tabloid, which at the time seemed to threaten all of Fleet Street's tabloids. In August, Maxwell launched a broadside against the unions using the anticipated appearance of *Today* to focus attention on the finite nature of their monopoly. As the Mirror Group losses mounted, Bill Miles noticed that the 'air of compromise disappeared. He became much more aggressive.' Maxwell's mixed blessing was that the appalling relations between SOGAT and the NGA, and between the national officials and the in-house shop stewards (FOCs), would enable him to play off one group of workers against the other. 'We realised that when Maxwell bought the *Mirror*, the writing was on the wall,' says Miles. 'I always believed his threats, but others didn't.'

At the beginning of August, Maxwell adopted the same tactics as at BPC. All the chapel leaders were summoned to the Mirror building and under the threat of a deadline began simultaneous negotiations to achieve voluntary redundancies. The crux of Maxwell's demands was that the *Sporting Life*, which was losing £3 million annually, should be printed by a subsidiary of Pergamon, which was not bound by Fleet Street's restrictions. At the end of two weeks, Maxwell struck a complicated deal with the NGA's general secretary Tony Dubbins, which allowed the printing of the *Sporting Life* to be moved. Hours later, the FOC of the NGA in the Mirror building refused to accept the agreement. To put pressure on Maxwell, NGA members, on 21 August, disrupted the

Mirror's production. Maxwell retaliated the following day by stopping production of all the newspapers and warning that 6,500 employees faced dismissal. 'The NGA were not like kamikaze pilots,' says Bill Keyes, 'because at least the kamikazes knew what they were doing.' When Maxwell's threat failed to persuade the NGA to surrender, he announced on 30 August that the *Mirror* would no longer be printed in Fleet Street. 'It is impossible to build success on anarchy,' he said. 'It seems equally impossible to be rid of that anarchy, so deeply entrenched has it become. . . . I believed I could change a floundering enterprise into a flourishing one. Regrettably, I must admit failure so far. . . . The choice facing Fleet Street and its unions is to change or perish. The unions, by refusing to allow me to publish except on their anarchical terms, have demonstrated their unwillingness to change.' The *Sporting Life*, he announced, was for sale. The union leaders were divided about the credibility of Maxwell's threats.

Bill Keyes believed that Maxwell was serious. After their violent stand-up rows about the closure of Park Royal, which the union had lost, Keyes had won a notable victory over Maxwell in their last dispute in April 1984. Printers had occupied the computer floor at Maxwell House. In retaliation, Maxwell issued a writ claiming damages from the union under the 1982 Employment Act. Keyes had been appalled that a socialist should use Tory legislation and was even more so when the Court imposed a £75,000 fine. 'I told Maxwell that we weren't going to pay,' says Keyes, 'and we'd never meet him again.' Keyes was 'shocked' that Maxwell could claim to be a member of the Labour Party. On a Sunday night, Maxwell phoned Keyes, Dubbins and Brenda Dean, the general secretary of SOGAT, and asked them to come to Oxford the following day to negotiate a settlement. All three arrived in adamant mood. 'If you don't pay the fine,' said Keyes, 'we'll go for broke and close down everything.' Maxwell refused. 'It was the same old Maxwell,' recalls Keyes, 'He'd say one thing and then change his mind.' All three walked out. The following day, Keyes travelled to Ayr in Scotland: 'That day, he and his lawyers phoned me seventeen times. We finally agreed a settlement which included Maxwell paying our fine.' They arranged to meet the following day at noon after the union's appearance in the High Court. At breakfast time Maxwell telephoned. 'I'm not paying,' he told Keyes.

'Then there's no deal,' answered the union leader.

At 11.40, Maxwell, according to Keyes, 'caved in'.

'Why did you do it?' Keyes asked his old adversary when he later collected the cheque.

'Because I'm a good socialist,' replied Maxwell smiling. 'Everyone's entitled to second thoughts.'

'It's like Russian roulette with you, Bob,' said Keyes, delighted to have won. 'You're an out-and-out bully.'

Yet when Keyes faced Maxwell about the future of the *Mirror* in August, the conditions had changed: 'Normally, his tactics were to never let us know where we stood. The sands were always shifting.' This time, Keyes did not think Maxwell was bluffing. 'We thought that he could recoup his investment by selling the Mirror building and do an Eddie Shah with the papers.'

The confrontation and shut-down coincided with the TUC conference in Blackpool. The unions wanted to talk and Maxwell agreed. He booked a suite of rooms and began non-stop negotiations. The very future of the Mirror Group depended upon Maxwell's tactics and personality. Although he had failed to organise alternative printing in Manchester, he was, Bill Miles noticed, unconciliatory about the *Sporting Life*: 'He said there was nothing to talk about. It was gone. Then he presented his "survival plan" for the rest.' For two days it was 'constant aggression, constant attack. It was exhausting. He would have closed the papers down.'

By 3 September, Maxwell's energy and tactics had won an agreement embracing the sale of the *Sporting Life* and the removal of some 'old Spanish customs', including the non-automatic replacement of the three hundred *Sporting Life* staff. The *Mirror* began publication the following day. Over the following eight weeks, there were isolated disputes and copies were lost. On 1 November, Maxwell claimed that the September agreement for uninterrupted production had been broken and announced that unless the unions agreed to an immediate cut of 2,000 out of the 6,500 jobs, of whom 1,100 were over sixty years old, the *Mirror* would close. Every employee was issued a dismissal notice. To take advantage of the new Employment Act, Maxwell 'awarded' the contract for the printing of the Mirror newspapers in Holborn after 31 December to a subsidiary of BPCC. Future disputes would therefore be hindered by the laws against secondary action. Combined with the constant reporting of the 'Shah revolution', the union leaders began to cower.

Maxwell imposed a deadline of 10 December and again, after a series of tempestuous conversations with the union leaders, corralled all the negotiators into a number of rooms to discuss how they would achieve his demands. By the final day, he had achieved an overwhelming victory. Most of the overmanning and excesses would disappear; 2,100 employees were made redundant and their payments would be largely funded from the surplus in their pension fund. The annual saving was £40 million. Maxwell's triumph was accompanied by the announcement that Mike Molloy was to be promoted and replaced by Richard Stott. Some *Mirror* staff believe that Stott made it a condition of his appointment that Maxwell would no longer interfere in the editorial process. Others believe it was Maxwell who proposed his own departure because he was bored with his toy. Although the centre of his operations was now on the ninth floor, his new ambitions precluded any interest in the daily management of a mere newspaper because he was now determined that BPCC would become one of the world's ten largest communications organisations and the *Mirror* would be just a small part of the Maxwell empire.

CHAPTER 14

On a warm June night in 1985, the concentric spheres of Maxwell's life gathered at Headington Hill Hall to celebrate his fortieth wedding anniversary. Inside the floodlit mansion, with the strains of the Salon Orchestra of the Royal Air Force playing in the background, Robert, Elisabeth and their seven children stood in a reception line to welcome five hundred guests to a gargantuan display of the family's wealth and happiness. Maxwell the celebrity is also a collector of celebrities and as he shook hands with dinner-jacketed politicians, bankers, businessmen, scientists, journalists, lawyers, trade union leaders, footballers and show-biz personalities, it was evident that their host had overcome his adversaries and fulfilled the ambitions which he had confided to Betty during their courtship in Paris. Clasping glasses of champagne, Harold Wilson, David Frost, Sir Robin Day, Ludovic Kennedy, Lord Rothermere, Lord Sieff, Hugh Scanlon, Ray Buckton and many other household names mingled to the beaming appreciation of their generous and good-humoured host as they awaited the year's most expensive dinner party. 'Many were his friends but the others came because they knew that everyone would be there,' says Richard Marsh, the former Labour minister and currently the chairman of the Newspaper Publishers Association. Displays of wealth are often vulgar but the natural vulnerability of a close family celebrating an admirable anniversary tempered the ostentation.

Just before 8 p.m., as the laughter and conversation reached a crescendo, the multitude were invited to enter a vast marquee which covered the swimming pool and a dance floor, to seek their places at one of the forty-four tastefully decorated tables. Each guest had been provided with a table plan and among the silver cutlery they each found a present from 'Bob and Betty' – an expensive leather toilet case. All agreed that it was a generous start to an unforgettable evening. As their hosts took their seats at the two main tables in the centre of the marquee, Robert Maxwell was pleased to reflect that the seating sensitively accommodated his guests' common interests and the perfection of compartmentalisation.

At a neighbouring table on his right was Jean Baddeley, his faithful assistant who had recently been appointed a director of Pergamon Holdings, with Detlev Raymond and Laszlo Straka, his close lieutenants from New York. Together, these three knew more of his secrets than the remaining guests combined although even their knowledge was strictly limited. Close by on his left was one of his brokers, Jonathan Bevan, his lawyer John Silkin and his old banking friend Charles Williams. They had laid the foundations for his BPC coup five years earlier. At his own table sat Sir Robert Clark of Hill Samuel, and Lord Kearton, to whom he was equally grateful for his recent successes, and, for sentimental reasons, Charles Hambro. Scattered through the rest of the marquee, his children were hosting tables which appropriately reflected their personal interests. His son Kevin, at twenty-four already the heir apparent, entertained the chairman of Pergamon's first merchant bankers, Lord Spens of Ansbachers, and its current analyst, Henry Poole. Maxwell's youngest daughter Ghislaine, twenty-two, who has ambitions to manage the Mirror Group, sat with journalists; similarly, his twin daughters Christine and Isabel, thirty-three, and his son Ian, twenty-seven, who all worked for BPCC, hosted tables of media stars; his eldest daughter Anne, thirty-eight, who had been an actress and was now a teacher, sat with educationalists; while his eldest son Philip, thirty-four, who is interested in science, sat with editors of Pergamon journals. If ever the constellations could be momentarily fixed in place around their sun, that moment was Friday 7 June 1985.

After four courses, there were the speeches. Elisabeth spoke movingly about her husband's achievements and of her suffering during the lonely years as he shuttled frenziedly across the world to build his fortune. All seven children stood, one on a table, as their own successes – 'O' levels, 'A' levels, university degrees – were recited for the guests to appreciate. Philip recounted his father's life story in a style which some thought faintly reminiscent of an impassive company report. (All the children, it was said, displayed an automaton loyalty to their father.) Harold Wilson, no longer in the best of health, praised the institution of marriage and his host, although he had personally denied his subject the prize he had most earnestly sought. Then Maxwell rose and spoke as a man who harboured no doubts that, after fighting a tough battle, he had won against all the odds. His words were unmemorable but the image was indelible. A huge man, in physique and personality, tinged with mystery, beaming in self-congratulation, but unable to conceal his impatience in the face of the elusiveness of the international status of Armand Hammer, Aristotle Onassis or William Hearst. His destiny – to become a national powerbroker and an international star – remained on the distant horizon, and he was sixty-three years old. Aristotle Onassis had died aged sixty-nine. Time was limited if he was to be more than a footnote in history. His large family would ensure that he was not forgotten but he wanted to enjoy his success before it was inherited. Those who were close and loyal understood his vision but only he could realise his desires. He wanted the world to forget his defeats and admire his empire. It was all implicit in his speech that night. After polite applause, the toasts were made, the champagne was drunk and everyone could dance to the music of Joe Loss's Ambassadors.

His guests began drifting away after midnight. Few could deny, even those glitterati who attend innumerable functions, that this occasion was memorable. 'A collector's item,' says one. 'Unbelievable,' opines another. There were comparisons with F. Scott Fitzgerald's *The Great Gatsby*, especially that immortal phrase, 'I was one of the few guests who had actually been invited. People were not invited – they went there.' Everyone had of course been invited to Headington Hall but who, some wondered, had refused invitations?

Two years earlier, for Maxwell's sixtieth birthday, he had hosted another lavish party. In preparation, Betty had sent hundreds of letters asking for contributions to a *Festschrift*, a collection of individual recollections about Maxwell's life collected in a book. The responses could be divided into four. Those who wrote a testimony and went to the party; those who wrote but declined the invitation to the party; or went to the party but did not want their name to appear in the *Festschrift*; and those who refused both to write and to attend the celebration. Two years later, many of those who had refused invitations to the birthday party were now quite prepared to be seen with Maxwell, since his aspirations and achievements had become impossible to ignore. The trappings of empire were being fast accumulated.

By this time, Maxwell had gathered close to him on the ninth floor of the Mirror building a diverse retinue reflecting his multifarious activities; they included several former Labour government luminaries whose past proximity to power appealed to him. Among them was Sir Thomas McCaffrey, an ex-Labour MP and formerly the press spokesman for James Callaghan at Downing Street, who had been appointed to perform the same function for Maxwell. There was Peter Jay, Callaghan's son-in-law and the last Labour government's ambassador in Washington who was Maxwell's chief of staff. After a costly debacle at Ansbachers, Charles Williams, who had become a Labour peer, was employed as a financial adviser to the Mirror Group. And there was Joe Haines. Although others in the original politburo found their influence had waned, Haines had been elevated from leader writer and political editor to become one of Maxwell's most trusted lieutenants with a clutch of directorships of Mirror Group subsidiaries. Haines's friends explain the conversion from arch-critic to idolater as consistent with the character they recall working for Harold Wilson: 'Joe needs to worship somebody and gratefully devotes himself to a powerbroker. He just convinced himself that Maxwell was right on every issue.' When McCaffrey resigned in anger about Maxwell's treatment of employees, Haines arranged for another former Downing Street press officer, Janet Hewlett-Davies, to replace him. She too would resign after one year. The frequent turnover of staff was a clear sign of an unsatisfactory working environment. Everyone was expected to adhere to the publisher's eighteen-hour working day, although the demarcation between sleeping and waking hours was never established. At all times, they were on call through the omnipresent communications network which each senior staffer accepts as a condition of service. There was no management structure. Everything revolved around and depended upon the emperor. 'It resembles more a Communist rather than a capitalist bureaucracy,' suggested one insider. In the outer office for the inner staff, his personal secretary Debbie Dynes had a list of those telephoners who could be connected to her boss irrespective of whether there was a meeting in progress. Telephone calls interrupted everything, including meals in his private dining room.

Eating had become one of Maxwell's preoccupations. There was a constant supply of lobster, salmon, caviar and other expensive dishes with the best wines and champagnes. His kitchen had a list of graduated menus, where the quality of the meal depended upon the importance of the guests. Those invited had no doubts about who ranked as the most important. Their host was always the first to be served by the liveried waiter, and he always received the biggest portion. At large parties, by the time the waiter had arrived to serve the guest on Maxwell's right, the host had already finished eating and was pushing his plate forward to demand attention for the discussion. Everyone thereafter ate in suspended animation. Maxwell's table talk varied between stimulating banter and heavy pontification. The latter predominated at the twice-monthly editors' lunches, at which policy was enunciated. Smoking was not allowed in Maxwell's presence, although he enjoyed Cuban cigars and, disconcertingly for some, habitually dipped the end into a glass of brandy. If the cigar plopped accidentally into his neighbour's glass, nothing would be said. Occasionally, as the meal ended, departing guests watched as the debris of salmon and champagne was swiftly removed to be replaced by beer and sandwiches, because a trade union delegation was about to be ushered in. The graduated menu was part of the performance.

Maxwell's diary was crowded with meals and meetings. Strand House, a neighbouring building in Holborn, was bought to be partially converted into a home and the roof to be transformed into London's only private heliport. The two-floor flat, on which no expense was to be spared, was designed as a miniature Xanadu, filled with priceless objets d'art and garish, gold-plated, modern appliances. Visitors found that it was less a home than a testament of wealth, where taste was not allowed to interfere with the spectacle.

Yet one man who was never present at the parties but whose ghost had nevertheless hung over everything for the previous two decades of Maxwell's life was Rupert Murdoch. Maxwell had striven to catch up with the Australian and his ruby anniversary party marked the moment when he believed that his opportunity might finally come. Within five years he would, if not eclipse Murdoch's empire, at least rank as an equal. In 1985, News Corporation's annual turnover was £1.5 billion, four times the combined equivalent of BPCC and Pergamon. Maxwell's target was to become one of the world's ten largest 'global information and communications' companies within five years. To realise that ambition would rank alongside Sir Edmund Hillary's ascent of Mount Everest.

Six days after the anniversary party, BPCC held its annual meeting. In his report, Maxwell unveiled how the company would be transformed from a traditional printing and publishing conglomerate into an integrated, technology-based corporation which offered newspapers, banks, brokers and packagers worldwide access through satellites to the most modern, computer-fed, colour presses and a wide assortment of other technical services. Everything depended upon increasing the fortune in his kitty to finance a buying spree for expansion. To some it seemed that there was no strategy other than rushing helter-skelter to be the biggest. The 1984 annual report explained, in his familiar vocabulary, where the money was to come from. Under the heading, 'Another Outstanding Year', Maxwell described BPCC's 'dramatic profit growth', which had risen before tax by 71.5 per cent to £37 million. But that huge increase was due, not to printing or publishing, but to property speculation. Although media companies do not usually depend upon property for their income, Maxwell said that property deals had become, and would continue to be, 'a significant profit centre for the Group'. His aggressive crusade did not start auspiciously.

In October 1984, Maxwell made a new £44 million cash bid for John Waddington, which he still identified as ripe for asset-stripping and incorporation within BPCC. Over the previous twelve months, he had denied that he had bought extra shares or that he had any intention of buying the company. Victor Watson, Waddingtons' chairman, had been sceptical of those hand-on-heart denials and tried to discover the fate of Maxwell's shareholding. The trail passed through the hands of Tiny Rowland of Lonrho but disappeared in New York. New shares, he discovered, had been purchased and were secretly owned by Maxwell's private American company, Pergamon Press Inc. (PPI). Consequently, at the outset of his latest bid, Maxwell owned a 23 per cent stake in Waddingtons. Piqued by the guile, Watson says, 'We decided to treat him to his own medicine and by God we wanted to hurt him.'

The merchant banker at Kleinwort Benson detailed to fight Maxwell on Waddingtons' behalf was Christopher Eugster, a mild-mannered, upper-crust Englishman who, with his colleagues, had perfected a strategy for defending companies against unwelcome predators. Eugster was surprised that BPCC could afford to pay for its spate of recent acquisitions because its borrowings, although cleverly dressed up by the accountants, were high. Since Maxwell was offering to pay the £44 million in cash, Eugster set out to follow the money trail. BPCC was owned by Pergamon, which was a private company, but Pergamon, as revealed in BPCC's annual report, was ultimately owned by the Pergamon Holding Foundation which was a trust incorporated in one of the world's most secret sanctuaries, Liechtenstein.

Maxwell had used trusts as tax havens for thirty years but few had noticed in 1982 that the ownership of Pergamon had moved from New York to Liechtenstein. Among Maxwell's reasons was the reform of American banking laws which had undermined the original guarantee of secrecy and freedom from taxation. The state of Liechtenstein, in contrast, promised its clients total anonymity since its law did not require that a trust be registered and the state did not provide a public record which indicated that a trust even existed. Such is the perfection of the service to guarantee anonymity that Liechtenstein law does not require the creator of the trust to identify who are the intended beneficiaries and even allows the founder to sign in a nominee name. Accordingly, the Liechtenstein government can honestly state that it remains unaware who created the trust and to what end, although the law requires the founder to promise that his trust has no criminal purpose. Nevertheless,

Liechtenstein is an ideal location for invisibly amassing and dispensing a fortune.

Maxwell's decision to cloak his activities in the secrecy of Liechtenstein was already public knowledge when Eugster began searching for ruses in Waddingtons' defence. The magazine *Private Eye* had four months earlier mentioned the transfer but such are the vagaries and weaknesses of British journalism that at the time the item passed without comment. Eugster consulted Anthony Cardew, a public relations expert retained by Waddingtons, about exploiting the Liechtenstein connection and received an ecstatic response: 'This story has got legs. It's going to run and run.' The fifty-six square miles of Liechtenstein represented the antithesis of everything Maxwell publicly claimed to espouse. Highlighting his use of a tax haven was the ideal weapon to embarrass a man who was a self-proclaimed socialist, whose newspapers thrived and survived upon exposing the intimate details of others' lives, and who campaigned on the slogan 'Britain First'. Eugster and Cardew dressed up the old as the new and hinted to friendly Fleet Street journalists that here was an area which was worthy of investigation. The first of a series of stories appeared at the beginning of December.

One week later, Dr Walter Keicher, a plump, ageing lawyer in Vaduz, the capital of Liechtenstein, was identified as the representative of the Pergamon *Stiftung*. When approached to reveal the trust's secrets, Keicher reacted with the embarrassment which might be expected of a young maiden tactlessly invited to lose her virginity. His doors were politely slammed and he grabbed for the telephone to call London. Maxwell could no longer ignore the intrusion but was furious that a take-over battle had once again degenerated into a smear about what he believed were his private affairs. In a statement, he condemned the 'outrageous and irrelevant smokescreen' raised by Waddingtons, which 'obscures the straightforward issues'. Watson countered that the obfuscation was caused by the Liechtenstein ownership of Maxwell's companies. Since it was impossible to establish the ultimate ownership of Pergamon because of Liechtenstein's laws, claimed Watson, no one knew what hidden financial liabilities Pergamon had incurred. 'If it was all as clear as Mr Maxwell says, then why does he keep it so secret?' he asked.

At the beginning of the second week of December, Maxwell's bid was delicately poised. He had already attracted 15 per cent acceptances which, in addition to his own 23 per cent, placed him in a stronger position than one year earlier. He would win the prize and humiliate Watson if a 15 per cent stake owned by Warburg Investments and held on behalf of the Sainsbury Group's pension fund were sold to him. As so often in his dealings, Maxwell had set a deadline of 13 December for acceptances and was convinced that Warburgs were bound to sell to him as the highest bidder. There was only the matter of disposing of the Liechtenstein embarrassment.

On 10 December, Ansbachers issued a statement on Maxwell's behalf about Liechtenstein. Keicher, it said, had represented Maxwell's interests for 'over thirty years and it is well known that the persons ultimately entitled [to the trust] comprise a number of charities and relatives of the respective grandparents of Mr and Mrs Robert Maxwell not resident in the United Kingdom'. The statement raised more questions than it answered. Although it was consistent with Maxwell's oft-proclaimed assurance that his children 'would not inherit one penny', it was pointed out that since his children were all French citizens (because they were born in France), it was possible that under Liechtenstein law they could be deemed 'not to be resident in the UK' and therefore inherit their father's business. Indeed, Liechtenstein law might not even apply because the secret trust document might contain a unique definition of 'residence'. The very reason for Maxwell's seeking the protection of Liechtenstein was to allow the trustees to enjoy the freedom of writing their own rules and it would be consistent with Liechtenstein's laws for Maxwell secretly to retain control over the trust. But the statement did explain why Maxwell had been anxious to correct his own front-page article in the *Daily Mirror* on 14 July 1983, which had declared that he was 'proud to be the proprietor of this group of publications'. A short time later, he had stated: 'I am the publisher, not the proprietor.' The legal difference was important for tax purposes in Britain. But since no one had seen the Liechtenstein trust documents and therefore could not authoritatively contradict his assertion until after his death, his denials were not treated seriously. To Maxwell's irritation, the mystery began seriously to undermine his ambitions.

On 12 December, however, Eugster's exposé only partially contributed to Maxwell's discomfiture. During that week, Maxwell had held a series of conversations with a senior member of the Sainsburys board about the sale of the pension fund's 15 per cent stake in Waddingtons. The tone of his remarks irritated the executive and triggered, just before the deadline expired, the sale of the shares to Waddingtons' bankers, Kleinworts. 'Maxwell knew that he blew it,' says a close adviser. Others blamed Ansbachers for failing to secure the stake. Maxwell conceded defeat but instead of consoling himself with the profit on his shares, his row with Watson rumbled on in public for some months under the heading in a circular, 'Damn the Truth – a New Waddington Game'. 'His lectures about the responsibility which a director owes to his shareholders and employees could have been called "Pot calls kettle black",' recalls Watson, who embarked on a popular lecture tour explaining how he had fought off Maxwell's bids.

The publicity surrounding Maxwell's defeat combined with the loss in circulation of one million newspapers in the Mirror Group was not enhancing his image at the end of 1985. The reverses were reflected in the accounts. BPCC's profits had fallen from £37 million to £25 million because the property deals which one year earlier had been described as a 'significant profit centre' had actually lost the company £1.8 million and other anticipated profits in publishing had dived, because of industrial disputes, from £4.3 million to just one quarter of a million pounds. The annual report minimised those reverses and Maxwell optimistically predicted that the worst of the expensive closures and redundancies were over. The report also contained an extraordinarily ambitious prediction: 'The aim of this reorganisation is to accomplish, from a British and European base, our great objective of successfully becoming a multi-faceted worldwide information and communications enterprise with revenues of £3/5 billion by 1990 with profits to match.' In 1985, BPCC's turnover was £265 million and gross profits were £79 million. Maxwell had forecast that there would be an eleven- to eighteen-fold multiplication of sales and profits within five years. Twenty years earlier, Oliver Marriott had said of Pergamon's huge profits: 'These are the sort of returns which all industrialists dream about.' The same could describe his new ambitions.

The first stage of his expansion plan was BPCC's purchase of Pergamon's 361 scientific journals, which in 1985 had earned £19 million profits. Automatically, BPCC's profits in 1986 would increase by 70 per cent. Because Maxwell's public company was buying his private interests it was necessary to assuage those who might be suspicious of inter-company trading. Bankers Trust was commissioned to value the journals independently and it set the price at £238.65 million. To reconfirm that this was a fair assessment, Maxwell announced that there had been 'stiff competition' from overseas buyers for Pergamon's journals 'but BPCC had won'. BPCC, of which Maxwell was chairman and chief executive, paid Pergamon, of which Maxwell was chairman, a new issue of 107.5 million BPCC shares. That meant that once more Maxwell personally owned over 70 per cent of the company and could embark on the next stage of his plan, which was to earn cash by quick deals.

In spring 1986, Maxwell was involved in so many bids that it was quipped, 'Maxwell has more fingers in more pies than most people have fingers.' By buying strategic stakes in companies which were in the midst of takeover bids, he hoped to profit by selling to the highest bidder. He was acting as an impromptu arbitrageur, when the term was still fashionable, posing as the 'white knight'. Ostensibly he would arrive to save a company from an unwelcome bid but the subjects of his warm embrace soon noticed that his bear-like arms had gradually tightened around their throat. The self-styled saviour would become a predator. 'There is no secret strategy,' commented Maxwell as his frantic burst of bids and deals provoked questions about his idiosyncratic methods, 'other than to make money.' The first intervention concerned Britannia Arrow, a financial group, and the second was for Extel, which provided financial information and confidential printing services. In both cases, Maxwell placed himself in the middle of a take-over battle to exercise decisive power and derive substantial profit from the predicament of others; and in both events he became allied with David Stevens, the chairman of United Newspapers, which had recently bought the Express newspaper group.

Stevens, whose diminutive stature and cool personality contrasted with Maxwell's, nevertheless shared his occasional partner's ambitions and some of his characteristics. 'Their combined aggression and rudeness is awesome,' recalled Michael Newman, the chief executive of Britannia Arrow, who, through Geoffrey Rippon, the former Conservative minister, initially appealed to Maxwell for help but was eventually forced by Stevens to resign. 'Maxwell was burned at the beginning,' said Newman, 'and appealed to Stevens for help. At the end, Stevens's profit was Maxwell's loss.'

'There is no friendship between those men,' according to Richard Marsh, who sees Maxwell, Stevens, Murdoch and Rothermere at the regular Reuters board meetings and the innumerable official functions which newspaper owners attend. 'They are street-fighters who don't particularly care if they are liked or hated. They have a common interest in forming temporary alliances and, whenever it suits them, to engineer another's downfall.'

Maxwell's bid for Extel started in his traditional manner. Extel was fighting off a bid from a printing company called Norton Opax and was hoping to attract the support of an Eygptian financier, Ashraf Marwan, who owned a decisive shareholding in Extel. Early in the morning of 12 February, Alan Brooker, Extel's chairman and an employee of the company for twenty-eight years, received a phone call from Maxwell. 'This is to inform you', said the voice, 'that you are no longer dealing with Marwan but with me. I have bought his stake. I think we should meet. I would like everything to be friendly and conducted in a gentlemanly manner.' Brooker is quite honest about his reaction. 'I was frightened. We were an independent agency and Maxwell is an interventionist. We knew his presence would frighten away our clients, who expected independent advice. Maxwell was as much an anathema to them as to us.' Brooker refused Maxwell's entreaties and expected a formal announcement of his bid. Instead, due to a breach of the Takeover Panel's regulations one month later, the Panel ordered Maxwell's bid to be frozen for one year.

'During that year, he harassed, chased and upset us,' recalls Brooker. He sought advice. 'Victor Watson was very helpful and we decided to use the "Liechtenstein defence". After all, the shareholders and employees were entitled to know who would own their company if Maxwell's bid was successful.' Like Watson, Brooker spent a fortune on lawyers in an attempt to unravel the ownership, only to discover that Liechtenstein's reputation for secrecy is well deserved.

On 13 March 1987, Maxwell wrote to Brooker to let him know that he intended to launch a bid the following month. Brooker replied with an onslaught of actions under the Companies Act 1985 to establish who was controlling the Extel shares owned by BPCC and the Pergamon Holding Foundation Corporation. On 31 March Maxwell responded to what he interpreted as harassment: 'I entirely fail to understand the pressure which Extel seeks to attribute to its demands [sic] ... and reserve my right to draw this matter to the attention of shareholders of Extel and to the attention of the regulatory authorities including the Secretary of State.' For Maxwell to threaten to appeal to the British government to protect a Liechtenstein trust seemed to Brooker richly ironic, but his bewilderment was compounded on 5 April. Keicher, the Liechtenstein lawyer, wrote to say that the Pergamon Holding Foundation did not control the Extel shareholding. Control, he explained, was exercised by its subsidiary, the Pergamon Media Trust, but 'neither our Foundation nor Pergamon Holding Corporation (which holds shares in PMT as our nominees) are so interested. This is because neither our Foundation nor PHC are entitled to exercise or control the exercise of one-third or more of the voting power of PMT.' Keicher had added to the confusion and accordingly Brooker asked Maxwell to explain the contradiction between the Foundation lawyer's insistence that he did not control the Extel shares and Maxwell's claims. On the same day Maxwell replied, 'There is no mystery,' but he revealed nothing more. Instead he attacked Brooker's use of the Liechtenstein ploy, criticised him for not giving the Extel shareholders the chance 'to choose to take a bona fide cash bid for their shares' (although Maxwell had still not made a bid), and finally announced that he would not after all bid for Extel. Clearly the exposure of the Liechtenstein connection was successful, thus exposing Maxwell's Achilles heel for those who wanted an easy defence in future bids.

Yet the fate and handling of Maxwell's stake in Extel displayed his rehabilitation in the City. He announced that the shares were to be auctioned and requested sealed bids. Acting on his behalf was his old contact Michael Richardson, who in 1969 at stockbrokers Panmure Gordon had represented Pergamon's interests but had resigned when Leasco's bid collapsed. In 1981 Richardson became a managing director at Rothschilds, the merchant bank which had fought on Leasco's behalf against Maxwell. In 1986 Richardson and Rothschilds were acting for Maxwell and were delighted to offer their services for his future deals. Apparently, the events of 1969 were forgotten. Maxwell was too important and was spending too much money for Rothschilds to spurn his business on an old matter of principle. Others in the City, discarding similar prejudices, would soon follow their lead. In the Extel case, Maxwell's shares were sold to David Stevens of United Newspapers at a profit, in theory, of £5 million.

In fact, it was impossible to ascertain what real profits were earned by Maxwell's interventions because, as will be seen shortly, despite his cultivated image of adroitly juggling a dozen balls which all produced profits, the truth was often different. While he dealt, a collection of highly paid executives waited permanently and forlornly outside his office for his decisions and approvals. Those delays caused incalculable losses. But it is a maxim of big business that one deal leads to another and that a high profile encourages a 'player's credibility'. Image is sometimes as important as substance and by August 1986 Maxwell had projected himself as a major and irresistible entrepreneur who led a corporation with surging profits. The key to that transformation was a 'corporate restructure' which, although dull in layman's terms, turned a sow's skin into a silk purse. The editorial section of Mirror Group Newspapers was legally separated from the printing presses, which had been transferred to a new subsidiary of BPCC, the strike-free British Newspaper Printing Corporation (BNPC). Accordingly, Mirror Group Newspapers, which was owned by Pergamon (Maxwell's private company), contracted with BNPC to print its newspapers. The contract increased the flow of money and new profits into BPCC, so enhancing the public company's balance sheet. Similarly, the sale of Pergamon journals increased BPCC's turnover and profits. Consequently, in August 1986, Maxwell could confidently announce that BPCC's pre-tax profits in the first six months had no less than doubled and Maxwell's image and substance coincided to pave the way for an important coup.

In City jargon, having your 'paper accepted' means that you are creditworthy. When Maxwell had tried to buy Waddingtons two years earlier, he had offered cash because no one would risk taking BPCC shares in exchange for Waddingtons' shares or 'paper'. After announcing BPCC's mid-1986 profits, Maxwell's credit-rating changed. BPCC shares, which in 1981 had traded at 12p, were worth 298p, and Maxwell's promises of greater profits to come were taken at face value. In August, Maxwell heard on the City grapevine that there was dissatisfaction with the management of the Philip Hill Investment Trust and that the Trust was for sale. He offered £355 million but said that he would only pay in newly issued BPCC shares. The Trust's shareholders were City institutions who for fifteen years had looked askance at the bidder, but after skilful lobbying by mutually trusted City operators they were prepared to concede that he now possessed financial credibility and to accept his offer. Within twenty-four hours of the purchase, Maxwell had sold most of the Trust's investments for cash and used the money to buy two American printers, Webb Co. Inc. and Providence Gravure, enabling him to become the second-largest printer in America. Within the Square Mile it was hailed as a masterstroke. Overnight, BPCC was bigger and richer, and the blitz of media attention devoted to the constantly photographed and interviewed Maxwell increased his self-esteem. The Midas touch could clearly, he felt, be extended to any venture. At that moment he was presiding over the Commonwealth Games in Scotland, which he had himself saved from catastrophe.

Edinburgh had been awarded the Games in 1980 and, at the time, the organisers had been told by ministers that, since the event was expected to be self-financing, they should not expect any government aid. The estimated cost was £14 million, a pittance compared to the Los Angeles Olympics, which had raised £340 million and had actually ended with a surplus. But six years later, on the eve of the opening ceremony, the chairman of the Edinburgh Games organising committee, Kenneth Borthwick, a wholesale confectioner and former Lord Provost of the city, privately acknowledged that he had failed to secure sufficient sponsorship contracts. Some blamed his amateurism, but excuses were irrelevant at the end of May. With just eight weeks left Borthwick was anticipating that the deficit might amount to £5 million. Without extra money the Games would not be able to start and the proud city would be embarrassed. In some panic, Borthwick secretly appealed to the government for help, but Malcolm Rifkind, the minister for Scottish Affairs, unhesitatingly refused and suggested that he might approach the nation's rich. Among Borthwick's thirty-seven pleading letters addressed to names culled from the *Financial Times* was one to Maxwell.

Maxwell and the Mirror Group had been approached for money more than one year earlier but, despite their profitable newspaper interests in Scotland, had refused their support. In the meantime, however, the Mirror Group in Scotland had been involved in a bruising battle with all its employees on the *Daily Record* and *Sunday Mail* to enforce an extension of the working week and obtain the unconditional acceptance of new technology. When the negotiations had failed, 1,050 printers and journalists were overnight deemed by Maxwell to have 'dismissed themselves' and, in a familiar pattern, a deadline was imposed to negotiate a survival plan. As the dispute stretched into the third week, barbed wire appeared around the premises and emotions became inflamed. Memories of Maxwell's behaviour at the *Scottish Daily News* were rekindled and he was castigated for resorting to Tory anti-trade union laws and for emulating Murdoch's methods at Fortress Wapping, despite his own jibe that the Australian's was 'not the British way of doing things'. Undeterred, Maxwell invited his 'ex-employees' to reapply for their jobs on his terms. Finally, in April 1986, the unions conceded a 30 per cent cut in the labour force and agreed to abandon their traditional work practices. But Maxwell's overwhelming victory had scorched his image, so Borthwick's request to save the Games came as an attractive opportunity to repair the damage and, in a favoured phrase, 'to be of service to my fellow man'.

On 19 June it was announced that Maxwell and a team from the Mirror Group would assume responsibility for the Games' finances. The *Mirror*'s front page blazed, '*Mirror* Saves the Games' and the *Record* trumpeted '*Record* Saves the Games', but both agreed that their owner would become chairman of the company managing the event, although the confusion over what his help implied was evident on the first day. For Borthwick, saving the Games meant that Maxwell would pour in a few of his many millions to remove the deficit. Suffice to say that this was neither Maxwell's understanding nor his intent.

Maxwell believes in self-help. In offering his money for the *Scottish Daily News* or for the Labour Party, he stipulated that he would match the amount raised by those seeking assistance. 'If I just gave,' he has said, 'they would do nothing themselves.' When he accepted Borthwick's offer, there was, in Maxwell's view, no commitment to contribute a penny.

'I guarantee unconditionally that the Games will go ahead,' he told a press conference on his arrival on 19 June, four weeks before the opening ceremony. 'I hope you will agree that there is nothing more important than that.' Attempts to extract from him an indication of whether he had promised to contribute any money were shrugged off. Instead he assured everyone that he would seek new sponsors so that the Games did not become a burden for the taxpayer. Under his command, he promised, 'There will be no deficit at all.' When pressed to reveal his secret plan, he smilingly acknowledged his financial acumen but urged his sceptical audience to understand that 'Jerusalem was not built in a day. We have got quite a few weeks left.' The sceptics remained unconvinced and suspected what he would repeatedly have to deny: 'I hope that will put paid to any nonsense about my being in this business to hijack the Games for the benefit of the *Daily Mirror* or that the *Mirror* and *Record* are going to have any special privileges or that I or any of my family will be handing out medals.'

For four weeks, Maxwell and his associates enjoyed a honeymoon period to produce the £4 million which had eluded the hapless Borthwick. On 18 July, six days before the Games started, it seemed that he had indeed performed a miracle. Maxwell announced his success to a group of what he now unlovingly called 'hacks': 'When it comes to elbow-twisting on a major scale I am particularly good at it.... The Games are financially secure. The job is virtually done.' In other words, he had found £4 million, and he even suggested that there would be a surplus. To prove how the money was pouring in, he pulled from his pocket a letter from a well-wisher in London which pledged the sum of two pounds. 'It is unbelievable,' he pronounced, alluding to the avalanche of donations.

During that penultimate week, the Games had become beset by a further albatross. In protest against Mrs Thatcher's refusal to countenance sanctions against South Africa, the Afro-Asian members had resorted to the same protest which she had encouraged for the Moscow Olympics after the Soviet invasion of Afghanistan. Thirty-two nations declared that they would boycott the Edinburgh Games. If the Games were now not short of funds, there was a definite lack of competitors. Caught in the maelstrom of international politics, Maxwell was spokesman to the world about the sorry fate of the competition. Only his irrepressible energy and unfounded optimism could support his pronouncements that the Games would go ahead, be a success and not incur an enormous deficit. But four days before the Games started, on 20 July, when the daunting repercussions of the boycott had registered, Maxwell suddenly acknowledged that there was again a deficit and that the Prime Minister would be expected to pick up the bill.

His contradiction inevitably provoked those whom he had labelled 'hacks who normally ask silly questions'. They could not tally the arithmetic and asked him to reconcile the statement he had made on 16 July that the £4 million deficit had been overcome with his latest claim that while the boycott would cost £1 million, the deficit was £2 million. Two Scottish journalists, Derek Bateman and Derek Douglas, persistently asked him for explanations since he had also earlier said that the Mirror Group 'had contributed £1 million to the Games'. Spotting an unequal equation did not require the skill of a City analyst, as Maxwell admitted when he rushed from their interrogation saying, 'I certainly needed this job like a hole in the head.' In all the newspapers other than those owned by the Mirror Group, Maxwell was attracting the blame for a disaster of others' making and was receiving neither sympathy nor gratitude for his efforts. Yet most would have acknowledged that without him the Games would have collapsed before their opening. But the goodwill was fast dissipating as the background to the bargain price became exposed.

During his many press statements before the Games, Maxwell had emphasised that the deficit had disappeared and he denied 'hijacking the Games' for his personal prestige and his newspapers' profits. Yet every day during the competition, the nation's television, radio and newspapers were saturated by his image and words. Edinburgh, a growing chorus chanted, had become the venue of the 'Maxwell Games'. Maxwell hung a gold medal around the neck of the decathlon champion Daley Thompson, he stood next to the Queen and Prime Minister on the dais, and the Mirror Group's red and white colours dominated the stadium and its scoreboards. His presence became so pervasive that at one crucial moment during the last day's closing ceremonies when Maxwell drew the winning ticket for the 'Save the Games' competition, the Queen had disappeared from the dais and BBC Television stopped broadcasting from the Games and returned to the studio. As Bateman and Douglas wrote, 'Immediately after the tombola drum and the Maxwell entourage had departed, normal service was resumed.'

Soon after the Games ended, Maxwell announced that the deficit was £4 million, which was exactly the sum when he had arrived. The company managing the Games had been bankrupt throughout the proceedings and it fell to Maxwell as its chairman to explain the discrepancies since Whitehall still refused to cover the deficit. 'If Mr Maxwell is really concerned about his creditors,' a minister confided to the press, 'he and his Mirror Group should make good the losses in recognition of the huge publicity he's got. It's a flea-bite to him.' Maxwell was clearly under renewed pressure to reconcile all his conflicting statements and, in the wake of the enormous publicity he and his businesses had enjoyed, to quantify his personal contribution. Before the Games, BPCC's accountants, Coopers and Lybrand, had estimated that if Maxwell contributed £4.3 million (that is, the whole projected deficit), 'it would produce a significant commercial advantage to yourself'. Yet Maxwell apparently (since at the time of writing he declines to quantify his contribution) was unwilling to pay more than £250,000 and possibly as little as £100,000. Instead, he tried first to raise money from national corporations. Now that the Games were over, his efforts proved even less successful than before the event. Secondly, he tried to extract money from the British government and those nations which had boycotted the Games. That also proved fruitless. His third target, Ryoichi Sasakawa, surprised everyone. Sasakawa, an obscure eighty-seven-year-old Japanese, had, according to Maxwell, 'devoted himself to world philanthropy' and claimed to control an $8.4 billion empire. Over the previous twenty years, Sasakawa had given away, said Maxwell, $12,000 million, a sum which reduced his own fortune to miniscule proportions and the £4 million deficit to a financial irrelevance. But considering the philanthropist's background, Maxwell's endorsement was decidedly odd. During the war, Sasakawa had commanded a sizeable fascist army and in 1945 he had been interned by the Americans for three years as a suspected war criminal. But imprisonment had been his good fortune since among his fellow inmates were the architects of Japan's peacetime prosperity who, on the basis of their close friendship, afforded him lucrative opportunities. Forty years later, on 13 October, Sasakawa authorised Maxwell to unveil their joint rescue package.

By unilaterally rejecting various accounts and charges from contractors, Maxwell claimed that the deficit had been reduced to £3.2 million. To settle the remainder, he announced that Sasakawa was prepared to contribute £1.3 million and Maxwell would personally pay £700,000 on condition that the British government paid £1 million. To his delight, the ball was firmly placed in Whitehall's camp, but only for the briefest moment. The government reaffirmed its refusal to provide a subsidy. By 1988, the deficit had grown to £3.8 million and there was still no solution in sight. Maxwell had moved on to many other ventures but he had enjoyed saving the Games.

The first casualty when Maxwell emerged from the morass in Edinburgh in September 1986 was a project which was very close to his heart – the proposed London evening newspaper. For years Maxwell had aspired to challenge the monopoly of the *Evening Standard*, which was owned by Lord Rothermere and which he had unsuccessfully sought to purchase. Although the sale of evening newspapers in London had declined from two million in 1960 to half a million in 1986, Maxwell believed that the capital was big and wealthy enough to support two newspapers. In April he had appointed Magnus Linklater as the paper's first editor and the projected launch date was set for October 1986. During those summer weeks while Maxwell was 'saving the Games', Linklater had great difficulty in gaining access to the one person who could endorse a series of vital decisions and authorise critical expenditure. By the time Maxwell emerged from Edinburgh, Linklater feared that his creation might be stillborn unless the launch was postponed.

Linklater, then forty-four, is an Old Etonian who, with a successful career on the *Evening Standard*, *Sunday Times* and *Observer*, was naturally ambitious for an editorship; Maxwell's proposals seemed very attractive. Although the newspaper's editorial offices would be adjacent to the *Daily Mirror* in New Fetter Lane, the venture was to be on what Maxwell described as a 'greenfield site' and would espouse his oft-vaunted ideals for printing a newspaper. The journalists would set the pages using computers while the traditional unions would be excluded by contracting out the printing to other national daily newspapers whose presses were idle during the daytime. Even distributing the paper from the five locations would be entrusted to a new organisation, Newsflow, instead of the established wholesalers who used union labour. 'We are breaking free of the *Mirror* and old Fleet Street attitudes,' said Maxwell, but his absence in Scotland had delayed crucial negotiations to contract three essentials: the printing, the computers and the distribution. On his return, Linklater and Bill Gillespie, the chief executive, faced the unpleasant task of persuading their employer to delay publication and therefore reverse his public commitment. Their problem was symptomatic of his organisation's weakness. 'No one ever says to Maxwell, "It's your fault,"' recalls one executive. 'There's fear in confronting him with reality and equally there is fear of being caught concealing reality. Even the strongest hearts avoid those face-to-face sessions because when he voices his anger it lacerates and bruises.' When the truth was unfolded, his explosion was predictable but he reluctantly agreed. Since it was close to Christmas, they recommended that the next optimum launch would be early February 1987. But in accepting their advice, Maxwell added an emollient which proved that there was a heavy price for his persistent juggling.

Among Maxwell's several reactions was to dispatch a team to the United States to investigate the feasibility of a twenty-four-hour newspaper. Eleven years earlier, one of the conditions he had set for his final contribution to the *Scottish Daily News* was acceptance by the unions of a twenty-four-hour newspaper, and his hankering for the concept had never dimmed. The commercial attraction was simply that, while the editorial content changed during the day, the advertisers were guaranteed readers in both the morning and the evening. The overriding disadvantage to the publisher was the increased labour costs. Maxwell's fact-finders, who included Linklater, travelled to New York, Detroit and Florida to taste the American experience and returned convinced that the idea was unprofitable, if only because, despite the propaganda, there were no genuine and profitable twenty-four-hour newspapers in America. 'Most of the newspapers we visited had abandoned or retained only a vestige of the concept,' said Linklater. Maxwell dismissed the findings of their report.

On 18 September 1986, Maxwell summoned a press conference at the Rotunda in which he would announce the delay of the newspaper's publication. His approach on that day would not differ from the countless previous occasions when his press office had sent summonses for journalists to attend for his latest communication. Maxwell wants these encounters to excite and interest his audience: 'He likes to believe their jaws have dropped and they're sitting up. He wants to be certain that he'll be the talking-point for the rest of the day.' Since Maxwell was always a 'good story', he normally achieved his object by calculating what would most surprise. That press conference was no exception.

'I have called you here today,' he began, 'to make an important and exciting announcement. The new London evening newspaper is to become Britain's first twenty-four-hour paper, which will provide the best possible service from breakfast to bedtime.' After explaining how the twenty-four-hour concept would revolutionise Britain's newspaper industry, he allowed a pause for the drama. 'This project has been so top secret that not even the editor knew about it until this morning.' The assembled journalists gasped. Linklater looked embarrassed and interrupted: 'That's a slight exaggeration, Bob.' 'Well, alright, alright,' conceded his employer unruffled. He added that accordingly the launch would be delayed to plan for 'this exciting new development'. Asked to reveal the anticipated circulation of the newspaper, Maxwell unhesitatingly replied, 'One million.' Again there was dismay on the dais, but this time it was felt by his other neighbour, Bill Gillespie, who was horrified. Advertisers' rates are calculated upon circulation and if the actual circulation falls below the amount guaranteed by the publisher the advertisers are automatically entitled to a refund. After heated whispering, Maxwell announced that the 'guaranteed circulation will be half a million'. Even that figure was higher than Gillespie had suggested. 'It was an unnecessary hostage to fortune,' said one of the team afterwards. As usual, Maxwell's optimism had outpaced realism. He had not assessed the full implications, especially the cost. Linklater and Gillespie consoled themselves with the knowledge that they had at least won another four months' preparation. Maxwell meanwhile stepped up another gear into more frenzied activity. During the week of 3 November, another of his ambitions was fulfilled. For seven days he dominated the news.

In the autumn, the buying spree to enlarge his fortune had recommenced, initially through Hollis, a small publicly quoted timber merchant and furniture manufacturer which Maxwell controlled but which was managed by his son Kevin. Hollis had recently bid for a diverse range of insolvent engineering companies, a crane manufacturer and an electronics specialist and had paid £30 million in an inter-company transaction for some Pergamon assets. But those deals were eclipsed on 3 November when Maxwell in the name of Hollis offered £265 million for AE, a well-known Rugby-based engineering group. AE was in the midst of an exhausting take-over battle and Maxwell presented himself once more in the guise of the 'white knight'. 'Publisher Rescues Engineer' was not a convincing headline that week (the AE bid in fact later collapsed) but in another bitter and much publicised take-over battle between two printers, the management of McCorquodale and Norton Opax, he maximised his interventionist role. He had bought a strategic 19 per cent shareholding in McCorquodales and he encouraged both sides to bid against the other for his support. The Dutch auction for his favours had continued for several weeks, often late into the night as he coolly haggled for a better price between two increasingly exasperated bidders. During the week of 3 November, as the climax of bid and counter-bid approached, Maxwell's name appeared daily in bold, large print in the news, financial and legal sections of every paper – 'In the centre of the stage', 'The global player', 'The big-league player who is no longer in it for the money', and 'The incredible all-performing Robert Maxwell'. It was also the week that a Chinook helicopter which was part of the fleet Maxwell had bought six months earlier from British Airways for approximately £14 million crashed in the North Sea killing forty-five people, the world's worst civil helicopter crash in history. Moreover when, at 2 a.m. on 6 November, he finally came down on the side of Norton Opax, he was spending his daytime in the High Court fighting a libel action against *Private Eye*.

Among the several paradoxes reaffirmed about Maxwell during that epochal week was his sensitivity about his reputation. *Private Eye* had falsely alleged in July 1985 that Maxwell had paid for the travel expenses of Neil Kinnock to East Africa in the hope that he would, as the Labour leaders's 'paymaster', be recommended for a peerage. When the item had appeared, Maxwell had denied the story (and was subsequently vindicated by the jury), asked for a published apology and a payment of £10,000 for the *Mirror*'s Ethiopian famine fund. The *Eye*'s editor, Shrewsbury-educated Richard Ingrams, had spurned his protest and had unwisely repeated the allegation. For many years, Maxwell and his wife had been a standing butt of facetious comment in the magazine and Maxwell was also the subject of a regular, laconic strip cartoon. The stimulus, he believed, was Ingrams's xenophobia and anti-semitism which sprang from the same 'forces of evil' which had pursued him since 1969. For Ingrams, Maxwell represented the worst type of humbug – a man who perpetually cried 'foul' but committed identical sins about which he vociferously complained. One of the *Eye*'s functions, which Ingrams had repeatedly expounded during his twenty-five-year editorship, was to expose what he thought to be the hypocrisy of the rich and powerful, who in turn were outraged that those beyond their employ did not display the respect which they desired. In 1985, Ingrams, who was contemplating retirement, viewed Maxwell as a prime candidate for that treatment and therefore ignored his complaint. Maxwell's lawyers served a writ alleging defamation. In reply, a member of the *Eye*'s staff swore an affidavit, which was presented to a judge, claiming that he would be able prove the 'peerage' story if the issue came to trial.

Maxwell's relationship with Kinnock was workmanlike despite the *Mirror*'s publisher occasionally posing as the alternative Opposition. With the exception of policies on trade union laws and defence, where his views had changed from two decades earlier (he was now opposed to unilateralism), Maxwell broadly supported the party leadership. His endorsement was welcomed by the Labour leader, who more than ever needed the *Mirror*'s support, although he was dismayed by the newspaper's rush downmarket, at the expense of political coverage, to chase the *Sun*. Maxwell, whose personal loyalty to the party was never in doubt, was clearly an important benefactor because there were few socialist millionaires who could afford to make large contributions. It was clearly within Kinnock's gift to recommend peerages and, after the elevation to the House of Lords of Maxwell's employees and fellow Labour Party supporters Charles Williams, Bernard Donoughue and Sam Silkin in 1984, the *Mirror*'s publisher might reasonably have expected the same recognition. Indeed, according to Maxwell, soon after the three appointments he was 'asked' by Roy Hattersley whether he too would like a peerage but he had rejected the offer. Maxwell would cite this exchange in the High Court case against the *Eye* as the second occasion on which he had refused the offer of a peerage, and as proof that he had no need to bribe the Labour leader. Hattersley insists that the question he posed at a social event was an 'obvious jest' and that Maxwell later privately apologised for mentioning the 'offer' in court. Kinnock is equally emphatic that he would only recommend Labour supporters as peers who would solemnly undertake to appear regularly in the House of Lords and dedicate themselves to work for the Opposition. Since Maxwell would be unable to commit himself to those long hours, he was therefore automatically excluded.

Nevertheless, such was Maxwell's obvious interest in power and recognition that when Ingrams was handed the story he approved publication because, even if he could not produce a witness to the alleged transaction, 'it seemed right'. Newspaper barons in Britain were customarily created peers and there was every reason to imply that Maxwell might expect the same. A jury, Ingrams calculated, would sympathetically interpret and share his prejudices against power and wealth and, even if the case were lost, the free publicity of daily coverage in the national newspapers would be worth a fortune. Since Ingrams had entered 'litigation' as one of his recreations in *Who's Who*, observers might have expected his familiarity with the law of defamation and the vagaries of the courts to make him hesitate to engage Maxwell in battle unless his case were stronger. It was a challenge to Maxwell, who readily accepted the chance to teach the public school establishment a lesson and to protect his standing in the Labour Party. By the end of the first day's hearing on 2 November, it was obvious that the same British cult of amateurism which had enabled Maxwell to earn his fortune had blinded Ingrams and his legal advisers to the interpretation which a jury of common men would put on their criticisms. The opening speeches in Court 11 showed that the trial would not be about buying a peerage, because the *Eye* could not substantiate its allegations. Its 'eyewitnesses' could not be named nor could they appear. Their case was a bluff. Maxwell *v* Pressdam, alias School Bully *v* School Sneak, became Nasty Outsider *v* Nasty Insider.

The magazine attempted, within the limitations of the alleged defamation, to put Maxwell himself on trial by probing his quest for publicity, his own newspaper's mistakes and how he might expect his support for the Labour Party to be ultimately rewarded. Maxwell, who had spent a lifetime defending himself against more formidable advocates armed with more incriminating allegations, not only withstood the attack without demur but turned the spotlight upon his accusers. On the third day, when he was giving evidence, Maxwell performed a remarkable somersault. Maxwell the ogre and bully became Maxwell the underdog.

The issue was a regular 'letter' purportedly sent by his wife to the magazine asking whether readers had noticed the similarity between two photographs. The personalities for comparison one week from 'Ena B. Maxwell' were the Duke of Edinburgh and Colonel Adolf Eichmann, who had organised the Third Reich's 'Final Solution' for the extermination of European Jewry. Eichmann had personally supervised the deportation of 400,000 Jews from Hungary for extermination at Auschwitz, and Maxwell's parents had been among those victims. The 'Ena B. Maxwell' letter was an example of the magazine's regular lampooning of the millionaire and Maxwell would probably have known in advance which examples his counsel would have offered him for comment in the witness box. No one, however, anticipated his reaction.

As he looked at the page, tears began falling down his cheeks and, according to the following day's *Daily Mirror* report, Maxwell 'shook with emotion and banged his hands on the witness box as he said, "My family was destroyed by Eichmann".... It was several minutes before he composed himself, wiped his eyes and took a sip of the glass of water handed to him. He then turned to the judge and said, "I'm sorry."' In the *Eye* camp, there was astonishment. 'When I saw him blubber, I knew that we'd lost,' confessed one of their heavier, hard-nosed investigators. Ingrams did not help his case by admitting in evidence his ignorance about Eichmann's role in the fate of Maxwell's family. The *Mirror*'s headline was the gravestone inscription over the *Eye*'s case: 'Maxwell Weeps over Family Massacre – Publisher's Fury at *Eye*'s Fake Letters'. As the case spun out from the expected one week into the third week, the champions of anti-privilege began massaging their brows: Maxwell was winning sympathy as the victim of gross insensitivity.

The jury's award against the *Eye* for the defamation was an unimpressive £5,000. But they awarded an extra £50,000 as punitive damages because the *Eye*'s journalist misleadingly swore an affidavit claiming that he would be able to prove his allegation. In addition there were an estimated £250,000 legal costs, which the *Eye* was ordered to pay. 'Bloody hell ... bloody hell' was the crisp reaction of the *Eye*'s managing director, the aptly named David Cash, as the jury recited the damages. In his own valediction, Ingrams, who was not in court to hear the verdict, advised potential litigants, 'If your lawyers tell you that you have a very good case, you should settle immediately,' and blamed the jury who 'while good and true [are] immensely thick'. Maxwell disagreed. 'People, family and friends', his voice boomed across the courtroom, 'have been recklessly attacked for years. We have exposed once and for all that they will publish anything for profit. They do not check their sources, they do not have the guts to apologise or withdraw. They are pedlars of lies and filth.' Asked what he would do with the damages, he answered, 'The money might go to AIDS research. After all it came from an infected organ and will go to help cure another.'

In November 1982, Maxwell had reviewed a book which recounted the history of the *Eye* and he had asked, 'Does it really make a valuable contribution to our society to destroy both in our own eyes and in those of the world at large our major national asset of incorruptibility in public life – to replace it with a belief that the instincts of the piggery motivate our public servants and successful entrepreneurs?' Four years later he went further and argued that the *Eye* should be closed down. The *Eye*'s readers did not agree. The alleged scandals surrounding the Guinness bid for Distillers (Maxwell had publicly supported Ernest Saunders for reneging on a solemn pledge about the composition of the new board), the endless corruption in local authorities, the chain of negligence which led to the sinking of the Townsend ferry at Zeebrugge and the admission of Britain's senior civil servant in Australia that he had been 'economical with the truth' pointed to a need for the *Eye*. Britain, the *Eye*'s supporters argued, does not enjoy incorruptibility but suffers from a lack of formalised accountability. In the vacuum of parliamentary power, the press was Britain's last safeguard against 'our public servants and successful entrepreneurs'. But, for Maxwell, 'The *Eye* has become the Joe McCarthy of British journalism [and it] cannot justify its continued existence.' His desire for its eradication revealed a limited understanding about newspapers. The *Eye* enjoyed sustained credibility, something which Maxwell's own newspapers could not boast.

'Watching Maxwell play with newspapers is like a child with a Meccano set,' says Keith Waterhouse, who resigned as a columnist on the *Mirror* in disgruntlement. 'When he's fed up with one toy, he looks for another.' By the end of 1986, Maxwell had successfully maximised the Mirror Group's profits. Having slashed its overheads in London, Manchester and Glasgow, BPCC entered 1987 aiming to fulfil his objective of becoming an 'enterprise with earnings of £3–5 billion with earnings per share to match'. The focus in early 1987 returned to his newspapers, although the omens were not encouraging. A new sports magazine, *Sportsweek*, launched in September 1986, had collapsed three weeks after its launch; he publicly alternated his views about continuing to print in Holborn; despite his announcement that the *Mirror* would be printed with colour pictures, no such pictures had appeared; and BPCC had lost the contracts for the colour magazines of the *Observer* and the *Mail on Sunday*. Balancing achievements were securing the contract for the *Sunday Express* Magazine, for satelliting the *China Daily* from Peking to distribute 20,000 copies throughout Europe, and the launch at last of the *London Daily News*.

The delay in launching the evening newspaper had probably improved morale among the newly hired journalists, who had wanted more time to prepare. Five weeks after the decision was announced, Maxwell organised a sumptuous weekend at Ettington Park where, to the delight of the 180 staff, the famed chef Michael Quinn served a gourmet's dinner which was eaten off an enormous refectory table. The highlight on Sunday was the arrival by helicopter of Maxwell himself with Betty and his after-lunch speech. 'You are the staff I have hired,' he averred, 'and I am going to stick with you through thick and thin. There will be no blood-letting. I am not the kind of proprietor who will close you down. You have my guarantee that you have two to three years to prove yourselves.' There were cheers and Maxwell began to take his leave when a note was thrust into his hands. The chef wondered whether he might have a ride on the helicopter. Proudly the publisher agreed and the two artistes flew off over the Warwickshire countryside. On the ground however, there was one man who was disturbed by Maxwell's whole approach – Bill Gillespie, the paper's publisher and the managing director of BNPC.

Until the spring of 1986, Gillespie had been working for Murdoch's News International. Maxwell had telephoned and offered him a high salary to manage the newly incorporated printing operation and oversee the creation of the London newspaper. Gillespie's credentials were impeccable. Under his supervision, all of Murdoch's newspapers had been moved overnight to Wapping, utterly routing the unions, and he had pioneered News International's own blueprint for a London evening newspaper. Since Maxwell prided himself on his ruthless and commercial unsentimentality towards newspapers, Gillespie was an astute choice. But by the summer Gillespie had become disconcerted by the contrast between working for Maxwell and working for Murdoch. Under the new regime, he was denied independence, initiative, information and access. While Murdoch had a deep understanding of newspapers, the foundation of a long-term strategy, Maxwell thought that creating a newspaper was similar to dealing on the Stock Exchange; he only needed to bark down a telephone 'buy' or 'sell' and the whole deed could be completed by his backroom 'number crunchers'. 'He was so arrogant', complained one executive, 'that he believed that if he just blew on the new paper, it would blossom.' Gillespie's confidence had already been shaken when Maxwell, without his knowledge, personally negotiated on a Sunday night in Oxford an agreement with the print union leaders (which later collapsed), and his unease was aggravated by the circumstances surrounding the delayed launch. Three years earlier, the collapse in the *Mirror*'s sales had exposed Maxwell's weak understanding of consumer journalism. The two months after Ettington Park tarnished his image as an innovator.

Initially, Maxwell's brief was that the newspaper operation would be a 'greenfield site', excluding not only the print unions but also the Mirror Group's management. His edict irritated the group's incumbents, especially his senior executives. 'Their constant criticism of us poisoned relations,' recalls one executive, 'and it got worse.' Gillespie became another casualty of compartmentalisation and of the confusion which surrounds many of Maxwell's ventures. The *London Daily News* was owned by Mirror Group Newspapers (MGN), which ultimately is owned by Pergamon. Gillespie was the publisher of the new paper and was therefore employed by MGN. Its printing was entrusted by MGN to BNPC, of which Gillespie was chief executive. But although Gillespie was simultaneously employed by MGN and BNPC and both companies were housed in the same building and were ultimately owned by the same man, Gillespie discovered that the relationship between the public and private companies was obscure, especially regarding the terms of the contract between MGN and BNPC. His efforts to establish the price BNPC would charge MGN for printing were unsuccessful and his requests to Maxwell were never comprehensively answered. Their relationship became strained, especially as the precise problems of managing a twenty-four-hour newspaper became apparent.

Maxwell had embraced the notion of such a newspaper without understanding that the term was a misnomer. Its theoretical attraction was the guarantee that the newspaper would be on sale early in the morning, before the *Standard*, with a large section containing classified advertisements for cars, homes and jobs, and that the same advertisements but with different editorial copy would also be read in the evening. To achieve that required fast printing, efficient distribution throughout London, and a sales force to attract the advertising. Maxwell, in Gillespie's view, was impatient with the implementation of that detail. As the telephone calls about all his other interests cascaded into his office, he brusquely swept aside Gillespie's queries and explanations. To his irritated executives, it seemed that he liked the architect's colourful sketches but did not understand that to fit the complex jigsaw neatly together needed meticulous calculations. 'The unseen foundations were left in the air because they bored him,' says one of the newspaper's founders. 'Since he refused to delegate and was rarely accessible, we never made decisions until it was too late.' Anxiety, about the delays and about Maxwell's indecision, grew. 'Gillespie was blamed for everything,' recalls an eyewitness, 'although it was Maxwell who was constantly changing his mind, possibly because he couldn't remember what he had previously decided. When he began to reverse his "greenfield" policy by ordering Gillespie to consult Mirror executives ['We have all the expertise here,' said Maxwell], that threw everybody.' Gillespie reluctantly agreed to the changes, but on one issue, the title of the newspaper, he was unyielding.

The market research agency had tested four possible titles: *The Londoner*, *London Newsday*, *Newsday London* and the *London Daily News*. Although the latter had been the working title, the researchers' reported that *The Londoner* evoked the most favourable reaction. Linklater insisted upon the *London Daily News* and was supported by Maxwell. Their choice might have been less controversial if Gillespie had not heard that Rothermere's managers were informally asking the *Standard* delivery drivers how much extra they would require for handling a second newspaper. To Gillespie that could only mean that Rothermere was considering the relaunch of his defunct *Evening News*, which would be a perfect spoiler against Maxwell. 'It was going to be a dirty war,' said Bert Hardy, one of Rothermere's senior executives, 'and we were going to meet Maxwell at every stage.'

On Saturday 22 November 1986, Maxwell had summoned yet another all-day conference at Headington Hall to discuss the newspaper's progress. Although all the editorial and commercial executives were summoned for 10 a.m., they expected to wait as usual for at least two hours before Maxwell appeared. True to form, he was delayed arriving from Heathrow airport but on this occasion, before entering his home, he encountered Gillespie waiting in the drive. The Irishman, whose attitude was by then quite jaded, issued an ultimatum that unless the proprietor reconsidered the newspaper's title, he would resign. Maxwell was unmoved and Gillespie departed.

Maxwell was unruffled when he greeted his remaining executives. 'I'll take over Gillespie's job,' he announced, and thereafter became more accessible. 'My problem now is that I can't get away from him long enough to shape the paper,' Linklater told his colleagues. Constant meetings were not a substitute for strategy and throughout those weeks what struck those incarcerated on the ninth floor was Maxwell's delight in his image as the skilled entrepreneur. 'Maxwell believes in the art of brutal buying,' observed one seasoned negotiator. 'A deal struck at the last minute, he thought, was sure to be the most profitable.' Deadline deals have their attractions for buying and selling, but they posed problems if hundreds of staff needed to be trained in the use of a computer system, if five editions of a newspaper were to be printed in five different locations every day and distributed throughout London, and if the paper needed a battleplan to fight for a place in a competitive and declining market place. Creating new consumer demand requires a peculiar intellectual skill which was not evident as the revised launch date of 10 February 1987 approached. Joe Haines probably understood Maxwell's nonchalance on such critical questions better than most: 'He has a touching faith in the printed word. He's one of the last men in the world who really believes in the power of the press.' Like many Haines misjudged Maxwell. The newspaper was just his latest toy.

By mid-January another of Maxwell's commercial innovations had been discarded. Experts were required to 'paste up' the newspaper pages and Maxwell ordained that redundant members of the NGA in the Mirror Group should be hired. His 'greenfield site' ideal was further contaminated. But the potential advertisers liked the 'dummies' of the new paper and for the journalists working a regular sixteen-hour day the omens still seemed promising.

Maureen Smith, one of London's more successful new band of hypists, was hired by Maxwell to organise a spectacular launch. Not unnaturally, since her new client thought big and regularly dispensed sums of money which resembled telephone numbers, she proposed a programme to match his ambitions. By chance, Smith discovered that the Albert Hall, which is normally booked for at least two years in advance, was free on the day prior to the launch. She found little difficulty in convincing Maxwell that the building would be an ideal venue for an unforgettable twenty-four-hour party to mirror the newspaper's novelty. Oysters and Guinness would be served to the newspaper's vendors in the morning, followed by a fashion show for the glitterati at lunchtime, a children's party in the afternoon, *Tout Londres* would be invited for a gala celebration in the evening and the 'young things' could dance through the night to receive the first edition in the morning. It would cost a quarter of a million pounds.

Everything had been prepared when quite by chance, ten days before the party, Smith heard that the launch had once more been cancelled. The reason was that the NGA 'pasters' had still not signed a contract, but cynics joked that Maxwell just wanted an excuse to avoid paying a fortune for a party. In reality, his newspaper was beset by an avalanche of problems. He had still not contracted for the printing, the distribution was still not settled and the new computer system for setting the pages was still troublesome. By the third and final launch date, 24 February, little had improved and the essential launch party was quickly improvised.

The organiser was Harvey Goldsmith: 'You want the biggest party London has ever seen? You've got it. You want VIPs? You've got them. You want a spectacular? Leave it to me.' The venue was the circulation department on the Mirror building's first floor which was gutted and reconstructed to resemble a fashionable nightclub. The centrepiece was an ice sculpture resembling the *London Daily News* masthead. Beneath stood a vast cake with the chef ready to inscribe in icing a facsimile of the first front page when it was agreed. Once again *Tout Londres* was invited, but the handful of celebrities who did come left before the appearance of the first edition, which had missed its deadlines. Among those who remained was a delegation from the Telegraph group of newspapers. Over the previous five months, Maxwell had been negotiating to use for the afternoon editions the Telegraph's new computer-fed printing presses in the converted London docks, but each time a contract was near to signature Maxwell began renegotiating. 'He always wanted more than his pound of flesh,' says one of those angered by his brinkmanship. By the night of the launch, there was a real possibility that the following afternoon's edition would not be printed. At the party, Maxwell was located by the delegation in a booth occupied by a fortune teller. 'Not the right place to discuss business,' he said jovially as he led his anxious guests to another part of the room where at last he signed. Most of the revellers around them were the worse for drink when, two hours after the deadline, the trumpets of four Life Guards heralded the birth. As the Guards slowly marched towards the centre of the room, the proprietor, clearly impatient with their melodramatic progress, gruffly pushed them aside and made his way to the dais, followed by an embarrassed-looking editor. As he made his speech, the Telegraph team hurried away, concerned about the need to hire and train the operators who would print the newspaper the following day and in the months ahead.

No Londoner was unaware of the arrival. Maureen Smith's team had persuaded every television and radio producer that Maxwell's exclusive appearance on their show was a once-and-for-all privilege which only the foolhardy could forsake. Every chat show from breakfast time to the epilogue featured the smiling proprietor and occasionally his editor. Even to the casual viewer, they propounded different messages and cast different images. Those who did not watch or listen were not spared exposure to the announcement because every doubledecker bus was covered with the slogan 'For the city which never sleeps, the paper that never stops'. Every publicity gimmick was tried and exploited with the exception of an irreverent proposal from somewhere in the *Daily Mirror* to launch a 'Win a Peerage' competition. The idea was understandably suffocated before it rose to the ninth floor for approval. Maxwell unveiled an unusual touch: '2,000 of the prettiest models will be walking around London looking for people holding the *Standard* and politely offer to exchange them for our paper. We'll then send them back to Bert Hardy.' Rothermere's agent was unmoved by the parvenu's tactics: 'No city in the world can support more than one evening paper and Maxwell will lose.' Twenty-five million pounds had been spent for Londoners to have the choice they had gradually rejected for twenty years, and to Maxwell's exclusive surprise their choice was trebled. As Gillespie had predicted, Rothermere, with a delicate preparation which Maxwell could only envy, launched his spoiler on the same day. The *Evening News* was reborn amid massive publicity, at 10p as opposed to the *News*'s 20p, and the *Standard*'s street vendors loyally agreed not to handle Maxwell's product. Rothermere's *Standard*, which had been substantially improved in the previous months, launched a 'Win a House' competition but majestically remained aloof. Those who could find the new *London Daily News* read a professional if rather worthy paper, which offered neither a substantial section of classified ads nor a good competition. In the streets, there was bemusement, but in the Mirror building there was panic.

Maxwell's much vaunted notion of contracting out the printing had proved to be disastrous. Deadlines which were missed in the editorial office meant that the papers were late off the presses and arrived in central London too late to beat the *Standard*. Some of the Newsflow van drivers had collected their loads and, after carefully locking their vehicles, had headed for breakfast. No one had explained to the newly recruited employees that speed was essential. Even those few street vendors who would accept the papers were, like the newsagents and the readers, confused by the idea of a twenty-four-hour newspaper. How could the reader in the evening know that he was not buying the morning edition? How could the casual buyer distinguish between the *London Daily News* and the *Evening News* when even Maxwell, in television interviews, said, 'I am very proud to have launched the *Evening News*.' Rothermere's spoiler was causing havoc and piles of discarded copies of the *London Daily News* littered the streets and were piled high in the newsagents. The first day's circulation of 400,000 began plummeting.

'We need more WOBs,' shouted Maxwell as he marched through the editorial offices one evening, suggesting remedies to improve sales. White headlines on black backgrounds was the latest advice he had heard from Mirror executives on how to improve the *News*'s design. On his return journey, he called them 'BLOBs', but everyone knew that he meant 'WOBs' – he just has a problem of enunciating names correctly. Later he wanted the masthead bigger and bigger still, and then smaller but the headlines increased. 'We need more subheads,' he boomed, when he meant crossheads, 'to break up the pages.' Then later he suggested changing the colour of the paper to distinguish between editions and after discarding that idea warmed to the notion that the stories should be in 'bite-size chunks'. The 'McNugget idea', as it was dubbed, was another ruse to relieve the paper's dense feel by shortening the articles and using more pictures. But nothing seemed to halt the inexorable decline in sales. The substance was of a middle-class newspaper which described itself as 'independent' but urged its readers to vote Labour during the General Election trying to appeal to London's right-wing electorate without a sufficient dose of dazzling magic. During those first weeks, it was not necessarily a fatal condition but it needed careful corrective surgery. Linklater and his senior staff were soon immersed in constant meetings.

Editorial changes were relatively easy to accomplish but the accumulated commercial handicaps were unmanageable. Bad distribution and late printing were still unresolved nightmares. There was an increasing gap where classified ads should have appeared. The massive publicity machine had fallen silent because no one had conceived a second stage for the launch strategy. The paper was losing half a million pounds every week. To rectify all those misjudgements required thought, time and discussion. Impulsively, soon after the launch, Maxwell had banged the table. 'I'm going to slash the price to 10p.' The universal reaction had been amazement. Every sinew of the professionals tensed as the arguments against were recited. The *London Daily News* would be competing with the *Evening News* instead of the *Standard*; the advertisers favoured an upmarket paper while the *Evening News* was so downmarket as to cause even the *Sun* editors to blush; the newsagents would not earn enough; and the loss of revenue would be excessive. Maxwell was unmoved. His grandfather's deals in Carpo-Ruthenia and his own deals in the late 1940s had all been won on undercutting the competitor. His chafing experience at the *Scottish Daily News* and the *Mirror* on the same issue had not altered his views. The price was cut, but in retaliation, the *Evening News* price was reduced to 5p and everyone was confused except Lord Rothermere. Sales of the *London Daily News* fell faster and further while the *Standard*'s increased. One further attempt to halt the haemorrhage by purchasing the *Today* newspaper and its presses from Tiny Rowland failed when Murdoch once again pipped his old competitor at the post. Maxwell's attempt to buy the loss-making tabloid confirmed that his repeated flourishes about BNPC's rosy future in supplying contract printing facilities for other national newspapers were illusory. By July, the economics were firmly against continuing the *London Daily News*, although the price was once again 20p. The newspaper was barely selling 100,000 copies and was firmly in a rut.

On 18 July Linklater presented to Maxwell his survival plan – a thick volume which had taken two weeks to compile. Linklater, who was admired by his staff, nervously awaited Maxwell's reaction. The wall-to-wall meetings had taken a heavy toll and some of those surrounding Maxwell had barely hidden their ill-will. Five days later, he summoned Linklater for the denouement. Using his favoured military analogies, Maxwell's opening remarks, spoken with unusual calm, were un-equivocal: 'I can't fight on two fronts, nor can I keep on pissing in the sand. The paper will have to close.' Further discussion was pointless and there would be no post-mortems. He personally told the staff at 12.15 the following day, Friday 24 July. 'No one thought it would go,' said Linklater, affected by the emotion of the moment. 'It was like a death in the family.' But about Maxwell he has few harsh words: 'He's an attractive man. A true human being.' Rothermere presented each of his staff with a bottle of champagne.

There are not many who can lose £50 million and a similar amount of prestige without feeling some hurt. The successful launch of the *Independent* newspaper had proved that new papers were not a foolhardy venture. But none of those around Maxwell would dare to confront their master with the truth: that his dream had died because of its parentage, and the same pedigree had borne other disappointments that summer.

On 24 May, Maxwell announced a $2 billion bid for Harcourt Brace Jovanovich, an American educational publisher which had diversified into theme-park entertainments in Florida. The offer, which was in cash, valued Harcourt's shares (which had been trading at below $30) at $44 each. If Maxwell were successful, he would at one stroke achieve the $3 billion status he so earnestly desired. Even if he failed, the financial community would be staggered that Rothschilds had been able to collect that huge amount of money in Maxwell's name. His credit seemed unassailable, except to William Jovanovich, Harcourt's sixty-seven-year-old chairman, whose response to the bid was of a style which Maxwell uncomfortably recognised. 'The sudden, unsolicited and hostile offer', said the American, 'is preposterous both as to intent and value.' He continued in a vein which caused Maxwell to reflect on his failure to bury the old skeletons. 'Mr Maxwell's dealings since he emerged from the mists of Ruthenia after World War Two have not always favoured shareholders – as Mr Sol [*sic*] Steinberg can attest.' A few days later, Jovanovich issued another vitriolic statement declaring that Maxwell was 'unfit to control' America's largest textbook publishers because he was not only a socialist with good connections in eastern Europe but was also tainted by 'hidden' sources of income. All the past vices had been resurrected. 'Mr Maxwell has money, but not enough. He has ambition but no standing. He ought to be sent packing to Liechtenstein.' Money, even billions, was not enough, Maxwell realised, to remove the stains. On 27 July, he backed off to prevent Jovanovich causing permanent damage. It was the latest failure to win a contested bid, and it was replicated three months later when Elsevier of Holland, the world's largest scientific publisher, also shunned his advances, albeit with less public malice.*

Credibility was Maxwell's problem. To deflect the weakness, he placed even more emphasis on personal appearances, especially alongside the great and the good. With his personal photographer in attendance as he ceaselessly flew around the world in a private jet, he arranged that after concluding contracts there would be a meeting and a photo opportunity with the country's prime minister or president. After television rights in France, Spain, Portugal and China had been secured, the photographer was present to record Maxwell shaking hands with President Mitterand and the other national leaders. But the appearances were misinterpreted as designed to boost his ego rather than confirm his importance. In a supreme effort to overcome the doubters, his new brokers, Alexanders, Laing and Cruickshank, published in September the first detailed analysis of BPCC. Its author was Henry Poole, who two months earlier had completed the issue of new BPCC shares worth £630 million which had powerfully enhanced Maxwell's kitty for another Harcourt Brace-type purchase.

Poole's report was called 'Unravelling the Melmotte Skein'. Melmotte was a character in Trollope's novel, *The Way We Live Now*, who though a tower of strength was thought by many to be built on sand. Like Melmotte, Poole suggested, Maxwell had suffered every wrongful accusation. The report, which Poole calculated took an average ninety minutes to read, reaffirmed its author's verdict at the company's June annual general meeting that Maxwell's empire was built upon secure foundations. To accept Poole's argument depended upon the reader's

---

* Pergamon remained the third-largest scientific publisher after Springer.

faith in Maxwell personally. No less than half of the anticipated pre-tax profits for 1990 were grouped in a column marked 'Other'. The understanding was that besides the profits to come from Pergamon's 'Orbit InfoLine', the computerised patent index and scientific information service and acquisitions, BPCC would earn over £100 million in one year from speculation on the world's stock markets and currency exchanges. Seasoned Maxwell watchers looked askance and reflected that no less than half of the £630 million raised in what was claimed to be the second largest rights issue in the city was in fact contributed by Pergamon. Citing Melmotte rather gave a hostage to fortune, but the brokers were apparently content to risk their reputation on the claim that their major client would create a £5 billion corporation by 1990.

On 25 September the new vehicle for that spectacular growth was revealed. BPCC, it was announced, was changing its name to Maxwell Communications Corporation. The name BPCC, said Maxwell, was confusing for a company which engaged in so much more than just printing and was spread worldwide. He wanted to be shed of the image of 'dark northern printing halls'. Peter Jay, his chief of staff, told the *Financial Times*: 'People said: We have read about you. We all know about you. For God's sake, even if it is personally embarrassing, you have got to get your name in the name of the company.' So Maxwell agreed, explaining, 'It's not an ego trip. I don't go in for ego trips. It's not my style. It was a decision reluctantly taken. I was forced into it by my colleagues.' Four weeks later a new eight-page glossy colour bulletin was published by Maxwell Communications to publicise the corporation's latest achievements. Maxwell's photograph appeared posing in nine different locations including one captioned, 'Robert Maxwell discussing world affairs with Henry Kissinger in Tokyo'.

Maxwell warms to Henry Poole's suggestions that he enjoys 'an acute sense of vision'. His detractors observe that Poole's 'reality of the vision' is merely a rapacious appetite to buy and become 'big'. Most of the new assets are established printers and publishers. Some deals, such as the purchase of a compact-disc manufacturer, defy logic but could produce profits. Other deals, like the attempted purchase of Watford Football Club, would seem not only to cater to his love of the sport, but also to have raised fears he might be interested in the potential land value; and Maxwell has an idea that when British soccer ceases to cater almost exclusively for the working classes and can attract the middle classes, as football does in America, it will be profitable. At Watford, his ambitions were stymied. The Football League in January 1988 blocked his takeover bid until he and his family interests divested themselves of their other interests in Oxford United, Derby County and Reading. Maxwell accepted their ruling with a minimum of complaint. His real businesses demanded attention and the City was again puzzled by the absence of any evident strategy. In late September 1987 he had announced the purchase of stock in an assortment of companies, banks and retail stores. A baffled inquirer on Thames Television's 'City Programme' asked Maxwell on 24 September to explain his motives. 'The rationale,' he replied curtly, 'could not be easier – to make money.' The stock market crash three weeks later, on 19 October, affected that ambition in Britain at least. Yet a deal concluded at an extraordinary general meeting on 31 December 1987 was one of the more peculiar in Maxwell's recent history, and reminiscent of the past. On 14 December, MCC had circulated to its shareholders a proposal to buy from Pergamon three companies – Orbit InfoLine, Molecular Design, an American data system for chemical information, and Pergamon Books. (There was also a separate transaction to purchase some property in New York state.) The initial price for what were called the 'Acquisition Groups' was £56 million in cash; but a further £15.3 million would be payable during 1988 if the companies' combined profits for 1987 exceeded £4 million, and an additional £28.7 million would be paid if 1988's profits exceeded £6.5 million. In all, the price could total £100 million. The proviso on profits was significant because in the first eight months of 1987 Orbit InfoLine and Molecular Design had earned a mere £579,000, although according to the prospectus this would increase substantially in the last quarter. (Pergamon Books had actually made a net loss.) Nevertheless, one stark fact was highlighted. Orbit's profits would have to increase substantially in just two years to produce the £100 million pre-tax profits forecast by his brokers three months earlier. Molecular Design had been purchased by Pergamon only three months earlier and few public corporations would hold special meetings on New Year's Eve or on the very last day of its accounting year to approve a takeover except for a special reason.

In the prospectus, MCC's board stressed that it 'engaged Bankers Trust to provide an independent valuation' of the three companies and that the Trust had stated that they were worth 'between £70 million and £107 million'. The MCC board had decided to pay £100 million if the profits came in on forecast. Yet the valuation report supplied by Bankers Trust showed that their scope for independence was severely curtailed by Pergamon: 'The estimates of sales and earnings for the years 1987 and 1988 have been prepared solely by Pergamon. No independent accountant has expressed an opinion on these estimates. Furthermore, we have not independently verified the financial results of the Acquisition

Groups.' In other words, the public company was buying assets from the private company on faith that the latter's valuation was accurate. Moreover, although most of the Acquisition Group's trade was based in America, the conversion rate to the pound adopted for the purchase was $1.60 while the actual rate at the end of 1987 was $1.86. Since MCC was paying in sterling, their purchase was already worth 13 per cent less.

Shortly before 10 a.m. on New Year's Eve, a collection of journalists gathered at the Mirror building to witness the meeting. Since Maxwell was faced with a conflict of interest, he was automatically deemed ineligible to exercise his 51 per cent shareholding in MCC to approve the deal. Hence it fell to the remaining independent directors to recommend the purchase as 'fair and reasonable ... [and] in the best interests of the Company'. It was an opportunity for the minority shareholders to voice their opinion. But, to the journalists' surprise, they were barred by security guards from entering the conference room and asked to leave the building. Maxwell, the self-publicist, was not only shy but positively irate at the scepticism with which some had looked on his latest deal. The press, said Maxwell, were 'ignorant and stupid' and were 'unjustified' in spreading 'misinformation'. Inside, within five minutes, the deal was approved without dissent even from the few pension fund managers who had earlier intimated their dissatisfaction. All that remained was for Maxwell to announce his plans for the future – to relaunch a London newspaper to be called *The Londoner*; to launch a Europe-wide middle-market colour newspaper; and the possible purchase of Murdoch's loss-making *New York Post*. None of these ventures would produce any profits in the foreseeable future and would just slightly add to MCC's size. 1987 closed with a cloud and a whimper rather than the bang he had anticipated.

The asset-stripper is creating a conglomerate, and like so many hybrids his empire will be broken up within a generation. His current weakness has been his historic strength – the vast fortune which he secretly accumulated in the Liechtenstein trusts. Britain's fuzzy lawmakers and indolent supervisory agencies have tolerated the confusions without demur. In America, the society which he so admires, his path is blocked by his past and especially by the legal uncertainties created by the trusts. He sought to allay suspicions by encouraging Rothschilds' bankers to meet Keicher and see the trust documents. That inspection revealed, according to the bankers, that no beneficiaries were listed. The mystery would seem to be compounded. In fact, his death will reveal that the anonymous trust which owns the Maxwell empire will continue as before. The empire will remain intact and will be 'managed' by his wife and children. Arrangements have also been made for a smooth transition, on Keicher's death, of Keicher's powers to another lawyer to manage the secrets. The catch-22 for Maxwell in the remainder of his life remains that, had he not accumulated his wealth in Liechtenstein, he would never have reached his present position; but the converse is that the Leichtenstein connection, his poisoned chalice, is the obstacle to his final ambition of success in America.

Among the several privileges of the rich is their freedom to indulge in fantasy and frivolity without accounting to their critics. There are many mortals of Maxwell's kind who have sought in their lifetime to ensure a secure place in posterity. Maxwell is unusual because he wants to write his epitaph in his lifetime and enjoy his assessment for years to come. Whatever his weaknesses and regardless of his sins, his achievements are sufficiently credible for him properly to expect a special place in the history of post-war Britain. If he remains tortured by the public humiliation, which cost him a valuable decade, it is understandable. The impressive size of his commercial creation is eclipsed only by the intensity of his family bonds. The public image is of a larger-than-life, occasionally laughing bully whose public successes, crushing failures and flashes of generosity elude most of mankind and create unpalatable suspicions. When nature takes its course and Maxwell travels to the next world, his parting message to those left behind will be, 'You haven't understood me.' Resounding from earth will be the reply, 'But have you understood yourself?'

'*For all is vanity. All go unto one place; all are of the dust, and all turn to dust again. Who knoweth the spirit of man that goeth upward, and the spirit of the beast that goeth downward to the earth? Wherefore I perceive that there is nothing better, than that a man should rejoice in his own works; for that is his portion; for who shall bring him to see what shall be after him?*'

Ecclesiastes 3: 19–22

The principal sources for this book were interviews with over three hundred and fifty people, access to a wealth of private papers, the three reports issued by the Department of Trade and Industry about the status of Mr Maxwell's private and public business affairs between 1971 and 1973, the annual reports of Pergamon and BPC/BPCC and the voluminous newspaper and magazine coverage since 1951. Mr Maxwell has consistently challenged many of the conclusions of the DTI reports but they are quoted as they contain the evidence given by the people involved at the time.

During May and June 1973, I spent considerable time with Mr Maxwell filming a long profile for BBC television. It was a critical period in Mr Maxwell's career and during those weeks we discussed at great length his ambitions, values and attitude to most of the criticisms which had been levelled at him. Nearly two hours of interview were recorded on film and the many other hours of conversation with him were noted. I retained those records and have drawn upon them for this book. Mr Maxwell also gave me access at that time to his huge collection of scrap books and some papers which were pertinent to his business affairs. These have also been very valuable.

In making the film, I asked Mr Maxwell to refer me to people whom he thought could contribute to presenting a full account of his life. Most of them agreed to be filmed and their interviews, both on and off camera, have also been used. The most important were Mrs Elizabeth Maxwell, Richard Crossman, Walter Coutts and Philip Okill.

We also interviewd in 1973 Saul Steinberg, the chairman of Leasco, Robert Hodes, his lawyer, and other Leasco executives. In the event, only the interview with Mr Steinberg was transmitted but other interview notes were kept. At the time, Mr Steinberg also made available a quantity of documents concerning his negotiations during

1969 with Mr Maxwell and Robert Fleming, the merchant bankers. These papers were clearly of great help in the describing of those events nearly twenty years later. All the quotations from Mr Steinberg and other Leasco executives emanate from 1973.

The interviews which I conducted in the past twelve months are clearly quoted and sourced. Inevitably, many requested that their comments be off the record and therefore I have not listed any acknowledgements for the enormous help, encouragement and kindness I have received from so many people.

One person who deserves special mention, however, is Michael Shaw of Curtis Brown, whose support has been invaluable.

The individual sources for each chapter do not separately mention newspapers or interviews. These are either apparent from the text or were off the record.

CHAPTER ONE

7   According to an historical survey. Herman Dicker, *Piety and Perseverance: Jews from the Carpathian Mountains*, Sepher Hermon, New York, 1981, page 58.

The best descriptions of the Jewish communities in Carpo-Ruthenia are in the third volume of S. Y. Goss and Y. Cohen, *The Jews of Czechoslovakia; The Marmos Book*; a special historic memorial about the Jews of Slatinske Doly (or Szlatfina) published by the Yad Vashem Institute, Jerusalem.

CHAPTER TWO

I have drawn upon the detailed records of Ferdinand Springer Verlag for the relationship between Maxwell and the publishers; and on interviews with the surviving but retired staff who negotiated with Maxwell during those years.

32   Maxwell's offer was 'the only hope for rebuilding our company'. Lange letter, 18 February 1955

32   Maxwell's own account. LSE Seminar, 25 February 1969

34   Von Eugen's protest to Kirkness. Public Records Office FO 371 1056/250

37   Springer's contract with EPPAC dated 16 September 1949; cf. Lange letter, 18 February 1949 and Maxwell, 14 April 1951

37   He threatened to renege on the whole deal. Historic summary of Maxwell's relationship with Springer, page 11

38   Maxwell sent Otto a menacing letter. Letter, 15 March 1949

41   Maxwell, wrote Tönjes, seemed to ignore any advice and was even signing letters as 'chairman'. Letter, 18 February 1955

41 'Maxwell gave us enormous and valuable help over those years.'
   Summary, page 14
45 'For Maxwell, it was the means to build for himself a huge business in
   London.' Summary, page 14
47 By November 1950 the outstanding bills amounted to £115,000. Letter,
   25 November 1950
49 Maxwell had overcharged Springer's old customer. Summary, page 24
51 'I deeply regret having to write this letter.' 10 October 1951

CHAPTER THREE

52 The various histories of Maxwell's companies have been obtained from
   the records at Companies House.
52 The best sources for the Simpkin Marshall affiair are the Reciever's
   Report, 1955; the reports in the *Bookseller*, 6 March 1941; 3 November
   1951; 3 March and 18 June 1956; and the Public Record Office,
   37034/5/6. The *Sunday Times* in 1969 interviewed Kurt Wallersteiner at
   length and took several sworn statements from him.
63 terminate the juggling act profitably. Springer letter, 14 April 1951
66 In 1969 Maxwell explained his motives in long interviews with journalists
   from the *Sunday Times*.
67 'Maxwell has proved to be a difficult person to do business with.'
   Springer letter, 21 September 1953
69 'a wide range of Soviet scientific books is now available'. Springer letter,
   21 June 1954

CHAPTER FOUR

85 Philip Wade's letter to the *Lancet*, 27 April 1963
86 'I do it because it ought to be done.' *Sunday Times*, 9 January 1966
87 Betty Maxwell has described those years of running a home. *She*
   magazine, 1987

CHAPTER FIVE

88 I have relied upon the Buckinghamshire local newspapers – the
   Wolverton Express (later the *Wolverton and Milton Keynes Express*) and
   the *Bletchley District Express* – for general coverage of Maxwell's local
   political career. Only a few contemporaneous documents of the Labour
   Party survive. Local members, however, retain a vivid memory of their
   experience.
90 '...I don't have any specific time or date.' *Midweek*, BBC TV, 1973
97 Christopher Booker's phrase, that he would be part of 'the dream after
   the storm'. *The Neophiliacs*, Fontana, 1970, page 64
98 'Now', he bitterly complained, 'our prized workshops are going to
   Steptoe's Knacker's Yard for pennies.' *Wolverton Express*, 6 March 1964

101 'I thought I was the cleverest thing on two legs there...' *Desert Island Discs*, BBC Radio, July 1987

103 'I have watched him frequently.' *Hansard*, 21 November 1967

105 Bernard Levin, *The Pendulum Years*, Cape, 1970, page 302

108 'has been pestering Hugh Cudlipp with phone calls'. *The Cecil King Diary 1965-70*, Cape, 1972, page 171

109 'That's the thing about me. I'm quick off the mark.' *Sunday Times*, 3 March 1968

CHAPTER SIX

114 Marriott's query, *Sunday Times*, 9 January 1966

115 Cecil King said subsequently. DTI, page 210

115 Their opposition was supported by Ansbachers. DTI, page 215

115 Maxwell ignored them both. DTI, pages 210/211

115 Maxwell felt that he had 'bought a bargain'. DTI, page 233

115 A 'satisfactory return'. DTI, page 20

118 He was to 'knock off the Caxton sales force'. DTI, page 11

120 ILSC's accounts were in a 'deplorable state'. DTI, page 74

121 its profits had, on its own admission, increased only 'marginally'. H. Kay Jones, *Butterworths, History of a Publishing House*, Butterworths, 1980, page 196

121 'to get lost'. Kay Jones, op. cit., page 226

122 the absence of reliable information about ILSC's finances. DTI, page 74

122 'irregular and insufficient'. DTI, page 73

122 'I was entirely at fault in not getting that as a copy for my own records.' DTI, page 73

122 'No accounts had been produced of any nature,' he said three years later. DTI, pages 78/9

123 Maxwell recalled that he had 'honestly believed'. DTI, page 234

123 'Mr Bennett took the initiative in these matters.' DTI, page 232

123 'heavily influenced by Mr Maxwell'. DTI, page 237 (and cf. DTI, page 231)

123 'Tell me where the £200,000 profit is?' DTI, page 268

123 the profits were considerably lower than officially anticipated. DTI, page 137

123 'was absolutely disastrous'. DTI, page 87

123 Maxwell fired both men and three other senior officials for alleged incompetence. (Although the DTI inspectors stated that Maxwell's allegations were erroneous (DTI, pages 138 and 154))

124 'The Board of ILSC has informed Pergamon that sales and profits... are running at the level forecast...' DTI, pages 48 and 143. The *Sunday Times*'s cautiously favourable comment was typical; cf. 20 October 1968

129 the profile concluded, he was 'surprisingly mild'. *The Times*, 23 October 1968

131 'This is a disgraceful affair and it is up to the Takeover Panel to do its proper job.' *The Times*, 26 October 1968. For Murdoch's attitude, see Michael Leapman, *Barefaced Cheek*, Hodder, 1983

132 Maxwell had suggested in his circular sent to shareholders on 15 May. DTI, pages 143/148

132 ILSC's accounts were 'unreliable'. DTI, page 160

133 complied with the takeover code. DTI, page 435

133 the price would rise very substantially. DTI, page 448

133 he would repurchase the shares at any time up to 31 January 1969. DTI, page 518

CHAPTER SEVEN

137 'I just used to think I was part of it.' *The Times*, 19 June 1969

139 'I wasn't sure that we needed his particular expertise.' BBC TV, 1 May 1973

142 'Maxwell knew more people than I did.' Steinberg, BBC TV, 1973

143 as we reduce our administration costs. DTI, page 163 and private

146 MSI (DS) was owned by Maxwell, his wife and Tom Clark. DTI, page 364

146 to collect Pergamon's debts, a task which had previously been undertaken by MSI(DS). DTI, page 365

146 for the benefit of Maxwell's sister. DTI, page 352

147 'They made a good case out to me and I was very happy...' DTI, page 602

147 'I certainly had no knowledge about terminating it.' DTI, page 602

148 Pergamon's profits were unaffected. DTI, page 607

148 'no ability and no experience and no know-how in this area'. DTI, page 610

149 'might be inflated or deflated as a result of such relationship'. DTI, page 600

150 he also managed Maxwell's private companies' accounts from the same office. DTI, page 462

150 with those of the private companies as 'basically impossible'. DTI, page 595

150 because all the accounts were chaotic. Pergamon *Annual Report*, 1970

150-1 one-third of Pergamon's total profits in 1968 would be derived from those two sales. DTI, page 492

151 the exact terms of credit between Pergamon and MSI Inc. DTI, page 483

151 'before the end of the year'. DTI, page 887

152 on a royalty basis if issues no longer available. DTI, page 577

152 the second was a confirmatory telex from MSI Inc.'s auditors. DTI, page 540

152 Maxwell's assurances that Pergamon had received a 'firm' order. DTI, page 579

153   a close watching brief on Pergamon's financial management. DTI, page 578

153   personally had the right to vet all major schemes. DTI, page 578

154   soon after his first meeting with Steinberg. US Court of Appeal Docket Nos 72-1638-41, 72-1654, page 9

155   he had disagreed with Maxwell's views of how the accounts should be prepared. DTI, page 200

155   a 'change of practice' in the valuation of stocks. DTI, page 578

155   'and I won't let you steal it'. US Court of Appeal Docket Nos 72-1638-41, 72-1654, page 9

156   a forecast of $1.4m profit if Pergamon owned ILSC completely. US Court of Appeal Docket No 71-1563, page 9

CHAPTER EIGHT

162   'I was amazed that it was so significant.' BBC TV, 1973

163   Maxwell, Crook or Paranoiac. A three-volume record of the correspondence and negotiations between Maxwell and the *Sunday Times* was compiled in 1973 by Alex Finer.

165   'fair game to try to bring them down'. BBC TV, 1973

168   'Maxwell was used to bullying people which our people didn't like.' BBC TV, 1973

169   'It was amazing that everyone else thought it was so significant to the world.' BBC TV, 1973

173   'But then Maxwell showed us the photo.' BBC TV 1973

173   This was a huge proportion of Pergamon's profits. DTI, page 619

173   the piles of old journals and books stacked on shelves. DTI, page 575

173   no distinction was made in the ownership of the stock between Pergamon, MSI Inc. and Robert Maxwell & Co. DTI, page 598

173   Anderson saw that Pergamon's major customers for back journals were the two private family companies. DTI, page 565

174   had the right to return all the stock it had bought from Pergamon and demand repayment in full. DTI, page 448

175   'no noise, no loss of face, just let's slide out'. BBC TV, 1973

178   'The internal management accounts show that ILSC is now trading profitably.' DTI, page 183

178   trading profit of just £40,000 at the end of the first eighteen months. DTI, page 174

178   to give ILSC £42,000 credit for services it had been charged for the use of the offices at Fitzroy Square. DTI, pages 176/7

179   'full information available and the points were not at issue'. *The Times*, 22 August 1969

179   The amount specified was just £40,000. DTI, page 185

179   Pergamon's recent purchases from ILSC worth £356,895. DTI, page 188

179 the accounts were proven to be in shambles. DTI, page 187
180 'I and my financial advisers are completely at a loss to understand why Leasco acted the way it did.' *Sunday Telegraph*, 24 August 1969
184 'has conducted himself with courage throughout the proceedings'. *The Times*, 29 August 1969

CHAPTER NINE

192 'I and my family have been through hell.' Transcript of EGM, page 10
197 Leasco would have had difficulty in establishing control over PPI. DTI, page 616
198 Ross, financed by Leasco, attempted to call a special shareholders' meeting. Supreme Court of the State of NY: Ross v. PPI and circular from Maxwell to PPI shareholders dated 4 November 1969
203 The issue, and Maxwell's reputation, were left dangling. See Select Committee on House of Commons (Services). Accounts of Refreshment Department 1965 to 1971; *Hansard*, complaint of privilege, 13 October 1969, column 44; First Report from the Committee of Privileges, Session 1969-70, 3 March 1970.

CHAPTER TEN

210 were quite intentionally private meetings. All England Reports, 1971, page 398
211 'up to two years...until the company was on its feet again'. *Financial Times*, 29 June 1970
213 When the Price Waterhouse report was finally published, it mentioned a further problem of a government export guarantee issued by the ECGD. This was also discussed by the DTI, page 75
214 Maxwell insisted that Pergamon had agreed to underwrite its massive debts. DTI, page 546
215 he told the *Daily Telegraph* after he returned. 21 November 1970
218 Price Waterhouse, the treatment of 1969 accounts was 'fair'. Report, paragraph 76
218 The inspectors prided themselves that they never sprang any surprises upon him. DTI, page 91
219 'I can see the value of these enquiries.' DTI, page 69
220 Maxwell, according to the inspectors, made no mention of that crucial sale. DTI, page 156
220 '...in the warranty period which ended on the 30th June 1968'. DTI, page 159
220 Maxwell vigorously denies. *They Must be Fair*, page 11
220 ILSC which was 'misleading and untrue'. DTI, page 44
220 he allowed important documents to be destroyed. DTI, page 105
220 that proper records were not kept. DTI, page 119

CHAPTER ELEVEN

On Labour Party affairs, I have used the local newspapers and the report issued by the Labour National Executive.

CHAPTER TWELVE

246 '...give the boys a break'. *Scottish Daily News*, R. McKay and Brian Barr, Canongate, 1976, page 8

249 The Council wanted to pay an additional £16,000, nearly double Maxwell's deal. McKay, op. cit., page 64

252 'Since Maxwell is pivotal to all the changes taking place'. The documents obtained by the *Bookseller* during litigation initiated by Maxwell for defamation against the magazine included all the *News*'s Council minutes and working papers. This was also the source for the documents regarding the industrial dispute at Pergamon.

271 sought to rescue Oxford United. John Ley, *Rags to Riches, The Rise and Rise of Oxford United*, Queen Anne Press, 1985

273 John Waddington. Victor Watson kept a diary throughout the battle and subsequently wrote various descriptive pieces.

CHAPTER THIRTEEN

278 thirteen trade unions. Simon Jenkins, *The Market for Glory*, Faber and Faber, 1986

CHAPTER FOURTEEN

324 The Edinburgh Games. Derek Bateman and Derek Douglas, *Unfriendly Games, The Inside Story*, Mainstream, 1986

331 Private Eye. *Malice in Wonderland*, Macdonald, 1986

GLOSSARY

AGM	Annual General Meeting
BBC	British Broadcasting Corporation
BNPC	British Newspaper Printing Corporation
BOAC	British Overseas Airways Corporation
BPC	British Printing Corporation
BPCC	British Printing and Communications Corporation
DPP	Director of Public Prosecutions
DTI	Department of Trade and Industry
EGM	Extraordinary General Meeting
EPC	European Printing Corporation
EPPAC	European Periodicals, Publicity and Advertising Corporation
FOC	Father of Chapel
HMSO	Her Majesty's Stationery Office
IBM	International Business Machines
ICI	Imperial Chemical Industries
ILSC	International Learning Systems Corporation Limited
IPC	International Publishing Corporation
JEIA	Anglo-American Joint Export-Import Agency
LMS	Lange, Maxwell & Springer
MCC	Maxwell Communications Corporation
MGH	Mirror Group Holdings
MGN	Mirror Group Newspapers
MIMC	Microforms International Marketing Corporation
MSI (1964)	Maxwell Scientific International (1964)
MSI Inc.	Maxwell Scientific International Inc.
MSI (DS)	Maxwell Scientific International (Distribution Services) Ltd
NASA	National Aeronautics and Space Administration
NGA	National Graphical Association
NUJ	National Union of Journalists
PPI	Pergamon Press Incorporated
PRISC	Public Relations and Information Services Control
R.M. & Co.	Robert Maxwell & Co.
SOE	Special Operations Executive
SOGAT	Society of Graphical and Allied Trades
TUC	Trades Union Congress
UNESCO	United Nations Educational, Scientific and Cultural Organisation

SCHEME OF MAXWELL'S COMPANIES

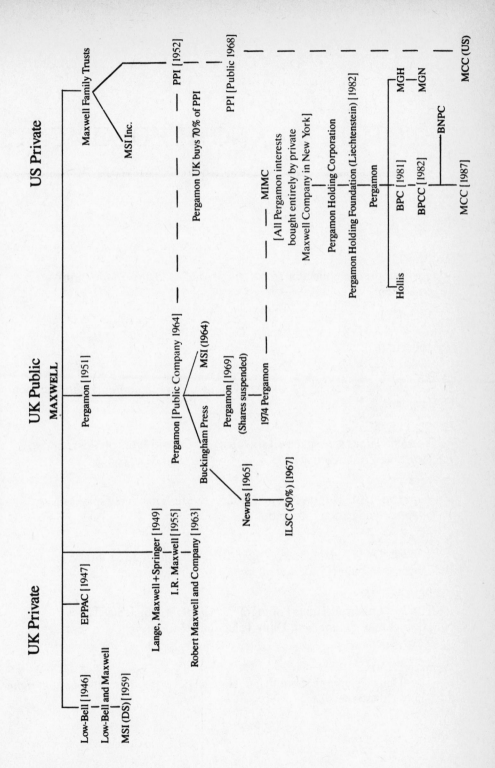

PICTURE ACKNOWLEDGEMENTS

PLATE I
Top left, private collection; *top right,* private collection; *bottom,* private collection.

PLATE II
Top left, J. H. Kisch; *bottom left,* Gunther Heyden; *bottom right,* private collection.

PLATE III
Top, Springer Verlag; *bottom left,* Gunther Heyden; *bottom right,* Gunther Heyden.

PLATE IV
Top left, Times Newspapers Ltd; *top right,* Central Press photos; *bottom,* Keystone Press Agency Ltd.

PLATE V
Top right, BBC Hulton Picture Library; *centre,* Times Newspapers Ltd; *bottom,* Syndication International.

PLATE VI
Top left, Daily Telegraph; *top right,* BBC Hulton Picture Library; *centre,* Times Newspapers Ltd; *bottom right,* Hill Samuel Group.

PLATE VII
Top left, Financial Times Photography; *top right,* Financial Times Photography; *bottom left,* Daily Telegraph; *bottom right,* Express Newspapers.

PLATE VIII
Top, Daily Telegraph; *bottom left,* Hailey Sports Photographic; *bottom right,* Times Newspapers Ltd.

INDEX

Jews: status in Czechoslovakia, 9; *see also* anti-semitism
Johnson, Walter, 62
'Jones, Private Leslie' (Robert Maxwell), 15-16
Jones, Robert (of *The Times*), 162, 172
journalism: and bingo games, 302
journalist: Maxwell as, 23
journalists: *Daily Mirror*, and Maxwell, 165, 289-90, 297-301, 304-5, 329
journals *see* scientific journals
Jovanovich, William, 343

Kalinski, Dr Felix, 211-12, 215
Kamienski, Tadeusz, 173
Kearton, Lord (previously Sir Frank Kearton), 136-7, 261-6, 271, 313
Keicher, Dr Walter, 318-19, 322, 347-8
Kellet, Elaine, 99
Kennedy, Edward, 141
Kennedy fellowship, 215
Kennedy, Ludovic, 312
Kennington, Ivor, 168, 171, 174
Kerman, Isidore, 70, 160, 179, 208, 221; testimonial for Maxwell, 143; and Leasco, 156, 182, 193, 199; and *Sunday Times*, 163-4, 171
Keyes, Bill, 58-9, 61, 74, 265, 281, 287, 309-10
Khrushchev, Nikita, 81, 92
King, Cecil, 96, 108, 115, 120, 278, 300
Kinnock, Neil, 287-8, 290, 332
Kirkness, Kenneth, 34
Kisch, John, 25-6
Kissinger, Henry, 345
Kleinwort Benson, 317, 319
Kosice: Maxwell in, 9
Kyllmann, Otto, 66

Labour Party: and Maxwell, 61, 88-9, 94-5, 97, 106, 203-4, 230-5, 243, 245, 288, 309, 333; science committee, 95; National Fund Raising Organisation, 97; working committee to improve productivity, 97-8; National Executive Committee, investigation into North Bucks constituency, 230-1; Maxwell at conferences, 235, 301; and DTI reports, 242; and Mirror Group, 280, 282, 286, 288, 296-7
labour relations: Pergamon, 268-70
Lancaster, Terence, 289, 299
Lancet, 85
Land Commission, 104
Lange & Springer, 48
Lange, Maxwell & Springer (LMS), 40-2, 44, 48-9, 55-6, 61-2, 67-9, 72-3, 78; and Springer Verlag, 49, 69-70; and Simpkin Marshall, 61-2, 72-3; name

changes, 146
Lange, Otto, 29, 36-8
Lange, Tönjes, 28-9, 31-3, 38, 40-1, 43, 45, 48, 56, 61, 67, 83-4
Lassen, Paul, 44, 56, 64-6, 73
Last Exit to Brooklyn (Selby), 105, 126,
Layton, C & E, 129
Le Bas, Hedley, 115, 118-23, 142, 170, 221
Leach, Rodney, 169-72, 177, 182, 187
Leach, Sir Ronald, 189, 200, 209, 219-22, 224-5, 229
Leasco, 137, 144, 148, 154, 157-60, 167, 190, 209, 239-40; and Pergamon, 139-40, 142, 154-5, 157, 160-1, 178, 180-2, 187-9, 211, 214; Maxwell's bid for,140; World Trade Company,160; and Takeover Panel, 181; writs against Maxwell, 199; suit against Maxwell in US Supreme Court, 241; *see also* Steinberg, Saul
Leasco-Pergamon professorship, 168
legal profession: and Maxwell, 3, 208, 210, 227
Leipzig book fair, 25
Levin, Bernard, 105
Levitch, Ben, 237, 239
Levy, John, 225
libel action: against *Private Eye*, 331-5
libraries: and pricing of Pergamon journal, 85-6, 238
Liechtenstein: Maxwell family trusts, 82, 96, 146, 317, 319, 322, 348
Linklater, Magnus, 329-30, 338, 342-3
literature: and Maxwell, 105
LMS *see* Lange, Maxwell & Springer
Lobl, Arnos, 24-5
London Daily News, 336, 339-43
London evening newspaper: Maxwell's plans for, 295, 328-30; choice of name, 338
The Londoner, 347
Long, Douglas, 279, 289
Lonrho, 317
Los Angeles: Pergamon in, 80
Loss, Joe, 314
Low, Toby *see* Aldington, Lord
Low-Bell Limited, 24-5, 44, 50, 63, 65, 73
Low-Bell, and Maxwell Limited, 146
Lyne, Major-General L.O., 16
Lyons, Jim, 104, 205-7, 230-1, 233

McCaffrey, Sir Thomas, 314
McCorquodale (printing company), 139, 331
McGarvey, Dan, 91
McGraw-Hill, 78
Mackie, Allister, 247-55
Macmillan Company of New York, 113, 147-8
Macmillan, Harold, 74, 88, 97
Macmillan Publishers, 72
McWilkins, Colonel, 15-16